... terrif...'
C.J. TUDOR, author of *The Chalk Man*

'Both tragic and chilling, *The Deep* perfectly blends
psychological thriller and eerie gothic ghost
story to create something truly haunting'
SARAH PINBOROUGH, author of *Behind Her Eyes*

'Full of surprises . . . a satisfyingly spooky
blend of history and horror'
SUNDAY MIRROR

'Masterly supernatural reimagining . . . eerie, haunting,
and filled with suspense, *The Deep* is a whirlpool
of a novel that pulls you in and doesn't let go'
DANIELLE TRUSSONI, author of *Angelology*

'As ghostly as Gothic . . . *The Deep* is thrilling,
rich, frightening, unsettling, and, best of all,
told from the heart'
JOSH MALERMAN, author of *Bird Box*

'Elegant and eerie. Alma Katsu really
is something rather special'
JOHN CONNOLLY, author of the
Charlie Parker thrillers

'Inspired by true-life tragedy . . . a sinister story that will leave you gulping into the darkness at bedtime . . . perfect spooky reading'
STYLIST

'Deftly mashes up spellbinding historical fiction, adroit commentary on class and gender, and a classic yet surprising ghost story . . . truly haunting'
PAUL TREMBLAY, author of *The Cabin at the End of the World*

'Blends the paranormal and historical fiction . . . a spellbinding tale where desire knows no bounds and death is only a beginning'
J D BARKER, author of *The Sixth Wicked Child*

'A terrifying paranormal tale'
BEST

'Katsu is a fantastic writer, with a unique ability to blur the lines of history, horror, humanity, and tragedy. Think Diana Gabaldon by way of Charlaine Harris'
MICHAEL KORYTA, author of *Those Who Wish Me Dead*

'Weaves together the true story of the *Titanic* and its sister ship *Britannic*, with a love story and a creepy tale of the supernatural'
SFX

ALSO BY ALMA KATSU

THE
DEEP

ALMA KATSU

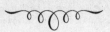

BANTAM BOOKS

TRANSWORLD PUBLISHERS
Penguin Random House, One Embassy Gardens,
8 Viaduct Gardens, London SW11 7BW
www.penguin.co.uk

Transworld is part of the Penguin Random House group of companies
whose addresses can be found at global.penguinrandomhouse.com

Penguin
Random House
UK

First published in Great Britain in 2020 by
Bantam Press
an imprint of Transworld Publishers
Bantam edition published 2021

A CIP catalogue record for this book
is available from the British Library.

ISBN
9780857504289

Printed and bound in Great Britain by Clays Ltd, Elcograf S.p.A.

The authorized representative in the EEA is Penguin Random House Ireland,
Morrison Chambers, 32 Nassau Street, Dublin D02 YH68.

Penguin Random House is committed to a sustainable
future for our business, our readers and our planet. This book is
made from Forest Stewardship Council® certified paper.

Dedicated to the memory of
the souls lost to the tragic sinkings of
the *Titanic* and the *Britannic*

THE
DEEP

For a moment, the falling feels like something else entirely—like a brief, wild glimpse of freedom.

But the surface comes too soon, shattering against her skin—a pane of glass—knocking the air from her lungs. Or perhaps it is she who has shattered. She is no longer herself, no longer a single person but divided and adrift in the darkness. The burn in her lungs is too unbearable; her mind begins to soften to make room for the pain.

Strange thoughts come to her through the cold: Here there is no beauty.

This much is an unexpected relief.

But the body wants what it wants: please, it begs. Her body begins to fight; her face seeks the sparse starlight above, already so far away. Someone once told her that the stars were merely sewing pins, holding the black sky up so that it did not come down on the world and suffocate it. Her brief calm gives way to panic. A powerful, unstoppable desire possesses her—it isn't life calling to her, demanding another chance, but love. We all deserve a second chance. The thought seems to arise not from within her but around her, even as the currents pull her deeper, as a frigid fog entangles her mind.

The surface is unfathomably high now, untouchable. The cold is everywhere, pushing, begging to be let in.

I can give you another chance, *the waters seem to say*. I can make all of this go away if you let me.

It is a promise. The waves are no longer pulling her down but holding her in their arms, waiting for her response.

She opens her mouth at last. Water floods in, forming the answer.

1916

18 September 1916
For the attention of the director
Morninggate Asylum, Liverpool

Dear Sir,

I write in the hope that you may be of assistance in a very sensitive matter.

My dear daughter, Annie, disappeared unexpectedly from our home in the little village of Ballintoy four years ago. My wife and I have been searching for her ever since. We have made inquiries of hospitals and convalescent facilities, as our daughter was in a distraught state when we last saw her and suffering from injury, perhaps of a more grievous nature than we thought at the time. We began with facilities close to us, in Belfast and Lisburn and Bangor, but when we failed to locate her, we worked our way out, eventually crossing the Irish Sea to Liverpool.

We wrote to fifty-five hospitals in all. Having met with no luck, it was suggested that we might expand our inquiries to facilities such as your own. Since childhood, our Annie has always been *extraordinarily* sensitive to the emotions possessed by all members of her sex. These emotions, however, can be both a blessing and a curse: a woman without these qualities would be a cold, heartless thing indeed, but to be possessed of *too* much love is no kindness. As her father, I at times cannot help but wish there had been a way to temper this quality in my dear Annie.

And so I write to you, kind sir, to inquire as to whether there might be a woman in your establishment matching my Annie's description. She would be twenty-two years of age and stand five foot six inches tall. She is a shy, soft-spoken lass who can go a week without a word to anyone.

I pray that you will be able to end our nightmare and return our Annie to us. Yes, in a word, she ran away from the home we provided for her, but we suspect that it is merely her own fear of censure that keeps her away. Please know, sir, that we are pursuing this matter outside the law in order to preserve Annie's privacy and dignity. I pray we may count on your discretion. I imagine, in your position, you see a goodly number of women in situations like my Annie's.

She is our only daughter and, despite her frailties, her weaknesses, *despite anything she may have done*, we love her dearly. Tell her that her brothers pray nightly for her return and her room remains exactly as when she left it, in the hope that we will take her again in her family's loving embrace.

Yours respectfully,
Jonathan Hebbley
Ballintoy, Civil Parish, County Antrim, N. Ireland

25 September 1916
Morninggate Asylum, Liverpool

Dear Mr. Hebbley,

I received your touching letter concerning your daughter, Annie, Friday last week. While I am not unsympathetic to your tragic situation, I regret to say that I am unable to cooperate.

The Lunacy Act of 1890 has wrought many changes in the legal constraints governing institutions such as Morninggate. The act has driven facilities to create hitherto unimagined internal policies, designed—in my opinion—to protect the institution against spurious legal claims rather than for the benefit of its patients. At Morninggate, these policies extend to safeguarding our patients' privacy. It is for this reason that I must respectfully decline to answer. It is a matter, you see, of protecting the privacy of the afflicted, who often suffer greatly due to the general public's prejudices against those with disorders of the nerves and mind.

Please do not construe this reply as either affirmation or denial of knowledge of your daughter's presence at Morninggate. *As administrator of this institution, I am bound by law.*

Your servant,
Nigel Davenport
Physician and Director, Morninggate Asylum
Byshore Mews, Liverpool, England

Chapter One

October 1916
Morninggate Asylum
Liverpool

She is not mad.

Annie Hebbley pokes her needle into the coarse gray linen, a soft color, like the feathers of the doves that entrap themselves in the chimneys here, fluttering and crying out, sometimes battering themselves to death in a vain effort to escape.

She is not mad.

Annie's eyes follow the needle as it runs the length of the hem, weaving in and out of fabric. In and out. In and out. Sharp and shining and so precise.

But there is something in her that is hospitable to madness.

Annie has come to understand the erratic ways of the insane—the crying fits, incoherent babblings, violent flinging of hands and feet. There is, after days and weeks and years, a kind of comforting rhythm to them. But no, she is not one of them. Of that she is certain.

Certain as the Lord and the Blessed Virgin, her da' might once have said.

There are a dozen female patients hunched over their sewing, making the room warm and stuffy despite the meagerness of the fire. Work is thought to be palliative to nervous disorders, so many of the inmates are given jobs, particularly those who are here due more to their own poverty than any ailment of mind or body. While most of the indigent are kept in workhouses, Annie has learned, quite a few find their way to asylums instead, if there are any empty beds to keep them. Not to mention the women of sin.

Whatever their reasons for turning up at Morninggate, most of the women here are meek enough and bend themselves to the nurses' direction. But there are a few of whom Annie is truly afraid.

She pulls in tight to herself as she works, not wanting to brush up against them, unable to shake the suspicion that madness might pass from person to person like a disease. That it festers the way a fine mold grows inside a milk bottle left too long in the sun—undetectable at first but soon sour and corrupting, until all the milk is spoiled.

Annie sits on a hard little stool in the needle room with her morning's labor puddled in her lap, but it is the letter tucked inside her pocket that brushes up against her thoughts unwillingly, a glowing ember burning through the linen of her dress. Annie recognized the handwriting before she even saw the name on the envelope. She has reread it now at least a dozen times. In the dark cover of night, when no one is looking, she kisses it like a crucifix.

As if drawn to the sin of Annie's thoughts, a nurse materializes at her shoulder. Annie wonders how long she has been standing there, studying Annie. This one is new. She doesn't know Annie yet—not well, anyway. They leave Annie to the late arrivals on staff, who haven't yet learned to be frightened of her.

"Anne, dear, Dr. Davenport would like to see you. I'm to escort you to his office."

Annie rises from her stool. None of the other women glance up from their sewing. The nurses never turn their backs to the patients of Morninggate, so Annie shuffles down the corridor, the nurse's presence like a hot poker at her back. If Annie could get a moment alone, she would get rid of the letter. Stash it behind the drapes, tuck it under the carpet runner. She mustn't let the doctor find it. Just thinking of it again sends a tingle of shame through her body.

But she is never alone at Morninggate.

In the dusty reflection of the hall windows they appear like two ghosts—Annie in her pale, dove-gray uniform, the nurse in her long cream skirt, apron, and wimple. Past a long series of closed doors, locked rooms, in which the afflicted mutter and wail.

What do they scream about? What torments them so? For some, it was gin. Others were sent here by husbands, fathers, even brothers who don't like the way their women think, don't like that they are outspoken. But Annie shies away from learning the stories of the truly mad. There's undoubtedly tragedy there, and Annie's life has had enough sadness.

The building itself is large and rambling, constructed in several stages from an old East India Company warehouse that shuttered in the 1840s. In the outdoor courtyard, where the women do their exercises in the mornings, the walls are streaked with sweat and spittle, smeared with dirty handprints and smudges of dried blood. Luckily the gaslights are kept low, for economy's sake, giving the grime a pleasantly warm hue.

They pass the men's wing; sometimes, Annie can hear their voices through the wall, but today they're quiet. The men and women are kept separate because some of the women suffer from a peculiar nervous disorder that makes their blood run hot. These women cannot abide the sight of a man, will break out in tremors, try to tear off their clothes, will chew through their own tongues and fall down convulsing.

Or so they say. Annie has never seen it happen. They like to tell stories about the patients, particularly the female ones.

But Annie is safe here, from the great big world. The world of men. And that is what matters. The small rooms, the narrow confines are not so different from the old cottage in Ballintoy, four tiny rooms, the roiling Irish Sea not twenty paces from her front door. Here, the air in the courtyard is ripe with the smell of ocean, too, though if it is close by, Annie cannot see it, *has* not seen it in four years.

It is both a comfort and a curse. Some days, she wakes from

nightmares of black water rushing into her open mouth, freezing her lungs to stone. The ocean is deep and unforgiving. Families in Ballintoy have lost fathers and brothers, sisters and daughters to the sea for as long as she can remember. She's seen the water of the Atlantic Ocean choked with hundreds of bodies. More bodies than are buried in all of Ballintoy's graveyard.

And yet on other days, she wakes to find plaster beneath her fingernails where she has scratched at the walls, desperate to get out, to return to it. Her blood surges through her veins with the motion of the sea. She craves it.

On the far side of the courtyard they enter the small vestibule that leads to the doctors' private rooms. The nurse indicates that Annie should step aside as she knocks and then, at a command to enter, unlocks the door to Dr. Davenport's office. He rises from behind his desk and gestures to a chair.

Nigel Davenport is a young man. Annie likes him, has always felt he has the well-being of his patients in mind. She's overheard the nurses talk about how difficult it is for the parish to get doctors to remain at the asylum. Their job is discouraging when so few patients respond to treatment. Plus, it's far more lucrative to be a family doctor, setting bones and delivering babies. He is always nice to her, if formal. Whenever he sees her, he thinks about the incident with the dove. They all do. How she was found once cradling a dead bird in her arms, cooing to it like a baby.

She knows it wasn't a baby. It was just a bird. It had fallen out of the flue, hit the hearth in a puff of loose feathers. Dirty, sooty bird, and yet beautiful in its way. She only wanted to hold it. To have something of her own to hold.

He folds his hands and rests them on the desktop. She stares at his long fingers, the way they fold into one another. She wonders if they are strong hands. It is not the first time she has wondered this. "I heard you received another letter yesterday."

Her heart trembles inside her chest.

"It is against our policy to intrude too much on our patients' privacy, Annie. We don't read patients' mail, as they do at other homes. We are not like that here." His smile is kind, but there is a slight furrow between his brows and Annie has the strangest urge to press her finger there, to smooth the soft flesh. But of course she would never. Voluntary touching is not allowed. "Here, you may show us only of your own free will. But you can see how these letters would be a matter of concern for us, don't you?"

His voice is gentle, encouraging, almost a physical caress in the stillness. Bait. She remains silent, as if to speak would be to touch him back. Perhaps if she doesn't respond, he will stop pressing. Perhaps she will vanish into air if she is quiet enough. She used to play this game all the time in the vast fields and cliffsides of Ballintoy—the recollection returns with startling clarity: the Vanishing Game. Generally, it worked. She could go whole days drifting in the meadow behind the house, imagining stories, without ever being seen or spoken to. A living phantom.

The doctor stretches his neck against his high collar. He has a good, solid neck. Hands, too. He could easily overpower her. That is probably the point of such strength. "Perhaps you would *like* to show it to me, Annie? For your own peace of mind? It's not good to have secrets—secrets weigh on you, hold you down."

She shivers. She longs to share it and burns to hide it. "It's from a friend."

"The friend who used to work with you aboard the passenger ship?" He pauses. "Violet, wasn't it?"

She starts to panic. "She's working on another ship now. She says they are in dire need of help and she wonders if I would return to service." There. It's out.

His dark eyes study her. She cannot resist the weight of his expectation. She has never been good at saying no; all she has ever wanted was to please people, her father, her mother. To please all of them. To be good.

Like she once was.

My good Annie, the Lord favors good girls, said her da'.

She reaches into her pocket and hands him the letter. She can hardly stand to watch him read, feeling as though it is not the letter but her own body that has been exposed.

Then he glances up at her, and slowly his mouth forms a smile.

"Don't you see, Annie?"

She knots her hands together in her lap. "See?" She knows what he's going to say next.

"You know that you're not really sick, not like the others, don't you?" He says these words kindly, as though he is trying to spare her feelings. As though she doesn't already know it. "We debated the morality of keeping you here, but we were reluctant to discharge you because— Well, frankly, we didn't know what to do with you."

Annie had no recollection of her own past when she was admitted to Morninggate Asylum. She woke up in one of the narrow beds, her arms and legs bruised, not to mention the awful, aching wound on her head. A constable had found her unconscious behind a public house. She didn't appear to be a prostitute—she was neither dressed for it nor stinking of gin.

But no one knew who she was. At the time, Annie scarcely knew herself. She couldn't even tell them her name. The physician had no choice but to sign the court order to detain her at the asylum.

Her memory has, over time, begun to return. Not all of it, though; when she tries to recall certain things, all she gets is a blur. The night the great ship went down is, of course, cut into her memory with the prismatic perfection of solid ice. It's what came before that feels unreal. She remembers the two men, each in their turn, though sometimes she feels as though they have braided together in her mind into just one man, or all men. And then, before that: fragments of green fields and endless sermons, intoned prayer and howling northern wind. A world too unfathomably big to comprehend.

A terrible, gaping loneliness that has been her only companion for four years.

Surely it is better to be kept safe inside this place, while the world and its secrets, its wars, its false promises, are kept away, outside the thick brick walls.

Dr. Davenport looks at her with that same wavering smile. "Don't you think, Annie?" he is saying.

"Think what?"

"It would be wrong to keep you here, with the war on. Taking up a bed that could be used for someone who is truly unwell. There are soldiers suffering from shell shock. Everton Alley teems with poor and broken spirits, tormented by demons from their time on the battlefield." His eyes are dark and very steady. They linger on hers. "You must write to the White Star office and ask for your old job, as your friend suggests. It's the right thing to do under the circumstances."

She is stunned, not by his assertions but that this is all happening so quickly. She is having trouble keeping up with his words. A slow dread creeps into her chest.

"You're fine, my dear. You're just scared. It's understandable—but you'll be right as rain once you see your friend and start working again. It's about time, anyway, don't you think?"

She can't help but feel stubbornly rejected, spurned, almost. For four years, she's managed things so that she could stay. Kept her secrets. Was careful not to disrupt anything, not to do anything wrong.

She has been so good.

Now her life, her home, the only security she knows, is being ripped away from her and she is once more being forced out into the unknown.

But there is no turning back. She knows she cannot refuse him this, cannot refuse him anything. Not when he has been so kind.

He folds up the letter and holds it out to her. Her gaze lingers on his strong hands. Her fingers brush against his when she takes it back. Forbidden.

"I should be happy to sign the release papers," her doctor says. "Congratulations, Miss Hebbley, on your return to the world."

3 October 1916

My dear Annie,

I hope this letter finds you. Yes, I am writing again even though I have not heard from you since the letter you sent via the White Star Line head office. You can understand why I continue to write. I pray your condition has not worsened. I was sorry to read of your current situation, although, from your letter, you do not sound unwell to me. Can you ever forgive me for losing track of you after that Terrible Night? I didn't know if you had lived or died. I feared I would never see you again.

To speak to the question that may still be weighing on your mind: I have received no further knowledge of what happened to the baby. Throughout the cold and miserable evening waiting in the lifeboat, silently praying to God to spare us, I held her tight to my chest to keep her warm. But when we were rescued by the *Carpathia*, as I mentioned in my last letter, I was forced to surrender her to the crew, and I have since gathered that she was likely left at an orphanage. You must consider that she may be lost to you and to me forever.

I'm so sorry, Annie.

Let me turn my attention now to you, dear friend. It grieves me to think of you wasting away behind the walls of an asylum. Whatever melancholy has possessed you since that fateful night, you must rise above it. I know that you can. I remember the girl who was my roommate on that doomed ship. I shall never forget the last time I saw you, jumping into those dark, icy waters. We thought you had lost your mind, made senseless by the terrible shock of it all. But only *you* had seen the baby tumble into the water. Only *you* knew that there wasn't a moment to waste.

Annie Hebbley is the bravest girl I have ever known, I thought that night.

That is how I know you will survive your current circumstances, Annie. You are stronger than you think.

I am no longer a stewardess but a nurse now, as part of the war effort. The ship on which I currently serve is a twin to that lovely one we both knew so well. Imagine if you can, however, that all its finery has been transformed, like Cinderella returned to her life as a scullery maid! HMHS *Britannic* has been fitted out as a hospital ship. The crystal chandeliers are gone, as is the flocked paper from the walls of the grand staircase. Now all is whitewash and canvas duck and everything smells of antiseptic, always antiseptic. The ballroom has been remade into a series of operating stations, the pantries made to hold stocks of surgical equipment. The wards can accommodate thousands of patients. The nurses and rest of the crew occupy many of the first-class staterooms, where you and I would've once made the beds and doted on passengers.

Annie, the *Britannic* is still in desperate need of nurses. I beg you, again, to consider reprising your career at sea to come to work with me. I shan't lie to you: we see injuries almost too terrible to be borne. What they say in the newspapers is true: this is surely the war to end all wars, for we could never surpass its horrors. These boys need you, Annie—to lift their spirits, to remind them of what's waiting for them at home. You will be the best tonic in the world for them.

And, if I am truthful, you will be the best tonic in the world for *me*. I have come to miss you terribly, Annie. There are few people who would understand what we have been through. Few people to whom I could admit that I still am haunted by that night, that it comes in my dreams monthly, weekly, and that I still sometimes cry out in fright. Who could understand why I still make my living on the water, why I am bound to it when it has shown me what awfulness it can do.

You, I am sure, will understand. I would be surprised if you did not suffer these same afflictions and fears yourself because you, too, are bound to the sea. I always sensed that in you.

Write, Annie, and tell me that you'll join me on the *Britannic*. I have already filed a letter of recommendation for you with the London office. We depart from Southampton terminal on the twelfth of November. I pray to see you before we sail.

Yours most fondly,

Violet Jessop

Chapter Two

11 November 1916
Southampton, England
HMHS *Britannic*

Charlie Epping is a man who respects a finely waged war, the way that others respect a well-made watch.

People so often misunderstand what war is—they think it's scattered, chaotic. But it is an incredibly sophisticated, constantly moving set of coded messages and information, quantities, commands, bodies, supplies, numbers, logistics. Those who can master the patterns can save countless lives. And what better business in the world is there than that?

He takes a long drag on his cigarette. The sky is wonderfully blue over Southampton, the kind of crisp autumn day that makes a man happy to be alive, though come night out on the open water it'll be brittle cold—brutal, even.

He leans forward, one foot on the railing, to watch the activity below. He's on the boat deck not far from his station in the radio room. From his perch a hundred feet above the froth of churning waves breaking against the piles, he has a clear view of all the activity, men on the other decks and the pier below. It's like a colony of ants, the men reduced to black dots, scrabbling to and fro to get the giant ship ready to leave tomorrow.

He has a million things to do, too, him and Toby Sullivan, the second radio operator: There are tests to run to make sure the fancy Marconi wireless telegraphy system works properly. Wireless is new. Like most Marconi operators, Epping volunteered for the training as soon as he joined the military. He likes the idea of learning a trade and sees a future in wireless.

Some days are busy for the radio operators, others less so. At sea, they can pick up transmissions only when they are in line of sight with another ship, or close to one of the wireless stations. The technology is cranky and mercurial. Weather affects transmission, as does the time of day. There are codes to memorize, numbers that represent standard commands. And then there is Morse code itself. Epping knows it so well that he finds his mind translating words into dots and dashes even in conversation, swears he hears the tap of the stylus in his sleep.

He throws the nub of his cigarette over the railing, his eye following its motion, like a flying dash against the repeating whitecaps. Then he checks his pocket watch: the morning pouch should've been delivered by now. Orders and intelligence reports come up twice a day from Southern Command at Tidworth Camp, and it's the radio operators' job to sort through them. Things will slow down once they are at sea, but for now he and Sullivan are hard-pressed to keep up.

The *Britannic* was converted from a grand ocean liner—the most luxurious ever built, or so at least they tell him. Unlike purpose-made military vessels, the ship has proper stairs instead of ladders. The alleyways are wide. There are plenty of portholes. You don't feel boxed in on this ship, the way you do on a cruiser or battleship. Epping's gotten so used to close quarters over the last few years that the sheer amount of open space on board the *Britannic* sometimes makes him feel as though he doesn't know what to do with his own arms.

Of course, the ship has a rather notorious sister. Command was upfront about the *Titanic* disaster from the beginning, assembled the entire crew to explain all the improvements that had been made to the *Britannic* in response to the tragedy. Doubled the hull and sealed all the bulkheads, all the way to the top. This ship is much safer than the *other one*, they were assured. No need to be nervous.

And Epping's not the nervous type. Can't be when you've got a floating ballroom that's been converted to a sleeping ward for the sick and dying: men torn to pieces like rag dolls, missing arms and legs, faces ripped apart by shrapnel, lungs destroyed by phosgene gas. The doctors say the carnage is greater for this war because modern weaponry is so much deadlier.

Having retrieved the mail pouch from its hook on the pier, Epping returns to the radio room, where Toby Sullivan points to a stack of papers at the telegraph station. "We forgot to send the updated crew list to Tidworth. Can you take care of it?"

Charlie doesn't mind; he's three times as fast on the stylus as Toby, who hasn't completely memorized Morse just yet and still gets hung up on letters—and not just the ones that are rarely used, like the *Q*'s and *X*'s and *Z*'s, but also the ones that are only slightly uncommon, like *J*'s and *V*'s. Charlie sits down in front of the crew ledger, picking out the names of those who came on board since the last report, and makes a check mark in pencil beside each. There is a list of information they need to send on each crewman: name, last held position, age, residence, next of kin.

Then he taps in the preamble: *From HMHS* Britannic *to Southern Command, Tidworth Camp . . . dot dot dot dot, dash dash . . .*

He moves his finger to the ledger and finds the first entry. *Edgar Donnington, Uxbridge Shoring, age 34, Ickenham, Mrs. Agnes Donnington (wife).*

Then to the next.

Anne Hebbley. Titanic . . .

He pauses. A survivor. Makes a mental note to find out more. The girl must either be a hardy one or extraordinarily lucky to have lived—or both. He can only imagine the stories she must have.

He goes on, tapping in her data: *age 22, Liverpool*. For next of kin, he quickly punches *dash dot pause dash dash dash* . . .

None.

Chapter Three

12 November 1916
Southampton, England
HMHS *Britannic*

It is easy to imagine, as Annie stands on the dock, squinting into the brilliant morning sun, a world without past, only future. Before her heaves the great *Britannic* and beyond it, the open sea.

Now that she is here, she feels the rise of determination in her—an urgency. She had been right to come.

The entire journey from Morninggate, she felt exhausted and exposed, worn down by all the *people* everywhere. Drivers and innkeepers, policemen and shoe polishers and street peddlers. Dr. Davenport had directed two nurses to take her into town a couple of times before the journey, to help her acclimate to crowds and noise. But since then, life has been a great roaring tide hurtling at her: the train to London, then Waterloo Station to catch another train out to Southampton to the great port. It was all almost too much at first, and she had to sit on the train with her eyes closed, clutching her little drawstring purse to her chest because she was afraid she'd misplace it—that she'd misplace *herself*. Fear was a chained dog, startling and rough and always dangerously close, stretching its leash, baring fangs.

By the time she got to London, the first leg of her trip behind her, she'd gotten used to the constant movement beneath her and the press of so many bodies. Gotten used to being surrounded, once again, by strange voices and smells and sights, even if she still felt them like a film of cobweb against her skin.

Even if everywhere she looked, she expected to see a familiar face in the crowds, imagined she'd spotted Mark—the wash of dark hair and the handsome cut of his face, the knowing gaze.

Even if every time it was not him but a stranger, she felt an old ache reopen in her chest.

Inside Morninggate, too, she often used to think she'd seen him among the other patients or strolling the lane outside the walls. But now she knows it's only her mind playing tricks. Mark died four years ago in the frozen black waters of the northern Atlantic.

Arriving in Southampton, she is again swamped by sensation. She remembers this feeling—somewhat—from that first time, when she came to work on the *Titanic*. She'd been in a complete whirl then, a child in disposition if not age, on the run from Ballintoy. That time, it was like an unseen hand had guided her—a guardian angel? She had known intuitively the right train to board, which street would lead to the White Star Line office. Strange men had offered to help the lost-looking young woman, and it was her guardian angel who told her which one would put her right and which one would try to lead her into a lonely alley.

It wasn't trust, or intuition, but something else that had swooped in, in the absence of both, to guide her.

The man in the White Star Line office is one of the good ones—whose eyes don't seem to judge, whose hands don't seem to linger. He leads her to the ship, insisting on carrying her satchel, a slight embarrassment for her because it is so light. All that's in it are a few objects of her personal possession—a Morninggate-issued hairbrush; a few barrettes and things accrued from inmates who'd traded them with Annie for favors; and of course, the brooch, a fine item far more valuable than the rest, and one Annie has held on to since her days on the *Titanic*.

The officer undoubtedly thinks she must be a very poor lass to have so little. She can't explain that she had nothing else but her gray linen Morninggate uniform, that the dress, hat, and shoes she wears were plucked from a stash of old clothes that had been donated to the hospital, and that the money for the rail tickets and meals came out of Dr. Davenport's own wallet. It is a different kind of Vanishing Game she is playing now, to dress in clothes meant for another woman, of another build and another time. To move among all these people as if she were one of them, even while knowing, deep down, that she is not one of them. That she is separate, somehow. That she is still alone.

Making her way across the docks takes her back to her first day on the *Titanic*. The crowds, the chaos. Bodies everywhere, each seemingly headed in a different direction. Lanes choked with wagons loaded with cargo and luggage. Carriages for the richer passengers picking through the crowds, drivers yelling to be heard over the hubbub, horses snorting nervously. Annie lifts her skirt so she doesn't have to look at her feet and can keep her eyes trained on the White Star Line man, who keeps disappearing in the crowds.

"Here she is," he says as they draw up on a dock. He hands her a piece of paper. "Give that to the first officer." He deposits the satchel at her feet. Then he leaves.

Annie claps a hand to her hat as she looks up, up, up at the ship's four huge funnels, like turrets on a castle. The *Britannic* is the spitting image of her sister, the *Titanic*—aside from the paint job, meant to distinguish it as a hospital ship. A familiar tingle washes over her, head to foot, and she is flooded with memories of that first ship. A floating palace in every sense: the grand staircase, the beautifully appointed dining rooms, the posh cabins. She remembers the passengers most vividly, of course, the first-class passengers in the twelve cabins she served as stewardess. They were rich; some of them famous. She remembers the Americans especially, with their peculiar accents and funny ways. So forward, so pushy, so unbound. But then she remembers that many of them are dead and she stops herself.

No. Now is not the time to mourn. If she looks back too long, she knows what will happen: How the black tides will once again close over her head, and she'll go under. How the grief and the loss and the horror will be too much.

For now, she needs to keep her wits about her and find the first officer and get on with things. After all, there is still a mission to accomplish.

There is still—somewhere out there—the child. Mark's child.

She marches up the gangplank. Everyone is in a uniform, without exception, and these are serious uniforms, not the White Star Line livery that she's used to. The men wear drab olive wool, the nurses in sweeping blue skirts with capes over their shoulders against the chill, faces framed by wimples. Everyone is busy, intent on whatever it is they've been set to do. No one pays any attention to her.

Inside, it's even more different. She finds it hard to imagine this ship was ever like the *Titanic*, it's been changed so much, like a woman just after childbirth—ragged and pale and vacant.

Inside, it could be any hospital. If you weren't near a porthole or door, you wouldn't know you were on a ship. Everything that made the *Titanic* sparkling and grand has been taken away. There are no deck chairs or card tables, no crystal chandeliers or wicker chaises. It is all antiseptic and uniform. Rows of cots for the patients, cupboards filled with supplies. And everywhere: bustle. Nurses supervise as men are loaded onto stretchers. Orderlies pass by with full stretchers, making their way to ambulances waiting on the dock below, then return with empty stretchers for the next lot. Some patients make their way on foot—arms in slings, heads wrapped, usually escorted by a nurse or orderly. There is as much commotion as on the *Titanic*'s boarding day. Annie remembers the crush of humanity that had come up the gangplanks that day and instinctively takes a deep breath. So many people, it had felt like she was being swamped by a giant wave. Swamped and sucked under.

But these are no guests, only survivors, each with a story tucked inside their bandages—wounds, pains, visions of shrapnel, explosions, and terrors she can't fathom. These are the half dead.

And the bustling staff have signed on to attend to them, to usher them either back to our world or into the one beyond. An altogether different kind of voyage.

Ahead, two men confer with a serious-looking man in a crisp uniform—probably an officer. She approaches, paper in her outstretched hand. "Pardon me, but I'm hoping one of you might help me find the first officer? I was told to report to him."

The trio stop to look at her. The tall one eyes her up and down with the disapproving air of a schoolmaster, then snatches the paper out of her hand, reading it quickly. "This says you're a new staff nurse, yes? A Miss Hebbley? Reporting for duty?"

"Yes, that's right."

"Nurses are matron's responsibility. Epping," he says, handing the paper off to one of the two men, a thin lad with hair the color of straw, "take Miss Hebbley to Sister Merrick, will you? We can't have her walking the decks, can we?"

She follows Epping in a haze as he picks up her satchel and leads her down passageways that are both familiar and unfamiliar. He ducks through traffic easily, constantly looking over his shoulder for her, a bright but crooked smile playing across his face, like sunlight on the water. "We just got in a few days ago, which is why things are so busy. We got over a thousand patients to discharge. We're about to head out again."

"Are you an orderly?"

"Naw. I'm one of the wireless operators." He sticks out his hand. "Charlie Epping."

They shake. His hand is not large but not small. His grip is warm but formal. His movements are precise. "Annie Hebbley," she says, her voice soft under his touch. "May I tell you a secret, Mr. Epping? I don't know anything about nursing." She's not sure why she said it—except that the light in his grin makes her feel safe. Or not safe but not invisible.

And after all, it's not strictly true. She has spent the last four years watching nurses and knows everything they do and say. She feels she could pass for one, at least. She often feels she has spent her life passing for something.

She's not sure what response she was hoping for, but he simply shrugs. "They'll teach ya. They'll assign a senior nurse to show you the ropes. You'll catch on in no time."

By now he has taken her to the grand staircase, which, she is happy to see, hasn't been taken down and replaced with something more sedate. It looks funny to her without the beautiful flocked wallpaper behind it, or plush carpets underfoot, and with the soldiers and nurses rushing by instead of ladies in fine silk gowns and men in evening dress, but familiar all the same.

"I remember this," she says, touching the carved handrail.

He gives her a skeptical look. "You been here before? That wasn't in the notes."

A blush warms her cheeks. "Not on this ship, no, but the *Titanic*, yes. I suppose now you'll think me a very unlucky person."

"Not at all! Now I remember you from the register. You must know Miss Violet Jessop. . . ."

"She's the one who encouraged me to come. We used to be good friends."

Epping smiles broadly. "She's like my big sister. Let me get you introduced to Sister Merrick and then we'll go looking for Violet."

But there's something about his generosity, his kindness, that makes her feel weighted down and sad. He is buoyant—of another dimension, one that does not experience the friction of the world in the same way she does. His fingers dart around the edges of a cigarette he twirls in his hand, and all she can think is *ease*. She has never felt that. She is more like the cigarette itself, passed from hand to mouth to earth, sucked dry and then forgotten.

Or perhaps she is the smoke, blown into the air, made invisible at the meeting of the lips.

Once they find Sister Merrick, it is quickly apparent that there will be no leisurely reunion with Violet, not for now, anyway. The woman looks down her long nose at Annie. "Thank you, Epping, for bringing her to me, but that will be all. I'm sure you're needed elsewhere." It's clear she doesn't want him to linger here in her domain, and so he touches his cap to them both and scurries off, leaving Annie with this imposing woman.

She turns to Annie, again peering down at her. Sister Merrick is tall and stout, with a sagging bosom that strains at the top of her pinafore. "First things first. We will get you a uniform and get you situated in a cabin. Then we'll start you on duty."

"Ma'am?" Annie is already dead on her feet. She was up at six o'clock at the boardinghouse in order to be packed and ready to catch the train on time.

The nurse gives her a withering look. "You're coming to us with no nursing experience, Miss Hebbley. In just a few days' time, we'll be in a war zone taking on fresh patients. You have a lot to learn and there's not a moment to spare." She calls over another nurse, a young one with kind eyes. "Find her a bunk and let her get changed into a proper uniform, and then I want to see her back here."

The young nurse's name is Hazel, a London girl whose sweetheart is fighting on the Continent. She has been on one run with *Britannic*, she cheerfully tells Annie as she escorts her to the quartermaster for her uniform, and then down to the crews' quarters on the lower decks. "The hours are long, but the work is very rewarding," Hazel says through the door as Annie changes into the nurse's uniform. "Sister Merrick is not so forbidding once you get to know her, but it does pay to stay on her good side."

Annie wishes for all the world that she could lie down on the bunk for a little respite from the bustle and noise, but she obediently follows Hazel back to the wards. For the next few hours, she is Hazel's shadow. The young nurse shows Annie where the supplies are, where to find blankets for the patients who are cold and water for when they are thirsty. The wounded wait to be taken off the ship, impatient to go, but there are only so many ambulances. They stop the pair of nurses over and over, demanding to be released. "You must wait for the clerk to come with your discharge papers. You're in the military, so everything must be done nice and proper" is what Hazel says to a man who threatens to walk off the ship. "Otherwise they'll consider you AWOL and they'll send the police for you."

Her most important job, Annie quickly sees, is to listen when they want to talk. At first, she finds the sight of the wounded unsettling—this is the first time she's seen men hurt this badly, and some are grotesquely disfigured. There are men without any limbs at all, or who've had half their faces blown off. Men who struggle for every breath, lungs damaged by gas, and men who know they won't live for very much longer. Men who talk to themselves in low, nonstop rambles—well, she's seen people like this at Morninggate so that doesn't bother her as much. And after a few hours of listening to the men as she changes dressings and straightens beds, fetches water and empties bedpans, she becomes less frightened of them. She finds the work surprisingly satisfying. It's nice to be on the other side for a change, the one helping instead of the one being helped. The men she has met are discouraged and frightened, not sure what waits for them. They're wounded and, in most cases, will be permanently handicapped. Their future is suddenly thrown into question. Will they ever be able to work again, or will they be a permanent burden on their families? Will their loved ones still love them? Some tell her about their families back home and—for a lucky few—the women waiting for them. She wants to tell the sad ones, *You think you've lost everything, but you're lucky beyond what you know. You're here, aren't you? On this grand ship?* She wonders what these men would say if they knew that just a few scant days ago, she was a patient herself. Maybe they would find it inspirational—but she fears not. She fears they would judge her, fear her, even, like the staff at Morninggate.

She comes close to telling one man with great sad eyes. He lies on the cot, staring straight up at the ceiling. He's not as young as many of the infantrymen, maybe in his early thirties. He rubs his thigh above where his leg ends. "What am I going to do for work when I get home? I can't be a burden to my Maisie," he says.

Annie knows her job is to stand in for his wife. "That's the last thing on her mind right now," she tells him as she plumps his pillow. "She'll be grateful you're alive and home with her. You'll see."

He kneads the leg. "You don't know my Maisie."

"But I'm a woman, aren't I? I know how a woman feels, and I tell you, all your wife wants is to have you home again." She feels a familiar dull ache in her chest. She wishes there were someone in the whole wide world who felt that way about her.

After four hours on the ward, Annie isn't sure she wouldn't follow the impatient young soldier down the gangplank, given the chance. She finds a chair in a corner and sits with her back to the mob, a glass of water pressed to her forehead. Her feet throb; the world spins.

Annie is just about to hoist herself to her feet—sure she'll cry out in pain—when Hazel runs up to her. "Come quick, you're needed on the floor," she says, pulling Annie's sleeve.

Annie can see there's a problem as soon as they enter the ward. A commotion in the center of the sea of beds. A man is thrashing and yelling, fighting off the orderly who is trying to hold him down. Even from across the room, Annie can see that there is blood everywhere. A sea of red. For a moment, she lurches, sickened.

Hazel gives her a little push. "Help Gerald. I'm going to find a doctor."

It's not until Annie is at his bedside that she can see what has happened: the man has tried to kill himself. He ripped the dressing off his fresh amputation and opened the sutures. He seems to have cut a ragged line across his throat, too, though Annie's not sure how he managed that. She stares at him, too stunned to react. Gerald, the orderly, soaked in the man's blood, has him pinned to the mattress but is helpless to do anything else. He looks bug-eyed at Annie over his shoulder. "Well then? Try to stop the bleeding. Hurry!" The blood loss is severe: the man is already swooning under Gerald's weight.

Blood blooms through the dressings, reddening, blackening at the edges. Annie is not sure what to do. She flails around for a second, then sees the man's stockings on the floor. She begins to move almost without thought: picks one up and cinches it around his thigh as a tourniquet, pulling the knot as tight as she can. Wraps the other around the man's throat—but not so tight that it will cut off his breath. She rips the sheet into strips and winds it around his throat like a mummy. That's as far as she gets before the man goes limp and Gerald is able to sprint to the equipment station for a proper tourniquet and bandages. She leans over the unconscious man, fussing with her work until Gerald returns.

And that's when she realizes she recognizes the patient's face. She had been talking to this man a few hours earlier. The one with the sad eyes. His wife's name is Maisie. He was a roofer before the war. How would he be able to work with only one leg? He couldn't climb up and down ladders. What could he do now? He was too old to look for another profession, he'd said.

Hazel returns with a doctor. They both look askance at Annie in her bloody clothing for a millisecond before falling on the patient, the doctor barking out orders for Hazel and the orderly. It's like a train wreck. She's crawled from the wreckage: her moment has passed, and Annie can only stagger backward in a daze. This is all her fault. Was there something she'd missed when she'd been talking to him before? She can't help but feel she should have known he was about to try to take his life. Should have felt it, sensed the will to live slipping away from him like a visceral loss, like a change in air pressure.

By some miracle, Violet Jessop finds her in the alleyway, swaying deliriously on her feet. "You can't stand out here covered in blood," she says, as chipper and full of business as she'd been on the *Titanic*— as if they've been working side by side ever since then, instead of parted all this time. She bundles Annie under her arm, and Annie, weak and overwhelmed, does little to resist. After some trial and error—Annie cannot remember the way to her room, despite the fact that the floor plan is the same as the *Titanic*'s—they find Annie's cabin. Violet sits on the bunk while Annie scrubs her hands and face and changes back into her discarded dress.

"I'm so sorry this had to happen to you, and so soon," Violet says, shaking out Annie's thick hair as though she could shake off the day's burdens. She takes a brush and begins to run it through Annie's hair. Annie sits on a stool like a schoolgirl. Numb. "I wish I could say it's not always like that, but the truth is that it can be brutal at times. The doctors say these are the worst battlefield injuries they've ever seen. It's heartbreaking, what's happening to those poor men."

"I'd spoken to him an hour earlier."

"You can't blame yourself." Violet begins pinning up Annie's thick hair. "If anyone's to blame, it's Sister Merrick. She shouldn't have pushed you so hard on your first day. Let's get you a good meal— Have you eaten anything at all today?—and then it's to bed with you."

Violet leaves to start her shift after dinner, so Annie wanders onto the promenade for fresh air before turning in. She looks over the water, the ceaseless rising and falling of it. She turns her face into the wind and she remembers what it's like being at sea. To be always moving forward, toward something unseeable—the shore again, or the idea of one.

"Look who I spy! So, tell me, how was your first day?" Charlie Epping is suddenly beside her at the railing, a hand-rolled cigarette pinched between his lips. The wind drags the smoke across her face.

"It's all . . . a bit much." She has trouble meeting his eyes.

"It's always rough at first. It will get better." He takes another drag off the cigarette. "You're a tough girl, you'll survive. And how do I know? Because you survived the *Titanic*. Why don't you tell me what it was like? Violet doesn't like to talk about it."

"Wouldn't it scare you?"

A stream of smoke is carried over their heads. "Naw. I figure they survived—that means if anything happens to this old girl, we'll survive, too."

What does she remember about her time on the *Titanic*? All she has to do is close her eyes and it comes back to her. The halls and the bustle and the noise. The fears and the whispers and the secrets. The hidden wanting. The thrash of the waves against the sides of the boat, so far below the deck that their foam seemed like a trick of the light and not the deadly cold it really was. The falling. The screams. The darkness of the night and the little rescue flares bobbing uselessly until one by one, they died out.

She picks a safe memory, one that won't frighten him. "Mostly I remember how cold the water was." She rubs her upper arms reflexively, as though she could rub this phantom cold away.

"Violet said you jumped in to save a baby."

She feels a thud at the back of her skull, like a mallet striking a bell. "Yes . . . That's right. I did." How could she forget that?

"Then you're a hero, Miss Hebbley," he says with a laugh.

Yet the recollection leaves her cold and hollow, not feeling like a hero at all. And she doesn't remember anything of what happened after that.

She looks over the railing again, into the waves pounding the side of the ship. Dark green-gray water, frilly whitecaps. The wind teases a few strands of her hair loose and into her eyes . . . and she can feel herself in the water once more, wrapped in it, succumbing to it, called by it, by some force she didn't know yet recognized intimately. Some voice calling her home.

1912

Chapter Four

10 April 1912
Southampton, England

Annie checked the tiny watch pinned to her apron and gasped. It was already 8:38 a.m. Passengers would begin boarding at 10 a.m. Captain Edward John Smith made it clear they would adhere to his schedule.

As she swept a strand of hair back, her fingers grazed the chain of the necklace she always wore, a slender gold cross. It must've slipped out from under the neckline of her blouse. She quickly tucked it back in place. The Catholics on staff had been warned to keep their religious insignia out of sight for the duration of the voyage: no rosaries, saints' medals, or crosses. But she found the cool metal against her skin comforting.

She returned to the task of putting away the last of the damask napkins, swanlike and fine. There was a time when the cavernous dining hall and its echoes made her shudder, but she had gotten used to the gigantic ship being empty. And it did feel empty, even with almost nine hundred crewmen. She couldn't imagine what it would be like once they were joined by the thousands of passengers.

The *Titanic* was more than her home now: it was her *world*. It felt as though her life had begun the day she stepped onto the ship, as if she'd crawled out of her past like a grave, reborn into the fresh sea air. It seemed, too, that she was learning everything for the first time, like a toddler: how to wear her crisp White Star Line uniform correctly, how to be understood despite her Irish accent, how to walk on the gently rolling ship.

She resolved not to be frightened by the newness of everything, instead immersing herself in work. There was no shortage of things to do on this massive ship. Stocking the linen closets with fresh-pressed tablecloths. Making beds; Annie had been told there were 7,500 blankets on board and there were times when it felt as though she'd smoothed, tucked, and folded each and every one. Counting the numbers of cups and saucers; glasses; sets of fine, expensive dishes—enough to have a complete set for every man, woman, and child in first class—entering the numbers in the quartermaster's ledger to be checked for breakage when they docked in America. The entire staff was busy from sunup to sundown, and this on an empty ship. Annie could not imagine how she would manage once her twelve assigned cabins were occupied by living, breathing passengers.

"You'll be on your feet for fifteen hours a day," her roommate, Violet Jessop, had warned. Annie was glad to have been paired up with Violet, a London girl who had worked on ships for years and was impossibly worldly in Annie's eyes.

At night, once they had finished for the day, Violet would coach Annie on what to expect from passengers. "I come from a small village in Ireland," Annie confessed to her on the first day. "We never had servants. I don't know how I'm supposed to act."

Violet was amazed that Annie had landed the job at all. "White Star is particular about the women they hire," Violet said, and Annie knew that Violet knew this firsthand. She'd heard all about Violet's troubles getting a position because the men who did the hiring suspected young, pretty girls like Violet would be distractions to male passengers and crew. Either that, or they'd quit within a year to get married.

Annie just shrugged. "Maybe he thought I was plain enough," she said. "And I told him I was eager to help."

"No surprise there." Violet narrowed her eyes. "It was probably your *solicitous* nature that persuaded the hiring manager to take a chance on you. Just remember not to be *too* solicitous—some men will try to see how much they can get away with, especially if they think you're naive." Then she arched an eyebrow. "Though, if you're going to fall for a passenger, better a rich man than a poor one. There will be some *very* rich men on the *Titanic*. Women with jewels so big they'll make your eyes water. Babies with gold teething rings. You'll see."

And now, in not more than an hour, she would.

Annie took a moment to marvel in the vast quiet of the empty room. She loved the ship, had never been on anything so big or so beautiful. She liked to touch the plates in the dining room—where she would be serving as part of the victualing staff—and wonder at the china as thin and delicate as paper. She liked to walk through the staterooms with their silk wallpapers and finely turned furniture, crystal chandeliers and mahogany appointments—modeled after the legendary Ritz hotel in London, Annie had been told proudly during her orientation—and pretend that it was hers, all hers. She could block out the occasional shout from a coworker or bang and crash of a hammer amid last-minute repairs, block everything out except the delicate ping of the crystal drops above her.

Were they ready for passengers? she wondered as she gave the tablecloth a final smoothing. Was *she* ready to lose the gracious quiet of her ship?

A steward appeared with a set of chimes at the far end of the dining room. Three bells. An hour till boarding. "Chief steward's called a meeting in the first-class smoking room," he called to her across the empty space, before abruptly withdrawing. Just her luck. The first-class smoking room was three decks up. She'd have to hustle.

As she hurried down the alleyway, she passed John Starr March going the other way, and smiled when he touched the brim of his cap and greeted her with a nod. John was much older than she, as old as her father. He was a postal clerk, responsible for the mailbags that were loaded on the *Titanic* for delivery to New York, but he was also to help out on the victualing staff. John was a bit of a celebrity among the staff, for he had survived eight incidents at sea. "One a year, regular as rain," he told her, laughing. "I don't even think about it no more. It's part of the job." Like many of the newer staff, Annie found John March's presence reassuring.

In the smoking room, Annie found to her relief she was not the last one to arrive. As she slid into place next to Violet, she was startled to feel her friend grab her hand. It was the first time, Annie realized, she had been touched by a single other person since she'd left home. She felt amazed by what this small gesture did—she felt suddenly anchored, secure.

The other assembled stewards reminded her of the poor of Belfast: gaunt, nervous eyed, anxious. A few were broad, bloated by drink and a diet of potatoes and cabbage. There were only about two dozen women among them, and she and Violet were among the youngest; the company was notoriously difficult when it came to young single women serving on board its ships, convinced it led to moral turpitude. She wasn't entirely sure they were wrong, judging by the behavior she'd seen on the staff decks after hours: Women as well as men wandering from cabin to cabin with a bottle of stout or whiskey, looking for drinking companions; card games and dicing in the alleyway. Men whispered temptations in your ear, when they thought they could get away with it.

But then, nearly everything about being on this ship surprised Annie—the aliveness of it all, the raw potential. The only other place where she'd been in the company of a large group of men at once had been church on Sundays, and there she'd known the names of each of them. Now, those names had slipped away into the light spring fog, evading her.

Her past: a dream of greens and grays, quickly blurring. All that remained was an acrid taste in her mouth.

Violet gave Annie's hand another squeeze as Andrew Latimer, the chief steward, cleared his throat, shouting for quiet over the nervous chatter of her fellow stewards and stewardesses. Annie hadn't had much time with Latimer but her impression was that he was a competent man who liked things done a certain way. Whether he was fair or kind, she hadn't a clue.

"From this moment until we dock at our destination, you must remember that the passengers' happiness is your paramount concern." Latimer's face was a florid red over the high white collar of his uniform. "Regardless of the demand placed on you, regardless of your other duties and tasks, regardless of the hour, the passengers' needs always come first."

Annie's stomach tightened. What did that mean? If she were fulfilling one passenger's request—fetching a meal for a passenger too sick to go down to the dining room, for example—and was stopped by another passenger who wanted her to retrieve an item from her stateroom, which request was Annie to obey? She'd been given a dozen staterooms in her charge: she was servant to a body of passengers nearly as robust as her old parish, bound to answer their beck and call, satisfy their every whim, in addition to cleaning up their rooms, making their beds, and serving in the dining room during meals.

"You must maintain for our passengers—our *first-class* passengers— the perception that they are residing at a world-class hotel. We are proud of the *Titanic*, yes—it's the finest oceangoing luxury liner in the world, we must never forget that!—but we should stress to our passengers the many amenities available to them. Make sure they know about the gymnasium, for instance, and the library." *There are one thousand books in the first-class library*, Annie recalled being told, statistics drilled into their heads so they would roll easily off the tongue. *Five hundred in second class.* The weight of the books alone, the massiveness of the stories contained therein, had seemed, to her mind, greater than what any ship could carry. The heated pool, only one shilling per visit. The children's playroom. The promenades.

"You must also be aware of what *not* to mention to passengers, as it would only detract from the enjoyment of their voyage." Latimer looked at each of them in turn, as though to make sure they were paying attention. "Familiarity with passengers is discouraged. Do not be drawn into talking about yourselves. Do not allow them to refer to you by your given name."

They'd already been handed a printed sheet of rules to memorize, but hearing them aloud had a different kind of power over Annie. Rules had always made her feel safe.

Latimer paused. His eyes were very dark. Annie felt, despite the color of his complexion, that there was something bloodless about him, something cold and hard. "Then there is the occasional passenger with a morbid turn of mind who will display a fixation with the natural fears and dangers of the open sea." Latimer continued his pacing. "You must do your best to discourage this line of thinking. If questioned, assure them that the White Star Line enjoys the finest reputation for safety in the industry, then endeavor to draw their attention to the evening musical program or the shuffleboard and ring toss sets."

Latimer had just finished when the bell sounded: the hour was spent and the moment they'd all been waiting for had arrived. In an instant, the din outside the iron bulkheads had swollen to a roar.

Latimer shouted something, but he had lost their attention. Annie rushed out to the alleyway with the rest of the stewards, catching herself with a gasp at the railing.

The dock below was teeming with people. Standing in lines, waiting to be let up the gangplanks, pressing impatiently at the chains. Spilling out of carriages. Lecturing the stevedores who struggled with their luggage. So many people, more than she had ever seen massed in one place. The sight alone made her dizzy.

They were divided by passenger class. At the far end of the ship was third class: mostly men in workaday clothing, albeit their best, duffel bags slung over their shoulders like sailors. Next came second class: again, mostly men, slightly better attired in their Sunday suits. Solid middle-class shopkeepers and preachers, teachers and the like.

But the first-class crowd was altogether different. Men and women in equal measure, all dressed in near-regal finery that she'd only seen in periodicals, clothing that no one in Ballintoy would be able to afford. Silks and satins and ostrich plumes, ribbon by the yard. Dresses that could only have been made by an expert seamstress, so closely did they follow the wearer's form. Most had a servant or two standing behind them, prim in black uniforms, carrying valises or attending to children. Annie strained to find a gold teething ring, though she was pretty sure Violet had been teasing her; even a country lass knows that gold is too soft to bite down on without damage.

At 10 a.m. precisely, the chains barring the gangplanks were lowered, and passengers flooded the gangplanks. It looked, to Annie, like a dark churning wave of people, overspilling the decks, foaming toward her. Annie hung back. The press of bodies and cacophony of voices: it was all too much after the relative quiet of the past week. She fought a mad desire to turn and bolt, to hide in the room she shared with Violet, and somehow sneak off the ship before it left the harbor. She took a breath. She might be frightened, but she felt it in her bones: this moment in time, this ship, was her destiny.

She turned around and then drew sharply back: a young man, only slightly older than her, had materialized in front of her, jogging a baby in his arms in an attempt to stop its fussing. Her heart went out to him immediately. He looked miserable, unable to stop his child from squirming, untethered and unhappy. She sympathized, too, with the infant—wishing itself back in the nursery, no doubt, where it was calm and sweet and cool.

"May I be of some assistance?" Somehow, she managed to get out the words.

His eyes opened, taking her in. They were kind eyes, the cool gray-blue of a hidden grotto. And, somehow, familiar.

"Oh—pardon me! I didn't see you standing there."

A burble from the child: suddenly there was white spittle all over the front of the man's wool coat.

"Please. Let me help." She pulled a cleaning cloth from her pocket as she reached for the baby. He surrendered the child to her readily, as if by instinct.

The child was not more than a few months old, a small but healthy thing with dark eyes and wisps of pale, honey-brown hair peeking from under the bonnet. The baby felt comfortable—almost familiar—in Annie's arms, even though she had little experience with infants, having been the baby of the family herself.

But the baby soon fell silent, squirming and nuzzling into Annie's chest.

The father dabbed the front of his coat with her cloth. "She has taken to you, hasn't she?"

He was handsome, she noticed, now that he was no longer so anxious looking. And there was something so familiar about him, she could almost think of nothing else. Something like alarm clamored in her head. *Have you ever been to Ballintoy?* she wanted to ask. But the idea seemed ludicrous. Londoners didn't go to Ballintoy.

"She's beautiful, and so healthy," Annie said instead. A tiny pink fist lifted toward her face, attempting to clutch at her chin.

The man shook his head, smiling. "Like a duck to water. Miss . . . ?"

"Stewardess Hebbley."

"Well, Miss Hebbley, you are a godsend. I am very grateful for your help."

"Shall I show you to your cabin, sir? Cabin number, please?"

He pulled out his ticket and showed it to her, as though he wasn't quite sure of the number himself. She was disappointed to see it wasn't one of hers.

Mark Fletcher. Another jolt of pure electricity went through her. *I know you,* she wanted to say. Though at the same time she knew she didn't, that they'd never met before, that this handsome man who seemed so familiar to her was, in fact, a stranger. "I would be pleased to show you the way, Mr. Fletcher. If you would just follow me . . . ?"

At that moment, however, a woman stepped off the gangplank and reached out a hand to her husband. Annie felt an irrational stab of disappointment. Had she hoped the mother of the child was out of the picture somehow? What a terrible wish that would have been. Yet the feeling Mark Fletcher had given her had been so sudden and sharp, almost primal.

She was doomed, it seemed, to be drawn to men who were out of her reach.

The woman who'd appeared at Mark's side was all brass and flushed beauty, fireworks in human form, confident of the power of her own happiness. She was dressed like a queen from one of Annie's imaginary stories; her hat alone, with its fine, delicate netting, the way the contours shadowed her face just so—would have cost a full year of Annie's wages. She was, Annie saw, the type of new young mother who seemed easeful and light, and the child not a burden but a pretty item to add to her collection of wonders.

"I'm sorry for the holdup," she said to Mark, and immediately Annie heard the sharp twang of her American accent, broad and easy and careless, "but I saw the Van Allens on the pier and I wanted to thank them for the other night. . . ." The woman turned her dark eyes on Annie, not unkindly. "And who is this?"

"I found a stewardess to show us to our room." Mark made introductions as he took the baby from Annie and handed her to an older woman who had appeared beside his wife. The nanny, of course.

Annie felt the baby's sudden absence from her arms.

"Shall we go?" Mrs. Fletcher took her husband's arm.

The Fletchers had a suite just beyond the row of cabins that had been assigned to Annie; theirs included a sitting room in addition to the bedroom. The nanny would be housed below with the other servants and crew. The luggage had already been delivered and was heaped to one side of the door: a huge steamer trunk and hatboxes, a half-dozen smaller cases. Two dingy valises—probably the nanny's. A small crib.

The enormity of the pile of luggage took Annie aback. "Will you stay long in America?" she asked, as the nanny hustled the baby into the bedroom, likely to address a soiled diaper. "Or is it home for you?"

The woman followed Annie's eyes and laughed. "All this, you mean? The demands of traveling with an infant." The woman pulled the pins from her hat and laid it on the table, fluffing her effortless waves of amber-brown hair. "And what about you, my dear? Is this your first trip to America?"

"It is, ma'am." As soon as Annie said it, she regretted it. Did this count as personal information?

"And are you planning to stay? I've heard a lot of the people signed on to work as a way to get to America."

Annie supposed this was true. She'd heard talk along those lines late nights in the crew quarters, once the stout and gin started flowing. She worried about saying too much, however, the chief steward's admonishment ringing in her ears. *No undue familiarity.* "Me? No, ma'am. I mean, I haven't yet decided." The truth was she hadn't thought of a single moment beyond right here and right now.

"But you're not against having a little adventure, are you?" The question was innocent enough, but it made Annie a touch uneasy, so she thought it best to say nothing. At that moment, Mark Fletcher began to move about the cabin as he unpacked. She was keenly aware of him behind her, going to and fro, his presence hot against her back, like the sun.

The woman smiled, warm and genuine, though there was a flicker of something behind her eyes that made Annie feel unease. "My name is Caroline Fletcher."

"Pleased to meet you, Mrs. Fletcher." Annie curtsied, and the woman laughed.

"Don't call me that. We're nearly the same age, aren't we?" Annie knew it wasn't meant to be a jab—it was simply more of that American friendliness—but she couldn't help but feel the sudden poverty of her situation compared to Mrs. Fletcher's. Alone, a stewardess, with only as much as would likely fit in one of Mrs. Fletcher's hatboxes.

"And what may I call you?" the woman asked, already milling about, unpacking her dazzling array of personal items with a comfort that made Annie almost dizzy.

"Just Annie is fine," Annie said. She watched Mrs. Fletcher open one of the largest trunks and begin to hang up more colorful dresses than she could possibly wear in a month, let alone a week's journey aboard a ship. Annie tried to make herself useful, taking up some of their books and stacking them on a side table, as Caroline then began to lay out jewelry boxes, opening the lids to display silver and gold pendants and rings—almost as if the suite were her personal shop. Who had need of such jewels? Not to mention the confidence to just set them out where anyone might ogle and covet them? Necklaces, bracelets, a shiny brooch nearly the size of Annie's fist.

Before Annie could comment, however, someone knocked at the open door. An older man peered into the cabin as though staring through the bars of the local zoo.

Mark, who had been laying out his hairbrushes and toiletries, straightened up. "May I help you? As you can see, this cabin is occupied. . . ."

The man seemed amused by Mark's question. "Thank you, my good man, but my cabin is right next door." There was something unsettling about the stranger. What the old women in Annie's village might call uncanny. Annie decided it was his beard, which was full and white, with straggly, unkempt ends, in odd contrast to his expensive clothing. His eyes, too, were constantly searching, lifting off and alighting again. "I heard your voices and thought I would see if there might be a steward about." His voice trailed off, but his eyes finally fixed on Annie.

The cabin next door was indeed her responsibility. She curtsied, a little relieved to be freed from Caroline's well-meant prying. "You are correct, sir, that would be my cabin. And if these passengers have no further need of me . . ."

The older man acknowledged this with a nod. "Indeed, indeed. I mean no inconvenience. I did not mean to steal you away. . . ."

"There is no inconvenience, sir," Caroline said brightly. Annie noticed the twitch of her hand as she waved it in the air. "We have no further need of Miss Hebbley, do we, Mark? She is free to go."

Annie repressed the urge to ask to see the baby one more time. She dropped into a curtsy, avoiding Mark Fletcher's eyes—not sure she could trust herself to meet them—and then followed the old man into the tumult of passengers flowing through the narrow alleyway, shutting the door to the cabin behind her.

"Am I really to have a female attendant?" He gave her a sideways glance. "It seems irregular for a man traveling alone."

Annie started, then folded her hands together to keep from fidgeting. "We are assigned blocks of cabins," she explained. "But I can ask the chief steward about getting a male steward to attend to you, if you'd prefer, sir." It would make for extra bother, running to different parts of the deck, but it could be done.

He canted his head, as if listening to a voice only he could hear. "Oh, never mind. I'm sure it will make no difference." Then, by way of introduction: "W. T. Stead. Do you know who I am?"

She didn't, of course, but she didn't want him to think so. She hesitated. "Should I, sir?"

He drew back, and she feared she'd hurt his feelings. "No, I suppose not, I suppose not. . . . It's just that people like to talk about me. They all have their opinions."

"And what opinion ought I to have, sir?" She'd meant it sincerely, but he smiled as though she'd told a joke.

"Well, I am a newspaperman, first and foremost." Then his face clouded over—again, as if some unheard voice had gripped him. He held open the door to his cabin and, as she entered, gave her a sideways glance she pretended not to see.

The cabin was a large one for a single person, Annie noted. Even larger than the Fletchers', its anteroom included table and chairs, and a door separating it from the bedroom.

Stead had a long list of things requiring her attention: additional blankets and ship's stationery, heavier drapes for the porthole, candles (electric lights being detrimental to health, he insisted), a pillow of duck and not chicken feathers. He gave her his preferences for breakfast (oats cooked in cream, two duck eggs—quail if duck was unavailable, chicken eggs as only the last resort—soft-boiled, all to be delivered to his door no later than 5:30 a.m.), and left strict orders not to be disturbed between the hours of 2 and 4 a.m. (whom did he think would disturb him at such an hour? she wondered, but did not ask). He used this time to work on his speeches and opinion pieces for the newspapers, he explained, and could not be disturbed. Once she promised to track down some misplaced luggage, she was dismissed.

Annie stepped into the alleyway to catch her breath. She had seen the eggs stored in one of the cool, dark pantries—forty thousand, a cook had said as he showed her the stack of trays reaching the ceiling—but she was pretty certain none were duck or quail. She wasn't sure what she would tell this man, who would likely run her off her feet every day. She hoped the rest of her passengers were not so peculiarly demanding.

So much bustle in the alleyway. Passengers a-dither and excited, rushing about in an attempt to see everything at once. Stewards running this way and that like rabbits flushed out of a hedgerow.

Violet stepped up to her. "Are you all right, Annie? Something the matter?"

"Just a bit overwhelmed."

Violet grimaced. "I don't blame you. Have you ever seen such crowds? It's like the entire city of London crammed aboard this one ship. Have you heard: there's a couple of prizefighters on board. I've seen them—a big, brown-haired one, and a smaller blond fellow. You've never seen a man with so many muscles!"

She was about to speak when Thomas Whiteley, one of the chief steward's assistants, walked up to them.

"Any problems, ladies? No? Then I suggest you get back to work. Now is not the time for dillydallying." He held up a finger as the women began to disperse. "A minute, Annie. Mr. Latimer asked me to tell you that the couple in C-85 has requested your help. They asked for you specifically. Said their nanny is overwhelmed and will require your assistance. On request only—it's not to interfere with your normal duties." He must have mistaken her face, because he added quickly, "They promised to pay extra for the service. If you think this will be a problem . . ."

She thought of the baby's downy hair, her sweet smell. Skin as delicate as a rose petal. She thought, too, of Mark's eyes, the coming storm inside them. "Oh no, not at all. It would be a pleasure."

"That's a good girl. That's what Mr. Latimer likes to hear."

But after Whiteley left, Annie felt a kind of dread seize her. She knew this feeling. The longing. The shame. *I will not be alone with Mark Fletcher, ever*, she promised herself. *I swear it*, she thought, reaching under the collar of her uniform to find the crucifix that had hung around her neck since she was a little girl. *Swear it on the cross, to all that is good and holy.*

The Lord favors good girls, Annie.

But she could not find the necklace. In the excitement of the day, the chain must have broken, and it had disappeared.

Chapter Five

David John Bowen twisted the ring off the pinkie finger of his sweaty right hand and placed it in his vest pocket before hanging his clothes on a peg in the gymnasium dressing room. It was a plain brass ring with a small engraved *B*, not worth very much, and he shouldn't even have bothered hiding it.

But habits die hard. And common as it was, the ring had a personal value to him. It had belonged to his father. He didn't know where his pop had come by it—he very well could've stolen it—but it was Dai's now, and he wasn't going to lose it. Not that he had reason to believe that any of the fine ladies and gentlemen in the first-class passengers' gymnasium would stoop to stealing a brass signet ring. Down below, it was a different story. There were some desperate characters in third class—he'd seen enough petty thieves in his lifetime to know.

Leslie Williams grinned as he stripped off his jacket and waistcoat. Les, the fearless one. The impetuous one. It had been Les's idea to buy tickets in the first place. America was where the money was. A man with Dai's talents would be a fool not to go, he'd said. He'd heard, for example, of a prizefighter who'd made *fifteen thousand,* just for a title bout.

When they bought their tickets, they'd paid extra to use the gymnasium. It was fine, but not at all like the one in Pontypridd where he and Leslie trained. That one was strictly for boxers. It had a proper ring. Punching bags. Medicine balls. It had smelled of sweat and cigar smoke and blood. This gym was for rich Londoners with its pommel horse, Indian clubs, and tumbling mats.

Word that two professional boxers were going to spar had obviously got out, and a small crowd had formed to watch. It wasn't unexpected. Les tended to draw crowds wherever he went. It was his smile, his bravado, his love of a good time—and something else, something that people couldn't name but wanted from him without ever knowing they wanted it. Women had a way of losing their underclothing and men their wallets or dignity when it came to Leslie Williams. There were few women gathered this afternoon; perhaps the rest were still focused on unpacking in their cabins, each the size of four third-class bunkrooms, or napping off a long lunch. Dai was disappointed. He liked the way these rich women eyed him. He was a different breed of man from their husbands and lovers. They liked his muscles, wanted to see how he would put them to use. *There's money in those eyes,* that's what Les would say.

Well, maybe there were few women, but there were plenty of men in the crowd; and Dai thought he recognized a few, swells who had been pointed out to him in passing: John Jacob Astor, said to be the richest man in America, and Benjamin Guggenheim, not quite Astor's equal in funds but twice the man in airs. Sir Cosmo Duff-Gordon, husband to a rich society dressmaker.

He and Leslie easily cleared a spot on the floor, the few others who'd already made it here for a workout in their gymnasium outfits vanishing sheepishly. The space became theirs. Dai flexed his hands; they were pugilists, bare-handed boxers. They were in their undershirts and their everyday trousers because it made for better theater. Loose buttons would fly. Sweat would soak through tight cotton.

Dai squared off opposite Leslie and raised his fists as he'd done a thousand times, framing Leslie's boyish face. Leslie made his living with that face, not his hands. Leslie winked, flashed a grin. *Let's give 'em a show.*

Dai threw controlled jabs that looked more impressive than they actually were. Leslie positioned himself so the punches seemed to come within an inch of his face. He knew how to dance back at the last moment. Leslie was incredibly light on his feet; *years of escaping*, is how he explained it. As a bantamweight, he was nearly two stone lighter than Dai, and had nowhere near the same hands. Leslie may have had the moves, but Dai had the skill and the weight. If they were to really fight, Dai would have Leslie beat inside of two rounds; sometimes he longed to show everyone the truth. The *real* truth.

Out of the corner of his eye, Dai saw the rich swells with their clean white hands huddled together, following his every move, already placing bets.

"I'll give two-to-one odds on the dark one. . . . Any takers?"

"Give me three to one."

"I'll take a piece of that."

After just a few minutes, they had worked up a good heat. Sweat plastered Leslie's blond curls to his face, made his undershirt transparent, made the muscles of his upper arms gleam like they were oiled. Dai liked Les best like this, his blue eyes burning and all his muscles raging hard, his breathing rough and rhythmic. Sparring like this, it was like having Les to himself. They'd been surrounded by strangers since boarding: in third class, they were cheek by jowl with people no matter where you turned, four passengers to a cabin. Still, better their crowded cabin than the dormitory taking up the middle of one deck, two hundred bodies crammed in double-decker beds.

He tossed off a jab and then left himself wide open, practically daring Leslie to step in and pop him on the jaw. But Leslie didn't take it. Dai tried again, hesitating for nearly a full second—something he would never do in the ring, where seconds were like lifetimes. It was as good as begging Leslie to hit him. To take the shot.

Leslie took the hint this time. He managed a swift uppercut to Dai's chin, knocking him back two steps. Dai felt his teeth grind together as a roar went up from the crowd behind them. Snuffing out the urge to hit back, Dai staggered forward and fell into Leslie's arms. Their damp chests pressed together. His bruised chin rested on Leslie's shoulder. Leslie's breath roared in his ear. Then Leslie pushed him away.

It was over. Behind them: cursing, the slap of paper and flesh. The sound of money changing hands. Dai picked up a towel. Damn, it was plush. Rich people's towels, and brand-new, too. The towels in steerage were like burlap sacks.

"That was a mistake, you know." Leslie poked a finger to Dai's chest. "You should've won. That's what they were expecting. We should've let them get complacent. Then we do the flip *after.*" Leslie looked over Dai's shoulder at the men settling up. "We woulda got better odds. This way, them are the only ones who benefit, and they don't hardly need it. . . ." He gave a sour look at the money changing hands but then—maybe sensing Dai's disapproval—broke away. He slapped Dai's midsection. "Never mind. . . . What's done is done. We'll get our turn again. When are we going to have access to this many stiff collars at once?"

Dai's stomach lurched. "No, Les. It's too risky."

Their audience started to disperse, making their way back to the lounges and their private rooms. Even as he toweled down, Leslie watched them: the women in their gymnasium suits with voluminous pantaloons gathered at the knee, looking vaguely childish, only to turn back into women, feathered and powdered, like exotic birds.

"What do you think," Les said, ignoring him. "The three-card molly?"

"We don't have Soapy," Dai said, stalling.

To run that trick, they normally worked with a confidence man named Soapy Marvin. Soapy was the one with the nimble hand. No boxer, with his busted knuckles and swollen fingers, had the dexterity to run a hand con. Dai and Leslie were the outside men, working the crowd. Leslie, with his natural charm, was usually the one who won the first round, good at crowing about his good fortune and making the game seem easy. Dai would be the capper, jumping in to outbid the mark if the mark happened to pick the right card, so they wouldn't lose a bundle. And he could be the muscle, too, if things got testy; but he didn't like to play that role, picking on men who were right to question them.

Growing up in the rough end of Pontypridd, nearly everyone they knew had been on the con at one time or another. Dai could understand the need for a trick. But Dai hated a lie.

"These are men of the world. They won't be fooled that easy."

"We won't try it on the whole. We'll pick our mark. A closed molly. Just between friends."

That jaw. That smile.

"No. Too dangerous." They'd be stuck with this group at least a week.

Leslie turned. It was like the sun had gone behind a cloud. "All right. I'll think of something else." Still, Dai knew how this would play out. He couldn't deny Leslie for long. No one could. Les was already walking away. Over his shoulder, he said, "Let's go up and try on our dinner clothes. If we're going to eat with the royals we might try and shape up a bit first—"

"Les, no."

"Tonight's the time to strike," Les went on. "These gentlemen just seen us. They'll be eager to talk with us professionals. Clean up and meet me on the deck."

It was Leslie, of course, who had talked him into having suits made special for the trip. They'd even missed the earlier sailing, the ship they were originally booked to take to America, because the damn suits hadn't been ready.

Leslie's hand was on the door to the locker room, but he'd paused, and now Dai saw why. On the opposite side of the gymnasium stood a woman in white tennis clothing. She was smiling at them—no, at Leslie. She was older than Les by a decade, maybe more, and not pretty, but anyone who could afford the clothing to play tennis was attractive enough for the moment.

Don't, Dai nearly said.

But Les had already pivoted. He was making his way over to the woman in white, no doubt to offer her some tips on how to hold her racket, the towel draped over his shoulders like a cape. That smile. *Dangerous.*

~~ellee~~

Chapter Six

The most excellent thing about being a kid was that no one paid any attention. And no one paying any attention meant you could mostly do what you wanted, no matter your station, just so long as you didn't get caught.

And Teddy was most excellent at not getting caught.

He'd been clenching his fists and making his muscles bulge up and down as he raced up the steep back stairs. Teddy had heard the Welsh boxers would most likely be up here on the big deck before the dinner hour, and he wanted to be the first to meet them. His mistress, Mrs. Astor, had been talking about nothing but the two boxers and their fight this afternoon in the gymnasium and Teddy sorely wished he'd seen it for himself, not least because he'd never been in any kind of gymnasium before and had only just learned the word.

A gust of cold air hit him as he shoved open the door to the promenade, but he didn't care if it was that cold and windy up here with no coat. Teddy was tough like that. No matter that he was supposed to be belowdecks taking care of Kitty, Mr. Astor's Airedale (Kitty! What a silly name for a dog). Here was where the action was: first-class ladies and gents were coming up from their cabins, and in no time Teddy was surrounded by bright silk skirts and thick wool coats and the hearty laughter of rich folk. As it happened, Teddy was at just the right height to find himself face-first in a sea of thick-knuckled old ladies wearing glinting rings, sometimes two to a finger. Before his mama died she'd taught Teddy to be a good boy and that taking things that weren't his wasn't nice. But Teddy had always thought that shiny things seemed most excellent, and he got distracted from looking for the boxers when he saw just how many shiny things there were to see up here, and wondered if anyone would notice if just one or two of them went missing, just for a little, while he got to look at them himself.

And then the most strange thing happened: he thought he heard a *tsk*, as if his dead mama had suddenly heard his naughty thoughts. He turned around, but of course his mama wasn't there and Teddy didn't believe in spirits no matter what his mistress said. His mama had taught him that, too: don't believe what those rich folk say. God knows there's only life and death and nothing in between.

But then: a woman's voice. It was thin, as though coming from a long way away.

Teddy turned and scanned the milling crowd but couldn't pinpoint where the sound had come from, thought maybe there was a performer out on the deck. He'd heard there was a famous singer on board and Teddy liked singers, though not near as much as boxers.

The soft melody continued, but he couldn't quite make out the words and yet the song reminded him of one his mama used to sing while shelling peas for their dinner mash, when he was real small. A real pretty song in the old tongue he'd never understood, but it always gave him chills.

Teddy felt those chills again and it wasn't just from the lack of coat.

The wind ruffled his hair and Teddy started walking toward it—toward the wind or wherever the song was coming from because suddenly he had to know. Had to see this singer who was invisible and was his mama but wasn't, of course, his mama.

His legs felt heavy. Colored skirts brushed against his arms but he couldn't feel them. He walked. There was a rail, and then, the sea: choppy and harsh. Waves like blue wolves. He could see their white fangs. Were the wolves singing? No, there was a woman who controlled the wolves, a witch of the depths, and it was her song. That's what he thought, though he knew it seemed like a kid's story and he was getting too big for kids' stories. The rail was there and no one was looking and the metal felt cold in his hand when he began to climb. Teddy was never allowed to see anything good, but this time he would be the first to see what there was to see. He would find the woman who was singing the beautiful song. The cold didn't bother him. He liked the cold now. He pulled himself up. The song became a roar of wind. Oh, he liked the sound of that roar.

Hands were pulling him off the railing, and at first he felt numb, but then Teddy started to struggle and fight. Whoever had grabbed him was holding him tight and now the song was gone, but he could hear gasps all around him and people were staring and Teddy wasn't used to being stared at.

"Settle down, boy, you're going to be fine," a man shouted.

Teddy's eyes cleared and a joy rushed into him, replacing the anger.

The boxer had found him! He recognized his likeness from the picture Mrs. Astor had been showing around.

"What are you doing?" the man said, shaking Teddy by the shoulders.

Teddy wanted to cry now because he was embarrassed, but he bit his lip instead. "Nothing," he said. "Please don't tell." He didn't want to be in trouble with the boxer, of all people.

The boxer, who people called "Dai," crouched so they were nearly eye to eye and he handed Teddy his handkerchief. "Look, I know. I heard it, too. It's all right. You're safe now."

He asked Teddy to tell him which of the people he belonged to—
Who is your mistress?—and for a second Teddy felt confused and he
almost answered *her*, pointing out to sea. But then he started thinking
straight again and pointed toward an outdoor table where Mrs. Astor
sat with a group of society ladies she'd only just met, all of them
dressed in silk dresses under furs, bright blue and cream and gold,
fingers crusted with more of those shiny jewels. Mrs. Astor was far
younger than the other two, closer to Teddy's age than those grown-up
women. One was Caroline Fletcher and the other was Lady Duff-
Gordon. Teddy knew who they were because all the servants had
been made to learn all the names of the Astors' new friends and Teddy
was fast at learning things.

The women were deep in conversation and Teddy got nervous, for
he wasn't used to getting caught and Mrs. Astor had gotten only tes-
tier as her belly had gotten bigger with that baby growing inside it.
He tried to hide behind Dai's legs, but the boxer pushed him forward
so he could be seen.

"Pardon the interruption, ladies," said Dai, "but would this poor
mite belong to any of you?"

His mistress let out a shriek. "Teddy! He's mine. Where'd he go
off to?"

"My goodness, what's this all about?" one of her companions
asked—that was the Lady Duff-Gordon. She was probably three times
Mrs. Astor's age, and she looked Dai up and down with the shrewdest
eye Teddy'd ever seen, then turned her gaze to Teddy, then back to
the boxer.

"It's nothing, ma'am. I'm afraid the boy had a fright at the railing.
A bit scared of heights, I'd say." Dai gave Teddy a wink and Teddy felt
a rush of pride. He stood up a bit taller. He weren't scared of these
ladies.

Mrs. Astor stood up with effort and as she did, her big belly poked
out over the table. Had to be near ready to burst, is what the other
servants were saying. She reached for Teddy and took his hand.

"Teddy, what are you doing up here, anyway? You're supposed to be down in the stateroom attending to Kitty while we're at dinner. Did you forget?"

"Madeleine, dear, don't trouble yourself in your condition," the woman named Caroline Fletcher said.

But despite her "condition," Mrs. Astor was capable of pulling Teddy's arm hard. She gave him a little jerk to get him to stand by her side as she sat back down.

"As for you," said Lady Duff-Gordon to the boxer, "you're quite the hero, saving that little boy."

Looking closely, Teddy could see that this woman's evening dress was dripping with beads and embroidery. A huge pink stone, ringed with shiny diamonds, glinted on one finger, looking most excellent, like it should be on display at the World's Exposition, a line of people paying a penny apiece to gawk at it.

"It's nothing, ma'am," said the boxer. "I really should be going."

"Nonsense. I'm not going to let you disappear, not before I've had a chance to get to know you." She extended a hand. "You're the boxing chap my husband told me about, aren't you? He said you took quite the drubbing today."

Teddy's mistress was still pulling on him. Though he wasn't bold enough to tug away, he kept his eyes fixed on the boxer, as if by doing so, he could make the man return his glance. "Did it hurt? Simon Chadley got me full in the nose once, and I didn't even cry." His free hand traveled to his chest. "Got blood on my shirt and everything. Mama near about killed me for that."

His mistress laughed, high and nervous. Teddy knew at once that he had embarrassed her. "That's enough, Teddy. You should know better than to speak out of turn."

Dai flicked his eyes to Teddy, a sympathetic smile on his face, then began speaking to the older lady again. "It was nothing, ma'am. Caught off guard is all."

"Cosmo was quite impressed by you, despite losing a few pounds,

I believe. Now, you really must join us for dinner. My husband will be cross if he learns I've let you slip away before he has a chance to meet you."

"I should be going—"

"I don't see why." Again, she fixed him with a crystal-clear, all-seeing eye. "You're not a first-class passenger, are you? Are you really in such a hurry to go back to—wherever?" She paused, and Teddy, watching it all, saw a hardness in her eyes. "Stay, and join us. I guarantee you'll have a marvelous time and an even better meal. And maybe I can make it worth your while . . . introduce you to an heiress or two. . . ."

The boxer smiled politely. "I'm not looking to be introduced to any heiresses tonight, your ladyship. . . . I'm spoken for."

"I'll have you know I'm not accustomed to men turning me down." The boxer bit his lip and made a face like he knew better than to argue with her anymore, and she burst into a comfortable laugh. "It's settled, then," she said. "Would you escort me to our table? I believe my husband will be waiting for us there. He was told there were *only* two thousand bottles of wine on board and he wants to put in his order before the best ones are drunk."

"He may have a point," Madeleine Astor said. "They told me there were thirteen hundred passengers on this sailing. That's less than two bottles a head for a whole week!"

"When you put it that way . . . you may be right. What an unconscionable oversight," Lady Duff-Gordon said with a laugh. She stood, leading the way inside, toward the grand, first-class dining room.

Madeleine Astor and Caroline Fletcher stood to follow, and Mrs. Astor tugged on Teddy to come along behind her. "Let's find Mr. Haverford and get him to take you back to the cabin," she said, adding in a whisper, "and I'll give you a sweet if you're good, just like I promised."

But as Teddy followed the ladies off the grand deck and into the warmth of the crowded corridor, he no longer cared to imagine the taste of sugar melting on his tongue. All he could think about was the way the water had sung to him. How it had called to him. How he'd felt, just in that moment, like he would do whatever the song had said, because the music had made him unafraid of everything. He shivered. He'd never had that feeling before—that feeling of wanting to fall.

Chapter Seven

10 April 1912 9:15 p.m.
Entered into the record of Dr. Alice Leader
Strict confidentiality
Patient: Caroline Fletcher
Age: 23

I was approached by Mrs. Fletcher late in the evening the first day on board. She told me that she had been using laudanum since the birth of her daughter some five months earlier to treat headaches and malaise, which sometimes takes the form of acute agitation and can be severe. She asked if I might write a new prescription for her as she had inadvertently forgotten to order more in time for the trip. It seems she must have planned it in quite a hurry. She added that she had to take twice the amount of laudanum as normal to get half as much relief.

I suggested that Mrs. Fletcher try cocaine as a preferable treatment to laudanum, and gave her a prescription for her husband to take to Dr. O'Loughlin's office for fulfillment, for an ounce in cake form. Instructions are to take no more than a quarter teaspoon in a quarter- to half-cup of water every two hours or as needed. The other advantage to cocaine is that it is not thought to be addictive, as is laudanum. Better to err on the side of caution.

I will follow up with Mrs. Fletcher in a day's time to see if the prescription agrees with her. Too, I harbor some suspicion regarding Mrs. Fletcher's excuse: Did she truly forget her medicine or had she exhausted it and was too embarrassed to ask her regular physician for more? I have seen many wives become addicted to laudanum. The stress and tedium of maintaining a household and answering a husband's demands. We shall see if cocaine proves a gentler remedy for her.

Chapter Eight

Caroline sat at the dressing table in her cabin after dinner that night, keeping her gaze strictly focused on her reflection in the mirror as she brushed her soft, golden-brown hair. One hundred brush strokes, like her mother once taught her. Her hand hardly trembled at all.

"I've never spent a less pleasant evening in my life." Mark tamped his pipe tobacco in fierce, sharp jabs. "If this is the way your people behave"—Americans, he meant—"then I have sincere reservations about what to expect in New York."

When he wanted to be charming, Mark could fill a room with his voice, his ease. When he wanted to be sour, however, he could curdle the blood in her veins. It was as if the suggestion of the séance, the childishness of it, had made *him* childish and pouty. "It was suggested in fun. They didn't mean to hurt the old man's feelings or to tease him. Besides, these aren't 'my' people at all."

The trouble had all begun with that old gossip Lady Duff-Gordon, showing off her new young hero, the boxer who'd apparently saved the boy from nearly going overboard. W. T. Stead had called the incident—What was it he'd said? "The call of the void." The old man believed in ghosts—he practically said so himself over dinner, waxing on about the spirit world and how it had been beckoning the Astors' little servant boy, raising the idea of a séance.

"The way they mocked poor William Stead," Mark huffed. "The man is practically an institution in England. They had no respect for him at all."

"Let it go, Mark," she said with a sigh. "They all agreed to participate, anyway, after Madeleine Astor insisted. I'm sure she simply can't think of any other form of postdinner entertainment. And you must admit you're curious, aren't you?"

There was more she could say, wasn't there? The weight and power of Lillian everywhere in their thoughts. He had to wonder, as she did. She tried not to admit how often she felt that woman's presence, looking over her shoulder. Would she follow them until the bitter end?

"It's disrespectful. A sick indulgence. I beg you, Caroline: let the dead rest in peace."

Caroline's hands shook as she smoothed her dress, and she refused to look Mark in the eye. *Let the dead rest in peace.* And yet he still carried Lillian's diary like some kind of dirty secret, kept it in his breast pocket close to his heart. As if Caroline didn't know. As if she didn't know everything—the horrible, shaking breath and piercing cry of his nightmares, the same ones, she was sure, that wove stealthily into her own on the nights she slept at all.

As for Stead, she heard he had spent time in prison for some ghastly offense, something to do with prostitution, though Caroline wasn't sure she had the entire story. She'd wanted to tell Mark that she had a bad feeling about Stead—it made her uncomfortable to travel with a newspaper man; they were always asking questions—but she held her tongue for now. You never knew anymore when a single word might spark a flame in Mark.

She was at thirty-seven strokes when the loud knock at the door startled her. She stood immediately, concerned about waking the baby. Mark gave her a quizzical look but said nothing, instead moving ahead of her to the door, as if to protect her from whoever was on the other side. Sometimes it made her want to cry, this playacting. As if she could still be protected. As if the sickness and the horror hadn't touched them both.

But it was only the stewardess, that pretty Miss Hebbley. It took Caroline a minute to understand why she stood in the doorway with a tray: it was the warmed milk they had requested be delivered at this hour every evening.

"Come in, please." Mark stood aside to let her by. That exact moment, Ondine chose to wake, shattering the quiet with a razor-sharp cry.

"The milk—would you like me to pour it straight into the bottle?" Miss Hebbley asked.

"Would you?" As the stewardess busied herself with the pot of milk and slender glass bottle, Caroline couldn't help but think that Miss Hebbley's small hands seemed made for such fussy, careful work. With their constant tremble, she didn't trust her own hands enough to pour—especially not in front of Mark.

Meanwhile, Ondine continued to wail—the plaintive notes repetitive as a metronome. Demanding, accusatory.

"Is there anything else I can do for you?" the stewardess asked. Her eyes went to the crying baby, as if she was wondering why Caroline hadn't yet managed to soothe her.

"No, thank you." The words came out more curtly than Caroline intended, but her frustration with Mark was morphing into a cloud of greater annoyance—at her husband's recalcitrance, at the baby, at the noise itself, inhabiting their small cabin like an additional presence.

She thought the medicine was supposed to help. This new drug barely took the edge off and made her thoughts fly faster through her mind instead of going still and quiet, as she'd wanted. She would go to the ship's surgeon if she had to and demand a prescription for laudanum.

After the stewardess had left, Mark turned on his wife. "That was uncalled for, don't you think? She was only trying to help."

"I don't like the way she was looking at Ondine." The thought came to her as she said it and crystalized into truth.

Caroline let Mark take the baby. The wailing, while it didn't stop, ebbed in intensity, like a violent storm wearing itself out. She watched Mark adjust Ondine's swaddle cloths with a degree of expertise that baffled her. She sighed. It wasn't Mark's fault that he was a natural with the baby. That he'd loved someone else before her. These things didn't mean he loved her any less. If anything, he had to love her *more*, didn't he? After all they'd been through together.

Did that make her a terrible person for the way she felt—itchy, entrapped in a web of her own making?

And then there was the baby. No matter how much help she received, she couldn't avoid the fact that motherhood simply wore her out. There was always this gnawing on the inside for a freedom she would never have again.

But the innocence and freedom of her past had died a gasping, strangling death, now hadn't they?

Caroline reached for her shawl, pinning it closed around her shoulders with the help of her favorite brooch. One of the few gifts Mark had given to her. Both of them knew who it had belonged to before. . . .

"Are you sure you aren't interested in coming?" she asked, knowing his stance on the séance had not changed.

"I don't believe in ghosts," Mark said, not looking up. He didn't have to. His words were like thorns. She knew better than to touch them.

By now Ondine had calmed and latched on to the bottle, Mark holding it at a gentle angle as she drank. He nodded at Caroline but stayed focused on the baby. His thorns had become a fortress of briars surrounding Ondine. Keeping Caroline out. She felt a pang of envy—though whether it was for that safety or that intimacy or both, she couldn't say.

Why wasn't the medicine working? It was supposed to soothe her.

It was too little, that was the problem. A pinch of powder, mixed in a thimble of water.

She touched the brooch, the smooth shape of the dangling heart, so close to her own.

She took the long way round the lower deck and up through a private staircase, presumably reserved for the servants. She was just at the top of the stairs when the Astors' servant boy, Teddy, slipped past her in a blur. Or maybe he'd not slipped by but stopped to say something to her in his secretive way. Had she, in fact, squatted down to his level to find out what he wanted? *What is it, Teddy? Do you have a secret for me?* But her head had been hammering, the passageway so narrow and dark, and she'd been unable to focus on what he was saying, desperate for the medicine to effect its magic, wanting only now to escape into the air and the night.

By the time she stepped out onto the promenade, thankfully, the dose began to do its work. She would take a breath of air before meeting everyone for the séance in Stead's room. Of course she was going to attend, despite her husband's misgivings and the apparent frivolity of it all. How could she not?

Besides, it wasn't just the call of darkness, the curiosity, the constant tremor of something following her from beyond the grave that made her seek out the gathering. She didn't want to admit how much she had *enjoyed* the company at dinner tonight. She hated to think that she simply wanted an excuse to leave her rooms, and her husband and child, behind.

It was much less crowded on the open-air deck at this hour than it had been earlier. A scattering of young couples, their murmurs drifting out over the water, strolled arm in arm or leaned on the railing to look at the stars—the great canopy of velvet blackness, punctuated by pinpoints of glittering light. Caroline sucked in a soft breath. The night sky was much more beautiful away from the city, and it made her want to cry, though no tears would come, she knew.

Her mother always said that beauty existed to make us feel life's perfect marriage of suffering and joy.

It was something her late husband, Henry, had never appreciated. That was one of the things that had drawn her initially to Mark: He understood. He was moved and awed by little instances of beauty bound with sadness: a torn page swept up in a sudden, swirling wind; a pigeon fluttering its wings as it bathed in an oil-streaked puddle; a crumbling ruin overgrown with swaying nettles; a stranger struggling to tamp down some secret sorrow. Henry had always called her a hopeless romantic, but Mark had seen it was something more than that.

Lillian had, too. Caroline understood Mark's love for Lillian. In many essential ways, she had loved Lillian just as fiercely. She had been complex, fiery, so full of *seeking*. Caroline had been drawn to her immediately, had envied the intensity of her and of Mark's passion for her. Had wanted—no, needed—to be part of that in some small way.

Lillian had been her friend first; that was how Caroline had met Mark. Lillian might've only been a seamstress—from a good family, but one that had fallen in society over the generations—and yet the two of them had become as close as sisters.

For a time, anyway.

A cold wind wriggled up her sleeve—she shivered. Her shawl had come loose about her shoulders.

The air out here was ghostly, craving something of her. Something she would never let herself give.

The truth.

She made her way to the railing and briskly rubbed her arms beneath her light shawl. The fresh-steamed evening dress she wore tonight was just one of the many she had commissioned while abroad, this one a shade of pale blue-purple that had made her think of the hydrangea blossoms that would burst up cloud-like in front of her family's vacation home in Nantucket.

Now, the choice of dress seemed naive—she hadn't considered the night winds. The torrent of dark memories.

They'd left their second stop of the day, in Cherbourg, France, sometime after dinner, and would be arriving tomorrow in Queenstown, Ireland. But for now, they were too far from land to make out its shape or the halo of its lights.

Dark ocean lapped on all sides.

She rubbed her arms, half thrilled and half unmoored by the idea of all that distance, all that darkness, everywhere she looked. There was something almost erotic about it, the incomprehensible massiveness of the world and one's small part within it.

Maybe they'd truly escaped the horror they'd left behind.

Maybe it was all new from here. A fresh start.

Tobacco smoke leaked from the portholes of the men's smoking room. There were eight thousand cigars available for the first-class male passengers' enjoyment, a steward had told Caroline proudly, as though she cared. It smelled as though all eight thousand were being smoked tonight. Still, it made Caroline feel guilty. Mark would probably enjoy the company of other men over brandy and tobacco, rather than being left to mind the baby while she was out taking a turn in the night air. She shouldn't have stormed out. She shouldn't treat Ondine like a toy, to be handed to someone else when she got bored. She wanted, desperately, for Mark to be happy.

But the truth came to Caroline with a shock of clarity as she moved past an older couple murmuring softly to each other: Mark *wasn't* happy.

And neither was she.

The marriage had been so hasty. It had all been theoretical before, a frantic mess of plans, urgent whispers, and last-minute purchases. Now they were encased in a swirling mass of secrets, bound together and making their way inevitably toward distant shores. There was no turning back.

~ele~

It was Benjamin Guggenheim who opened Stead's door when Caroline knocked. She recognized him from dinner and was relieved to see him again.

The smile he gave her told her that he was pleased to see her, too. He was cloaked in tobacco smoke, a half-finished cigar smoldering in his hand.

"Are you alone, Mrs. Fletcher?"

She recognized the look in his eyes: hesitantly flirtatious. He was married, with children around her age, if she was correctly remembering a newspaper story she'd once read, but he was known to be sailing with a mistress, a French singer. Caroline wasn't naive; she knew such arrangements were common, even if rarely conducted this openly. And yet Guggenheim had impressed her at their dinner conversation and didn't seem the kind of man who was interested in women only as conquests.

Feeling her face flush with the thought, Caroline surveyed William Stead's cabin. He had transformed his stateroom. Caroline imagined it had started out exactly like hers: a square box paneled in wood, with a table and four narrow chairs, cheerless electric sconces on the walls. But here, the lights had been turned off and a pair of elegant silver candelabra brought in, the long tapers topped with wavering flames. Additional chairs formed a ring around the table, which was now graced with a flowing white tablecloth. The porthole had been unlatched and left slightly ajar. Sounds from the ship drifted in through the open window. Muffled talking and laughter. Somehow, this Mr. Stead had managed to conjure up the right atmosphere; well, Guggenheim had said the Englishman was a noted occultist. Maybe he kept all the accoutrements with him in a box, like a traveling salesman.

Caroline felt a tremor of nerves run through her, despite the powder.

Madeleine Astor had evidently been able to persuade her friends to join them. Sir Cosmo and Lady Duff-Gordon were already seated at the table, Lady Duff-Gordon with a puckish smile on her face. *She doesn't expect anything to come of this. To her, it's a lark.*

The Astors were already at the table. John Jacob gave her a nod, but he looked miserable. Caroline couldn't tell if he might be there only to indulge his wife. Madeleine was beside him, her chin jutted proudly. Her face was done up with all the fashionable paints—dark arched brows, and pouty reddened lips—yet the sweet roundness of her face made her look more like a schoolgirl than a society lady. She was so *young*. And pregnant: the swell was evident, even under the skirts of her cleverly designed evening dress.

No sign of the boxer Mr. Bowen. Undoubtedly, no one had thought to invite him even though he was the one who'd saved the boy. For a moment, she thought of what Mark would say: that to these rich people, anyone who wasn't in their class was invisible.

"Can I help you to a seat?" Guggenheim asked her, shuffling her forward toward the table, his hand resting on the small of her back. "Occultism is a fad among my friends," he muttered, "but I must admit that I find it a bore." He whispered that last part, his warm breath tickling her ear.

"You don't believe in life after death?" It was a true question; Caroline felt herself hope he'd have some superior knowledge of the truth. *Could we ever escape?*

He held out her chair. "I'm not opposed to the concept, mind you, but no one has proved it to my satisfaction. *Yet,* anyway." He released a wobbly smoke ring into the air and a mischievous smile crept over his lips. "But if we're trying to find out what was responsible for that little boy's spell earlier . . . my money would be on sirens. I've always been partial to the idea of them. You know, those sea nymphs who bewitch men with their song until they crash their ships onto the rocks and die." He laughed and shook his head. "I'm not sure what such a fascination says about *me*."

"It means you're a romantic."

"That would be the *kindest* interpretation, Mrs. Fletcher. I'm not sure everyone would agree with you, however." He grinned and she felt briefly dazzled by the brightness of his teeth.

As Stead pulled items from an open trunk, the various conversations at the table died down. First, a bowl decorated with a beautiful Oriental motif. He put something in the bowl and then struck a match. A thin trail of smoke lifted toward the ceiling and a musky smell filled the room.

"Incense, William?" Lady Duff-Gordon asked.

"A special blend I picked up in the Himalayas. Used by the monks when they wish to communicate with their dead."

Next came a large, shallow dish that Stead placed in the center of the table. The interior of the bowl was luminous, as though lined with mother-of-pearl. Stead filled the dish with water from his ewer. "Have you seen a scrying bowl before?"

"I should say not," Cosmo Duff-Gordon replied, presumably speaking for everyone.

Stead dipped a finger into the water. "If we are lucky, the spirits will show themselves there. Or we will be allowed to see the spirit world through this surface."

"Like a portal?" Guggenheim asked.

"Exactly, sir." Stead beamed.

Last came a plate. It held a small, crusty loaf of bread.

"Did that come from our dinner table?" John Astor guffawed.

"It's for the dead. Spirits of the dead come to us looking for things. Sustenance," Stead said, gesturing to the bread. "Light, warmth." He gestured to the candles. "Everything on this table is here for a reason."

"I see," Lady Duff-Gordon said, arching an eyebrow.

Caroline, too, had become restless. Cynical. What were they all pretending?

"There's one more thing I must tell you." Stead looked to each one in turn as he spoke. "We don't know the provenance of the spirit that made contact with the Astors' servant today. We don't know if it is someone related to their servant boy. It may be someone else entirely— perhaps even someone looking to make contact with one of you. In all likelihood, if we are contacted by a ghost, he or she will be known to someone in the room. Have any of you lost someone close to you recently?"

Once again, Caroline shivered. It was a silly question, though: *everyone* had, not just her. Disease, pestilence, accident, war: death was never very far away. Still, trepidation seemed to flare briefly on everyone's faces.

"Very good. Our dear departed, the beloved dead," Stead said. "Remember those names."

The room suddenly felt small and close. Even with the porthole open, there was not enough air, and what little they had was thick with incense and the salty perfume of the sea.

Stead looked around the table. "Let us take our places." It seemed much more solemn once they were all sitting, faces bathed in the flickering candlelight. "Now we hold hands," Stead said. "But, ladies, I must ask you to remove your gloves. The contact must be skin to skin."

Caroline undid the rows of tiny buttons at her wrists before tugging off her gloves. She wriggled her fingers; her hands looked naked. When she pressed her fingers into Guggenheim's warm palm, she felt a frisson of electricity pass between them. It wasn't often she felt a strange man's bare flesh.

"Silence, please." The table settled. Stead closed his eyes, solemn as a priest. "We are gathered tonight to commune with the dead. Today, a boy on this ship was contacted by a spirit. The people now gathered wish to understand what lured that boy to near death. If that spirit is present, we ask that you make yourself known. . . ."

Caroline peered through narrowed eyes. The flames stood with only the faintest flicker; the water in the scrying bowl lapped gently in time with the movement of the ship.

Stead tried again. "We wish to speak to any spirits now present. We beg you to make yourself known to us. . . ."

Sounds from elsewhere on the ship started to worm their way into her consciousness: a woman's laughter; snatches of violin, high and sweet.

"Please, make yourself known. We are believers. We invite you to come among us." Strain was creeping into Stead's voice.

Madeleine Astor coughed. "Must there be so much smoke? I don't know that I can stand this much longer—" *Not in my condition*, she meant.

"My dear, this was all your idea," John Astor said in a voice that Caroline couldn't quite read. Was it reproachful or teasing?

"Yes, it was," Astor's wife replied testily, fixing him with a glare. "I take it very seriously and I wish you would, too—"

"Quiet, please." Stead cleared his throat. "We encourage any spirit here in this room tonight to reach out to us."

Caroline was almost relieved when nothing changed.

Then she noticed that the room had grown colder.

Sea air, because the porthole is open. It's nothing.

The faint trails of smoke rising from the candles seemed to be swirling together, chasing one another like children around a maypole.

Again, it's the porthole. Driving the air into some kind of vortex. A simple explanation.

"There's a spirit in the room with us," Stead said, as excited as a boy on Christmas morning. "Spirit, give us another sign. Confirm your intention. If you are here with us, knock on the table. . . ."

The table trembled beneath Caroline's hands, skittering like water thrown into a pan of hot oil. She had to clench her teeth to keep them from chattering.

Madeleine whimpered. "Is it Teddy's parents? Please let it be Teddy's parents."

The candle's flames reared high, suddenly, illuminating everyone's face. A low moan shuddered through the room.

It's only the wind whistling through the porthole. That's it.

"Again! Speak! Tell us your name!" Stead prompted. "Are you known to one of us? Why have you contacted us? Why?"

The surface of the water in the scrying bowl went choppy, like a storm at sea, then splashed from the scrying bowl onto the white tablecloth. It spread in gray patches.

"Speak, spirit! What are you trying to tell us?" Stead was nearly shouting now, his hands gripping his partners' so tightly they had gone white. "To whom would you speak?"

The door flew open, suddenly. Electric light fell like a dagger from the alleyway.

Anne Hebbley was in the doorway, drawn back like a frightened cat. "Good God, what is going on?"

Wind swept through the room, lashing the flames. Then—they were out, twisted plumes of smoke rising from the wicks. They were plunged into darkness, the only light spilling in from around Anne Hebbley's form, silhouetting her.

Hebbley curtsied and Caroline's eyes began to adapt to the darkness. "Begging your pardon, but Mrs. Astor's lady's maid, Miss Bidois, sent me to find Mrs. Astor and Mr. Guggenheim. I do apologize for the interruption, sir, but she asks if you might bring your physician to the Astors' stateroom right away."

The Astors exchanged looks, Madeleine's hand going reflexively to her belly. Astor narrowed his eyes as though suspecting someone was playing a trick on him. "I don't understand. . . . Surely whatever the problem, our presence is not necessary. Tell Miss Bidois she must handle it on her own—"

"It's the boy," Hebbley blurted out. Stead flicked on the lights at last, and there was terror in Miss Hebbley's eyes, Caroline realized. "Miss Bidois said Teddy's having a seizure. She's afraid he might—"

There was a fluttering of white chiffon as Madeleine Astor leapt up from the table, followed by her husband as they dashed from the room.

Their cabin was only a few doors down, and yet Caroline couldn't make herself follow, feeling fixed to her chair and unable to move.

Far away, a door opened. The sound of concerned murmurs leaked into the alleyway—a dream's distance away. The rest of the Astors' servants? The door must've been left open as Caroline heard Madeleine's voice, then—the timbre if not her actual words, muddled as if through thick, undulating water. For a single moment, everything was quiet and still.

And then there was a scream. Madeleine Astor's. A scream of such terror and sadness that Caroline had no doubt as to what had happened, even before she'd followed the sound, in an out-of-body rush, to the room and seen it for herself.

The little servant boy she'd seen running around the promenade earlier, no bigger than eight or nine, lay still on the floor, the coverlet from the Astors' four-poster bed yanked partway onto the ground beside him, as though he'd tried to clutch at it to pull himself up but failed. A physician had two fingers to the boy's neck and was staring at the rest of them with a distant look in his eyes. Out of habit, Caroline reached for her brooch but found it was gone. Instead, she did all she could think to do: she went to Madeleine and held her close. After all, the girl was only eighteen—practically a child, herself.

Chapter Nine

The cloying scent of incense hung in the air like a reproach. Stead would never get the smell out of his rooms tonight, but that disturbed him far less than the sight, just now, of that small boy askew on the floor of the Astors' bedroom, where he must have no doubt sneaked to play. His eyes had been open, until the physician bent down to gently close the boy's lids.

A seizure, the physician had determined, after hearing the accounts of the servants who'd witnessed it.

Stead pushed the porthole out as far as it would go. The air against his face was chilly and damp. Wisps of fog floated above the black water, looking like clouds. The clouds of heaven and a cold, brackish hell.

He turned his back on the porthole. The séance had been unsettling. He snatched the bread off the table and threw it out the porthole. He lost sight of it in the mist but was sure it had fallen into the ocean.

With any luck, the wraith would follow it down.

The electric lights filled his room with a bright yellow glow. He normally detested electric lights but was glad for them now.

He stood at the table and deliberately unfocused his eyes. He had seen enough tonight and would see no more. What had happened at the table? He had no doubt that it was supernatural—he had been attending séances for fifteen years, had seen bald fakery as well as the unexplainable—but struggled to make sense of what had transpired tonight. These smart society people had ridiculed him at dinner, but at the first sign of disturbance, to whom do they run? To him, of course. Then they wanted his help. Or at any rate, the young (far too young) Madeleine Astor had wanted it, and what Madeleine Astor wanted, she got.

As he cleared the table, he thought of calling for the Hebbley girl, the stewardess, for help—or perhaps just to distract him from the weight of this silence—but he could barely stand to be in her presence. That was the real reason he'd asked about getting a different steward for his cabin.

Though he could hardly admit it to himself, the girl reminded him of Eliza.

Which was ridiculous. He hadn't seen Eliza Armstrong since *The Maiden Tribute of Modern Babylon* had come out in the *Pall Mall Gazette* in 1885. She had been thirteen then, which meant she would be forty today.

Besides, Eliza and this Anne Hebbley looked nothing alike. And yet there was something about the stewardess that unsettled him. Made him feel sad and . . . guilty. Terribly guilty.

A guilt he was unable to escape. He thought he'd made his peace with that. Had served three months at Coldbath Prison for what was, he insisted to this day, an honest miscalculation. But apparently that was not enough.

Was the presence that had visited him this evening . . . Eliza?

That would mean she was dead. But the private investigator's report had said otherwise. And it had to be right. Stead had staked everything on seeing her again, one last time. In America.

He pushed the idea away.

Besides, what possible connection would there have been between Eliza and the Astors' servant boy?

No, what had happened to the boy was something else.

Guggenheim's physician tried to argue it had been a fit of epilepsy following a delirium that had perhaps set in much earlier in the day, but Stead knew better.

A seizure was one of the most common signs.

There was no doubt in Stead's mind: a demon was lurking on board this ship. While they'd all been distracted here in Stead's room, attempting to reach out to the spirit, it had evaded them, had found the boy alone, lured him somewhere private, then swirled its ghostly fingers into the boy's chest—had wound its way up until it was choking the child from the inside.

The boy had died, as if it had been fated to be so.

And the spirit was still among them—a spirit who wanted something badly, though it was still anyone's guess what that could be.

Chapter Ten

Mark Fletcher had been in bed for an hour when his wife returned, but he hadn't been sleeping.

He'd been thinking instead of that itch that traveled through his hands, that longing for a deck of cards, a room full of smoke, the momentary high of the risk. He'd been thinking of numbers in red and black, teasing him with their offerings of fortune or failure. Of watching the horses run at Epsom and Newcastle, all flash and thundering hooves. But there were also dogfights and cockfights in dirty London alleys. He'd even bet on ratcatchers in corner pubs on his more desperate days. But he'd given all that up.

Had given up, too, a respectable if underpaid barrister's position so that he could be here now, embarking on something new, with her. With Caroline.

When she'd stormed out, he expected she'd be back before too long, but then the minutes became hours, and still Caroline hadn't returned. He wasn't angry, really; it was something else—restlessness, maybe, like his skin was too tight. Big as the ship was, full of a thousand mazelike hallways, they were stuck here on it. Not even a day into the journey and Mark was already sick of this ship, this overstuffed and bloated behemoth. Gilded, embellished, excessive in every way. Mark wasn't used to such dizzying luxury. He found it obscene. An insult to the dignified grandeur of the ocean on which it rode.

Maybe that was all it was. His sensibilities were worn raw.

When Caroline finally slipped into their bedroom, however, relief washed over him. He leaned back on his elbows to face her. "Where have you been? I was worried about you—afraid you'd gotten lost down one of those endless, twisting corridors, or . . ."

"I didn't intend to be gone so long," she said, pulling off her gloves. She started to undress, but he noticed that she was acting strangely. Distracted. "A terrible thing happened tonight. Maddie Astor's little servant boy died."

What does Astors' servant have to do with you? he wanted to ask, but she looked so distant at that moment—like she was not in fact in their rooms but floating out in the water, in danger of drifting away into the night fog—that he couldn't. "Is this the boy who almost fell overboard?" he said instead. "The one saved by that boxer?"

Caroline was still blank faced, as though she'd seen a ghost. "I suppose it's the same one. He had some sort of seizure in his sleep. They called in a doctor, but . . . it was too late. I—I *saw* him, Mark."

"Saw who?"

"The *boy!*"

"The child must have been ill from the start of the day and disoriented. That could explain it." The near falling, then his death. Surely the two were connected, each too odd in their own right to be coincidences.

Caroline sighed, slipping a thin silk nightgown over her head in the darkness as he watched. "It was awful. He's so young. His eyes looked very strange, clouded."

A child dead. Mark felt like a bucket that had plunged down an empty well.

The gentle, almost ineffable sway of the ship suddenly seemed too much for him. Ever since having his own child, he'd noticed he'd gotten more sensitive to mortality—he used to be aware of it but brazenly so. Now it whispered to him, tapped his shoulder, and distracted him when things were quiet.

"I'm sorry," he said to his wife. He didn't know what for—for their fight, for his mulishness earlier, for the fact that she had encountered this terrible occurrence on her own without him there to help. For the fact that whatever she'd seen, she wouldn't be able, now, to unsee it.

He reached for her as she came toward the bed; he was usually so drawn to her body but right now saw her as something soft and fragile, in need of protection.

"I'm sorry, too," she whispered as his fingers grasped her wrist and drew her in. She sat on the bed with her back to him.

He ran his fingers down her exposed shoulder blades, so crisp and so perfect in the moonlight from the window. He kissed the shadow there, and felt her shiver. "I'm sorry," he repeated, whispering it against her skin, stroking her arm.

He pulled her toward him, taking in her smells. The perfume she always wore but mixed now with briny ocean air. Cigar fumes. And something else: a smoky botanical he couldn't place, though it reminded him of a man's cologne.

His wife's body always made him hungry, and now more than ever. The hollow in the small of her back. The perfection of her breasts, which filled him with a boyish awe.

That possessive layer of musk that shouldn't be there, on her skin.

He began to kiss her neck, below the hairline. He loved her hair. Slowly, she responded, arching her back slightly and tilting her head, until finally she turned, and kissed him. The consolation of her return gave way to a sudden urgency—he had to have her. If he didn't, she might slip away again, vanish forever. He had to hold her down, to keep her.

She gasped slightly as he grasped her thighs, pushing up the flimsy nightgown. She was on his lap now, her legs parted around his waist, but he turned her over onto her back, riding the wave of need that had possessed him. Her hips rose and he was holding her wrists over her head now and they were moaning, breathless, and it was all too fast, and she cried out—from pain or pleasure? He suddenly didn't know. There were tears in her eyes. He kissed her cheek, pushing up inside her until he had finished with a kind of force that shook him.

"Shh," she whispered, her voice trembling when it was over. "We could have woken the baby."

He was still catching his breath. Had she felt the intensity between them just now, or had it all been in him? Usually he knew; usually he had a sense of her body, of the way it responded to his. But tonight everything was a sea, dark and inscrutable and strange. "The baby," she was whispering.

"She's asleep," he assured her.

But Caroline rolled over onto her side and sat up. "Mark, why didn't she wake up? We were too loud, we . . ."

She was agitated, hadn't calmed down. He knew her nerves were sensitive. It was because of the boy, certainly. A terrible thing to have seen.

"I'll check on her," Mark said, partly to comfort her and partly to get out of the bed. He felt suddenly unsettled by her, by the way everything seemed to be unraveling spontaneously and inexplicably, without a moment's notice—their marriage, the thin threads of intimacy he thought held them together. Something else was bothering Caroline tonight, besides the boy's death.

He pulled on his sleeping pants and entered the connecting chamber. The entire room was quiet. There was not even the soft intake of breath he often heard in the nursery back in London. When he bent over Ondine's crib, he saw that she had somehow wriggled under the blanket. Alarm rang through him. The blanket covered her face completely—no, it was *in* her mouth, like a gag.

He was yanking the blanket aside before he could even stop to think it—the baby wasn't breathing.

Ondine was at his shoulder in a second and he was banging on her back and at last she cried out, waking up, and only then did his heart seem to start beating again. He was never so happy in his life to hear her cry. For that instant, everything else disappeared and all that mattered was this tiny being.

Had he imagined it? No, she'd been suffocating, he was sure. If they hadn't thought to check on her . . .

He stood there with the baby in his arms—wailing in his ear—for several minutes, just breathing, feeling her hard little breaths, fear coursing through him. He thought he might sob. But she was okay. She was fine. They were all fine.

After he'd gotten over the dizziness of his brief panic, he brought her back to the bedroom.

"What was it?" Caroline asked on his return, but he didn't answer, not wanting to alarm her.

He placed the baby in Caroline's outstretched arms.

"Don't cry now, everything's all right," she murmured, pressing her pinkie finger gently into the baby's mouth. Ondine calmed, latching on to Caroline's finger. A contented smile spread over Caroline's lips. Then she began to sing a lullaby. Mark loved Caroline's singing, untrained but sweet and pure.

He curled back into bed and lay on his side, an arm tucked under his head, beside his wife and child for some time as she sang and sang, the melody pouring into his ear like warm honey, soothing away the strangeness of the evening, melting down his momentary fear.

His eyes were soon too heavy to keep open. He was warm beneath the blanket. His mind drifted, floating on a raft in the middle of the ocean. Bobbing gently, rise and fall. Black water all around him. Rise and fall. Lapping at his arms, then his chest. Then up to his neck. Steadily rising until he was enveloped by it. The water touched him all over like the hands of a curious lover, but an unfamiliar one, a new mistress, whose ways he couldn't yet anticipate.

But then the water slipped over his head and he was being pulled down, down, down. There was no getting away, but he didn't want to, even as the hands came over his mouth.

Down into the inkiness he sank, Caroline's beautiful voice falling further and further away, until it was nothing but a whisper.

At the bottom, where all was blackness and silence, waited Lillian, whom he never expected to see again. Lillian, whom he tried not to think about. Yet here she was, waiting for him, and he came to her with a final gasp of certainty.

1916

Chapter Eleven

17 November 1916
Naples, Italy
HMHS *Britannic*

One by one, Annie throws back the heavy curtains draping the massive windows all around the main ward, which had been the first-class dining salon on the *Titanic*. It takes her the better part of an hour to make her way around the entirety of the room, with all the patients who begin to wake up and call out to her, asking for things she can't provide. Assurances of their fate. An extra dose of morphine. She's not even allowed to have her hands on the wound dressings, for fear of infection, which makes the hours longer and more exhausting— this perpetual feeling of helplessness, even as she is put to work delivering breakfasts, spooning porridge and wiping mouths, emptying bedpans, changing sheets, spreading vinegar into the cracks in the floors to try to clean out the remains of blood or vomit or urine. And, above all, *listening,* until the stories and litanies run together, a constant murmur of fury and fear and pain.

It surprises Annie how quickly this new existence has become routine. It's almost as though she's back on the *Titanic*, as though the terrible tragedy and the past four years were only a long nightmare. The two ships are so much alike that the two experiences begin to meld into one. Here are the same long, broad passageways, the same layout so that she can make her way around almost effortlessly. The same ceaseless undulation underfoot as the ship slices through the waves. The same bracing salt air filling her lungs and blowing her hair about her ears. On the ship, she is in a waking hallucination that she never left the *Titanic* and that she has always been at sea. That the sea is her home.

Of course, the people and the circumstances are vastly different— and oddly, she prefers being on *Britannic*. She'd rather wait on patients than pernickety rich passengers.

She secures the tieback and moves on to the next curtain. Dust lifts into the air, swirling about in the dove-gray light of dawn at sea. Rain batters down hard on window glass. It has now been nearly five days aboard the *Britannic*, but the days have begun to run together the same way just now, memories blur by as she watches trails of water slide into one another, then streak away.

At least, she *thinks* they are memories. Sometimes she can't distinguish between her actual childhood, ancient fairy tales told by Grandmother Aisling and spontaneous fantasy, morphing, fleeting, and strange.

In these memories, a girl wears a muslin dress and thick wool sweater and sprints through the rain, out to the vast bluffs overlooking the Irish Sea, the air cold and stinging on young skin. But the memories bleed together, and then she is a young woman, dancing in the noisy, crowded streets of London, nearly knocking over a stand of roasting chestnuts as she laughs, turning her face to the sky, opening her mouth to the rain made bitter by coal smoke. Then both become a third—a girl who is part seal, part human, her body undulating with the curves of the tide as she swims toward the surface, rain pelting it like bullets. She transforms: the slickness of her animal hide becoming the tenderness of a child's flesh, and two legs frantically kicking as she breaks the crest of a wave and comes up, heaving her first human breath.

Beside Annie, a man gasps for air. She swivels away from the window and the rain, dashing to the side of the nearest bed, where a patient appears to be suffocating, something in his throat seizing.

He's an older man, with white mixed in his hair and in the bristles on his face. His eyes have gone round and wide with fear. Annie tries to help him sit up—Is he choking on something?—and within seconds is joined by a nurse and doctor on the shift. Quickly and efficiently, the doctor checks the man's eyes, looks into his mouth, and feels at his neck for his pulse before declaring the man is fine.

"It's just a panic attack," the doctor says to Annie as they step away from the bed to confer. "I'll give him a dose of morphine. Keep an eye on him until he falls asleep."

Annie tidies up the area around his cot waiting for his eyelids to begin to sag, but a few minutes pass and there's no sign that he's getting sleepy. Is it possible to be immune to morphine? She could ask the doctor for another dose, but he and the nurse are busy attending to a much more serious case on the other side of the ward and she hates to bother them.

"I don't mean to be such a baby," the man says sheepishly. He nods in the direction of the windows. "It's just that I'm afraid of the sea. I don't travel by boat if I can help it, but the military don't ask you your druthers. I never did learn to swim. And it looks like we could go under any minute, doesn't it?"

The gray ocean outside the windows looks particularly bad, indeed. She can understand why anyone would be afraid of it.

"Don't worry. You're perfectly safe. This is the *Britannic*, sister ship to the *Titanic*—"

The man brays like a donkey, cutting her off. "And that's supposed to make me feel better? We know how that turned out, don't we?"

"This ship is different. Better. They changed things, based on what they learned from the sinking," she says. She hopes that is not too inaccurate. She's not sure what White Star Line may or may not have done; as the story went, they blamed the iceberg more than the

ship's inadequacies, its too-few lifeboats and disregard for safety pre-
cautions. The jammed wire signals. A million theories had flown
about over the last few years and she'd lost track.

She squints at the man's sunburned skin, the patches across his nose
that look like freckles trying to reassert themselves on fresh skin.
"Irish, are you? Then you know the story of the dubheasa." He fur-
rows his brows at her. "Never heard of the dubheasa?" she says, the
Irish pronunciation—*deh vah sah*—easily tripping along her tongue
like her grandmother had always said it. "Didn't your nan tell you
these stories? The dubheasa looks out for all the sailors and men at
sea." That's not the whole story, but she doesn't want to frighten him
further, and he doesn't seem to have heard of the one thing that everyone in Ballintoy is taught to respect and fear practically from birth.
"Don't worry—as long as you've been good, she will save you, should
you ever need it." She smiles at him so hard her cheeks ache. "And
you seem like a good man."

He looks at her doubtfully. "I don't know about that, my dear. I
was fighting in a war, after all."

But he does seem to be comforted, and finally, the old man falls
back to sleep. With the shift change, Annie is free to go on her breakfast break. She walks down to the dining hall, where she takes a bowl
of porridge out of habit and sits down beside Violet at one of the long,
unadorned tables, staring at the slop with no real appetite. Some
mornings, she can hardly recall what it is to feel hunger, as if in the
night she has forgotten.

"And he couldn't get out?" Violet is asking the radio man—Charlie
Epping.

Charlie nods. He's straddling the bench on the opposite side of the
table, one elbow propped beside his fork, gesturing with a coffee mug
in the other. "Apparently he'd been knocking for the better part of
three hours. Bastard was bloody lucky Mortimer happened by and
heard him—could've starved to death in the supply closet, and what
a way to go, eh?"

"Who could've starved?" Annie asks as she stirs the contents of her bowl.

Charles leans toward her, conspiratorially. "One of the orderlies. Stanley White. First, a whole tray of scalpels goes missing from the operating theater, and then, when he goes to replenish them—"

"He walks into the supply room and the door locks behind him!" Violet finishes. "No one realized he was gone!"

Another orderly, sitting at Epping's far side, pipes in, "It was no accident, that. You gotta know this lady's haunted." He gestures at the air, suggesting he means the whole ship.

Violet laughs. When she laughs, she puts Annie in mind of the perfect Irish lass, with her thick auburn hair and smiling gray-blue eyes. A sweet, bonny lass who is always up for fun. "Naw, I wouldn't go that far and you best be careful with that kind of talk. The captain wouldn't like to hear it, for sure." But Annie didn't miss the quick look Violet threw her way first.

Annie swallows, unable to eat her breakfast. This isn't the first rumor of a ghost, which she now knows must be standard fare. Aren't there stories attached to every large ship, every mansion, every deep and dark wood? Just yesterday, one of the firemen swore he saw a man in a tuxedo walking down the alleyway toward him, only to disappear into thin air just as they would have collided. Said he could swear he felt the air chill as he passed through him and was gone. Claimed he could still smell cigar in the alleyway.

Then again, Annie knew plenty of the crew hung out in the alleyways at night, passing around a cigar, sharing a bit of comfort, so that's probably what accounted for the smell.

"Well, some of the patients are no longer in possession of their faculties," Violet had reminded Annie last night when she brought it up before they went to bed. "It's no surprise they're hearing and seeing things. So long as it's only the patients and not the rest of us, there's nothing to fear," she added, clearly intending it to be a joke. But she must have realized the hidden insult—Annie had, up until less than a week ago, been living in an asylum, after all. Violet clamped her mouth shut with a small smile.

She is not mad.

But there is something in her that is hospitable to madness.

Now, before Annie can find her words, Violet turns toward her, clearly wanting to change the subject. She gently touches the brooch pinned to Annie's pinafore. "Ooh! That's a lovely one. Have I seen it before?"

Annie fingers it. A tiny gold heart dangling from an arrow. Heat forms in her cheeks—the embarrassment of being paid attention.

Violet apparently sees her silence for coyness because she winks at Epping and the other orderly. "Must've been a gift from someone *special*."

Now Annie can feel her blush deepen.

"Ha! I knew it. It's not the kind of piece a woman buys for herself, and I should know because have I ever told you about . . ." And then Violet's off on another story of an admirer on one transatlantic crossing who'd taken a liking to her and offered her his mother's favorite bracelet, but Annie loses the thread, still touching her brooch and keeping her eyes tilted downward.

Why *had* she worn the brooch today? Perhaps she'd just needed a little reminder of who she was.

Like a small gold anchor.

Only now instead it makes her feel exposed and vulnerable, a blazing scarlet letter on her chest, like something out of a forbidden novel. She looks up to see Charles Epping eyeing her, an amused look tossing across his boyish face. She smiles back, and the heat moves down from her face to her chest and her abdomen. A man looking at her like that has always felt like fire—part comfort and warmth, part danger.

There is something uncanny in the feeling, in the way he looks at her. In all the stories of hauntings. In the whole spirit of this ship. In the memories that continually rise around her like a dark tide.

Something terrifying, some buried, rotting truth that wiggles its way into the core of her, like maggots eating a carcass.

With that thought, she cannot bear to choke down her porridge, so she gets up and clears her tray.

～ℓℓ～

Rain pelts down hard as the hospital ship pulls into Naples that afternoon. Annie comes out onto the deck with a handful of nurses, everyone eager for land after five days at sea. The town that sprawls beyond the harbor looks dirty and squalid; the rain has painted all the buildings in muddy browns and sodden grays, dark alleys slanting down the hillside, veining the city. On the docks, packs of children dressed in tatters run from ship to ship, begging for coins or food.

Charlie told her they were stopping to take on coal and water, but looking over the side, Annie spots a caravan of men and stretchers approaching the gangplank. They will be taking on wounded, too, then.

With war raging across the continent, this strategic port town is overstuffed with troops. The base's hospital is likely overrun with casualties. Apparently, they weren't looking to miss the opportunity to off-load their worst cases.

Annie huddles under her cloak, playing the Vanishing Game in her head—*I am here; I am not here*—as she waits for Sister Merrick, the head nurse, to decide where each patient will go and which nurse will escort the man down to his appointed ward. The parade hobbles up to Merrick one at a time, a long line dressed in mud brown and olive drab to match the streets from which they've emerged. Many are on crutches, some strapped to a stretcher. All have the unanimated faces of the shell-shocked, half ghost.

It always jolts Annie, the smells. In the trenches, the men have sometimes spent days—even weeks—surrounded by their own feces, rampant rats, and the remains of their dead comrades. Many of their wounds are so deep, and already festering with bits of shrapnel and filth that nothing can be done but hold them down as they scream, as their fevers rise.

"This one to D ward," Merrick says to Annie. She points at the man on the stretcher as though Annie is a field dog and expected to trot out smartly on command. Merrick acts as though she is the head-mistress at a girls' school and her nurses are obedient students.

Annie is glad to bend to the head nurse's iron will. Obedience is something that has always come easily to her. Almost always.

She gives Merrick a curt little nod and mutters, "This way, please," to the orderlies carrying the stretcher.

She is sad, though, to get out of the cold rain, which reminds her so of a time before, when she was whole and young and altogether different. Rain's always done that to her when it touches her skin. Like the kiss of the sea.

Her gaze alights briefly on the face of the next man in line and in that sliver of a second, she thinks she recognizes him. There is something familiar about his face.

No. It is nothing more than longing. The same longing that made her see Mark's face on the journey to Southampton from Liverpool, that made her see his face in train stations and on street corners.

They're only taking a handful of men on board, but they're Annie's first actual patients and now she has an idea of what it will be like when they dock in Mudros in a few days' time and she is surrounded by wounded. She imagines it will not be unlike when she was a stewardess with more than a dozen passengers to take care of.

Out of the rain and settled into the wards, some of the men become more animated. A few even joke with the nurses, ask when the tea cart comes around. The patient on the stretcher whom Annie has been escorting is a young man with the fair skin of the English, spangled with golden freckles. His eyes are open, but he stares past her. When she undoes the straps and strips back the blanket, she sees that he is missing both legs below the knee. She bends to help him onto a cot, struggling to get both her arms underneath him without jostling him too badly. She's learned the hard way that often even those who don't seem to be in pain may cry out in agony if you handle them too roughly. And something as simple as moving a man's body from one surface to another can take an enormous amount of effort. She is breathless by the time she tucks his newly issued blanket up around his chest, making a note to reserve one of the ship's wheelchairs for him.

"Water?" she asks, and when there is no answer she simply holds the glass to his lips, tilting it back until he takes a few sips. So, he is responsive, not catatonic.

She puts the water glass on the tiny stand beside the cot. "Do you need a bedpan? Would you like an extra blanket?" she asks patiently but gets no answer. She spreads the blanket over him and tucks the ends briskly under the edge of the mattress. "There you go, nice and cozy. . . . Please signal if you need anything, but a doctor should be with you shortly."

The young man still says nothing, eyes downcast. "You're safe now." The words slip out in her desperation to comfort him. Perhaps to comfort herself, too. The ill feeling from this morning still clings to her, a shadow. "This is the HMHS *Britannic*. The largest, grandest hospital ship in the fleet. It's unsinkable, you know."

Nothing.

She stands and begins to move away. And then she sees the man that she mistook for Mark Fletcher across the room. Two orderlies lift the soldier from a stretcher and settle him into a bed.

Though she knows it's foolish, heartache pulls her toward him. She wends her way through the wounded, pulled by some invisible force.

A nurse Annie doesn't recognize stands between them now, tucking a blanket tightly over her patient.

"How is he?" Annie asks over the woman's shoulder.

"Unconscious," the nurse answers without turning around. "A head wound. They said he slipped into a coma yesterday, poor man."

Finally, the nurse steps away, leaving Annie with him. Now she can study his face all she wants, to satisfy her curiosity and be assured that her eyes were playing tricks, that her fantasies have taken over once again, that—

She stares.

She stares for what feels like an hour but can only be seconds, wondering if another vision has come over her, something half memory, half dream.

But no.

It *is* him.

This man is Mark.

He looks like Mark but older, as Mark of course would be by now. Flecks of gray at his temples, the mouth more drawn, a few lines at the corners of his eyes, like delicate crackling on a vase, making it even more valuable for its fragility.

But there's no denying.

A vibration of knowing moves through Annie's body, even as other nurses bustle past her, ignoring her.

It's him.

Mark has come to her.

Mark Fletcher has come back to her.

This—this was the purpose of everything. Why she knew she had to answer Violet's letter, had to be here, on this ship, for this strange voyage with the dying.

Somehow, she willed this. Somehow, there was a silent call between them. Even after all this time. After everything. And now: here he lies. Half dead, but not dead.

And this time, he belongs to no one else. He is alone.

He is hers.

1912

Chapter Twelve

11 April 1912
Queenstown, Ireland

Annie stood on the open deck, shivering under her cloak against the cold and damp. The stern was swathed in fog so dense that it dimmed the pale dawn light, so thick that she could barely make out the activity twenty feet in front of her. A clutch of bodies ahead, dark and indistinct, appeared and disappeared in the shifting white. They had to be servants; you couldn't expect the Astors to be up at this hour, not for the burial of staff.

It was as though the sea were conspiring in this funeral for the dead boy by conjuring up the fog to hide him from prying eyes. Cosseting him in the softest blanket of cloud for his last journey.

Annie herself felt foggy headed. It was only the second day of the *Titanic*'s journey from Southampton to Cherbourg to Queenstown. After today's final stop, it would just be open sea. According to the itinerary, they'd spend five more nights at sea before docking in New York, unless bad weather set them back. She'd had a poor night, unable to sleep after fetching Guggenheim and helping him find his physician, then leading them to the Astors' stateroom. Violet had already been asleep, and, as much as Annie craved conversation, she hadn't the heart to wake her. She tossed for what seemed like hours before falling asleep, only to be tormented with wild dreams—one in particular involved a man that she was certain was Mark Fletcher. While she could recall no particulars beyond the heat of someone's breath against her skin, hands tracing her neck, it left her feeling shameful and burning.

She pulled her cloak tighter to her body.

Annie crept closer, moved by piety for the dead but also—to be truthful—curiosity. She'd seen the dead before, of course, but only after they had been washed and dressed by the old grandmothers in the village and set out in the family's parlor, ready to receive visitors. There was no coffin for the Astors' boy: he had been wrapped in sail-cloth and weighted down with ballast from the bilge. He made a compact white package, small enough to be mistaken for laundry or a bundle of life belts, improbably bound in heavy iron chains.

The Astors had requested the body be buried at sea, as quickly as possible. The boy had been an orphan; no reason to keep the body on board—there was no family waiting to receive him, and it would be a good six or seven hours until they reached Queenstown, the last stop before New York. More likely, they simply wanted to avoid a scandal. Still, it all seemed overly hasty to Annie; on the back of the boy's sudden and unnatural death, it left her unsettled.

When she heard that the Astors' servants were to attend the service, she decided to go, too, to swell the meager ranks. She counted heads: there was the head butler and Mrs. Astor's two lady's maids, Mr. Astor's valet, and two young under butlers, all of them bonneted and buttoned up in shades of black and charcoal, plus two sailors to help with the body. The mourners were as fidgety as she, hovering, pacing, wringing hands. No one, it appeared, knew what to do or what to expect. Protocol called for the captain to preside—but certainly that wouldn't apply to a little servant boy.

Finally, an elderly man in a black suit with a Bible tucked under his arm appeared out of the fog, whom Annie recognized as one of the ministers in second class. The head butler walked up to him and, after a minute's engagement, shepherded the rest to form up around the shrouded body.

The minister opened his book and began the service, but Annie, standing to the back, could barely hear his words, swallowed up by wind. She edged forward a few steps, as close as she dared without disturbing the mourners. She liked the bit that she was able to hear, how the dead in the sea sleep without monument and so there were no distinctions between rich and poor. Theodore Wooten—a name too stiff and formal for the tiny boy—would rest with kings and peasants, all of them the same in the eyes of God.

When the minister closed his book, the sailors crouched on either side of the body, then raised the board carrying the sailcloth bundle to their shoulders. With some awkwardness, they lifted it over the railing, then tilted the board and, just like that, let the bundle slide into the sea. They were high over the surface of the water and Annie heard the splash as the body met the waves. She shivered all over.

Annie had always been a good, strong swimmer; her mother insisted on it after her uncle had died at sea. She used to love to hold her breath and open her eyes beneath the warmth of high tide in late summer, where, it always seemed to her, lay the ultimate truth, the fractured light of it. And yet . . . as she watched the ocean close itself over the pale shape, she imagined it was her own body plunging into the frigid water, being wrapped in cold, the chains pulling her down in a terrible embrace.

One of the young footmen let out a muffled moan and the older of the lady's maids cried noisily into a handkerchief, but Annie was surprised to feel no urge to join them. It was, she supposed, because they knew the boy and she did not, but it bothered her that she felt so little. Only regret that he'd died so young. She wondered if that meant there was something wrong with her.

It was then she noticed William Stead standing beside her, dressed as though out for a morning country walk in a tweed jacket and brown trilby. He appeared to have observed the entire thing. Annie was taken aback; as a man of his station, he stood out.

"Astor's boy, I take it?" he asked without emotion.

"Did you come for the service?" Annie asked.

"No . . . I was working and thought I might stretch my legs. I saw the gathering and . . ." He gestured to the group. As they watched the mourners straggle away, Stead turned to face her. "I'm glad to see you, Miss Hebbley. I wanted to thank you for your assistance last night, procuring the items I requested."

She remembered only hazily, amid the blur of anxiety around the child's sudden death. A few curiosities: plain bread, extra candles, a large shaving bowl.

It seemed he wanted to tell her something. "I'm happy to help provide whatever you need." It was one of the sentences she'd been trained to say when the first-class passengers were feeling conversational.

He shrugged but didn't make eye contact. "I will likely need more of the bread and candles tonight."

"Of course. Were they not enough?"

"The waves will be hungry for more, I'm afraid," he said, staring out at the water.

"The . . . waves?"

"The bread was not for me, you see, but for the dead, who have come back, hungry. One offers them bread in order to appease them— or perhaps to hear what they might say."

A sickening shock moved through her. Was the man insane?

Perhaps he saw the way her face had changed, because he smiled, as if to reassure her. "I have been practicing séances for years now. I assure you, I know what I'm talking about." He paused and she said nothing. "Have you ever attended one?"

"No, sir," she replied hastily. "Nothing like it up in Ballintoy." At least as far as she could recall. Back home, the priests wouldn't have approved of such things.

He squinted toward the ocean, invisible in the fog. "I take all my holidays at the seaside. It's very restorative, walking the shore, watching the waves. . . . I can see how, sometimes, the wind over the water might sound like a woman's voice. There are stories, you know, of creatures who try to lure men to their deaths in the sea. Some call them sirens; others call them mermaids."

Annie knew all of these stories. Ballintoy was a town of fishermen, with fishermen's superstitions and fishermen's tales. Men claimed to hear the sirens' call when they were far out at sea. Lost men were said to have let themselves be swept overboard in storms, to meet them.

A memory came to Annie—one she was conscious of having tried to bury, though now it somehow seemed like the *only* clear memory she had of her past, blotting out all others. She'd been very young and wandering on the beach at Ballintoy not far from her auntie's cottage, where they were having a picnic. Her auntie Riona was a fisherman's widow and lived by the sea with her mother, Annie's granny Aisling, a short walk from where Annie lived with her mother, father, and four brothers. Normally Annie loved the sea, despite the fear her parents had tried to put in her, told her she would never be able to fight the strong tides if she were to get swept out and that she would be lost to them forever like Uncle Wilmot.

But as she scampered over the rocks that day, Annie's head started to hurt and her vision went white and blurry. It had been a bright spring day, cold and clear. Still, there was something about that day that left her, even now, with a feeling of terror. . . .

She'd had a vision. There was no other word for it. A terrible vision that had made her run back to the picnic, to seek out her father and try to climb into his lap, hiding her face against his chest. But he would have none of it. She was too old to sit in his lap, he'd told her. And when he'd demanded to know what had frightened her, she'd told him what she'd seen: the dubheasa. The dark lady of the water. The sea goddess. The demon. The one who longed always for her coveted girl children, to keep and protect them, never allowing them to surface from the water again. Or so the stories went.

Rather than comfort her, she watched as his bearded face grew red with fury, the kind that always seemed to be boiling just below the surface of his skin. He shouted in front of everyone, *See what comes of these daft fairy stories,* he'd yelled at Annie's mother. *What would Father Mulroney say? It's all your mother's doing. . . .*

It's the old ways, Auntie Riona had said, jutting out her chin, wild black curls whipping all around her face. She was the only one in the family who stood up to Jonathan Hebbley.

It's pagan nonsense, and I forbid it in my house. Do you hear that, Annie?

That was the last family picnic with Auntie Riona and Granny Aisling, and Annie wasn't allowed to visit her grandmother ever again, the woman who told her of wee folk and fairies and her favorite of all, selkies: women who could slip in and out of their beautiful coats of sealskin, to walk the earth in search of those they had once loved.

With effort, Annie pushed the memory away. She was not in Ballintoy, and she was not a little girl anymore.

When she opened her eyes, she saw that Stead had left her side without any word, continuing his walk along the promenade, his figure just disappearing into the mist.

As she regained her senses—she had to get belowdecks; there were passengers to attend to—she was approached by a sailor. She recognized him as one of the pair who had sent Theodore Wooten's body to the deep.

He touched the brim of his cap. "Begging pardon, miss, but you're one of the first-class stewardesses? I was wondering 'f I might give this to ya." He reached into his peacoat and pulled out a handkerchief. It seemed to be wrapped around something, the small, white lump reminding her of the shrouded body on the deck.

He placed it in her hand. Unwrapping the handkerchief, she saw a piece of jewelry. A brooch in the shape of a heart dangling from an arrow, the clasp fashioned into the arrow's back.

"I was part a' the detail that made the body ready, and I found that on 'im," the sailor explained. "Piece as nice as that, I figured it must belong to one of them first-class passengers. Kid mighta pilfered it. Could ya see that it gets back to the rightful owner?"

Annie looked from the object to the sailor. A man on funeral detail would be among the lowest ranks on the ship. He could've pocketed it himself, sold it. No one would've known. She was touched that he trusted her, that he saw the decency in her. "Yes, of course."

As he shuffled away to his next task—shoveling coal, oiling machinery in the bowels of the engine rooms—Annie turned back to the jewelry. It was a fairly large brooch, made of gold but no gemstones, with finely detailed designs all over. She struggled to remember where she'd seen it before. All her female passengers brought jewelry with them, strewn across their dressing tables with little concern, as though they were mere baubles and not the most precious things Annie had ever seen. She had to ignore them completely or risk temptation—but she'd made an exception for this piece, of which she had been immediately covetous.

And now it seemed the boy had been unable to resist that temptation, she thought sadly as she turned the piece over in her palm. Would a boy so young be of a mind to sell it? she wondered. No, more likely he'd stolen it because he liked it, because it was the prettiest thing he'd ever seen and had decided in a rash moment that he couldn't live without it.

And then she remembered where she'd seen the brooch: on Caroline Fletcher's dressing table. She recalled thinking it was curiously unlike the rest of Caroline's jewelry. Could the boy really have stolen it? He would have had no reason to be in the Fletchers' rooms, no reason at all. It wasn't easy to get into the cabins; people didn't leave them unlocked and, besides the occupants, only the stewards had keys. It would have been impossible for Teddy to get into the Fletchers' room—unless the Fletchers invited him.

Which was absurd.

She ran a finger over the brooch's face, thinking. What if it were the other way around—not that Teddy went into the Fletchers' rooms, but that Caroline went to see Teddy? Could she have sought the boy out for some reason? Given him the brooch? That, too, made no sense.

But that was probably always true at the start of a mystery.

As the ship heaved onward through the thick waves, the irking anxiety that had been lingering in her chest ever since the boy died—no, ever since seeing Mark board the ship—billowed into a vague, cold dread. Something was not right; she could sense it at the core of her, an echoing suspicion, a discomfort she couldn't find a single source for. It was everywhere on this ship. It was in the cool air sliding along her skin even now, like one of Stead's hungry spirits.

Annie covered the brooch with the handkerchief again, afraid that someone might see it and leap to the wrong conclusion: that *she'd* stolen it. Because she wasn't going to return it to Caroline Fletcher, not yet. She would hold on to it a while longer. *Had* to hold on to it, for it was proof of something, even if she didn't know what.

The oddest thing was that—holding the brooch now, being reminded of the Fletchers—Annie had the strongest urge to see Ondine. To hold the baby in her arms, cradle her close, breathe in her delicious aroma, warm and sweet. To protect her, to make sure she never ended up like poor Teddy Wooten, his body now entrusted to the care of the sea.

She stuffed the wrapped brooch deep in her pocket—the gentle weight of it there kept her anchored amid all this bad feeling and fog—and ducked down into a darkened stairwell to prepare for her morning duties. The rest of her passengers were sure to be waking soon.

Chapter Thirteen

11 April 1912 10:30 a.m.
Entered into the record of Dr. Alice Leader
Strict confidentiality
Patient: Madeleine Astor, née Talmage Force
Age: 18

Condition: overall health is good; patient is five months pregnant by the patient's reckoning, though judging by distention of belly she could be at later in term (six months? Seven? Note: Perhaps an attempt to obscure that conception took place prior to the wedding?). Patient lacks color; but temperature fine, breathing and pulse in acceptable range. Notable swelling of the joints to be expected with pregnancy.

I did not intend to practice while on this voyage; indeed, I tried to explain to Mrs. Madeleine Astor when she came to see me that I am on holiday with my friends the Kenyons and Mrs. Margaret Welles Swift and not prepared to see patients. But Mrs. Astor had developed an antipathy to Dr. O'Loughlin, the ship's surgeon, and insisted on seeing me, feeling she would be more comfortable consulting a female doctor. Given her condition, as well as her state at the time, I did not think it wise to upset her further.

Mrs. Astor came unaccompanied to our meeting, insisted on coming without her husband. (Note: no evidence of husband's permission. Follow up with him separately?)

The patient was visibly tired and had the appearance of not having slept well. Her hands were restless. When asked why she had come to see me, she did not answer, asking instead if I believed in occultism. I told her, truthfully, that while not overfamiliar with it, I had several friends who were avid practitioners. That seemed to put her at ease.

She told me she believed there was an evil spirit on the ship that was trying to harm her. When I asked her why she thought this, she told me that one of her servants, a young boy, told her that he had heard "a woman on the water calling for him to join her" shortly before he died. I assured her that children often claim to see and hear the dead. Given the child's circumstances—a recent orphan, by Mrs. Astor's accounts—this is not surprising at all. That seemed to calm her somewhat, but she told me that she, too, believed there was a spirit and, what's more, that this spirit had designs on her unborn child. She admitted she believed it had something to do with her marriage to Mr. Astor and the scandal around his divorce, though she refused to go into further detail. However, she hardly needed to. Though I myself care little for gossip, I have seen the newspaper articles about Mr. Astor's shocking whirlwind romance with the much younger woman.

In any case, knowing that indulging her delusions would do her no good, I advised Mrs. Astor that she was apt to feel unsettled after her servant's death. It was only natural to be upset. But she was at risk of developing a hysteria: the excitement of her recent marriage and subsequent attention from the newspapers; her pregnancy.

Prescribed dilute of laudanum with instructions to further dilute in ratio of 1:20 and take a quarter cup over the course of two hours. Skeptical but visibly calmer, Mrs. Astor left my room after making plans to meet again the following day.

Chapter Fourteen

Sunlight broke like a golden egg yolk through the Astors' porthole, flooding the stateroom in sparkly shards of light, refracting off every surface, from the set of silver and ivory combs to the jewelry tossed carelessly across her dressing table, diamonds and emeralds and sapphires strewn about like children's toys. Light glinted off the crystal perfume bottles and faceted whiskey decanters. It lit up last night's discarded gown in a blaze of pure white, so blinding that it was impossible to look at for more than an instant. It was as though they'd awakened inside a mirrored lantern.

Madeleine Astor winced in her chair in their private breakfast nook by the window. These days, her body simply couldn't get comfortable, even snuggled deep in her voluminous robe, which was like wearing a velvet tent. She couldn't warm to the day knowing that Teddy's body had been dropped into the sea at dawn, long before they'd even awoken. The thought of it made her queasy. She'd wanted to be there, but John Jacob—Jack, as he liked to be called—had put his foot down. "You're emotional enough about it. . . . The last thing we need is for you to faint at a servant's funeral," he'd said.

She'd gone to speak to a woman doctor about her queasiness, worried it might be a pregnancy-related nausea she was experiencing. But

Dr. Leader had been clear-eyed, if unsympathetic, and suggested the events of last night, and Maddie's lingering feelings of guilt and horror, were to blame.

She shouldn't feel guilty, the doctor had assured her. After all, Teddy's death hadn't been her fault. Bad things simply happened sometimes. It didn't have to be part of a pattern. It didn't have to *mean* something.

But it *was* her fault. She knew it as surely as she knew anything.

"We're out of tea, Mrs. Astor. Would you like me to send for more?" a maid was saying, though the words felt a bit as if they were moving toward her through water.

Her husband rattled his newspaper. "Dear—Miss Bidois is asking you a question. Do you want more tea or don't you?" Jack was looking at her in a way she had learned to dislike only a few months into their marriage. As though he were a schoolteacher and she a disobedient and not very bright pupil.

"No, thank you."

The maid nodded and exited the room.

The protracted honeymoon to Europe and Egypt had been a way to avoid the press—so much speculation about the timing of their marriage, so much sniping—but it had been much better than she'd expected. They'd had a wonderful time. Everything—even the . . . *intimacy*—had been easy and immediate between them. Though he was nearly three times her age, and some of her school friends had whispered and giggled about what *that* would be like, she'd been surprised to learn it wasn't so terrible. Jack sought her pleasure with the patience of one who has never known hurriedness, never known need. One who had built a life instead around the joy in, and pursuit of, things not needed, only wanted. He was generous with her— physically, emotionally, financially.

All he asked for in return, of course, was complete and utter loyalty.

And she had no reason not to offer that to him—except the

workings of her own mind. She sometimes wondered if she'd been designed purposely to push against things. She used to think it was curiosity. That's what her father had called it. Her teachers hadn't always been so generous. "Don't be willful. It's an unattractive quality in a lady," they'd said to her on more than one occasion.

Now she wondered if the teachers had been right. If what resided inside her was something more like resistance.

Surely, others would call her spoiled. But could a person simply have a predilection for unhappiness? Not suffering, mind you—she had no desire to suffer—just a quiet, tickling dissatisfaction with the way things were—no matter how wonderful things *actually* were?

If so, that was Madeleine's illness, her personal curse.

And now, after six months, they were on their way back to New York, and a dark, fluttering worry had begun to inhabit her chest, moth-like, invisibly eating, eating, eating. . . .

Something was *wrong*. Did no one else see it?

She clenched her eyes shut, trying to chase away a coming headache.

Jack let his newspaper droop. "Are you feeling unwell, dear? Perhaps you should go back to bed."

The bed *was* calling. How late had it been when Madeleine had finally been able to get to sleep? She'd tossed and turned for hours, thinking of the boy. And, too, of the prophecy . . .

"Perhaps you're right." She rose and made her way slowly to the bedroom on swollen, tender feet, though what she wanted more than to sleep was to be *home,* not in Newport but in New York, among her real friends, the girls she'd grown up with. Not the young women who fawned over her in her travels, the other heiresses and new wives and society connections who'd become their natural companions on the trip.

For so many years, *marrying well* had been her vocation, her calling, she thought as she slipped in between the silken sheets of their bed.

There had never been any pretense otherwise in her family. She had been given the best the family could afford, private schools and finishing classes, lessons in dancing and singing and tennis. Parties in the homes of the very best people and vacations in the right places. It had worked for her sister, Katherine, gotten her an enviable marriage and social standing. It would work for her.

And this expectation had never bothered Maddie. She loved school, had been an eager student, a natural leader among her set, and a social butterfly. Things had come easily for her—but she always found herself craving a challenge.

Some people talked about her family, called them social climbers and jumped-up merchants, but her parents paid no heed. "It's been this way for centuries," her mother sniffed whenever they were snubbed by some matron or other. "That's how you get ahead, through strategic alignment. That's how great families are forged." Theirs would be a great family, it went without saying.

She'd met John Jacob at Bar Harbor the summer of 1910. Madeleine had been seventeen and Jack forty-five. They were vacationing at the summer home of mutual friends, Maddie playing tennis with one of the other girls, showing off her fine form. Jack retrieved an errant ball and walked all the way over to the court to return it to her. She knew what was meant by the look in his eye when he handed her the ball and introduced himself. Her mother nearly fell all over herself afterward. "Mr. Astor has taken an interest in you, my dear! We must play this very carefully, very carefully indeed!"

She didn't need her mother to tell her that. A long game was Madeleine's very favorite type of game. She, like her friends, had been groomed and bred to wed princelings. Being a debutante was a blood sport. And she had succeeded, gotten the richest man in the world to propose to her. It made her the envy of all her friends. One even had a nervous breakdown over it.

Maddie's maiden name was *Force,* after all.

Kitty, Jack's Airedale, lay by her feet—she always slept on the bed with them. Now the dog whined lightly, as if echoing the restlessness in Maddie's head.

A sick tumult of guilt and dread rose up from her stomach, acidic against the back of her throat, remembering that Teddy had been responsible for Kitty. The dog was probably crying for her missing friend.

"The two of you are miserable wretches this morning," her husband observed, standing over them.

"Surely you can't expect me not to feel *something* for the poor boy."

"It's not like he was your child," Jack said under his breath.

She got up and moved to the wardrobe, ornate mahogany, stewing quietly as she attempted to select a daytime dress.

She was angry, she realized—and even afraid.

It was all the fault of Ava, Jack's first wife. Her husband didn't want to believe it—Maddie hadn't wanted to believe it herself but came to see that the ugly little story her mother had heard was, in fact, true. Jack's divorce had been ugly—it was before she met him, thankfully, but that didn't stop Ava Willing Astor from being vindictive. She'd gotten terribly angry at her former husband when he announced his intention to remarry. They'd divorced less than a year earlier; he was remarrying scandalously soon—and, of course, someone scandalously young. Ava was afraid of what it might mean for her son and daughter when there was a second set of Astor children, younger and cuter and living with their father day in and day out.

Maddie's mother learned through her spy network that Ava had hired a gypsy to put a curse on her. Maddie would've thought it laughable if occultism wasn't the biggest fad of the day, if she hadn't known for a fact that many society ladies went to mediums to speak to the dead and have their palms read. Ava's gypsy was well-known among the Manhattan set, keeping an exotic little atelier in a chic section of the city, advertising in the *Times*. Maddie's mother's operative gave them a full report on the supposed curse. "Your husband and his new wife will never know prolonged happiness," she'd said, mimicking the gypsy's Slavic accent. "He will never have a child that he loves more than the children he already has, and the new wife will lose everyone she has ever loved."

Jack had laughed it off. "Ava? A gypsy? Impossible. She's the most sensible woman I've ever known." But men often dismissed the power and importance of prophecies, of anything they could not see or hold—or own.

Maddie had waited until they'd arrived in Cairo to consult her own mystic, a one-eyed crone known to the expat set. The woman told her she could see the malignant spirit following Maddie, bound to her by the gypsy's curse. "Get rid of it," Maddie had said, her voice rising as she tried not to cry. "I have a child to protect. I'll pay you anything." But the crone had insisted that Maddie had to drive off the evil spirit herself. "You must prove stronger than your foe." Her English had been poor, though, and Maddie wasn't sure what that meant. Maddie wasn't one to back down from a fight, but how was she supposed to drive off something she couldn't see or touch? She had resolved to hire a medium in New York, a famous psychic.

Now she was sorry that she'd waited.

And something had to be done now, before they got to New York. She didn't like the shadow Teddy's death had cast over her, over everything. The ugly suspicion that it would not be the last of the curse's working.

She had grown very close to Teddy, in fact, feeling bad for him after she learned his parents had died, insisting they give him a place in the household. He'd become like a member of the family. Almost. She'd fancied adopting him—not in the formal way; Jack would never stand for that, nor would his two children from his former marriage, who weren't much older than Maddie herself, and who, she suspected, truly only saw dollar signs when they looked at their father. She'd imagined taking Teddy in like a nephew, providing him with nice clothing and warm food, imagined how he'd dote on her, would love her, even. He'd come to embody all the good she was capable of.

Now, of course, that would never happen.

The worst part was she knew she was to blame, no matter what Dr. Leader had said to soothe her. Teddy wouldn't have come on this tour if not for her. He would've remained behind at Beechwood with the rest of the staff, polishing the silver and running errands, waiting for their return. Jack had raised his eyebrows when she'd asked but gave in to make her happy. He hadn't complained, not even when Teddy lost Kitty in Egypt, the dog getting away from the boy, who was then too scared to tell them. Jack had paid to have a suite of servants stay behind and look for the dog, to no avail. It was only through sheer dumb luck that they ran into the dog some days later, stowed away on the barge of another group of wealthy American tourists. She'd been sure that Jack was going to insist they get rid of the boy, but he didn't.

She had loved Teddy—in her way—and the evil spirit had taken him away. Just like Ava's crone had said.

Her husband caught her looking at the dog as she slipped out of her robe and began to dress for the day. "I know you feel bad about Teddy," Jack said. "I quite adore seeing your sensitive side. But you must try to put it out of your mind. All this melancholy can't be good for the baby."

She rolled her eyes. As if *he* knew what was best for the baby.

They took their time with everything, the Astors. Even getting ready for the day was an event; and today was no different, despite the awfulness of Teddy's death hovering over them. So it was well into the afternoon by the time Madeleine's hair was set just right and they found their friends gathered around a table in the Verandah Café, playing cards and drinking.

No, not *friends*. Their *circle*. Their people. A few of them, stragglers who didn't normally meet the standards of the rest but had risen momentarily to their ranks via the strange shuffling together that occurred on a ship, would be forgotten as soon as they had disembarked, shed like an unneeded umbrella.

The Verandah Café reminded Maddie of her trip to Florida, taken when she was thirteen. Indescribably exotic then, the palm trees and sand beaches and cute little alligators now paled in comparison to what she'd seen in Cairo and Alexandria. Still, the room conjured up that happy family trip, with miniature potted palms and wicker furniture, and great fans circling lazily overhead. The bright greens and corals of the cushions gave cheery respite from the unending gray of the ocean and sky outside.

And yet, seeing the crowd gathered in here gave her another moment of ill feeling—W. T. Stead and the Duff-Gordons; Caroline Fletcher and her husband, a handsome young man named Mark, his face always creased with worry. It was the séance group re-created, almost exactly, but with the addition of Dr. Alice Leader. Last night had ended in tragedy; it seemed a bad idea for them to be gathered again. This unspoken *thing* united them. The way the candles had all snuffed out.

The way the scream had torn from her throat when she'd first seen Teddy, strewn on her bedroom floor.

Maddie sank into a wicker chair, grateful for the plump cushions, and watched the men gravitate to Kitty, their careless hands petting her too aggressively. Men liked their pets, the implicit permission they felt in handling them however they wanted.

"There's a good thing," Sir Duff-Gordon said to the dog as he cuffed her chin.

"Why don't you join us? If you both play, we could make up another foursome," Lucy Duff-Gordon said, not taking her eyes off the cards. Though she was a year or two older than Jack—nearing fifty—she looked no older than thirty-three. She had an elegance—and arrogance—that made most women wither, but Maddie had noticed that her humor, though cutting, was always warm. She was beautiful, savvy, quick, and not easily impressed—all qualities Maddie hoped to cultivate in herself over time. And a successful businesswoman, a rarity, to be sure. One of the biggest stories of the day was that she'd fitted Gaby Deslys, the French stage actress, with an entire wardrobe of nightgowns and negligees that she wore during her courtship by the king of Portugal. After that, everyone in Maddie's circle back at home had ordered similar slinky, silky garments though none, that Maddie knew of, had dared to wear them.

"We can put Mr. Fletcher and Mr. Stead to good use, instead of letting them sit around like wallflowers at the ball," Lucy said.

"I'm a far more skilled observer than player," Stead said with his characteristic aloofness.

"That's not what *I* hear," Lucy clipped back, with the arch of a perfectly shaped eyebrow.

Madeleine knew what she was referring to: Stead's history as a newspaperman. The scandal of Eliza Armstrong in particular. Everyone knew about it. Everyone whispered. How he'd been far *more* than an observer. How he'd gone undercover to purchase a *hired* girl—a girl of only thirteen, no less—and taken her to a boardinghouse for the night, all in the name of "research." His goal had been to expose the ease with which the sex trade was conducted right under everyone's noses, right there in civilized England. And yet what he'd succeeded in accomplishing was causing ripples of suspicion and outrage among the elite.

It had been, when you thought about it, positively *American* of him.

But this had all been before Maddie was even born, and she grew restless thinking about it. Again, she felt a sudden desire for her real friends back home. Six months traveling had been an awfully long time.

She wanted, desperately, suddenly, to be off this ship.

"I don't like bridge, in any case," Jack was saying. "I've always thought women are far more skilled in the counting of cards than men. Just one of their many hidden mysteries." He scratched Kitty's belly, the dog on her back with her legs in the air, tongue lolling from the side of her mouth. Kitty knew how to make Jack love her. It struck Maddie that she and Kitty occupied the same level in her husband's affections. She knew how to make her husband purr like a kitten. You learned the ropes very quickly.

"I wonder, then," said Lucy Duff-Gordon, "that more of us aren't operating businesses, with all our mysterious talents."

Her husband, Sir Duff-Gordon, coughed into his sleeve. "Surely not all young women share the *interest,* my dear. Mrs. Astor, you can take my hand if you wish." He rose from the table, offering his cards to Madeleine. "Though that does mean partnering with my wife. Bid high at your own peril."

"Nobody finds that funny," Lucy said as she rearranged the cards in her hand.

"I couldn't," Maddie said, demurring quickly. The truth was that she didn't like bridge. She associated it with her mother's set. Hours exchanging gossip in the sunroom over tea and sherry, the snap of cards played against the glass table topper. She didn't want that to be her future, as much as she knew it would be. Even though she'd benefited from that gossip.

She preferred more active games. Tennis, horseback riding, even yachting. She had heard there was a squash court on board, with a balcony for people to observe the game. A professional instructor and everything. She wished she were in a position to play, but running was out of the question. Lord knew she needed a bit of movement—they'd likely be sitting on their rumps all evening, between dinner and the scheduled piano concert in the reception room that everyone seemed to be planning on attending later. At least the reception room was lovely, with its Aubusson tapestry and leaded-glass windows.

She stayed to watch them play a hand, however: a foursome of Lady and Sir Duff-Gordon, Mrs. Fletcher, and Dr. Alice Leader.

Mostly to see if Lucy would say anything tart about anyone else on the ship. The one thing Madeleine hated more than gossip was being left out of it.

Besides, she liked to observe people. There was so much you could guess about a person when they didn't know you were watching.

However, Alice Leader made her uncomfortable in a way she couldn't quite articulate. It seemed funny to see the doctor with this group, in her somber brown skirts and staid spectacles, hair pinned up primly. In contrast to, say, Lady Duff-Gordon, who always dressed so beautifully. Today in pale pink silk and tiny rosebuds. The two women were like chalk and cheese.

"Where's Guggenheim? Taking voice lessons from his French chanteuse?" Jack asked, the men sniggering. Was that a tinge of envy Maddie detected in his tone? Everyone knew the hired singer he'd brought with him was not spending her nights teaching him French. At least, not French *music*.

"I expect that's it," Sir Duff-Gordon said as he discarded. His choice of card elicited a groan from his wife.

"Maybe he's sleeping in after the excitement of last night." Mark Fletcher was being deliberately arch.

Dr. Leader looked up from her cards. "Excitement?"

Don't mention the séance in front of the doctor, Maddie wanted to say, but knew it was hopeless with this crowd.

"We had a séance last night," Lady Duff-Gordon said with her usual bluntness. "It was quite . . . lively."

"I suppose you object to such things." Mr. Stead took preemptive offense, as Maddie expected he would.

"Many of my colleagues find spiritualism intriguing," Dr. Leader said.

"What a diplomatic answer," Lady Duff-Gordon replied with a crisp laugh.

"But not you, I take it," Stead said. "Even a disbeliever wouldn't deny we had contact from the other world last night. We had . . . a presence." As he spoke, the words crept underneath Maddie's skin, the coldness sweeping into her bones. The old man knew the truth of what had happened, just like her.

"The table shook under our hands," he went on, and she remembered it. The night had seemed a dream, but now she knew it had been real. Too real. "A wind came in and blew out the candles," Stead was saying, "and the room grew cold. All the classic signs of the presence of a spirit." *Stop talking*, she willed him, subconsciously afraid that they'd summon up the spirit by merely talking about it. *This spirit isn't a toy, a curiosity. It's dangerous.*

"I've been practicing occultism for many years now," he continued, "often in the company of great mediums, and I can honestly say I have never felt a presence as strong as the one I felt last night."

Maddie sank farther into the chair, growing more and more desperate for escape. The chill was winding through her now, stirring in her belly and up into her chest, like ice-cold seawater.

"It could be because we are over water. Water is easier than earth. The spirits encounter less resistance. Yes, that could explain a lot of what we saw last night." He nodded even though no one was refuting him.

He was talking about it like the spirit was a physical presence. . . .

"So, you're saying spirits over water are more powerful than they would be on dry land," Caroline Fletcher asked as she picked through the cards in her hand, "because they would encounter less resistance? Like with electricity?"

"Precisely," Mr. Stead confirmed. "Like telegraphy. Like that Marconi machine. Except"—he paused, and in the silence, Maddie shivered—"spirits can live not just in air but in *people*."

"What?" Maddie said, the interruption bursting out before she was aware of it. Her husband gave her a sidelong glance.

"Do you mean like a possession of some kind?" asked Lucy.

"I do indeed, madam," Stead answered. He looked from one to the next dourly. "And it's when they possess the body of another that they're at their most dangerous. Because, you see, then they are *corporeal*. Flesh and bone. They can act on their desires, whatever those may be."

"Excuse me." Maddie shot to her feet—as much as she could shoot up in her current state. The urge to flee was overpowering. She would cause a stir leaving so abruptly, but she couldn't sit there any longer. "I'm not feeling well." She smiled faintly, with a gesture toward her belly, knowing they wouldn't ask for details.

She pushed through the glass doors and scurried down the promenade, ignoring her husband's calls. She would claim that she was about to be violently ill and she couldn't wait for him. He wouldn't get mad at her for leaving. He wasn't good with illness of any kind. He was good with a great many things—playacting and dogs and inventing useless things—but not sickness. It wasn't in his nature.

She just couldn't take it a minute longer. They could all make fun of the séance and act as though it was some kind of trick, but she knew it wasn't. It had been *real*.

They had touched the malevolent spirit that had taken Teddy; and you could tell it was pure evil, whatever it was.

And it was still here, hovering on the ship. What if it had taken the form of someone here, someone in that room, someone lurking in the halls, waiting for the next victim? Stead had just said this was possible, that this evil spirit could slip inside the body of a living, breathing person, bend it to its will. Those near misses and misfortunes during their grand tour made sense in retrospect: the servant who'd let Kitty out of the hotel suite in Cairo, causing all manner of anxiety, the trail guide who'd given her that too-spirited mount in Montreux. The thief who'd chased her into an alley off the open-air market in Florence. Jack had said he was a common cutpurse, but Maddie had seen something more sinister in his eye. Demonic cat's-paws, all, sent to fulfill the curse.

Of course: that's how Teddy had died. At the hand of someone on board this ship, someone who might not even be aware of what they'd done. Could that be why she still had this ugly, sinking feeling lurking within her?

Some might think her young and naive—spoiled even—compared to all those vaunted, celebrated people upstairs, laughing and playing cards, but Madeleine Astor knew complacency when she saw it. They wanted to believe in spirits and ghosts, but they were blind to the danger. They were ignorant of the shroud of death that hung over them.

Over all of them.

Footsteps had caught up to her and she swiveled. Caroline Fletcher had followed her. "Are you all right? I thought I should make sure you got safely to your stateroom—you gave us quite a fright." Before Maddie could say or do anything, however, Caroline rushed forward and took Maddie's arm firmly, in a way that reminded Maddie of her mother.

She let Caroline escort her. It was reassuring, at that moment, to feel a warm human body beside her, anchoring her. "I find all this talk about spirits very unsettling," Maddie said. "It's just that Jack and I had several *frights* while we were traveling. Traipsing from one old castle to another, each of them haunted, to judge by the stories." She choked back a sob. "And then losing poor, dear Teddy . . ."

"Don't underestimate the effect of pregnancy." Caroline nodded at Maddie's swollen belly. "It makes you so much more sensitive to everything around you. Almost *unbearably* sensitive."

"Yes . . . You understand. . . . It wasn't so long ago for you, was it?" Maddie thought of the Fletcher baby, a beautiful little thing; too bad she was usually off with the nanny. Maddie wouldn't mind a little practice handling an actual infant. Caroline merely smiled, one of those beatific smiles that only recent mothers could give. Maddie looked forward to smiling like that herself. Saintly.

They had fallen into a rhythm, their steps in cadence like horses paired together in harness. At that moment, Caroline could've been one of her old friends—and was certainly closer to her in age than any of those other ladies—and her companionship was a comfort. "I feel it, too. There's a presence on board this ship. It's not just you: everyone is talking about it."

As frightening as it was to hear her fears confirmed, it was also reassuring. It wasn't all in her head. "It seemed every place we stayed in Europe was haunted. Jack kept telling me there was nothing to be frightened of. . . . 'Ghosts can't harm you—just a lot of cold air and humbug!' But you heard Stead. Could it really be possible for a ghost to take possession of someone's body?" If this was true, the danger from Ava's curse was real.

And present: on a ship with more than two thousand souls, how would she know which ones meant her harm? She was surrounded by potential enemies. Like the newspapers with their insatiable appetite for stories about them, with their swarms of reporters ambushing them in Europe and Egypt. Waiting on the docks to waylay them as they boarded the *Titanic*. The world, it seemed, meant her harm.

Caroline was leading her now, clamping Maddie's arm firmly to her side. Caroline wasn't looking at her any longer, no: she was looking down at their feet as though following a path Maddie couldn't see. "In the town where I grew up, there were a lot of Catholics. One of my Catholic friends told me a story about one of the parish priests, an old man who had done a number of exorcisms in his day. But there was one case in particular. . . . He wouldn't talk about it, but the parishioners did. It had to do with a young man who had lived a couple of towns over. . . . The man had been accused of killing his brother in a fit of jealousy because the brother had married the man's sweetheart, the girl he'd hoped to wed."

Maddie was beginning to tire—she got winded so easily with the pregnancy—and tried to slip out of Caroline's grip, but Caroline held tight, continuing to pull Maddie down the long, empty hall. Pulling

Maddie along as though she were a stubborn child. "The family was convinced that their son was possessed by his brother's spirit. He'd moved into the dead man's house, slept in his bed, enjoyed his wife— the dead man using his brother to have the life he was otherwise denied."

Maddie snorted, unable to control her tongue. "That was stupid of them. It obviously wasn't possession: it had been the killer's intention all along. He killed his brother to have the girl he loved, and used possession as an excuse. The family just couldn't accept that their son was capable of such evil—"

"That's what the constable thought, too. The family was in a position of influence in the town, however, and was able to buy the priest a few days." The pressure on Maddie's fingers grew painful. "He tried all the usual things: tying the man down, praying over him for hours at a time, sprinkling him with holy water, making him kiss the crucifix. Nothing worked.

"Finally, knowing time was running out, in a fit of desperation, the priest took the man to the pond behind the family's house and . . . submerged the man. Completely, totally underwater. He wanted to trick the spirit into thinking that the man was going to die, to drive the spirit out."

Maddie gasped.

"That's what the priest did. He held the brother down. Held him down, even though he thrashed and fought. Held him down to *save* him."

Maddie was nearly faint with pain. Caroline was squeezing her fingers together, squeezing them into a pulpy mash.

"He almost drowned the man—almost—but pulled him out of the water at the last minute. The man sputtered and wheezed, but he was alive. The priest was relieved to find that it had worked: he'd driven the dead man's spirit out of him. It was the brother once again."

"The killer," Maddie clarified.

They'd come to the end of the alleyway. Caroline steered them through a door onto the promenade. They stood at a railing at the ship's stern, the gray-green ocean spooling away in two spiraling wakes. Maddie looked down at the cold, dark sea. Into the fathomless abyss. It was a long, long way down.

Where was everyone? In this lonely corner, it was like they were the only two people on the ship. A chill descended on Maddie. Why had Caroline Fletcher brought her here? They'd walked right by the stairs that led to the Astors' stateroom with its cozy, safe bed.

Finally, Caroline released her hand. Maddie rubbed life back into her fingers as the two stood at the railing and stared at the sea's hypnotic undulations.

"The spirit driven out, when the brother—the killer, as you say—came to his senses, he was horrified. Because while he was under the brother's influence, he'd killed the girl. The dead brother had driven him to do it, he told the priest. He swore the brother's vengeful spirit had been inside him. Had seen the happiness on the girl's face as they fornicated—she'd wanted the first brother all along—and the dead brother flew into a rage when he saw it. Killed the girl, and wanted to kill the brother, too. Such is the power of a jealous heart, even from beyond the grave."

The power of a jealous heart. It was only a story, but Maddie didn't doubt the truth of it. She could feel the brother's pain and confusion all around her.

Caroline continued to stare at the sea. "And now the brother, seeing what he'd done, what the vengeful brother had *made* him do, he was beside himself with rage and regret. What else could he do but kill himself? He stabbed himself in the heart as soon as he stepped back inside his parents' house." She settled her gaze on Maddie. Was it Maddie's imagination, or was Caroline Fletcher's normally warm gaze a trifle chillier than before? "When you hear a story like that, you can't doubt whether possession is real. There is no other explanation for what he did."

The deck moved beneath Maddie's feet suddenly, and she grabbed the railing to steady herself. Was it the ship, rising and falling on a gigantic wave, or Caroline's insidious story? The vengeful spirit, coming for her?

It was a long way down. The gray-green waves lashing the ship, clawing like wolves.

Maddie saw, in that instant, what she had to do to save herself and her unborn child.

Chapter Fifteen

There was a faint rattle of crystal drops as Dai Bowen entered the Astors' stateroom that evening, a step behind Les and Violet. If someone were inside, an Astor or one of the servants, Dai would not be able to explain their presence. Violet Jessop, who'd opened the door with her passkey, was the stewardess assigned to the room, of course, but if the Astors were to return early from the concert, they'd be surprised to find the two boxers with her.

Could Violet have miscalculated the length of tonight's piano concert? Or might one of the Astors' servants have remained to polish shoes or lay out tomorrow's outfits?

No: all was still. It was nothing more than the rise and fall of the ship rattling the crystal. They'd made their final stop in Queenstown, Ireland, earlier this afternoon, and had already by now struck out for open sea, New York bound.

They tiptoed into the room. Dai had to hand it to the girl: Violet had nerve and cunning, planned it all to a T. All the first-class passengers' servants were being treated to a special meal (eels in aspic and pigeon pie) in the crew's mess. She'd known the rooms would be empty and decided to use the opportunity to offer them a little sightseeing tour.

Not that he was surprised—he knew the effect he and Les had on girls. Once they fell under the spell of it—the smiles, the subtle flexing of the muscles, the teasing in his voice, the mention of his workout regimens—they all became the same to Dai. A sea of sweet laughter and perfume and confidential tones of voice. They became standing too close and smelling too floral, all haloed hair and pink lips and white teeth.

Dai wasn't proud of it. And he certainly could take no credit for the way his hair curled just so across his face or the symmetry of his dimples—his pretty mama had given him those. And he knew there were plenty of other men with curls and chins and muscles—but they were not boxers. Modern-day gladiators.

And he didn't like to lead her on—*you're not my type, miss*—but it was good cover. He had to play the game.

Besides, he had lured her in as a favor to Les.

Dai fancied he and Les looked out of place in the pretty room of mahogany paneling and plush carpet, chairs upholstered in velvet, enough bedspreads and robes to keep an entire village in Wales warm through the winter. It was nothing like the room in steerage they shared with two additional men, not enough space to turn around without whacking your head on one of the bunk beds. As a matter of fact, he felt out of place on the entire ship and had the sneaking suspicion that the ship had come to the same conclusion and was secretly displeased whenever he set foot on any of the upper decks. *Know your place, guttersnipe.*

Violet went about the room lighting another two lamps—the first-class passengers had such excesses of *light*, it occurred to Dai—and Les traced her path. Dai didn't like the way Les's eyes glittered as he surveyed the Astors' possessions. He watched Les pause before the dressing table laid with Mrs. Astor's nice things: ivory and jade combs and a set of silver brushes. A Chinese lacquer tray holding Mr. Astor's everyday jewelry. Two pairs of cuff links and a watch on a chain. It made Violet nervous, too, Dai could tell, and why shouldn't it: it was her job on the line if something went missing. Now he understood why Les had been keen for a little tour: it wasn't to see how the other half lived. It was to case them.

The bed had been turned down by some dutiful servant—probably Violet herself—but Dai approached, recalling the gossip that had circulated the second- and third-class quarters all day. The story of the little boy—the one he himself had rescued from falling into the water only yesterday.

"So, this is where he—where it happened," Dai said, not wanting to bring the word *died* into the room with him, as if it might leave a stain. A pang of sadness moved through him—the boy had looked at him so admiringly on the promenade yesterday. For the moment, Dai had been his hero. And yet . . .

Whatever had troubled the boy enough to cause him to first climb the railing had continued to call to him, until the boy succumbed to his own death by another means. It was uncanny.

"I wish you hadn't mentioned that," Violet said. "I've been thinking about it all day, every time I'm in here by myself. It gives me the willies."

"Are you the superstitious type?" Les asked, poking around in a cabinet. "I heard some of the swells think the ship is haunted," he added, looking over his shoulder with his half grin.

Violet swayed toward him, as if to stop Les from prowling through the cupboard; then thinking better of it, she lingered instead near Dai. "The crew, too," she said. "There's a strange feeling on the ship, there's no denying."

Les laughed. "How could it be haunted? It's brand-new. Nobody's died on it, except for—"

"The boy." Violet rubbed her upper arms like she had a chill. "And it isn't just the boy—there are deaths on every voyage, it's just that most passengers don't hear about them. Crew members, mostly. Accidents. There's something different about this crossing. I been on plenty; I should know better."

He wasn't sure if Les believed in hauntings. Dai had grown up with it all around, belief in fairy folks and malicious spirits, mostly embraced by the poor and uneducated and, ironically, the most religious, in his experience. The kind of people who would call for his public execution if they ever found out the desire he harbored in secret, so he had resolved early to have nothing to do with them, including their embrace of magic.

"Aha!" Les said, and swiveled around, with a bottle of what looked to be mighty fancy American whiskey—bourbon, he'd heard it called. "Vi?" he said familiarly, rummaging out a glass. "And don't worry— we'll just add water to the bottle. He'll never know the difference."

"Oh no, I couldn't," Violet said nervously, though Dai noticed she didn't tell him to stop. No one ever told Les to stop.

"Well then, just the gentlemen," he said lavishly, pouring a drink for himself and handing one to Dai.

Dai sipped on it—the stinging warmth felt good, loosened him up. He had a simultaneous rising of contradictory emotions, both wanting to get drunk with Les on rich men's whiskey with not a care for the consequences, to laugh with abandon . . . and on the other side of it, a tiny current of dread. A voice that said, *Brace yourself. Here we go again.*

Les poured a third, smaller serving, and set it on a side table. "In case you should change your mind," he said to Violet with a wink. She blushed.

He plopped into one of the cushy purple chairs by the porthole and crossed his legs, leaning back. "I know we shouldn't," Les said, with that wicked grin again, "but rich just feels so *right*." He was rubbing the side of the chair as if petting an exotic animal. Then he produced a pack of cards. "Let's have that hand of poker, shall we?" Les had joked that he'd show Violet how to play a game called strip poker, a game he'd learned in the gin halls of Pontypridd. "It's nothing an upstanding young woman like yourself would know about," he'd said, teasing her, but she'd scoffed. If she wanted to pretend she was tough and wild, that was her choice. She had no idea what she'd be getting into with Les, but Dai knew why girls like Violet were attracted to boys like him and Les: they made her feel wild and free. They made her reckless.

They made her feel as if her life were different than it was.

Kind of the way Les made *him* feel.

So they all sat at the table where the Astors took their tea. Les dealt, cards gliding over the shiny, polished table like birds over a lake.

The girl either could not play cards worth a lick or was deliberately throwing the game. She lost three hands in a row. She started timidly, arguing that jewelry should count and surrendering her White Star Line service pin and a comb, but then on the last hand, shed her apron with abandon. Her hands lingered over the buttons at the front of her blouse, too, a promise of things to come. Les's eyes settled on those breasts with a big smile, making Dai's stomach go tight.

Dai lost two hands, taking off his necktie and his signet ring. When Leslie finally lost at last, he magnanimously took off his waistcoat and—for extra measure—his shirt. He rolled his neck until it cracked, and Dai noticed the way his biceps pumped, just subtly enough that Dai knew he'd done it on purpose. By this point, Violet was giggling hard, her face flushed, and even Dai had to bust out a laugh or two at Les's jokes.

He felt hot, and needed to move. He got up to stretch and poured another round of drinks. As he topped off the bottle with a splash from the water decanter, he looked over his shoulder and noticed Violet batting her lashes at Les. She seemed to recognize that Les was the one paying attention to her, and had begun to respond. Adaptive, women were.

Eventually, Dai began to relax, to imagine they were at any old pub back in Pontypridd or perhaps one in New York, where they were headed. As long as they neatened up and sneaked out of here before eleven, they'd be fine. He looked at the fancy brass clock on the mantel—it was only half past eight. The Astors would only just be getting served their entrées.

The whole time they played cards, Leslie looked about the room, remarking on this item or that. The room was chockablock with the Astors' possessions, as though they needed to put their mark on even temporary surroundings. Trunks of Mr. Astor's suits and Mrs. Astor's dresses stood open for perusal. Books were piled messily on a side table, along with stationery, an inkwell, and an assortment of pens. Jewelry was scattered across the dressing table, as though Madeleine Astor had changed her mind several times before heading out that evening.

Leslie rose to his feet. "Let's switch games," he announced all of a sudden. "I have too much respect for your mutual prudishness to continue in this way." At that, Violet laughed again.

He wandered the room, and Violet swiveled in her chair to watch. "You can tell so much by a man's possessions, don't you think?" Leslie's fingers danced in the air above the stack of books but settled on a leather-bound journal left open to an ink-smudged page. "What's this?"

"Don't be messing with his things," Violet said. "You're a naughty one, Leslie."

"I'll be careful. These hands," he said, waggling his fingers at her, "are ever gentle, I assure you." At this, she blushed and laughed again. "He'll never know." Les lifted the book for examination. He skimmed a page, then flipped to the next. "Your Mr. Astor is quite the thinker. Not one to let his brain sit idle, is he? There's all kinds of notes here for a piece of equipment. Something to do with a bicycle." He flipped another page. "This actually looks like . . . an invention." He dug into the earlier portion of the book, brows furrowed like a terrier catching the scent of vermin.

Violet swept the cards up. "I overheard Mr. Guggenheim say something to Mr. Astor once, congratulating him on a patent he'd just got or some such thing. He must be very clever."

Leslie was flipping pages furiously now. "There's more here. Bits of prose . . . Maybe he fancies himself a poet, too." He returned the journal to the table, careful to leave it open to the correct page. Next, he went to the clothing trunk. At least he wasn't rough with Astor's things, Dai noted with relief. He treated them respectfully, like he owned them himself. "Very flashy clothing for a society swell, wouldn't you say? Here's a man who likes to be looked at, admired. A man who likes the limelight. Who acts like he's on stage."

As he did his little performance for Violet—because that's certainly what this was—Dai felt himself spooling away from the scene, floating above it, just him and the whiskey heat and the watching. Les was always like this, seemingly able to read a person from a glance, like a fortune-teller. As much as he *exuded*—warmth, energy, danger—he *absorbed*, too, took you in, made you feel seen and lit up and alive. He saw things—details, opportunities, hopes, and wishes—that others overlooked.

It was part of what had drawn Dai to him in the first place. Their trainer, George Cundick, had introduced them. They were just boys hanging around the boxing gym, though Dai occupied a higher rung than Les because Cundick had seen early promise in him. Les was just a street urchin who had gotten it into his head that he could be a boxer, with his broomstick arms and concave chest. Dai had given him wide berth at first, being prone to mistrust posers and opportunists, but over time they became friends, mostly because he'd come to see Les's love and admiration of Cundick was real. And if Cundick saw something in the skinny, blond kid, then maybe Dai should, too.

They'd become roommates after that—until, one day, it had become something altogether different. Somehow, Les had known something about Dai that Dai hadn't—at least not *really*, not in words—known about himself.

It made Dai feel exposed around Les, made him feel like Les *knew* . . . knew and yet never made any effort to say if it was the same for him, or if Dai was just a passing interest among Les's myriad sources of entertainment.

A sound of clattering down the hall broke the spell Les had woven over the Astors' room, and Dai remembered again the kind of disaster it would be if they got caught. He and Violet, both drunker now, it seemed, than Les was, frantically moved about neatening up the room, and the three of them slipped out the door with stifled laughter, waiting until they hit the back stairwell before sprinting down it, Violet giggling between her hands.

But the fun wasn't over. "Come on, this way," Les said with a glint in his eye as he pushed open a narrower door at the end of the passageway that cut through the first-class suites, leading them down to steerage. Les led them, guileless and obedient, through crowded corridors like enchanted children following the Pied Piper. Dai could tell by the way she kept leaping out of the way of people, startled, that this was the first time Violet had been down here, so different from first class, where she normally spent her day. The air was thick with the smells of sweat and beer and homemade sausage carried in luggage. Children ran by in a string like feral puppies giving chase. They had to step around card games played on the floor in the passageway. The sound of a concertina drifted down the hall, behind it the rhythmic stump of a jig.

They ducked into a deserted passageway at last, not far from the boilers. Dai could hear the murmur of the coal men up ahead, the sound of coal being shoveled into furnaces, but did not see anyone. They were alone.

"Have you got another game for us, then, Leslie?" Violet was asking, catching her breath.

"Do I." Les leaned into her, hips nearly touching hers, eyes not far from the well of her cleavage. "You're my kind of girl, Violet." She sucked in a sharp breath. "Smart. You're not fooled by those rich toffs upstairs, are you? I mean, they think nothing of the likes of us. So, it's not like we owe them anything."

He had slipped his hands around her waist. Dai knew the magic in those hands. Les was a man who knew what he wanted. She squirmed in his grip, but she didn't run, not yet.

Dai's heart began to sink. This was it, Les's plan.

"What are you getting at, sir?" she asked playfully, throwing a quick, cautious glance at Dai. Dai was the reliable one. Dai wouldn't let anything *too* crazy happen. That's what her expression seemed to say.

Les gave her a brilliant smile. "I've got a proposition for you, Miss Jessop. Say! I just noticed your name sounds like *julep*. Mint julep, that's what we should call you. Anyway, this idea of mine, it will make you a bit of money, much better than the tips you get from those rich swells."

"What are you talking about?" Another glance at Dai. Dai did his best to smile and shrug. He really didn't know. At least, not exactly, though he had a feeling . . .

"All you have to do is let me into their cabins—"

"No, Leslie. If anything goes missing, I'll be the first person they'd suspect. This is my job, Leslie," she said. "You don't know how hard it was to get an interview. They didn't want me because they said I'd be a distraction to the male passengers traveling alone." There was pain in her voice. The injustice hurt her still.

Les leaned in closer, so they were practically touching. "And aren't there times when you're afraid it will all be taken away from you? That some woman will complain about you because she doesn't like the way her husband looks at you? Or when some fussy old matron misplaces her cheap paste brooch and blames you rather than admit she's starting to forget things?"

Violet sniffed and that's when Dai knew Les had her.

"Nothing is going to go missing. Trust me," Les said, his lips inches from her cheek. "What I have in mind, it's as safe as houses."

"Hmm," she said, but didn't nudge him away this time. There was a faint smile twitching at her lips. When she let out a little sigh, Dai knew it was time to slip away. He had no idea what Les was planning and was pretty sure he didn't want to find out. Whatever the con was, he didn't want to witness Les sealing the deal.

He was in no mood for company as he climbed the stairs all the way to the top deck. Les would be kissing that stewardess right now. He almost felt sorry for her. Violet was an innocent, probably never kissed by a man like Les. Probably only had dry, chaste ones from boy cousins and a belowdecks engineer who kept promising that he'd marry her. Passion was unknown to her, was something she'd only imagined, but Leslie's kisses would stir it in her. There was something about the way Leslie Williams kissed that made you want more— want all of him, and more than that even.

He made you want whole, impossible worlds.

As though wanting Les Williams wasn't impossible enough.

Chapter Sixteen

It had been a long second day of the journey—the sun had already sunk beneath the sea, leaving a bloodstain that finally turned into the black of night—but Annie knew she wouldn't sleep just yet. Something was very wrong. First the boy's death, then the mysterious brooch. Annie felt dizzy with the weight of it; she had to tell someone. If only to alleviate her own worries. But her schedule was overwhelming and left her numb from racing about the ship's many decks.

Now, she was on her way back to the first-class cabins for one last check-in before bedtime. She'd been carrying the heart-and-arrow brooch, wrapped in a handkerchief, in her pocket all day long, and the suspicion stirring in her own heart had only grown. It was time to return the piece to Caroline Fletcher and, if she found the courage, to ask her what the Astors' boy had been doing with it last night before he died.

Annie paused at the top of the stairway. It was a long climb to the boat deck, the ship's top level. She stood outside the first-class passengers' lounge to catch her breath. Here, women walked in pairs and threesomes along the promenade in their smart dresses, most with a fur stole wrapped around their shoulders to keep off the chill. You could see the lounge through the windows, the Verandah Café made up with a tropical motif, wicker tables and chairs, groups sitting together drinking their after-dinner coffee or playing cards—those who hadn't attended tonight's concert in the reception room, that is.

As she passed the door to the lounge, her gaze fell on a figure sitting in a corner. It was Mark. She recognized him through the window. He was curled around a book, alone toward the back of the room. Annie took a quick scan of the crowd, but Caroline was nowhere to be seen.

Annie had of course resolved to avoid Mark, not to let herself get into trouble—*the Lord favors good girls, Annie*—but this seemed like fate. She found herself curiously drawn to him. She had turned this attraction over in her mind since they'd first met—Why was she so fascinated with this stranger?—and the best she could come up with was that he reminded her of a man back home, the only man she'd allowed herself to fall in love with. They didn't look much alike, aside from the kindness in their eyes and their shy, easy smiles. There was something about the way he spoke to her, however, so gently and warmly, and the way he treated her that she couldn't help but feel close to him. To feel as though they already knew each other. And no matter how many times she silently reminded herself that Mark was not Desmond, and not allow herself to get too familiar, it was all forgotten as soon as she looked into his blue eyes.

He might know about his wife's brooch, anyway, she reasoned. Surely it couldn't hurt to go talk to him.

She shivered, and out of habit, felt for the crucifix just below her throat before remembering that she had lost it. She felt naked without it, undone somehow.

As she slipped through the door, moving through the crowded lounge toward where Mark sat, a story swirled into her head: an old tale of a girl with a green ribbon tied permanently around her neck. *No matter what*, the girl was forever warning people, *never untie the ribbon*. To untie her ribbon would be the end of everything: it held her head in place, you see, and without it, she was but a walking corpse. The tale had always chilled Annie—its taunting nature, the embedded warning; and yet she could never decide what its warning *meant*. Was it that girls were fragile—fragile as a single-knotted bow—and must be protected at all costs? Or was it that the only way they may prove their story true was to die for it?

Or was it that they were a pretty package and tied up with a bow, but once the wrapping had been undone, their magic would be released and they were no longer valuable?

Across the crowd, Mark looked up just then and smiled at her—and it was as if the moon had shifted through a porthole and flooded the room in warmth and light, the memory of the green ribbon fluttering away on the night breeze.

She curtsied when she reached his side. "Good evening, Mar—Mr. Fletcher. I'm sorry to interrupt your reading."

"Don't be. I was looking for a distraction," he said.

"Surely there are plenty of distractions on this ship." *One thousand books in the first-class library. A swimming pool, one shilling a visit.*

"I need to take my mind off something, not merely fill my time." His eyes twinkled, but she felt something shifting and restless behind them. "Actually, I wonder, Miss Hebbley—might you have a moment? There's something specific I'd like to discuss with you. It must be highly unusual for a passenger to seek your confidences so readily"—his cheeks went pink—"but I feel I can trust you, and I hope you feel the same way."

She took a breath. He felt the bond between them, too; it wasn't just in her head. "Of course," she found herself saying. He started off through the crowded room and she followed as though there were an invisible thread pulling her. They pushed through the door at the end of the hall and stepped back out onto the promenade. It had gotten quieter out here, and darker. It had to be past 10 p.m. Passengers would be retiring soon; many already had.

Outside, in a quiet corner away from the hubbub, he turned to her.

They were alone together, only the ship's gentle sway beneath their feet—something you normally couldn't notice, except in moments of perfect stillness. "I witnessed something I can't explain, and I was wondering if perhaps you had seen anything similar. It's to do with Ondine. This morning when I first woke up, I could swear that I saw what looked like *scratch marks* on the baby's face. But then . . . *they disappeared*. Right before my eyes. Went from pink, bloodied grooves to fine white lines to . . . nothing. Just smooth skin." He held his breath, obviously bracing for ridicule.

Her first thought was alarm: Was he accusing her of harming the baby? "Could she have scratched herself? Babies do that."

"I checked her fingernails myself, and they were trimmed neat. Miss Flatley is good for something, it would seem." He pressed his lips together tightly. Started to speak, stopped, then relented. "I hesitate to admit it, but, yes. It's most . . . unusual. Almost . . . supernatural. There's more. . . . Something else happened last night, Annie— Ondine's all right *now*, mind you, but at the time it was . . ." He shuddered.

An icy finger ran down Annie's spine. A push, a prod. *Speak up.*

"We woke to find Ondine *choking*. . . . My wife—" he began, but then stopped, as though there were hands at his own throat.

Had Caroline been choking the child? Did he think his wife was responsible for the scratches? Annie had heard stories of what mothers sometimes did to their babies. Bad things. Caroline Fletcher did not *seem* like such a woman. Still—what else could it be? Annie's heart went out to Ondine. The helpless one.

Then again, there was her brooch, found on the dead boy's body, which still sat, wrapped in its handkerchief, in Annie's pocket.

The poor man was tormented, that was plain to see.

He suspects his wife. The thought came to her and she couldn't erase it, even though it turned over sourly in her gut.

"Is there something I can do to help?" There was such sadness in his eyes; she would do anything to make it go away.

"Let's find someplace quieter. There are too many people here," he said, even though it wasn't true—the crowds on the promenade had thinned out vastly, the night sea was dark and twinkling. Still, he pulled her farther into the darkness, to a deserted spot—a guilty spot, a place where it would be hard for a stewardess to explain why she'd been found there with a married passenger—and then turned again to look at her, the wind whipping his hair around his face, making something inside her soar. "I hope you don't mind my confiding in you, Miss Hebbley. I realize it's inappropriate and a terrible imposition but . . . I feel as though I have no one to talk to. . . . These people"—she supposed he meant the first-class passengers—"are my wife's people, not mine."

"Oh?" she asked, though instantly she felt she had *known* this about him—that this was why she'd been so drawn to him initially. It wasn't just the intensity of his eyes, pulling on something within her. It was that feeling she sensed, that he was just to the outside of things, like her. That this boat, for all its comforts, was not her world, and not his, either.

"I wasn't born to money," he explained, offering a strained smile. "Those who've always had it can't understand what that's like. To feel so . . ."

"Helpless," she whispered.

"Desperate."

"Trapped."

"Yes." He blinked. "Yes, that's it exactly. Ironic, isn't it? A ship so massive, and here we are, trapped on it, nowhere to run."

She shivered. "One is always trapped within oneself, though." She wasn't sure where the thought had sprung from. It was something she'd heard somewhere or read in a book, though she'd never remember where.

He stared at her, concern wrinkling his brow. Had she spoken out of turn? But then she watched as the corners of his eyes crinkled and a smile, far brighter and more genuine, broke out across his face.

"What?"

"Nothing, it's just." He shook his head, the smile still playing across his lips like sunlight on water. "Someone I once knew used to say that very same thing."

"Who?"

For a moment, Mark Fletcher was transformed. No longer sullen, his face radiated with the kind of warmth that only comes from re-membered love, so strong that Annie felt a pang of jealousy. "She was very special to me. Her name was—" But then he stopped, and the smile was snuffed out in the wind. "Never mind. I'm doing you a dis-service, Annie. I shouldn't trouble you with the intimate details of my life. It's an imposition. You are staff on this ship."

She felt slapped, even though what he'd said was true: they should not be alone like this. They should not be confiding in each other. She had no right to feel so close to this man, this stranger. "I—I'm sorry, sir, I—"

"I didn't mean it that way. . . . You have no choice if a passenger comes to you with his problems. . . . You must do your job. It is I who am sorry. I'll take up no more of your time. You may resume your duties."

She curtsied, feeling sick to her stomach. She had begun to take leave of him when he called out to her. "Annie?"

She turned. "Yes?"

He was quiet for a moment, only stared at her. Once again, she felt as though he were seeing her for the first time, studying her features so intimately but without recognition. Whatever he'd hoped to see wasn't there. "Never mind," he finally said.

As she watched him return to the lounge, the joy went out of her, like a soul departing the body. She wanted to sit for a moment, sink onto one of the chairs set out for passengers, and have a good cry. She felt confused and overwhelmed: far too guilty now to approach the wife, though she still had Caroline's brooch and it suddenly felt wrong, almost dirty, that she'd kept it so close. It was a wonder she herself didn't reek of death from it. It had come straight off the boy's corpse, after all. And again, desire to see Ondine tugged at her sleeve.

"Miss Hebbley! There you are," a voice called out from the across the deck. It was John Starr March, the postal clerk. He jogged toward her, an envelope in his hand. A flush of guilt poured over her, but surely he couldn't tell in the darkness.

"I've been looking for you, Miss Hebbley. I have something for you." He thrust the envelope at her. For a moment, they both stared at it. Crumpled and twisted, as though it had been wet once but had dried. He smiled sheepishly. "You know we're not supposed to deliver mail while we're at sea. I hand 'em over to the U.S. authorities when we dock, but this one bag got wet and I was drying them, to minimize the damage, when I saw one had your name on it! Addressed to the ship. I didn't think there would be any harm in giving it to you now. . . ."

More likely, he'd been bored, trapped down there in the mail room, had looked for any reason to snoop on people's mail and then to skirt about on the upper decks to deliver it.

She turned the envelope over. The flap was unsealed. Clearly, it had been opened. She looked at March, too anxious to be angry at him for invading her privacy.

"You should read it, Annie. That's why I brought it to you."

She pulled out the letter. She recognized the handwriting, though the lines were bloated by water and nearly unreadable. It was from Father Desmond Flannery. He had been on her mind because of Mark but now, seeing his name written out like this sent a dark current of memory through her. Dark blue eyes the color of an angry ocean. A lean but strong frame. Delicate, long hands, like those of a musician.

Annie—Can it really be you? Safe and alive, on a ship to America? You must know, I have searched for you since the day you disappeared . . .

Annie lowered the letter, feeling March's eyes on her. "You must swear to me that you'll tell no one about this letter—no one."

"But this man is worried sick about you. I don't know what happened at home to make you end up here—"

Annie drew back from him. "I don't want to talk about it. I've put it all behind me. I don't want to reopen old wounds. Can you understand that?"

"Aye, I understand only too well. But did you ever stop to wonder that maybe life doesn't want you to move on, and that's why this fellow found out about you? You know, after my wife died last year, my daughters pleaded with me to give up the sea. 'You've had enough close calls,' they said." John Starr March's near misses were legendary among the crew. The man had endured an accident on each of the ships he'd served. "But I returned because this is my destiny. I wanted to make them happy, but I knew in my heart that if I left the sea, I'd never be able to make peace with it. So here I am, where I belong. You might ask yourself whether the same is true for you, girl."

March's words crashed down on her like a great wave, dragging her under and holding her down. He was wrong, she knew: the past would drown her if she stopped running. It was all well and good for him to make peace with his past. He hadn't done anything nearly as bad—as damning—as she.

When she thought of Desmond Flannery—*Father* Flannery—she panicked. She couldn't say why exactly. There was something standing in the way of her memory, like a curtain, hiding whatever stood on the other side. She could remember the sound of his voice, though, gentle—and persuasive. His boyish smile, the curve of his lips. She knew the feel of those lips, the feel of his hands. His name, whispered on her tongue, *Des.*

"What you saw in this letter is not my destiny," she said as she returned the letter to its envelope and stuffed it in her apron pocket. Strands of unruly strawberry hair had fallen out from her cap and she brushed them impatiently off her face. "As you said, it's not your business and I'll thank you to keep it to yourself. Now, excuse me. I'm late seeing to my rooms."

She rushed away without waiting for another word from him, down the passageway of first-class cabins. But as soon as March disappeared, she walked on, not paying attention to where she was going, and it wasn't until her feet stumbled over a threshold that she realized she was in the first-class smoking room. She had no business here, could not say why she'd come. The few passengers puffed on their cigars and eyed the lone stewardess with detached curiosity. She scanned the smoky room, not sure whom she was looking for—until she realized she was hoping to find Mark again. She wanted to see his face light up, the way it had for the woman he'd mentioned, surely a former lover. Mark would comfort her, take care of her.

She wanted Mark and it had nothing to do with Desmond Flannery.

There was no denying it.

Mr. March was wrong: she had been drawn to the *Titanic* because it *was* her fate. She was fated to meet Mark. He was her destiny. She felt the truth of it in her blood.

As for her past—she'd made up her mind, hadn't she, by traveling to Southampton and talking her way aboard this ship?

She reached for one of the cigar lighters—a heavy brass affair designed especially for the fancy smoking room—and set a corner of the envelope on fire, then dropped it on top of the logs that had been carefully arranged in the fireplace for the evening crowd. She watched the orange flames stretch heavenward and said a little prayer. Fire would cleanse her past, taking Des—his words, his promises, even his faith—away on a furl of smoke.

Chapter Seventeen

Mark needed a smoke.

Where had Caroline gone? He couldn't remember if she had promised to meet him in the lounge or the reception room. The nanny was there to watch Ondine during dinner and had long since put her to bed. Mark himself should go to sleep, too. But something irked him.

First, the conversation with the stewardess, Miss Hebbley, and the odd thing she'd said to him. *One is always trapped within oneself.* He couldn't count the number of times Lillian had said something similar to him. She considered the soul to be one's true self; but unlike many people, she sometimes longed for her soul to be freed from its mortal shell. "Wouldn't it be wonderful to be free of one's own self?" she had asked on a number of occasions, a desire that he frankly didn't understand. She had moments of disliking herself, voicing the strange craving to be rid of her fine body and beautiful face. It was absurd, especially when many women would give their eyeteeth to be her—raven haired and sparkling eyed. Lillian was, sometimes, a paradox. Her mind was so strange and dark that way. He knew he shouldn't be drawn even to her melancholy, to her moods, but he was. He loved her moods. He loved the stir he felt in her, even from across a room.

The swirling rise of tension, when he knew without even knowing how he knew—simply by the angle of one of her eyebrows or the tapping of her foot—that a fight was about to brew.

Lillian loved to fight. And she fought ruthlessly, too. With verbal claws. She'd told him once that that wasn't true—it wasn't that she was vicious, only that he chose to believe every cruel thing she ever said to him in the heat of the moment.

But of course he had believed. Her word had been God to him, and he didn't even believe in God. He believed in Lillian. Cruel, dark, strange, wonderful Lillian. He knew that he had loved her too much—in the same way he loved gambling. He loved too deeply, and one day it would drag him under.

He had to stop thinking of her. What was it about being at sea that made him feel so *close* to her all over again, like she was *here*, hovering nearby?

He shook his head—felt drunk even though he'd had only a single brandy after dinner. He'd been good tonight. Had avoided the itch to play, though it had called to him like a high whine of a dog in the distance, persistent. He'd brought a book and kept his nose in it until Miss Hebbley pulled him out.

No matter.

What he wanted—what he *needed*—was his damn wife.

But since they had set foot on this ship, Caroline had been disappearing a lot. When she finally did turn up, there would be a sly little smile on her lips, but she refused to talk about it, insisting he was imagining these absences.

He knew now what else had distracted Caroline the night of the séance: Guggenheim. She'd let slip that they'd spoken that night and since then, the millionaire seemed to turn up in random spots throughout the day with annoying regularity. He'd taken the table next to them at breakfast, slipped into a bridge game that afternoon, his gaze always returning to, and lingering on, Caroline.

If he were honest with himself, Mark could see why Caroline

would respond to the attentions of a man as famous and rich as Benjamin Guggenheim. Guggenheim was more like Henry, Caroline's late husband: older, with a wise paternal air that Mark—being close to Caroline's own age—would never attempt with her. And confident: Guggenheim exuded the self-assurance that came with vast amounts of wealth.

He pushed his way into the smoking room. It was only when he saw the room was deserted—everyone off to bed by now, certainly—that he realized his heart was pounding. Shame poured over him like a sheen of sweat. He'd come in the irrational hope of catching the two of them. He wanted to have it out with the millionaire, to make him stay away from his wife. Which was absurd, he knew. Nothing had happened. Why was he acting like this—like a possessive maniac?

He never used to be like this: jealous, petty. Not with Lillian. With her, their passion had been mutual and matched. It had never occurred to him to think otherwise. Lillian had been the jealous, volatile one. And now . . . it was like the memory of her was at his shoulder, whispering envious thoughts into Mark's head.

He should go back to his room. Caroline was probably there already, humming lullabies to Ondine. It wasn't Caroline who was even missing, was it? It was him. He was the one lost, roaming, adrift.

He moved to the door, but the acrid scent of smoke stopped him.

He turned, wary.

A spark from behind one of the heavy, polished oak tables.

A snap.

Behind the table, the hearth glowed hot.

The flicker of shadows on the wall, orange light dancing behind a cluster of club chairs.

Oh my lord.

Fire.

Crackling and hot and . . . out of control.

Mark acted without thinking, darting across the room straight toward the hearth, nearly tumbling over the table that stood in his way.

There was no one else around. No crew, no stewards. He had to do something.

Buckets of sand hung on the wall beside the servants' entrance. Mark hoisted two from their hooks and ran back to the conflagration, which had already spread now, beyond the lip of the hearth, eating away at one part of the soft rug. He threw the contents onto the fire. That helped dampen the flames.

He ran back twice more before the fire was out.

Sweat streaked down his face. The carpet was gritty with sand. Soot streaked up the wall. Seemed awfully strange for a fire to blaze out of control inside a fireplace—though there had been a string of odd occurrences on the ship. Out of instinct, Mark reached up to check the flue. His hand sizzled at the touch, and he had to pull back quickly, but he'd been able to tell it hadn't been opened. That was damned careless of the staff.

Fire had almost ruined his life once. Only by the grace of God had Lillian avoided what could've been a terrible tragedy. The factory where Lillian spent all her daylight hours burned to the ground, killing nearly every one of the women she worked with.

But Lillian had been spared, called away unexpectedly by the owner to run an errand. At the time, Mark had seen it as confirmation from the Fates that this woman, this perfect creation, was not meant to die.

This miracle was somewhat ironic, because she was gone less than nine months later.

Mark reached into his pocket for a handkerchief to wipe his face and spied, from the corner of his eye, a piece of paper jammed into the half-devoured stack of firewood. Most of the paper had been consumed by the flames. A singed, tattered remnant remained.

He pulled it out. The first thing he saw was Annie Hebbley's name.

He couldn't make out much else, only a string of desperate words in a man's handwriting.

Mark staggered to one of the club chairs, the paper already forgotten. This night was too much—the fire brought it all back, his past life, the life he had expected to have with Lillian.

He knew he shouldn't, but he did anyway. He reached into his coat and drew out a slim, worn journal. Lillian's. Her essence poured into its pages.

It was the last bit of her to survive, and he couldn't bear to let it go.

1916

Chapter Eighteen

17 November 1916

Naples, Italy

HMHS *Britannic*

He is hers and yet not.

He has not awoken. She doesn't know if he ever will.

Annie sits on a campstool next to Mark's bed. She can still barely believe Mark is beside her, close enough to touch. Alive, after believing for years that he was gone. He lies in bed, his head heavily bandaged. He has changed, though not so much that she couldn't recognize him. Annie studies him. He's aged far more than the four years that have passed. He looks like the Mark he was to become in middle age. His hair is military short, what's exposed beyond the bandages, very smart and crisp, but she misses the way he wore it before. Slightly longer, it gave him a bohemian appearance, like one of those British expatriate artists living in Paris whom you hear about, ruined by absinthe and syphilis.

Still, the age—the pain and suffering—etched onto his face only make him more handsome, more a man than he was before. He can only be in his early thirties, yet he has seen unthinkable things now. Has been on the front lines. Has risked his life.

Has survived.

The last time she saw him, she realizes, was *before*. Before any of the terrible things that followed.

The memory of that night on the *Titanic* comes back to her too readily: screaming and panic, crewmen grabbing at her as she ran by, exhorting her to get in one of the lifeboats. The black water rushing up the slanted promenade, clawing at her . . .

She shudders. Mark's hands are folded on top of the blanket. They are scarred and white—and ring-free. He wore a wedding ring on the *Titanic*, but there's no ring now.

Wake up, wake up, she wants to say. She wants to shake him by the shoulders, see those blue eyes pop open. She has news to tell him, news that will make him happy. And he will be so grateful: he will scoop her up in his arms and press her to his chest and maybe . . .

A flash of fantasy—another vision or memory or something else—flutters at the back of her mind. His lips against hers. His hands in her hair—her hair much longer than it is now. She can feel his hair twined in her fingers, too, his hair, his face, his body familiar to her in ways that . . . cannot be. An old hunger in her, but as sharp and precise as the edge of a knife.

She shakes her head, dispelling the image, the desire. Wishes she still had her crucifix to ground her. To anchor her.

But the brooch—it's still on her lapel, and she strokes it now, to calm herself, tracing the heart and the arrow. To remind herself.

She has a *gift* for Mark. He *must* wake up, if only so she can tell him:

His daughter, Ondine, did not die that night.

She is still alive.

Violet had said this in her letter, assuring Annie that her plunge into the ocean that night had not been for naught. Violet had held Ondine all through the night, right up until the lifeboat drew up alongside the *Carpathia*. In the chaos of disembarking, however, someone had plucked the baby out of Violet's arms. She'd assumed it was one of the *Carpathia*'s crew acting in an official capacity. Once they arrived in New York City, it was chaos: the press descended on the survivors and, in the swirl of fetes and speeches, Violet lost track of Ondine. The White Star Line front office assured her that all the children orphaned by the sinking had been reunited with family or placed under the care of the proper administrative offices. There was nothing more she could do.

Annie looks at Mark's still face, flat and blank. Ghostlike. She will be the one to bring joy back into his painful, joyless life.

She reaches forward and takes his hands. "Mark, I've got something very important to tell you," she says to him as though he can hear her.

Hours pass this way. They blur together as the *Britannic* sails from the port in Naples, and still, Annie remains by his side.

It is not until sometime very late in the night that she senses a stirring in him.

She leans closer to him.

"Mark?" she whispers so softly, so carefully.

His eyes open.

She's so startled that she almost yelps.

"Lord in Heaven . . ." she whispers, as he blinks at her.

He stares at her. His eyes move over her like he's seeing a ghost. He takes in her smile, her hands, even the shiny gold brooch on her lapel.

And then . . . a spasm of some kind.

He's ill. Unwell. Something's wrong. What's happening? She wants to call for one of the doctors, but it's so late; she was told not to bother them but for emergencies . . . but surely they would want to be alerted when a comatose patience awakens?

Mark is frantic, practically crawling backward, recoiling at the sight of her. His eyes roll like a spooked horse's. For a moment, her chest feels crushed by a great weight—Why isn't he as happy to see her as she is to see him? This reaction is normal. Is it because he's woken up in a strange place; one minute, he's in an army hospital in Naples and the next minute he's listing and rolling on a ship at sea? Yes, that's it. He's disoriented. He doesn't know what's happening to him.

"It's me, Mark. It's Annie, Miss Hebbley from the *Titanic*. You remember me, don't you?" she says, trying to reassure him, rubbing his hands, patting his cheek. That only seems to make it worse. He pulls his hands away. He is trembling. Poor man.

Why hasn't he said something? He can't seem to speak, even around the bandages. He's had a head injury, so that could be bad news. It could be brain damage, a stroke. She's seen catatonic soldiers, immobile in their wheelchairs even though they've got perfectly good legs, staring emptily into space. Very bad news, indeed. *No, please God. You've just reunited us. Don't take him away from me now. I've been a good girl. It's time for my reward.*

"Wait here, Mark," she says, turning to leave. "I'll fetch a doctor." Dawn is breaking by now anyway, and night shifts will be turning over soon. "I'll be right back. It will be okay. You're going to be fine. I promise. We're together now. That's all that matters."

Chapter Nineteen

19 November 1916
HMHS *Britannic*

The radio room is kept deliberately dim at night. Only one light burns, low. Charlie Epping likes it that way.

This hour—just before dawn—is his favorite time. Nothing stirs. All is quiet but for the soft tapping of the occasional wire dispatch, rhythmic, soothing. The sea is like a vast silver field laid out before him.

He works alone. Toby Sullivan, the second radio man, was supposed to pull shift with him, but Epping told him to take the night off. There's not much that needs doing and Charlie prefers to keep busy. Besides, he would rather have silence than listen to Toby's bored, nervous chatter.

Epping sorts through yesterday's pouch of dispatches from command headquarters, getting them ready for Assistant Commander Dyke in the morning. There are the mundane, such as changing hours for the mess hall and new rules about using the recreational facilities, and the important. He reads through each report and puts them in a rough priority order, according to his own taste, but Dyke will decide which pieces are important enough for the commander's attention. Everyone knows that Captain Bartlett lets Dyke handle the day-to-day things. Bartlett fancies himself a big-picture kind of man, doesn't like to be distracted.

Behind Epping, the stylus starts to tap. Strange: they don't get many telegraphs at this hour. He starts to take down the message. A few message groups into the transmission, he realizes that it's in code. It's an intelligence report. That means it's not so simple. He will need to decode it and then type the whole thing up for Dyke to read when he gets up. Command would've sent the report in this morning's pouch, but the *Britannic* has already put out to sea, a bit later than scheduled, the storm having passed enough to make it possible.

Before Epping sits down to start decoding, he lowers the blinds. That way no passerby will be able to look into the radio room while he writes out the secret words in plaintext—not that anyone's awake, save for the some of the night staff. Still, it's protocol. It's his job to protect classified information, and he takes it very seriously. After lowering the blinds, he unlocks a drawer, pulls out the codebook, and looks up the key for that day. The key sets up the transposition of letters that creates the code. It changes every day and if you don't use the proper key, you'll end up with gobbledygook. Then he gets a sheet of grid paper and a sharpened pencil and starts entering the encoded letters.

It takes the better part of an hour, but Epping decodes the entire transmission. While he's decoding, he doesn't pay attention to the words that are being formed. It's all about chasing the letters. Now that he's finished, he sits back and reads the report through, wanting to make sure that he did everything correctly and that it makes sense. But he's also curious as to what it's about.

A German informant has told the British that Kea Channel has been mined. Epping consults the navigation map pinned to the wall, though he doesn't really need to. They've made five trips to pick up the wounded at Mudros and each time, they've gone through the Kea Channel. There have been rumors of mining in the channel before and the captain decided to take his chances. It could be that the

Germans were spreading disinformation in the hope of tricking England into diverting some of the minesweepers that were keeping the English Channel open.

He runs his finger over the worn paper map, tracing the lines of longitude and latitude in the intelligence report to the island-studded passage that is the Kea Channel. The supposed mines lie right in the path *Britannic* is to take. Staring at the spot on the map, Epping—who is not prone to nerves—feels a tremor through him. Like someone walking over his grave, his ma would say.

He sits down at the typewriter, threads in a fresh piece of paper, and starts typing. Dyke will want to see this first thing in the morning.

1912

WESTERN UNION, April 12, 1912

To: MR. AND MRS. ARTHUR RYERSON,
first-class passengers

Please be assured that arrangements have been made to your specifications for the funeral of your son Arthur, Jr. The funeral is scheduled to take place on April 19 at 3 p.m., at St. Mark's Episcopal Church on Locust Street. How regrettable that you have had to cut short your travel to attend to this heartbreaking tragedy. The town has been rocked and saddened by this tragic accident. You have our deepest condolences.—White Funeral Parlor, Cooperstown, New York

To: CHRISTOPHER MITCHELL,
Seventh Avenue South, New York City

I wish to secure your services for a confidential consultation. I have been assured by mutual acquaintances of your discretion. I am currently en route to NYC, scheduled to dock on April 18, and will be in touch shortly thereafter. This is in regard to a matter most pressing on my mind. Again, I am relying on your absolute discretion.—Mrs. Madeleine Talmage Force Astor

To: BENJAMIN GUGGENHEIM,
first-class passenger

Advising discretion when disembarking in New York. Your wife's lawyer has conveyed that she will initiate divorce proceedings if Miss Aubart's name appears in the papers. It might be a good time to send Miss Aubart on a vacation in the country. Perhaps two weeks at a resort in Pennsylvania? With a private car picking her up at the dock? If you concur, we will make the arrangements immediately.—Joseph Sebring, Law Offices of Manchester and Coates

~ellee~

Chapter Twenty

12 April 1912
Titanic

Rise and fall.

The ground swells beneath her, rising, rising until there is a moment of suspension . . .

A gentle tip . . .

And descent, floating down, down, down.

It is rhythmic, like the motion of the ship.

Like riding on horseback. Rising a great swell of muscle and power.

There is a body close to Annie. Warm, firm, strong. They are rising and falling together, they bump, bump again, and then are locked together, their bodies entwined. Hands, arms, legs. Their skin is clammy with sweat. Heat streaks through her like fire in a furnace.

But there is something else in her, a yearning so deep that she feels hollow inside. The Lord loves good girls, Annie.

Annie blinked her eyes, her vision swimming and cloudy, before finally clarifying.

She was in the alleyway outside the first-class cabins. Tiny electric lights glowed in the darkness like fireflies. Annie was wearing only her thin cotton nightgown, no robe or slippers. Her pale hair was down around her shoulders. Her skin was gooseflesh and her teeth chattered against the cold. It might've been the chattering that woke her up.

She rubbed her eyes. She must've been sleepwalking. She'd never done this before.

She wrapped her arms over her chest to hide her breasts. Where was she? She tried to read the cabin numbers in the miserly light, but she was pretty sure she knew where she was: outside the door to the Fletchers' cabin.

Noises seeped under the door. She recognized these sounds: they were the sounds of a couple making love. She even knew their voices though not one word was said, recognized the timbre and pitch as they growled and giggled, sighed and moaned. Mark was pleasuring his wife in the ways he'd pleasured Annie in her dreams.

The cold disappeared, replaced by an embarrassment that set her aflame. She couldn't deny her desire for Mark, so deep that it took control of her in her sleep and led her, step by step, to his door. And the worst part was this feeling she couldn't shake, after hearing the two of them in their room. That she had caught Mark cheating on *her*.

Annie hurried away, hands tucked in the warmth of her armpits, cold tear tracks on her cheeks. She prayed that no one would see her wandering the halls like the ghost of an insane wife. No one may have seen her, but Annie caught herself thinking that the ship knew. *The ship knows and will be disappointed in me now. It'll know I'm not as good as it thought I was.*

As she made her way to the crew's quarters, she muttered promises to herself. She would think no more about Mark. She was done with him. And Caroline, too. The only Fletcher who needed her help— the only Fletcher she would let herself care for—was Ondine. Poor helpless Ondine. Annie knew—she *felt*—that the baby needed her from the moment she'd seen her. Those innocent eyes searching her face, as though she were trying to tell Annie something. A message in those eyes. *Protect me. Save me. I need you.* And hadn't the baby been looking worse lately, paler, seeming to waste away before their eyes? No, Annie would never be able to deny Ondine.

~elle~

Sometime later, white light clawed at the edges of Annie's eyelids, trying to pry them open.

It was the cold white light of early morning, she knew as a servant who had to rise early every day.

Who had to rise *before dawn*.

She had overslept.

Annie sat up abruptly. Instinctively, she looked at Violet's narrow little bunk on the other side of the room. It was empty. Violet had risen and not bothered to wake her.

She threw back the covers and ran to the ewer. The water was ice-cold, but for once she was grateful: the bracing cold woke her up. Eyes squeezed shut, she groped for a towel and scrubbed warmth back into her face.

When she opened her eyes, a small rectangle of white on the floor drew her attention. It was a folded piece of *Titanic* stationery, by the looks of it, slid under the door. She snatched it up. She didn't recognize the handwriting. Shaky and light, it looked like a very sick person had written it. And it made no sense; all it said was:

You know who I am.

You know what I want.

For a moment, all she could picture was the face of the woman she'd seen once on the beach as a child. Naked, beautiful, basking against a rock, seaweed strewn on her body and through her hair. How she'd stared at Annie with dark, endless eyes. How Annie had known in that moment who and what the woman was—dubheasa. The lady from her grandmother's tales. The dark spirit of the sea, who collected innocent girls, kept them safe far beneath the waves, her immortal children.

Annie shuddered.

She flipped the note back and forth, looking for something more, but there was nothing, not so much as a drop of ink. Her mind struggled to make sense of it. Could it have been meant for someone else and slipped under her door as a mistake? No, it was a sick joke—it had to be. One of the crew teasing her for her shyness. Some of the boys working the boilers were as immature as schoolchildren. Once dressed, Annie stuffed the paper in the pocket of her apron. She would get to the bottom of this.

She saw Violet later that morning as they worked on their assigned rooms. "This," she hissed at Violet, shaking the note at her. "What do you mean by this?"

"I don't know what you're talking about," Violet said after giving it a cursory look.

"You didn't write it?" Annie looked at the spidery writing and felt her stomach skittle like water on a hot griddle.

"I've never seen it before."

Cleaning up in Stead's stateroom, Annie was staring at the note when William Stead walked in. He nodded at the paper in her hands. "What's that, my dear? Did you find it in here?"

He had spoken kindly enough, but it was clear he thought she had been going through his things. The thought of being taken for a thief made her stomach even worse. "No, sir. It was on the floor of my cabin."

He gave her a grandfatherly smile. "A love note, is it? One of the crew taken a fancy to you?"

"No, sir. It's not like that at all . . . but, honestly, I don't know what to make of it." She handed it to him in a moment of confusion, pure reflex.

As he read it, his smile dissolved into a frown. He thrust it at her. "It makes no sense. A hoax, surely."

"Who would do such a thing?"

"It's the ship's stationery, so it could've come from anyone." He watched as she pocketed the paper. "An enemy among the staff?"

She shook her head. She felt guilty; she didn't think Mr. Latimer would approve of her discussing such things with the passengers, but it seemed natural to confide in Stead. "I was wondering, sir—you know so much about these things—if you think it might be a spirit trying to reach me?"

"A spirit?"

She took a step back, wringing her hands. "They said the dead boy heard a woman calling to him from the water and it reminded me of a story my grandmother Aisling told me when I was a child. Of a spirit of the sea—"

"My dear," he said in a kind voice, "as a resident expert on spirits, I can tell you that they are incorporeal beings—"

"Incorporeal?"

"They have no flesh, no mass. They are specters. They cannot hold a pen or push a note under a door. Hence, no spirit could've written this note to you, Miss Hebbley. Unless of course they found someone to *inhabit*."

She felt hot again, this time so hot she thought she might have a fever. "Like I said, my grandmother told me a story—and, and I know that spirits exist out on the ocean because I met one once. A tremendous great one, the witch queen of the sea she was—"

Stead shook his head. "A queen of the sea, is it?"

"It happened when I nearly drowned one day, at the shore outside my grandmother's cottage—"

"Drowned? Well, that's it, you see: a hallucination brought on by trauma." Stead's tone was kind but distant—that of a practiced journalist. "But didn't you tell me you were an expert swimmer? That you swam every day for miles when you were a child? Which is it, Miss Hebbley? It can't have been both."

She drew back. She felt faint with fever. The room spun around her. She was sounding crazy, wasn't she? Even to a known occultist, her fears were unfounded, silly. She wanted to argue with him: she knew what she knew, but the Englishman was twisting it all around, making her doubt herself, even as he spoke kindly and softly, like she was some spooked animal. . . .

She touched her forehead; it was clammy with sweat. The witch queen of the sea—Where did that come from? Had someone said it to her or had she read it in a story? A ghostly figure danced in her memory, faceless and indistinct, but how could she be sure it was real and not a hallucination? The more she thought about it, the more it seemed like a dream.

Nothing made sense. Perhaps she *was* sick. The story had come from someplace inside her, a mischievous little story bubbling out of her like air bubbling to the surface from an underground lagoon. Her hand found the crumpled piece of stationery in her pocket. *You know who I am.*

She wiped her sweaty forehead with the back of her hand and curtsied unsteadily. "Forgive me, Mr. Stead, I don't know what I'm saying. I don't know what's come over me. I must be ill. . . ."

He took her elbow and tried to usher her to a chair. "You *look* unwell, dear. I didn't want to say anything but . . . perhaps you should see the ship's surgeon. . . ."

"No, I—" She pulled away from him. "I just need air."

She rushed into the passageway, leaning against the wall to keep from falling to her knees. She couldn't afford to see the ship's surgeon just yet: the watch pinned to her apron said it was time to bring warm milk to the Fletchers.

She stumbled down the stairs to the kitchen, ducking about to avoid the busy head cook while she fetched and warmed the milk in a small pan, careful to make sure the milk didn't become too hot and curdle, testing it with her pinkie finger before taking the pan off the heat. For a moment, she hovered there, waiting for the milk to cool a tiny bit. She pulled Caroline's brooch from its now permanent spot in her pocket. Ran her fingers along its smooth shape. Then she put it away, before the milk would have time to get too cold.

Annie rushed to the Fletchers' cabin, barely able to keep from dropping the tray. She knocked on the door harder than she meant and stood, nervously waiting to be let in. Listening to the noises on the other side of the door, murmuring and hushed tread on carpet. No longer the sound of moaning and sighing, though the memory of that still tugged at her chest, made her feel hot and dizzy again.

She rushed in as soon as the door swung open, not waiting to be invited. She knew what to do and set the tray down in the same place as before, pulled the cozy off the pot, turned to fetch the glass bottle.

Caroline had set the baby on the bed, lying in the center of a white blanket. There was something different about Ondine. Annie could tell right away. The baby was abnormally quiet. Listless. And there were ghastly-looking half-moons under the child's eyes. The baby was sick. Obviously, something was wrong. Mark had been right, last night, to be worried.

Annie studied Caroline reclining on the bed with her daughter. She wasn't sure that was the way a mother should look at her newborn, at something so defenseless. There was something calculating about that look. Studious. It made Annie frightened, yet again, for Ondine.

"Did you hear me, Annie? Miss Hebbley?" Caroline was speaking to her. "You can go. I'll take it from here." There was a coldness in Caroline's voice. She had become a different person—not the vivacious, chatty one who'd boarded the ship two days ago.

"Yes, ma'am, of course." Annie walked slowly down the alleyway, clutching the metal tray to her chest. Caroline's sudden change chilled her, while Stead's words still rung in her head. Spirits were incorporeal.

Unless they were not.

Changeling. Every mother in Ireland knew about changelings. How fairies sneaked into nurseries at night and plucked babies out of their cribs, would take your innocent child and replace it with a fairy baby. Sick babies were thought to be changelings. The deformed, babies that were inhuman in a way. Her father called it ignorance, to say such things. It was nothing more than an excuse to deny responsibility for bringing the poor wee one into the world.

The ship lurched underfoot, bucking like a wild horse and throwing Annie against the wall. She clutched the railing to stay upright, the world spinning around her.

Nothing made sense to her anymore.

What if it wasn't the baby who was a changeling, but the mother? Could the fairies—or an unkind spirit—have whisked Caroline away and left one of their own in her place? Because Caroline was acting differently; in the short time Annie had known her, she'd gone from smart and warm and caring to cold and evasive. She looked different: paler, warier, her hands trembling when she thought no one was watching. Her own husband had said as much to Annie, or implied it anyway.

The spirit had been trying to find a way into the corporeal world. . . . First, the dead boy. Now Caroline.

Annie shook her head, as though she could shake off the poisonous thought of it. That was too wild. Fantastical. She knew what her father would say of such thoughts. He would say she was crazy, as crazy as his mother-in-law with her belief in magical powers.

Maybe she *was* crazy.

Annie smeared a hand over her sweaty face. No, not crazy—ill. She had been on her way to the ship's surgeon, hadn't she?

But it seemed to her that there were only two possibilities: either Caroline was possessed by an evil spirit, a wicked thing from the fairy world, or she, Annie, was losing her mind. And she did not believe she was losing her mind. She had an important job. Dozens of passengers depended on her and she remembered everything with perfect clarity. She cleaned her rooms, served her passengers, remembered who wanted a pot of tea delivered to their room at night, who preferred candles to electric light. There had been no complaints, no mishaps.

She was fine. Perfectly fine.

That left only one alternative.

Chapter Twenty-One

Maddie Astor no longer knew herself.

In a matter of months, she'd become someone the former school-girl wouldn't recognize. Not just in status but in shape. Her body was no longer her own.

She groaned and rolled over in bed. She couldn't take another morning of lying in, especially not with the way Jack's hands had roamed all night, even in his sleep, wanting her—no matter that her girlish form had stretched and gone taut and round at the middle, that her feet were swelling enough that her favorite shoes had begun to pinch.

Last night's piano concert played an insistent march through her brain and she found she had hardly slept at all, visions of Stead's spirits rustling through her thoughts, unsettling.

She kept thinking of Caroline's frightening story of the possessed man. Kept replaying the séance they'd had, two nights ago now, racking her mind for clues. The spirit had been about to manifest itself, but the séance had been cut short—by that stewardess Miss Hebbley asking for the doctor. For Teddy. That implied that the evil spirit Ava Willing Astor had sent after her wasn't in Stead's room but with Teddy. She wished she knew how these things worked. Could a spirit be in two places at once?

She recalled what Stead had said, that a spirit might possess a body. Could Teddy have been possessed by the spirit?

She replayed it all again: the chanted questions, the candles. And then, the sweep of air as Miss Hebbley had burst in on them, causing enough of a breeze to snuff out all the candles at once.

She sat up—carefully, so as not to stir Jack.

Had Miss Hebbley's entrance caused the candles to blow out? She remembered the sudden eerie dampening of flame, as though all had been snuffed out simultaneously by the same unseen hand. She pictured Annie Hebbley's pale face in the darkness—like a ghost.

Could *Miss Hebbley* be the possessed one?

The idea seemed outlandish, of course.

But there was no disputing there was something odd about the stewardess. She had a strange effect whenever she came into a room. No one stayed long in her company. Just the thought of her needy, searching gaze gave Maddie a chill.

She thought again of Caroline's words. Surely Maddie was not alone in suspecting that something terrible was afoot here. She wasn't wrong to believe in the prophecy. She was not hysterical, as Dr. Leader would call it. This was real.

Wasn't it?

She got out of bed. She needed to be among *people*.

She couldn't stand being pregnant, she mused as she dressed herself, in such a hurry that she didn't bother to call her maid for help. She hated the idea that the child would have to somehow wrestle its way out of her at the end. Like a demon being exorcised from its victim's body—Wasn't that human birth?

She snatched a black shawl from the pile in her trunk—she was in mourning, after all. Not just for Teddy but for her former self, the one who'd played and studied and socialized and *flirted*. The girl who'd been alive with possibility, all of it *ahead* of her. Strange—terrible—how you could turn a corner from young and vibrant and on the brink of everything, to being tired all the time, stretched tight like a balloon filled to bursting.

She made her way to the bedroom door, just as her husband was rolling over with a yawn, beginning to stretch. "Don't wait for me to head up to luncheon," she said over her shoulder. "I'm going to find the girls and take a turn on the decks. The walking is good for my poor swollen ankles—Dr. Prendergast told me so."

In the lounge on the A deck, she found the Fortune sisters—Alice, Ethel, and Mabel—heads bowed together over some piece of gossip, no doubt. The Fortunes were in their early to mid-twenties, far closer in age to Maddie than some of the other women in their set. In fact, she sort of enjoyed playing the worldly-wise married lady around Ethel, who was engaged to be wed when they returned to Winnipeg. They had all sorts of questions about what they termed the Bedroom Arts.

It was certainly an effective distraction from the prophecy.

"Oh, Maddie, do join us." The sisters were flattered by her attention, she knew. Mabel patted the chair next to her while Alice poured tea.

She lowered herself into the chair, grateful for the thick seat cushion. "What are you up to?"

Ethel leaned in. "We're going to see if we can't find Mr. William Sloper— You've met Mr. Sloper, haven't you? He's developed quite a crush on Alice."

Alice lowered her lashes and blushed, as was required of a properly bred young lady, but Maddie could tell she was as proud as a lioness making her first kill.

"We met in Paris," Alice said softly. "Just two Americans making the grand tour."

"He rescheduled his passage on an earlier ship so they could be together a little longer," Mabel said. "Isn't that romantic?"

"Is he handsome?" Maddie asked. Might as well get to the heart of the matter. This was the face you would be looking at across the breakfast table for the next twenty or thirty years.

"Very," Ethel said. Alice lowered her lashes again and blushed twice as hard.

"Then by all means, let's find him. I'd like to take a look at him myself." The thought of a handsome man made Maddie's pulse quicken. It wasn't that Jack was ugly but—God help her—he just wasn't her type. He wasn't very distinguished looking. He had a youthful, almost *silly-looking* face, in her opinion. She deserved at least to look at handsome young men whenever she could. It was her secret pleasure.

They were in luck: they didn't even need to make a complete lap of the boat deck afterward to find Mr. Sloper. He was in the gymnasium with a crowd of other first-class passengers watching the boxers spar again. Oh, the boxers—people couldn't get enough of them, it seemed. To the men, they were nothing more than a prize racehorse or a fast car: an object to be admired. They watched for form and athletic prowess. The women on the other hand . . .

Maddie knew why there were as many women here as men. How often did you get to see a man in such good physical condition stripped down to their drawers? They were wearing special boxing outfits, scanty linen drawers and a shirt without sleeves or collar to keep them cool. Women rarely saw this much of a man's body—artists didn't paint them as often as they did half-dressed women—and now that she had the opportunity, Maddie couldn't stop looking.

Perhaps she was not pregnant with a girl after all, she thought, but a boy. The rush of desire she sometimes felt these past few months was positively *masculine*.

Both men were definitely good-looking. The blond was more to Maddie's taste. The other—while somewhat baby faced—was too big and hulking. Easy to imagine being crushed underneath all that muscle. The blond was smaller and slender. He looked like he'd be a good dancer. He was more sophisticated looking; with the right clothes, he could be positively debonair. There was cunning to his face, too.

If she went up to talk to him, she was sure he'd snap to attention because of who she was. Mrs. John Jacob Astor. It would be amusing to have this handsome specimen of a man on her arm for the rest of the voyage, fetching drinks and plumping pillows and rubbing her feet—*he'd* rub her feet, if she asked. But it would likely be far too maddening, this handsome bloke fawning on her out of show and not *true* interest.

Out of the corner of her eye, Maddie saw the stewardess Annie Hebbley. The sudden appearance when she'd been thinking of her only an hour earlier sent a chill through Maddie's veins. The fantasy of showboating around with the blond boxer evaporated into thin air: Maddie's attention was riveted on the pale wraith in the gray uniform making her way through the crowd. That searching, empty face with hungry eyes was like something in a mausoleum frieze. No one else seemed to pay any attention to her. It was almost as though no one could see her but Maddie. Like she wasn't really there.

There was something else, too. The stewardess was passing in front of a row of windows that looked out over the promenade, and yet she cast no reflection on the glass. Maddie blinked and strained to focus as hard as she could, and yet she saw no trace of Annie Hebbley. Not a streak, not a ripple. Not a wisp of the strange Irish girl.

She went cold all over.

Chapter Twenty-Two

The truth was, Dai felt miserable.

Society women surrounded Dai and Leslie at the dinner table, in their colorful silks and satins, arms enclosed in long evening gloves. A blond on the right and a redhead on the left, and three brunettes like charms on a bracelet across the table from him. From their expressions, Dai couldn't tell what they were thinking; society men often came to the boxing halls and engaged him in chitchat, but he had little experience with their women. They may have been smiling, but their eyes were sharp, like pointed daggers searching for a chink in Leslie's facade. As though they knew he was not what he was trying so hard to appear to be.

Word had gotten out already that Leslie had telepathic abilities—he worked quickly. Dai had to imagine Violet had been essential in planting the gossip so well—and now these women flocked happily around him, clamoring for him to divine something about them. *Me, me, me*, rang the voices, high and pretty and sweet. Les wouldn't, of course; he'd only had time to slip into a few cabins and so his marks were preselected. But let them think he was only demure.

That was part of the game.

At the moment, his target was Miss Ethel Fortune, eldest daughter in a family of wealthy Canadians. Les had been able to find out all kinds of things about her from one quick trip to their suite. The family—three daughters, a son, a pair of stolid parents—had just completed a grand tour of Europe and Miss Ethel had used the trip to amass her trousseau. But he had found a few interesting things among her dresses and silk nightgowns.

"Oh, come on," Dai said, right on cue. "Leslie, they'll never believe it unless you show it off. I swear, ladies, his ability *is* uncanny, much as he may deny it."

Les gave a fake groan, but the sparkle in his eyes made Dai warm. Even when he hated a con, it still felt good in the moment, to be in it with Les. To be on the same side.

"Oh, all right, all right, I'll do one—only one!" Les turned to Ethel, holding her gaze. "I sense that there is a man waiting for you back home, Miss Fortune," he said slowly, as if the thought were gradually dawning on him. Dai swore he had the skill of an actor; where in the world had he learned to control his face like this, so serious but with a faraway, almost pained look?

Miss Ethel's younger sisters gasped, though other members of the audience exchanged skeptical glances. "Oh, that's true!" Mabel Fortune said, clapping her hands together. "She's got a fiancé waiting for her in Toronto. They're going to be wed as soon as we return."

"But this fiancé is quite a bit older than you," Les said sternly.

"Yes, he is," Ethel Fortune replied. "What of it?"

"I meant nothing by it . . . but I see many suitors surrounding you, Miss Fortune." His hands fluttered, like he was sifting through thoughts as they came to him through the air. "Many young men have tried to win your heart. Some are still trying."

Ethel's sisters giggled again while Ethel herself grew red in the face.

"There is one in particular . . . A young man who is very . . . special to you." Les closed his eyes and touched his forehead, as though he were concentrating very hard. A swami who could command spirits, make them whisper answers in his ear. "He is very fond of riding, isn't he? Quite the horseman. And I believe his initial are . . . R . . . J . . . no I'm sorry, is it R.K.? I can't quite get it. . . ."

Mabel Fortune shrieked. The high-pitched note echoed off the crystal chandelier drops, the wineglasses. Heads turned from across the dining room.

Their table exploded in chatter. Ethel Fortune retreated behind her handkerchief and refused to confirm Leslie's pronouncement, despite the pestering of their guests. But no confirmation was needed, really: Ethel Fortune's bright red cheeks were proof enough.

It had been so easy. Les had found a box from a fancy London saddlery containing a fine hand-stitched riding whip, on the handle a silver button engraved "RJK." A note slipped inside, written in Ethel's hand. The only present for the fiancé among Ethel's many artifacts was a cheap silver-plate gentleman's toiletry set. It wasn't even engraved.

Me, me, me, the other women at the table clamored, thrusting themselves toward Les, all painted lips and eyes and skin smooth and white as poured cream. After whipping them into a frenzy by his last stunt, Les held them off with a cunning smile. Les had proven his genius for deceit: three of them had stood in the Astors' stateroom, dazzled by a rich man's finery, but only Les had seen the opportunity. Dai didn't know if he should be amazed or frightened.

In the midst of this, Les slipped Dai a quick nod, his signal to scout for their next victim. The journey would end in a few days and they needed to identify their targets as quickly as possible. The daughters of well-to-do American merchants might be gullible enough to believe in Leslie's telepathic powers but had little to offer as payment beyond a piece of jewelry or a peck on the cheek (though Dai was afraid that Les would be only too willing to take those pecks). But there were a number of fairly wealthy men on board who might be bored or curious enough to fall for Les's spiel. Dai made his excuses and rose from the dining table. It was his job to eavesdrop, to make small talk with first-class passengers, and ask probing questions. The most gullible tended to like to talk about themselves; it was a fact learned in the con game.

He headed to the first-class smoking room, where most of the men retired after dinner. The room was enveloped in a bank of thick, acrid smoke. Dai didn't smoke and, like many athletes, thought it bad for his wind. Simply surveying the room was unpleasant.

There was a good number of men there, though it was nowhere as full as it would be once the second dinner seating was over. Smokers sat in companionable pairs and trios, lifting glasses of brandy and whiskey between puffs. Men played cards at tables toward the back. As he walked the fringes of the room, Dai had a brief worry that they were out of their depths here. This wasn't like running a card game on the street. He recognized few of the faces. He was pretending to be looking for someone while he eavesdropped, and avoided the waiters, sure they would ask what he was doing in first class. But no steward approached him and so he kept his head down and kept moving. Maybe the suit had worked its magic and he was blending better than he thought.

When he judged no one was looking, he picked up a half-empty whiskey glass and carried it around as if it were his own, to better melt into the background. He milled about, listening in on conversations, looking for, what? Signs of gullibility, desperation, anything that could be exploited as a weakness. A "hook," Les liked to call it—a way in. Dai thought of it more like a vulnerable spot, an Achilles' heel. Their coach, George Cundick, taught them the same: to watch not just for their opponents' strengths, their patented moves, but what those moves *hid*. The way they'd favor one angle due to a weaker back leg.

Go for the weak spot.

George had given them both their lives, their livelihoods, a way forward in a world that didn't always offer solid paths to success for boys like them. Everything George had taught him, Dai held sacred.

Go for the weak spot.

Dai concentrated extra hard to decipher the American accents, of which there were many. Americans, it seemed, would talk only of business back home—small-town interests, feedstores and lumbermills, a steel foundry—and other dullnesses. A sport called baseball. No one spoke of boxing. These were all stolid, potbellied men, content to puff on cigars and stare glassy-eyed into space, waiting for their wives to send for them. He almost wouldn't feel bad feeding one of them to Les.

He was about to approach an older, portly gentleman with a propensity to laugh after everything that came out of his own mouth when a holler went up from a table nearby.

Dai turned to see a group of men arguing over cards. Among them was Mark Fletcher. In fact, he was trying to calm the other four men down. Someone must have called out an unfair play. Dai had seen Mark about yesterday—he'd seemed a nice enough young fellow, if slightly out of place among all those industrialists. Dai thought him an odd match for the wife, who definitely came from quality.

Mark reached into his pocket and pulled out a ladies' bracelet, laying it on the table. It was modest though unmistakably of good quality. A strand of delicate gold links with a heavy ornamental clasp. It could only have belonged to his wife.

Dai felt a quick, almost familiar wash of shame, as though he'd stolen it himself. He watched as one after another the men at the table peered at the bracelet and shook his head, each in turn, refusing it as payment. Mark had no choice but to scoop up the bracelet and return it to his pocket, toss his hand on the table, and leave.

Dai found him a few minutes later at the bar nursing a drink. "Ah, fancy running into you here, Mr. Fletcher. I didn't take you for a smoker."

"Nor I you." Mark fished a bill out of his pocket and put it on the bar as the bartender came up with a second drink. Whiskey neat. "What are you doing here?"

"I was supposed to meet a man who claimed to be in the boxing business in America, but it looks like he didn't show." Dai realized with a pang that lying came easily to him these days. Les would be proud. He caught the bartender's eye and nodded at Mark's drink. He'd ditched his fake drink but decided he would have a whiskey to be sociable, even though it would be pricey.

They drank in silence for a moment as Dai struggled for something to say. Only the most banal thing came to mind: "Where is your lovely wife this evening?"

Mark sighed. "I don't know," he said, his voice carrying a hint of ice. "She slipped away from the dinner table."

"Ah. I hear wives can be independent creatures. I wouldn't know myself. I've never been married."

Mark finished his first drink and reached for the second. "I've barely been married a year and I can't say I recommend it."

"It can't be as bad as that."

Mark chuckled ruefully but offered no explanation.

"She seems to be a lovely woman. Surely you love her or you wouldn't have married her."

Mark made the muscles in his jaw pop. "To be honest, I'm not sure listening to one's heart has ever gotten anyone anywhere good."

"I'm no expert on it myself." He wasn't sure why he was talking about this with Mark Fletcher. The man was practically a stranger. But Dai felt close to him at that moment. He knew what it felt like not to trust your own heart. So many times, Dai told himself he was a fool. And yet he stayed. There was no release from love, anyhow. There was only learning how to live with the hurt.

Dai tipped the glass to Mark in a salute, then swallowed the last of his whiskey. Warmth spread through him in waves. "You married her because you love her," he went on, growing bolder as the heat blossomed inside him. "You chose her, and now you belong to each other. There's no going back from that, no matter how hard . . . how *bad* things get."

"You make it sound like punishment," Mark muttered into his glass.

Dai laughed, surprised at himself. Mark laughed then, too.

"That it is, Mark Fletcher. That it is—sometimes. But it's also the most mysterious, most wondrous experience a man can have." Dai waved off the bartender as he came to refresh his glass. He'd decided he couldn't use Mark as a—well, as a *mark*. The coincidence made another laugh bubble up.

Mark at last smiled—and Dai could see that he was a very handsome young man, when he chose to show it. And he had it so easy, though he didn't seem to know it, married to that lovely woman, da to a beautiful healthy baby. He'd followed his heart and had landed in clover. Men like him, Dai thought, ought to be able to find happiness, if anyone could.

Chapter Twenty-Three

A sharp rap at the door woke Annie from sleep—thick and gauzy, full of rain and the mutations of memory into dream: *emerald fields of clover slashed through with city streets; the ocean crashing against the cliffs of Ballintoy; the ocean baring white fangs; the ocean stretching out white arms; the ocean calling, crying, the voices trapped inside it—*

She blinked and rubbed her eyes. She couldn't imagine she'd been asleep very long; it felt as though she'd just peeled off her uniform and crawled into her narrow bunk. Her body felt small and bare in her thin nightgown. In the dark, she heard Violet moan across the room. Whoever was outside the door had awakened both of them.

She opened the door to see Alexander Littlejohn, Chief Steward Latimer's second, leaning in the doorway. He was in charge of the night shift, overseeing the small team that readied the ship for the following day, straightening deck chairs and polishing handrails, restocking supply stations, emptying ash cans and spittoons. Littlejohn squeezed his hat in his hands, apparently more than a little apprehensive knocking on stewardesses' doors in the middle of the night.

"I'm sorry to be waking you, Miss Hebbley, but the call bell in the service room's gone off for you." Annie and Violet exchanged a look: it was highly unusual for passengers to ring for their stewards after a certain hour, and if they did, usually one of Mr. Littlejohn's team answered.

"Which cabin?" Annie asked as she reached for her shoes.

"It's Mrs. Astor."

That wasn't her room at all. Littlejohn had made a mistake. "Well, then you want Violet."

Littlejohn sighed. "I know that, Miss Hebbley, but why do you think I've come down here? Mrs. Astor asked specifically for you. You know they're friends of Ismay?" He was referring to J. Bruce Ismay, chairman of the White Star Line, aboard for the *Titanic*'s maiden voyage. "What Mrs. Astor wants, Mrs. Astor gets."

Annie hurried down the passageway in just her nightgown and a light overcoat. The ship was so very dark at night, the flicker of the hall lights dancing in and out of her vision. Urgency coursed through her. The last time she'd been called to help the Astors was the night of their servant boy's death.

She felt for the brooch but remembered it was in the pocket of her work apron. She felt unmoored without it, somehow.

What reason could Madeleine Astor have to ask for her? And the look on Violet's face . . . Clearly, she suspected Annie was trying to steal one of *her* passengers, hoping for generous tips at the end of the trip, no doubt. It didn't matter that Annie swore this wasn't the case and that she barely knew Maddie Astor. She couldn't erase that hurt look from Violet's face.

Mrs. Astor was already wearing a fur-trimmed coat when Annie arrived. There was also a shawl over her shoulders and her shoes buttoned on her feet, lace-trimmed cuffs of her nightgown peeking out from her sleeves. Otherwise, the stateroom looked normal for this hour, dark and still, with the husband and Airedale, Kitty, probably fast asleep in the next room. "I've got insomnia." She gestured to her belly, which Annie knew was full with child, though underneath the heavy, tentlike coat she wore, you couldn't quite tell. "I need to take a stroll, and I want you to escort me," she said.

Why me? Annie wanted to ask. *Why not one of your servants or your husband or even Violet?* This whole episode was strange, very strange indeed. Stranger still was the way Madeleine's eyes seemed so distant, as if she were sleepwalking . . . which reminded Annie that she herself had sleepwalked only last night . . . which gave her the brief flash of worry that she might be dreaming *all* of this. Perhaps she was simply sleepwalking again? Could it be that none of this was real?

It certainly didn't feel real. At this hour of the night, with dark dreams still hugging the edges of her thoughts, Annie could swear she could feel the sway of the boat beneath her more sharply, could feel the way they were suspended above depths and depths of seawater merely by the hubris of man's progress, of invention. There was no sensible reason that a ship of this size should float. She had no under-standing of physics, and could not fathom how it was possible.

But that was modern life: full of impossibilities.

And if life was a series of impossibilities . . . Annie shivered. It meant anything was possible, that you could be haunted or pursued, or succumb to madness at any given moment. All or none of those things might be true.

Maddie's hand on Annie's arm was light but firm, and Annie couldn't help but feel that they weren't just casually wandering the halls, that this was more than just a relaxed midnight meander.

Was Maddie leading her somewhere?

"I wonder, is something in particular bothering you?" Annie asked. She tried to reassure herself—her nerves were unjustified. This poor girl, actually *younger* than Annie but married and with child, was probably just lonely. Maybe she was distraught over the death of the boy, Teddy. He was closer to her age than her own husband, after all.

"It's the pregnancy, I'm afraid. I'm too uncomfortable to sleep. Warm milk doesn't help, reading doesn't help . . . the only thing that helps is to take a long walk. My mind is . . . Have you ever read Shakespeare, Miss Hebbley?"

Annie felt the question like a pinprick through her clothing. It stung. Girls like Annie did not read Shakespeare. They were lucky to be able to read at all.

"No, ma'am."

"Well, never mind that, but there's this line in *Macbeth*—oops." She put her hands over her mouth. "You're not supposed to say the name of the play out loud, Jack told me it's bad luck, not that I'm superstitious. Anyway, there's this line I love," she whispered as they turned a corner into another vacant alleyway.

"Yes?" Annie was, quite honestly, mystified by everything Maddie was saying.

"*O, full of scorpions is my mind.* Isn't it just perfect? To describe those restless thoughts we have at night?"

The image was disturbing. Though Annie had never seen a scorpion, she knew what they were. "Yes, Mrs. Astor," she said, even though she didn't agree—just the thought of a heap of venomous creatures writhing and twisting and crawling over themselves made her skin prickle.

"Please call me Maddie," the girl replied. More of that American familiarity, like it fooled anyone. They were not equals.

Behind a door came the faint sound of a man snoring. Such an odd sound, gentle and rough at the same time. Familiar and yet disquieting. Angry and yet reassuring. It reminded Annie of her father, a terrible snorer who could be heard throughout the house. A tyrant who could make his wife and children cower with a few snarled words.

Walking with Maddie on this night was like being a fairy, a sprite, or an elf, drifting noiselessly through a house after everyone has gone to sleep. Looking for a child or a gold coin to steal. Or maybe it was most like being a ghost, trapped on another plane, held captive apart from the living.

She looked for numbers posted over the doors as they passed, but it all muddied together. She couldn't place them. Where were they? Maddie had said she wanted Annie to accompany her so she wouldn't get lost, but she'd insisted on leading and Annie was now so mixed up that she wasn't sure she'd find their way back.

"Now tell me, Miss Hebbley, where do you come from? That's not a British accent I hear."

Do not allow yourself to become overfamiliar with the passengers. "I come from a little village in Ireland. You wouldn't know it."

"You're probably right, seeing as how I've not been to Ireland. What about the ordeal of pregnancy? Do we share that in common? Do you have children?"

For reasons she couldn't recognize, the question bothered her, caused a swirling chill in her gut. "No, ma'am," she answered slowly. "I mean, Maddie. There is no child. . . ."

"And no husband, either?" she pried. "Or . . . sweetheart?"

"No, Maddie," Annie answered, the cold swirl becoming colder still, ice crystalizing in her chest.

"Yes, I supposed not."

"What do you mean?" Annie asked quietly.

"Oh, just . . . there is something very . . . *untouched* about you."

"Untouched?" she asked, but she knew what the heiress meant.

"Innocent. Childlike."

She felt sick. *The Lord favors good girls, Annie.*

"But surely," Madeleine went on, "you've got interests, have you not, Miss Hebbley? Hobbies? Practices?"

"Practices?"

"Beliefs, you know. Do you believe in spirits, for instance?"

They were in a deserted back stairwell.

"We ought to turn around now, I should think," Annie said quietly. "Surely you don't want to have to go up and down so many steps. It can't be good for you."

"Oh, to the contrary, let's explore," Maddie said, with a strange determination. Like she was pretending to be delighted but in fact had led Annie here with purpose. But that was impossible, wasn't it?

Or was all of life one great impossibility?

Once again, Annie was beginning to feel that she didn't know what was true anymore and what was not. She didn't feel safe—that much she knew.

Slowly, they descended the stairs, which led them farther into the darkness of the ship.

"I have been meaning to ask you about something," Maddie said suddenly.

Here it was, then, the reason she had asked for Annie tonight. Annie held still, waiting.

"When you came into Mr. Stead's room two nights ago, to . . . to ask for a doctor. What did you . . . well, I only mean to know what you saw. I wanted to explain to you what we were all doing there."

Annie already knew what they'd been doing. She'd helped garner the supplies for Stead. But she listened anyway.

"We were having a séance. To call forth spirits. It was mostly for a lark—someone had said they'd heard a voice calling to them over the water, that sort of thing. But then, you appeared, and then Teddy . . ."

"I'm very sorry for what happened, Mrs. Astor. It must have been terrible for you," Annie said cautiously.

Maddie clutched Annie's arm more tightly. "Yes, well, it isn't just that. I think there's something dangerous here. Something onboard that means us all harm. Can you not sometimes *feel* that?"

She wanted to balk, to tell Maddie her worries were foolish and unfounded.

But Annie herself had been saying, just this morning, to Mr. Stead himself, that she believed the same thing.

Could it merely be coincidence?

"I don't deny . . ." she answered slowly, trying to think of what Mr. Latimer would consider an appropriate response. "I don't deny that sometimes on a ship this size, one can feel very . . . vulnerable."

"And very trapped, too, don't you think? None of us could escape, were something terrible to occur among us."

Annie *was* feeling trapped, now especially.

"We should probably get you back to bed," she said softly.

Maddie brought them to an abrupt halt. "Ooh, look," she said.

They were standing, Annie realized, just near the doors to the pool. It was closed at this hour, of course, but the doors had round portholes that glowed a wavering green-blue from the lights surrounding the pool. It had an otherworldly feeling.

"Come on," Maddie whispered, pushing on one of the doors. It gave. Annie knew the doors to the common rooms were rarely locked. The library, the smoking rooms and game rooms, even the children's playroom: Nothing was kept off-limits to the passengers. The first-class passengers, that is.

"Let's go in. It's good for the pregnancy," Maddie said as she pushed her way in.

"I don't think we should," Annie said, but it was obvious Maddie did not intend to listen to her.

She followed the socialite into the empty room. It was cavernous. The white-tiled walls glowed eerily in the dark. The light bounced off the gently sloshing water and played randomly on the ceiling, making it seem as though something alive was in there with them, a beast waiting for them in the shadows.

Maddie unbuttoned her heavy coat and let it fall onto a chair. Then she pulled her nightgown—voluminous, sheer, and undoubtedly made of the finest imported fabrics, delicate as gossamer—over her head. The richest woman in the world stood in front of Annie in her pantaloons and a French silk camisole.

Annie had no choice but to get down on her knees and help her off with her shoes.

After she'd undressed, Annie took off her own coat and slid into the water first, sucking her breath at the cold. The water was supposed to be heated but it was still cool and not at all what she expected at this hour. She helped Maddie down the steps and into the water, wondering all the while why this woman was doing this. She didn't seem to be enjoying it. She gritted her teeth as she lowered herself, inch by inch, into the water.

"So, tell me about your upbringing," Maddie said through slightly chattering teeth.

Why was she going on like this, asking personal questions? It was wearying. "There's nothing to tell," Annie said, holding Maddie's elbow to steady her as she took baby steps along the slippery marble floor. "I'm an ordinary country girl, like hundreds of other Irish girls."

Maddie gave her an enigmatic smile. "I'm sure that's not true. I'm sure there are many interesting things about you. I want to know the *real* Annie Hebbley."

"I don't know what you mean, ma'am." This was starting to go beyond merely annoying; Annie was starting to get frightened. It was as though there was something wrong with the woman . . . well, girl. Despite the fine, fancy clothes and the swollen belly, Maddie Astor was little more than a girl. Even Annie could see that. "Please don't ask me about my past anymore, Mrs. Astor. I don't like to think about the past."

"How can you say that?" Maddie scoffed. "The past is who we are. It's where we come from." She waded in deeper. Once again, Annie had no choice but to follow.

Easy for a rich girl to say that. Her past was full of rosy memories, no doubt. Nothing to make her cry, nothing to make her wish she'd never been born.

Annie could feel her lips going blue and her flesh all goose pimply. The water was now mid-chest level.

"Feeling sleepy yet, ma'am? Perhaps it's time to get you back to your stateroom—"

But the young woman stopped abruptly where she stood. "I brought you here for a reason, Miss Hebbley. There is something I simply have to know the answer to." The hand on Annie's arm became suddenly fierce, stronger than Anne would've imagined. She was holding Annie now by the upper arm as though she thought Annie would run away.

Why would Annie run away? These people were her charges. . . .

"And that reason is to find out if you are who you say you are."

It was a strange accusation, one that sent a dagger of fear through Annie's heart. She shuddered from the cold, from the feeling that she didn't know what to answer. Didn't, sometimes, even know who she really was. Her past wasn't just painful, it was a haze. Her future, too. She was caught in a kind of time cloud, she existed only in the moment, in this strange passage between lands.

Who am I? she thought as she stared at Maddie's mouth, which was twisted into a kind of fearful pinch. She wasn't looking at Annie but staring at the water. Like Stead and his scrying bowl, as though the future could be divined there.

Maddie Astor tugged Annie's arm. "Look, Annie. You don't have a reflection."

Annie peered at the water. It was dark in the pool room. There was no light to see anything, let alone their reflections.

"Why don't you have a reflection? Don't you think that's odd?"

"I don't understand what you're talking about—"

The water around them was broken by their movements, circle upon circle of rippling away from them.

"Oh, Annie," Maddie whispered softly. "I'm so sorry."

And then she was pushing—pushing so hard. Shoving Annie's head below the surface of the water.

Annie was so shocked she bucked, uncertain what was even happening. But as Maddie's hands grew only fiercer, more determined, Annie saw that what was happening was very purposeful.

Madeleine Astor was trying to drown her.

She had her hands in Annie's hair and was holding on tightly as she held her under the water. Because she'd been pushed under before she knew what was going on, Annie's mouth, her eyes, her nose filled instantly. Her eyes stung from salt the stewards put into the water.

She tried to free herself, but Maddie was strong for her size. The hands on top of Annie's head held her in place no matter how much she thrashed. Too, Annie had enough presence of mind to be afraid of hurting the pregnant woman or—God forbid—doing something that ended up harming the baby.

Seconds passed in agony. She choked on water. Her chest started to burn.

Something heavy—the fur coat, she thought dimly—came down like a weight over her, and though the pool wasn't deep, Annie struggled, shoved down toward the tiled floor.

She had to breathe or—

This was really happening. She was thrashing but slowly losing the will to fight it.

In some ways, it would be a relief to die. The thought startled her—Where had it come from? Annie was tired of fighting. Tired of running. Tired of trying to forget everything that had been done to her.

The Lord favors good girls, Annie.

Would He even have her?

The bubbles in her wake, as she thrashed, seemed to lift her. Seemed to want to carry her away.

Take me, she thought.

And then, a twin thought, coming from inside her but not—from the water itself . . .

No. You're not done yet.

She heard the words as clearly as she'd heard anything in her life.

You're not done yet.

She had heard that voice before.

In those frantic seconds, fighting the force pushing down on her, fighting the urge to suck in more water, to breathe, it came to her: that day on the beach when she was a wee girl, scampering along the rocks. The pretty lady with the long, dark hair waiting for her lover, the lover who would never come. The queer shimmer of her legs, like opalescent fish scales. Annie heard the voice again, with its background note of loneliness, her longing for her Innocents.

You're not done yet.

She was transported out of the water, bursting through the surface of the pool like she was lifted up by a giant hand. Shooting up, the force knocking Maddie Astor off her feet, plunging her under.

Sputtering, Annie made her way to the edge and pulled herself out. Crawled, coughing and purging up pool water. Cold, sodden clothing weighing her down, pinning her to the tiled floor. Hands pressed into the tile surrounding the treacherous pool as though she could hold herself there by fingertips alone. Grateful for the floor beneath her. Sucking in great gulps of air, sweet air as water coursed down her face in rivulets.

Maddie fell to the ground next to her on her knees, a sodden Madonna. She was shaking. "Annie, forgive me! I don't know what came over me. I'm so sorry, I only thought—"

Annie recoiled from her instinctively. "Don't touch me—"

Maddie lifted her hands in surrender. "Don't you see? It's the only way to be absolutely sure. That's what they say. You didn't have a reflection, Annie. That's how I knew something was wrong. I thought—I thought you were possessed."

"What?" Annie spat.

Maddie was, oddly, crying now. "I wasn't going to drown you, Annie. I was only trying to drive the spirit out. . . ."

That's right; she had almost died. Annie looked at the pool, surface still tossing from their struggle, white shimmers winking at her.

"There's an evil spirit following me. I was convinced—convinced"—Maddie took a deep breath—"that it was inside you. That it had possessed you. I was trying to protect my baby. That's why I did it, don't you see? A mother will do anything to protect her children, surely you understand that. . . ."

Annie clambered to her feet, nearly tripping over her sodden nightgown. She refused to look at Maddie Astor. The only thing she wanted was to get away from the madwoman as quickly as possible.

"The medium said that everyone I love will die. You must believe me." Maddie padded after her a few steps, clutching her bare, wet arms against the cold. "Teddy was like a little brother to me. He was all I had! I couldn't lose my baby, too. You see that, don't you? You won't tell Jack—Mr. Astor—what happened, will you? He would be so upset. I don't know what he might do. The newspapers, they print so many awful things about us. . . . You must promise not to go to the newspapers with this. I'll pay you—"

Maddie Astor's voice thinned away to nothing as Annie jogged down the alleyway, coat over one arm, shoes dangling from the other hand, a thin trail of water marking her path.

Maddie Astor was safe this time, though she didn't know it. The crazy rich woman didn't understand that Annie would never go to the newspapers. You don't go to the papers when you're running away from your own demons.

And besides, there was something so plaintive, so pathetic, in Maddie's thin, pleading voice, that Annie almost, *almost,* felt the pang of sadness and desperation in it as if it were her own.

1916

Chapter Twenty-Four

19 November 1916

HMHS *Britannic*

The ship lurches under Annie's feet. Outside, the swells have reached thirty feet. They lift the hospital ship into the air. One minute, the bow is pointed nearly straight up at the sky, the next minute, it's the stern. They stayed an extra day at Naples, trying to wait out the storm, but after it stalled and showed no signs of moving, the captain ordered *Britannic* to sea. Half the patients are completely seasick, lying flat on their backs, vomiting into pails, moaning and whinging to the few members of staff left on their feet. Water sloshes in from the deck, seeping under doors and spilling across floors, making walking extremely hazardous. Patients are asked to keep to their beds as much as possible to avoid injury.

Between wet wool—a steward managed to get all the blankets wet, and they're holding water like sponges—and buckets of vomit, the ward smells terrible, sour and musty at once. It's stomach turning and hangs heavy in the air, like a miasma. They're down to a skeleton crew, many of the nurses and orderlies succumbing to seasickness and holed up in their quarters. There is grumbling that some are gold-bricking, using the rough seas as an excuse to put their feet up before they take on the bulk of their patients in Mudros, that there are many injured waiting for them there. Not that it should make a difference: with the ship at a third of capacity, there are more doctors and nurses than needed for the patients on hand.

Annie works; she doesn't mind. She prefers to stay busy. This way, she can keep an eye on Mark while there are fewer people to question why she's lingering around this one patient. She's heard he regained consciousness again, and her chest feels tight as she remembers how disoriented he seemed before, so . . . *frightened*. But he should be better now. She'll be able to assure him. Everything will be as it should.

She stops by the canteen trolley for a cup of tea and soup crackers to bring to him. Standing in line, she overhears a couple of nurses ahead talking about the handsome lieutenant with the head injury who's just woken up. *That must be Mark.* It seems he's asked Sister Merrick to move him. Something about wanting a different nurse to look after him.

The two nurses prattle on—*Since when are patients allowed to decide who will take care of them? The nerve of some men; of course it was an officer, don't you know, they think they're in charge of everything*—but Annie is knocked for a loop. She almost forgets where she is, for a second. Mark is in her ward. *She* is his nurse. There must be a misunderstanding. Perhaps this has to do with a girl on a different shift. Surely he wouldn't ask for a change if he knew he'd be losing her.

On the other hand, it means he now can speak! Suddenly the thought of it is almost too much to bear; she can hardly breathe.

But when she enters the ward, she sees his bed is empty. Anger rips through her for a wild instant: *No, not when we've been reunited. Not when we've come so close.*

After twenty minutes spent visiting each ward, Annie finally comes upon a small, private area, with a half-dozen beds, only two of them filled. No nurses. No movement at all, really. A heavy feeling hangs in the air, and Annie wonders if this is a special ward for more serious cases: bandages cover the heads of both patients; both of them lying eerily still, except for the gentle rise and fall of their chests beneath their matching blankets.

Annie hovers for a moment in the doorway, almost afraid to go in—afraid for it to be him. She looks over the roster, recognizing the names of the nurses assigned to this room—Miss Jennings and Miss Hawley—both women with lots of previous medical experience. Proper types who would give her a bit of hassle if they returned and saw her.

In the corner lies Mark.

As she approaches, he rotates toward her. His face is unmistakable, even with the bandages along his jaw, and an ugly wound ravages his right cheek. His eyes are open.

And in that moment, her stomach drops. Because she can tell, can feel it from the change in energy in the room, the way his body seems to go stiff, that he is unhappy to see her.

So, the rumors are true. He asked to be moved away from her. But why?

"I'd heard you were awake," she says with forced cheerfulness.

He shifts under his blanket, uncomfortable. Trapped. If she didn't know better, she'd almost say he seemed frightened again. It suddenly occurs to her he could simply be traumatized. The idea of lying supine on another massive ship, after what he—what they both—had been through. Her wariness softens into sympathy.

"Annie," he says.

"So, you *do* know me," she replies, her voice suddenly swelling with relief, with joy.

"You've tracked me down."

"Fate has brought us together, more like." She feels her cheeks heat.

"I've long stopped believing in such a thing as fate."

Poor man. She moves to his side, tries to take his hand, but he pulls it away. "As you can see," he says, "they've moved me to another ward. I guess that means I won't be your patient anymore."

"We can change that. I'll tell Miss Jennings to—"

"No—please." He licks his lips, hesitating. An unruly lock of hair falls over his forehead; it has a streak of gray in it. "It's for the best, don't you think? It's no good for either of us. The memories." He shudders. "Best to let the past go."

A foreign memory floods her—not one he speaks of. Not from the *Titanic*, all those screaming souls fallen into the icy deep. But an earlier memory. Something from . . . the great gray wash of *before*. She has so few connections to the time before that it could simply be a dream. She remembers: the bark of rifles against the dawn. Her father and brothers dragging home a red deer; watching as they skinned and dried it, removing the innards—the epic process of it. Remembers the words of a man she thought she'd erased from her mind forever, echoing back to her. The soft voice of a young priest as she knelt before him weeping. *It's too cruel,* she'd said to him—of the hunting. Of the slain deer. *No,* he said soothingly. The touch of a warm hand against her hair. *No Annie. Let the dead be dead.*

But, Des—

"But, Mark—"

"Please." His voice breaks. "Leave it be. Leave me be."

"But there is so much I must tell you."

He lifts an eyebrow. Curious, but he's not going to invite trouble by asking.

"You and I both know what happened between us on the *Titanic*." The words come out in a rush. She doesn't want to be so forward, especially within earshot of another patient, but she has no time. Mark's been moved out of her reach and the nurse on duty could come back at any minute.

"What are you talking about?"

"You can't have forgotten. The way—the way you touched me. Held me. That night. When we found each other. The smoke of the fire." Her words, and the images they held, are disordered. A chaos of touch and feeling, of desire and confusion buried so deep inside her that none of it makes sense anymore, if it ever did. "In the smoking room. That *night*. The things you did to me," she goes on breathlessly.

"That we did together." She's whispering hotly now, fighting back tears, fighting off the torrent of memories. The heat of his mouth. How she'd gone light-headed at his touch, had cried his name into the side of his neck. The flame in her is so alive she's surprised it hasn't broken out across her skin, lit her up in a burst of desire.

But he's staring at her as though she is speaking in tongues, as though she has dropped from the sky. As though he has never seen her before.

"I don't know what you're talking about. *Nothing* happened between us, Annie. Maybe there was a bit of flirting. I can see where you might've thought that. But there was nothing else."

If he had struck her, he could not have hurt her any worse. She cannot believe he can deny it to her face. The look of incredulity is genuine. He is perplexed and angry.

Instinctively, she clutches at her neck for the crucifix. But of course, it is gone. She lost it on the *Titanic*, four long years ago.

"Mark . . ." She stares at the stern set of Mark's jaw, the bandage still bound tightly to his head, hoping he will smile at her, will take back the sting of his denial. And then she realizes: his head injury. That must be it. Whatever knocked him unconscious and damaged his jaw must've affected his memory. That's why he doesn't remember what they've been to each other.

He doesn't remember, that is all. He will in time! And yet—the shame of it, the way he stares at her as if she is a liar—it takes her breath away.

Just then, a set of footsteps creep up behind her. Miss Jennings has returned, a narrow blond woman with a tiny nose and eyes close together. "What are you doing here, Miss Hebbley? This isn't your room, is it?" She crosses her wiry arms over her chest. She will have been warned about Annie.

"Of course, I must have been turned around," she mutters hastily, spinning away from Mark's side and moving quickly past the beds. Needing suddenly to be far, far away from Mark and his cold stare.

"I'm so sorry to have troubled you," she whispers, feeling as though she has trespassed on a grave. The layers of sin, and hurt, and betrayal heave over her like piles of dirt. No trespasser, then. The grave is hers.

~~~

It is late. Annie stands over the surgical tray. Beyond the portholes, it's still night but going as silvery as the row of neat metal instruments winking up at her.

She is supposed to be taking inventory before surgery but is so distracted that she cannot concentrate. To force her mind from wandering, she touches each instrument in turn—*clamps, retractors, forceps, scalpels, lancets, trocars*—as she goes down the checklist.

It is no use, however; her mind keeps skipping ahead to what will happen next. Mark will come around. This is just a phase, a disorientation. In any case, he will see that he *needs* her. He will need her to go with him to America to look for his daughter. He will need Annie's calming influence, her good cheer. Too, he will need someone to vouch for him with the authorities, someone who knew him as Caroline Fletcher's husband. And he will need a woman to help raise his daughter.

Too late, she realizes she has cut her hand. She wasn't paying attention when she reached for one of the scalpels. The blade is so sharp that she didn't feel it slice into her flesh, but she looks down and all she sees is shiny wet red. Blood streams down her hand, drips onto her skirt.

Her head floods with panic. It must be a bad cut for there to be so much blood. She will need stitches. She should go for a doctor, but she can't bring herself to do it. She'd have to explain how it happened, admit she'd been daydreaming.

Holding up her hand to slow the flow, Annie runs to the bandage cabinet. She pulls one from a stack and knocks several others to the ground. They bounce and roll and unravel all over the place like balls of yarn. She curses under her breath, leans down to pick them up, realizes that, no, she should take care of her wound first, and starts to wrap up her hand—only to realize there is no cut.

No blood. Her hand is fine. Fine.

She squints and looks closer. Could it have healed? All by itself?

But there is no blood: not on her hand, not her sleeve or her skirt. Annie doesn't understand. What could've happened? Was it a miracle—another miracle?

The floor of the operating room lurches up at her. She feels like she is falling. The lights are bright, too bright. What is happening to her?

Annie . . .

Someone is calling her. A voice that cannot be heard.

Fear floods Annie's mouth, sour.

You didn't think you could hide from me forever, did you?

It is the sea. The sea has spoken to her since she was a girl child standing on the beaches of Ballintoy, the gray foamy water clawing at her bare feet.

She goes cold, so cold.

I've come for what's mine. For what you owe me. You remember, don't you?

There is no fighting the ocean. Only a fool would try.

In her panic, she recalls the night Madeleine Astor tried to hold her down beneath the surface of the great ship's pool. How she ran to William Stead—good William Stead—the next morning looking for an explanation. "Maddie Astor said I was possessed," she told him. A shameful secret, that anyone could think this of her.

"It happens," he told her then, of no comfort at all. "I've witnessed it: mediums willingly letting the soul of the departed inhabit their body, so they can speak to the living. But I've heard of times when a dead soul inhabits a body against the person's will. An ordinary soul, under extraordinary circumstances. It's never easy, possession. The

214 | ALMA KATSU

souls will fight for control of the body, you see. And at night, the spirits are stronger. They find it easier to take control of the body when the mind is asleep. Dormant.

"We must tread carefully, now," he said to her then. "This malevolent spirit may be responsible for one death already. We may all be in danger."

She thought she'd escaped all this. Escaped all the fear and confusion of the *Titanic*. That had been her solace during those four years in the asylum. The conviction that whatever had been haunting her had gone down with the ship itself. But now, here she is, alone with the whispering and the horror, the certainty that it isn't over after all.

1912

WESTERN UNION, April 13, 1912

To: LADY LUCILLE DUFF-GORDON,
first-class passenger

Lucy, I'm afraid the fire inspector's office isn't quite done with us. They were not pleased to hear that you had left the country, but I assured them that you were prepared to answer all questions to their satisfaction. I am dispatching by post their latest list. Do not despair! This ordeal will be over eventually. Give my best to Cosmo.—H. Benedict Ridgely, Esquire, Offices of Banks and Banks

Chapter Twenty-Five

Caroline was by no means meticulous when it came to her personal possessions—one's best items were meant to be worn and admired and enjoyed, she felt, not stored carefully away and kept in waiting for another day—but even she could see in the fresh light of morning that two of her ruby-studded combs had gone missing. She flipped through the tray that held her more common pieces of jewelry. She found them, but it gave her the opportunity to look through the majority of her things and frankly, she was alarmed. Quite a *few* pieces were missing. She might've left one or two behind, or packed them in crates of household goods being shipped back to her father's house, but she was certain of several personal items she'd packed for this trip and they were missing. A couple of bracelets, a ring . . . and the gold heart-and-arrow brooch.

Her pulse picked up on realizing the latter was missing: that piece was important. Lillian had loved that brooch, had commented on it the day she came to fit Caroline for the blue dress from Lucile of London. They chatted the afternoon away, like real friends. Caroline, on her grief tour, knew few people in London, just a handful of her father's associates to make introductions, and there had been teas and museum visits and a few musical salons but no real friendships. Until that day.

She poked through the compartments of her little jewelry case, growing increasingly irritated. With the anger came jitters, like spiders were crawling all over her. She felt as though she could jump out of her skin. What a disaster this trip was! She nearly threw the case against the wall.

Caroline wasn't a suspicious person. She was used to having many servants come and go, was often known for leaving her valuables unlocked, out in the open. Even for leaving her first-floor windows ajar when she was not at home. She wanted air and sunlight to come in, and bad energy to go *out*. She was like that, herself: an open window. Which only made her feel more offended—more *hurt*—that she'd been taken advantage of. She was leaning against the dressing table, fighting tears, when she heard the door open behind her, the scent of stale air and unwashed linen following close behind. "What was that racket?" Mark asked, his voice still sleepy. Clearly, he expected an apology.

Not today. "I'm glad you're up. There's something we need to discuss."

Mark went rigid, not used to that tone from her. But instead of rising to the bait—*What are you talking about?*—he looked around. "Where is the baby? She's not in her crib."

"Ondine was fussing, so the nanny's taken her for a stroll on the promenade. I thought fresh air would help settle her," Caroline said. She clasped her hands, trying to sound calm. "Mark, some of my jewelry is missing."

His reaction was an odd combination of shock and anger, those two emotions seeming to struggle for domination. He staggered back a step, his face flushing bright red. After a moment where he appeared speechless, he said, "Are you sure?"

"Am I sure? Of course." She fought the urge to snap.

"I didn't mean to doubt you. It's just that . . . it seems so unlikely, doesn't it? I mean, who would steal it on board this ship?"

"Oh, please, Mark. It's not as though we have much privacy. People are tramping through here night and day. And don't act as if I'm being *unreasonable*."

"Caroline, I can see you're upset, but let's keep a cool head. First thing is, we'll give the rooms a thorough search. . . ."

Don't say I just misplaced it, like I'm a child.

"You've probably just misplaced it, whatever it is."

She suppressed the urge to scream.

"You think I'm being unreasonable, don't you? Unstable? Isn't that what you said of her, too? Isn't that what you thought of Lillian, in the end?"

"Caroline." His voice broke as it dropped a register. From the rictus of pain in his face, she could see she'd gone too far. They'd promised not to say *her* name again.

But Caroline couldn't slow down. Her anger had reached the breakaway point. She could only pivot and keep going. "Where were you last night? I woke in the middle of the night and you were gone. I waited up for hours and you never came back."

He gave her the queerest look, as though seeing her for the first time. "I couldn't sleep, that's all. I went for a walk and got lost."

Hard to refute that. But she didn't accept it, either.

Rather than explain his absence, however, he switched the subject. "I think Ondine has taken a turn for the worse, don't you?"

"What are you talking about?"

He went to the empty crib, looking into it forlornly. "The listlessness, lack of appetite . . ."

Caroline had no patience for this. "You're not suggesting that we take her to the ship's surgeon, are you? The man is worthless. I'll take her to a physician once we're in New York."

"Yes, yes, very well . . . But what do you think the problem is? I'm worried about her. I must admit, after talking to Miss Hebbley—"

The stewardess's name was like nails on a chalkboard. "You were talking to the stewardess about our baby?"

"Surely, there's nothing wrong with that. She *does* help care for Ondine—"

At first, Caroline couldn't speak, she was so mad. Anything she tried to say would be gibberish. But Mark was staring at her as though she'd lost her mind, so she forced herself to reply. "I want to stop that arrangement, Mark. I think there's something wrong with the girl, to be frank. I don't like the way she's always hanging around, showing up at all hours. It's as though she's developed an obsession with us. And it might be more than an obsession. Maybe my jewelry—"

"Obsession? It's only been three days. You can't possibly suspect the stewardess—"

"Who else could it be?" They both glanced in the direction of the chair where the nanny usually sat. "We don't know what Miss Hebbley does when she's in here by herself. I must say, Mark, that I resent that you're taking the stewardess's side."

"That's not fair. I'm not taking anyone's side—"

"Do you think I'm a fool? I've seen the way she follows you around like a lovesick puppy. And you do nothing to discourage it. I think you enjoy the attention."

Now she'd done it: she'd managed to make him angry. She was becoming more like Lillian, if that were possible. His head snapped up, and it was like he had to forcibly stop from rushing at her. He quivered where he stood, hands on the belt of his bathrobe. "Tell me where you were last night?"

"I couldn't sleep, I told you. I walked the halls."

"Did anyone see you?"

"To corroborate my story? Is that what you require—witnesses?" He laughed hollowly. "It was late. Most people were asleep. I suppose I might've crossed paths with a crew member here or there. . . . Then I saw Miss Hebbley. She'd had a mishap. She was sopping wet, and I helped her back to her room."

"A mishap? What kind of mishap?" What he was saying made no sense.

He froze. "I'm sorry—she asked that I not speak of it."

Caroline roared. "Isn't that ridiculously convenient? My God, Mark. Honestly, how do you expect me to react?"

"I expect that, as my wife, you would believe what I tell you."

He could've been a stranger standing there in front of her. Her fingers twitched with the urge to dig up another dose of her medication—her nerves felt as if they were on fire. But she wasn't in the mood for Mark to comment on it.

It occurred to her that maybe Mark wasn't the stranger before her. Maybe *she* was the stranger. A few short days on this ship had changed her. Possessed her. Maybe she was mad.

"I just . . . need to be alone. We can talk about this later."

She left him standing in his bathrobe, mouth agape; felt the knob cool and firm in her hand as she pulled the door closed behind her.

Chapter Twenty-Six

You could hear the squabbling all the way from the grand staircase.

William Stead took a deep breath before going inside.

He couldn't wait for the voyage to be over. It wasn't the ship's fault—it was a beautiful machine, so well-built, real pride of craftsmanship—but its misfortune was to be filled with such disagreeable people. And his misfortune to have no means of escape from them. He'd headed to the Café Parisien for breakfast and there they were all were: grouped around the wicker table, the Astors and the Duff-Gordons. The insufferable lecher Guggenheim, smelling of an assignation with that French woman he had brought with him and kept in a separate cabin, as though no one was wise to his little game. And beside him, newly seated, was Caroline Fletcher.

As Stead approached the table, Astor signaled for a steward, who came instantaneously. They must have an eye peeled for Astor wherever he was on the ship, so he wouldn't have to suffer even a second's want. "We'll need another chair," he said, gesturing to Stead. The steward hurried over with a chair, as though Stead were an invalid grandfather. He took it gruffly.

Astor cast an eye at Stead, deciding whether to address him. "We were discussing the event tonight. Do you plan to attend?"

"Event?" It was the first Stead had heard of it, but then he tried to avoid the petty amusements. He had work to do: an editorial he had promised to the *Pall Mall*. A speech he intended to give to the Theosophical Society in New York a few weeks after his arrival.

"The captain's ball," Sir Cosmo Duff-Gordon said.

"They should call it the Joseph Bruce Ismay ball and be done with it. I'm sure he's the one behind it. He wants to do something splashy for the maiden voyage," Lady Duff-Gordon said.

"Free advertising for *you*, is it not? I can only imagine you'll set the standard of attire. Ladies will be in line for your next collection," Guggenheim said.

"Ever the capitalist!" Lucy laughed. "I shall do my best to dazzle."

Stead resisted the urge to scoff. Overpriced rags for women with too much money and not enough modesty were just one of society's many failings. Capitalism indeed. Avarice and frivolity, more like it.

Lady Duff-Gordon turned to Caroline, who had just started nibbling on a piece of leftover toast in the rack on the table. The plate in the center was scraped bare, though by the looks of it they'd dined on caviar and scrambled eggs. Streaks of cream obscured the blue decorations on the china. "We have another clotheshorse among us. Have you planned your outfit for tonight?"

Caroline lowered the toast and smiled wanly. "I'm sure I'll think of something. My full wardrobe is in the hold, so my options are a bit limited. And I can't seem to find my favorite bracelet—I searched for it all morning."

Astor went suddenly alert. "Mrs. Fletcher, are you sure it wasn't stolen?"

"Stolen?"

"There's been a *rash* of burglaries in first class, Caroline," said his wife, Madeleine. "Had you not heard?"

"Well now," Stead inserted. "A rash of them? That sounds a bit extreme. Let us not jump to—"

"It happened to me, too!" proclaimed Lucy. "I didn't know it had been a *pattern!* But I'm convinced someone has stolen my ring, the opal and diamond. It is one of a kind. Irreplaceable. I wore it when we boarded!"

Of course, Stead recalled it: the way the woman had been flashing it around, there wasn't a soul on the ship who *hadn't* seen it. She might as well have asked to be robbed.

"I thought it was just me." Caroline looked around the table. "I'm missing a few things, too. Nothing as valuable as your ring but of sentimental value all the same."

"You don't suspect the staff, surely," Guggenheim said. "It would be foolhardy, with them trapped on the ship and no way to hide the evidence."

"Criminals aren't usually the type to think ahead, are they?" Astor said. He twirled champagne in a glass, releasing its aroma. Stead watched the golden swirl of it in the morning light. He'd never understood it, how men could put so much poison into their mouths, even at this hour. And do it with delight.

Stead made a stern face, the one he reserved for when he was speaking at public events as the Famous Newspaper Editor, the living legend. "Many strange things have happened on this ship in the few short days we have been at sea. That there may be another party responsible, one that none of you have considered—"

Caroline put down her cup. "Are you saying, Stead, that I don't know what's going on in my own cabin? My jewelry is missing. That's a fact."

He felt uneasy. He didn't like sparring with young women. He remembered the picket lines outside his trial. Protestors outside his newspaper office.

She raised one eyebrow. "You don't think much of the female sex, do you, Mr. Stead?"

Stead cleared his throat. "That's not true. My record speaks for itself, I believe. Why, I am a champion of women's emancipation.

You're an American, you wouldn't know, but there's a British law that bears my name—"

"The Stead Act. We know all about it, and the Eliza Armstrong case," said Lucy Duff-Gordon.

There was something about the way she said Eliza's name that worried him.

"You went to jail over that case, didn't you?" Astor said with a slight laugh.

It felt like a noose had tightened around Stead's throat, though he should have been used to his past being thrown in his face by now.

"You're going to argue for your innocence, but I doubt they send famous men to jail in England, not if they are innocent," Caroline said with a harshness that surprised him. "From what I read, it wasn't until another newspaper found out the truth that you owned up to it."

She was at least familiar with the details of the trial, he had to give her that. "What is it you want from me, Mrs. Fletcher? I wish I could take back that night—in hindsight, I realize I made a terrible mistake with some aspects of it. But I paid for those mistakes with three months at Coldbath. Which is more than the libertines who routinely exploit young women like Eliza Armstrong can say."

He sweated for a moment under her appraising eye. But if she was going to bring up another point, it was lost when her husband came up to the table. It didn't take a detective to figure out within seconds that things were strained between them that morning.

"I suddenly find I am not hungry," Caroline said, rising. Stead had seen this scene play out many times before, but the husband only watched, openmouthed, as she walked away.

"Oh, dear." Stead felt rather sorry she'd left. Mark said nothing, only sat down forlornly in her seat.

The Astors and the Duff-Gordons made polite escapes as the waiters came round to clear the used plates.

Now, it was only Stead and Mark. "I suppose you ought to go after her and apologize."

"In a minute, perhaps. She needs to cool off."

"If you don't mind my saying, you seem particularly sad this morning."

"Do I?" Mark's smile was wistful.

Stead finished his coffee. "I hear your wife has been . . . having difficulties? Her things trifled with by an unseen hand? Have you considered the possibility of spiritual intervention?"

Mark paled. "What do you mean? Are you talking about . . ."

"Ghosts," Stead said plainly. "Someone from your past. Someone who has recently died. Can you think of anyone like that, someone you've been thinking of?"

Mark furrowed his brow. "I can see Caroline has told you about Lillian."

Now this was a turn. "Lillian," Stead repeated. "Your . . ." *Former wife? First love?*

"Yes, Lillian. My . . . we were very close."

Stead leaned in. "What happened?"

Mark stiffened. "A terrible accident, is all."

"I see," Stead said softly. "Mr. Fletcher. The living are often anchors for the dead. Sometimes, when our feelings for the dead are very, very strong, it keeps them tied to us. It prevents them from moving on to the next world. Your love for this dead woman, whoever she is, might be keeping her spirit trapped here with you on earth. On this ship, even. Have you considered it?"

As Stead watched Mark absorb his words, he thought again of Eliza Armstrong. The spare young figure in the bed and his own distraction haunting him still.

But Mark snapped the napkin with a flourish before laying it over his lap. "No, I haven't considered it because I don't believe in this nonsense, and I'll thank you not to speak of this again," Mark said, as the waiter approached again.

Stead bit his tongue. He wouldn't give voice to the thought that ran through his head at that moment, that Caroline Fletcher's anger with her husband seemed justified. He simply stood, shoving his napkin aside. "You might take a long, hard look in the mirror. There's obviously something preying on your conscience and you must address it before it consumes your life—and your marriage."

And then he left without a backward glance, passing through the corridors that seemed alive with fluster and activity. Obliviousness, everywhere around him, he thought. They were in danger, that was obvious to anyone who would take the time to see, but all these silly, frivolous people could talk about was this captain's ball. He could hear the peal of bells as passengers rang for service throughout the ship: the jangle of vanity, high and tinkling, like a million chimes caught in a fierce wind.

Chapter Twenty-Seven

13 April 1912 5:45 p.m.
Entered into the record of Dr. Alice Leader
Strict confidentiality
Patient: Annie Hebbley
Age: 18

I was relaxing in my cabin when I was approached by a stewardess named Annie Hebbley. She looked exhausted, having been
on her feet all day with the servants' bells ringing nonstop as the
ladies of first class readied themselves for the captain's ball. I
can't say I have any interest in it myself, so I was passing the time
reading when she stumbled in, flustered and wild-eyed.

There is something strange about this one. She reminds me
of the lower-class maids and factory girls I treated at the Willard
Asylum. It seems a baby in her care had exhibited long red welts
like scratches, frightening the stewardess. Perhaps she had
scratched herself. Infants are known to do that, I told her. Then
she got to the heart of the matter: there were rumors that this
same phenomenon had happened to the dead servant boy. She

was afraid something uncanny was happening on the ship. Miss Hebbley's eyes were fevered, like the eyes of many patients I have known. She clearly has not been sleeping.

I pressed her on the rumors she "claimed to have heard" and she had no answer, of course, other than to mumble something nonsensically about Madeleine Astor. My point was to challenge the paranoia at play in her mind. For now, I merely cautioned the stewardess not to spread rumors of disease on a ship. People might panic.

As it stands, I have my suspicions that both Mrs. Astor and Stewardess Hebbley suffer from low-grade hysteria. I know firsthand how easy it is for this kind of thing to happen in a confined space with few distractions. Someone gives voice to a concern and before long, it's on everyone's lips. Paranoia is itself a kind of contagion. Humans are predisposed to it. I have long held that it is a learned behavior from our primitive ancestors, a defense mechanism. Cautious humans stay alive longer than incautious ones.

I have seen similar cases in the asylums. There are many reasons why women succumb to hysteria and, while they sometimes try to hide behind stories of visitations by angels or demons or (popular now) visits from the dead, more often it is some shameful secret that has turned their minds against them. We are all, men and women, creatures of desires both good and bad. But everything has a price, and the price of indulging in that which is bad for us is often guilt; and too much guilt results in a sickness of the mind. We have poisoned our conscience, and something poisoned will need treatment one day—or it will rot.

But the stewardess Miss Hebbley . . . She worries there is something wrong with her, I think. She will not admit it, but I saw her lips twitch and eyelids flutter when I told her the troubled mind can never know itself; that this is the sad truth of madness. For so many who are mad do not see themselves that way. I cannot guess what is behind her speculations. Looking into those frightened, haunted eyes, I could almost believe in demons and spirits myself.

Chapter Twenty-Eight

"I like you in this," Les whispered, close to Dai's ear. "Though I'd like you better out of it."

It was a stupid line, Les knew, but Dai didn't seem to mind.

Les stood back then, and picked imaginary lint from the shoulder of Dai's suit. "Anyway, don't look so long-suffering. This'll be good practice for when we're in America, meeting with fight promoters. You need to go to a mirror and see how handsome you are." Dai turned to look at himself, straightening his tight bow tie as Les ran down a checklist in his mind of the four marks he'd selected for the evening's play. The past day had been a whirlwind of meeting Violet to slip into strangers' staterooms and riffle through their belongings. He was afraid of mixing up his marks—there had been so many details to keep track of—that he made notes on a slip of paper. There was Henry Harper, a gadabout who lived off his grandfather's largesse to travel the world. He and his wife were returning from a trip with an interpreter they'd picked up while in the Middle East, a handsome man named Hassab. Les scarcely needed to look twice at the detritus around the cabin to know what the two men had been up to.

Then there was Miss Helen Newsom, the debutante who was afraid of her mother, and her lovesick beau, Karl Behr. The silver watch had been so beautiful, so touching—exactly what he would like to be able to give Dai one day, when he won his first big match in America, perhaps—that he couldn't help but lift it.

And then there was the old newspaper fellow, W. T. Stead.

Dai turned back to face him. "What are you puzzling on about?" he asked, looking directly into Les's eyes.

Les shrugged. "Potential marks. I was just thinking about old Stead."

"The journalist?"

Les nodded. "He's made no secret that he's afraid of drowning on board a big ship like this one. He's told anyone who would listen that the newspapers ought to write about the dangers of sailing with too few lifeboats, or some such. Might be able to offer a clairvoyant reading, something to ease his mind, or—"

"Have you lost your mind?" Dai took a step backward in their tiny quarters, bumping into one of the bunks. "Stead's no fool, Les. And he's not the type to sit quietly if he thinks you're pulling a con on him. He's a crusader, right?"

There was nothing like telling Les something shouldn't be done to make him dig in his heels. "He's gullible, that old man. Believes in haunts and ghosts and all that nonsense. He's the perfect mark for this, I tell you."

"No, Les. Not Stead."

"Then help me find another," Les said as he worked on his bow tie, trying to tamp down his anger. "This is our one night to score. We have to make the most of it. Find me another while I'm working these plays."

Dai looked like he'd rather drink poison.

"Get Violet to let you in one of the rooms, take a look around, and report back to me. Easy as can be. I'll take care of the rest."

"I don't want to be sneaking around people's staterooms." Dai looked down at the tips of his shoes, something he always did when he was having trouble deciding. "I might know of someone . . . or it might be nothing. I don't know rightly—"

"Tell me, and I'll decide," Les said, trying not to sound impatient and scare Dai off.

"First of all, you've got that all wrong," Dai said, reaching over to wrest the bow tie from Leslie's hands. He took over fastening it around Les's collar, and Les found himself both grateful for the help and for Dai's gaze—the weight of it a welcome sensation. There was nothing so gratifying as knowing Dai was looking at him. Was with him.

While he fumbled with the tie, Dai told him how he'd seen Mark Fletcher in the card room using his wife's jewelry to cover his debts. How sad faced he'd been, trembling with guilt. Les had to admit, he was a little shocked. He'd pegged Fletcher as someone who played by the rules because he was afraid of being caught. The more he thought about it, he could see it: a barrister, used to trying to find a way around the law to further other people's causes.

"Well, well, well," Les said. "I'd say that sounds promising. A guilty man with a rich wife."

"The man is struggling, though—"

"If you didn't want me to know, why'd you tell me? He's perfect, Dai. And I swear to you, he'll barely feel the sting."

"I shouldn't have said anything." Dai swung away from him with the raise of an arm like he wanted—no, *needed*—to punch something. There was no shortage of things to punch in that tiny, crowded room, but he somehow managed to contain himself. "Les, I'm sick of it, all the scheming and lying and cheating. There's got to be a line somewhere."

"And I'm tired of you always being the Samaritan." It came out before he could stop himself. "We grew up in the same neighborhood, Dai. You know what happens to Samaritans."

"Yeah: they get swindled by people like you."

That hurt worse than any punch he'd gotten from Dai. "You don't like what I do—but I've done it for *us*." He got up close to Dai again. "Everything I've done, it's been to keep us going. We won't be able to box all our lives. Eventually, we won't be able to take a beating for a living. I, for one, don't intend to die in the ring like some old workhorse dying still hitched to the wagon."

"All this lying and cheating and conning . . . I feel sometimes . . . like I don't know you. Like I can't trust you."

It was a blow from a cannon right to Les's chest. "How can you say that? To me? After everything I've done—"

But Dai was already slamming the door shut behind him and Les was left with only the scent on the air of his sweat and pomade, and the tiny room, heaped with ragged clothing and stinking of herring: a reminder of how small and trapped their lives were. This was his life in a nutshell, this constant starting over, constantly losing ground, no matter how hard he fought. And he fought so hard it was wearying. So hard he thought maybe he wouldn't ever be done until he was dead, like that workhorse.

The part that was true was that he did it for them. For both of them. Wouldn't it be the height of irony if it became the reason he lost Dai Bowen in the end? Because that was his greatest fear. That one day Dai would finally realize the truth: that Leslie Williams had never been good enough for him in the first place.

Chapter Twenty-Nine

As the deep cream silk of her dress—bedecked with bugle beads and crystals—fell around her swollen body like a soft stream of water, Maddie worried her hands together. They'd become chapped in the night, after . . . the thing she had done—cracked and dry, despite the primrose-scented oil she'd rubbed into them repeatedly. Luckily, she had the perfect pair of evening gloves to match her gown: pale walnut, and a diamond choker to match.

In the mirror, she studied her face, painted to cover the rings beneath her eyes. It had been a very late night. Her nightgown—soaked through and still pungent with the scent of salt from the pool, had had to be disposed of, of course. No one could know what had happened last night. Which meant that, once she'd managed to pull herself back up the servants' stairwell, dripping wet, she'd returned quietly to her rooms, stripped down, wrapped the soaking nightgown in a pillowcase, donned an overcoat (plain brown wool, it was an effective disguise), then sneaked back out and threw the incriminating bundle over the railing, watching it disappear into the black of night and sea. It had taken a lot of strength, and the wind had been fierce, but it was done. All traces of her momentary madness gone. If only it was as easy to erase it from her mind.

By the time she'd returned to bed at last, the sun was piercing the horizon. She'd drawn her silk eye mask over her face and fallen into a fraught, dream-tormented sleep—dark salt waves choking her, the eerie glow of the lights in the pool swimming around her, glowing orbs that became, when you looked closer, pale faces, crying out *help us . . .* or had it been, *join us*? Because she had briefly joined some sort of communal madness, of that she was sure. For this, she blamed the ship: the tight quarters, the inability to escape the collective. It was like living in a hive.

She'd awoken only after the maid had come to clear away her husband's lunch tray sometime that afternoon. It had left her groggy and disoriented—with very little time to make arrangements for tonight's ball.

There was no question of abstaining, of pleading a headache and staying in her rooms. The Astors were the pinnacle of the social pyramid; Jack would insist on making an appearance, and he wouldn't risk the scandal of going without her. She would have to attend if only to show that she wouldn't be cowed by the matron society in New York, that she was Mrs. J. J. Astor now and she would have her due.

Maddie rubbed cream into her hands furiously. What had possessed her last night? The reasons were clear in her mind, but it would be impossible to make anyone else understand. She had played right into the hands of Ava and her cronies, and if the papers caught wind, could absolutely ruin her. Jack would be furious with her and might be moved to do something—baby or no.

She managed the final buttons on her dress alone. Miss Bidois had found a seamstress in steerage to work on it all night to get it ready for the gala. It was a shame to let it out at the waist and hips, but it could always be put back the way it was after the baby was born. She made a mental note to make an appointment with Lady Duff-Gordon once she'd set up her atelier. Have some dresses made especially for the pregnancy. She was sure the Englishwoman could come up with something chic. So many maternity dresses were so dowdy; she didn't want to end up looking like a sack of flour. It was important to keep up appearances, no matter what.

"Are you ready?" she called out to her husband, in his dressing area. If there was one thing she could change about her husband, it would be his fussiness over clothing. Jack took longer to dress than she did. He had more clothes than any society woman she'd known; it went back to his theatrical streak. He loved dressing up.

A vague murmur came from his dressing room. She knew what that meant. "I'm going to head down. I promised some friends I would see them there at nine o'clock and I don't want to be late." She didn't wait for an answer.

Maddie found Helen Newsom by the grand staircase, as arranged. They knew each other from the tennis circuit in Bar Harbor. A lovely girl; too bad about the overprotective mother. That was sometimes the way with widows (though Helen's mother had remarried profitably): they were hell-bent on their daughters marrying for security. The mother had lined up a good catch back in the States, but Helen had fallen in love with an American tennis player while touring Europe. The poor fool, Karl Behr, was even on the ship, trying to ingratiate himself with the old battle-ax. Helen was from comparatively modest means and Maddie could sympathize with her entirely. Who doesn't wish to marry for love? Sometimes she felt like a broodmare: carefully bred, valuable for one thing and one thing only. And if she did this one thing, if she was compliant, she would have a life of relative ease for the rest of her days. To marry for love seemed incredibly wild and rebellious. She wasn't entirely sure she approved—She'd made her bed, hadn't she?—but it was fun watching someone else try.

They kissed each other's cheeks like Frenchwomen. Maddie admired Helen's lilac frock. The girl was so statuesque that she could look good in anything, even an old gunny sack. And how she managed to do her hair without the help of a lady's maid—Maddie would have to ask Helen for her secrets.

They were quickly joined by Mabel Fortune. Maddie didn't really know the Fortunes, but Mabel had attached herself to Helen like a lost-love cousin and there didn't seem to be any way of shaking her off. Maddie was pretty sure Mabel made the attachment after she noticed Helen was an acquaintance of hers. She didn't like to be suspicious, but it was impossible not to notice, really.

"Where's Mr. Astor?" Helen asked, looking around.

"He's coming later. Some business thing." She waved a hand airily. "Let's go downstairs, shall we?" Though the ship was as claustrophobic as ever, the company of her friends made it bearable. Her nervousness began to lift; being in that swirl of activity—pretty gowns, men in black, bright chatter—she was like an old warhorse responding to the sound of gunfire and the smell of powder. She was made for this, born and trained. The banquet hall was her war table, the ballroom her battlefield.

The reception area had been reasonably transformed into a ballroom. The damask-covered couches and armchairs had been taken away, though the Axminster carpet remained. The chandeliers threw off a beautiful faceted light. Music drifted up from the far end, where the piano normally sat—the ship had a good assortment of musicians, she'd been happy to see. The room was already filled with passengers all turned out in their best. Most of the men wore swallowtail coats with black waistcoat and white tie, though she was charmed to see some of the men in the trendier white waistcoat, and a few daring, fashion-conscious souls in black tie and white waistcoat. A fair number wore dinner jackets instead of swallowtails; it was only a captain's ball, after all, and not as demanding. She spied Guggenheim decked out in a swallowtail and white waistcoat, a notched collar on his coat, not the shawl collar that was quickly falling out of style.

"Let's find Lady Duff-Gordon, shall we?" Normally, Maddie wouldn't have given Lucy of London a second thought, even if she claimed to dress the aristocracy and famous singers and actresses of the day, but now that she'd seen the clothes herself, up close where she could get a sense of the workmanship and quality of the fabrics, she was intrigued. Besides, it might be a good idea to ingratiate herself with the older woman: she could be a formidable ally if word got out about the episode with the stewardess. What happened at the pool.

What she saw when she found Lady Duff-Gordon took her breath away. The outfit was like nothing Maddie had seen before. It most closely resembled a Japanese kimono in shape and the way it was draped. The Englishwoman's dress was a long column of the most exquisite purple silk. The fabric for the bodice had a glorious pattern of tiles embroidered in gold, with sleeves the same shade of purple. There was a sash of pale gold and another of ivory doubling the waist and hanging to the hip. It was both effortless looking and highly designed—breathtakingly beautiful.

Maddie was almost breathless addressing Lady Duff-Gordon. "I must say, your dress is exquisite."

"It's from my latest collection. Inspired by *la Japonaise*." Lady Duff-Gordon's eyes shone like a mischievous schoolgirl's. "I would be happy to design one for you, my dear."

What a clever one she was. This transatlantic crossing was a way to drum up business. She had a wealthy and captive audience.

Out of the corner of her eye, Maddie saw her husband descend from the central staircase. Maddie squeezed Helen's hand as she turned away. "Let's go, girls. I'm in the need of a drink."

They were making their way deeper into the room when there was a bump from behind. A male voice said, "I'm so sorry, ladies—I beg your pardon." Maddie turned and was happy to see the boxer who had pulled Teddy down from the railing.

"Oh, Mr. Bowen, how nice to see you this evening," she said.

He held a dripping cup to one side. "I'm afraid I wasn't watching where I was going and seemed to have spilled some punch on this young lady's dress," he said, gesturing to Mabel Fortune. Mabel looked down at the hem with a frown.

"Oh, it's nothing Mr. Bowen, and I'm sure she'll do worse herself before the evening's out," Maddie said, ignoring Mabel's insulted glare.

The boxer was suddenly very solemn. He bowed, still managing to hover over her with his great height. "Mrs. Astor, I wish to extend my sympathies. I heard about the passing of your little boy. I'm sorry I didn't have the chance to tell you sooner."

"Yes, poor little boy. But he was just a servant," Mabel blurted. "It wasn't like he was *her* son."

"Still, it was very sad nonetheless," Helen Newsom said.

"Thank you." Maddie did not want to talk about it. She didn't want to hear one more word from Mabel Fortune's mouth. She was beginning to feel very self-conscious. People were staring at her belly, doubtless replaying gossip from the papers in the back of their mind. *How pregnant is she? And* when was *the wedding?*

"It's a shame to see such beautiful women on their own tonight. Lady Duff-Gordon had said there was a shortage of eligible men on board this ship, but I didn't believe her," the boxer said, all smiles.

"We're not in need of eligible men," Maddie said. "I am married, as you are aware, and Miss Newsom here has a beau. We are merely, for the moment, unescorted."

"Then we need to find you an escort. Women as lovely as you need someone to protect them from unwanted attention." He reached out and snagged the sleeve of a passing man. The man was handsome and blond, about David Bowen's age but not nearly his size. Where Bowen was sweet, however, something about this one was off-putting, she noticed now that they were close. He practically exuded cunning. "Allow me to introduce my friend Leslie Williams," Bowen said. "I don't believe you've met."

"We know Mr. Williams!" Mabel put a hand possessively on Les's arm. "He read my sister's fortune! He's a swami."

Maddie looked at him with fresh interest. Maybe she didn't have to wait until she was back in New York to engage someone to help her, after all. "Is that true, Mr. Williams?"

He ducked his head in a show of modesty. "I've been told I have a talent in this area."

"Perhaps you can help me," Helen said. It was her turn to move closer to Leslie Williams. "I've lost something of great importance to me."

The blond man stepped up to her. He conveyed an immediate air of intimacy, reeling her in as though he'd thrown a net over her. "Certainly, if I can be of help."

"It's a watch, a man's watch. Made of silver." She blushed under Mabel's stare.

He took her hand without asking permission first. "And had you handled this watch recently? It may retain something of your aura—and that can help me locate it."

"It was with my jewelry."

"So, it was in close proximity to your own things." He spoke with a mesmerizing smoothness. At the same time, he was stroking her hand like a cat. He closed his eyes. "I—I feel something. A presence, but it's very weak. But now I know what its aura should feel like. I will hold on to this feeling, though, and who knows? Maybe it will lead me to your watch."

Helen clutched his hand. "Oh, Mr. Williams, if you could find it, I would be so grateful. And, of course, I would give you a handsome reward."

"No reward is required—that is, any compensation is solely up to your discretion." He gave her a big smile.

Maddie knew she ought to be wary of this man, and yet the need for answers was stronger than any trepidation. Before she realized it, she had taken his arm and drawn him a few steps away from the others. What she had to tell him, she didn't want the others to overhear.

"I heard about the reading you gave to Ethel Fortune." Thinking of Ethel inflamed her momentarily. She'd heard of Ethel's spending spree in Paris, the gowns she'd bought for her trousseau at the House of Worth. Maddie hadn't been able to do anything like that for when she'd wed Jack. It'd had to be all hush-hush lest his first wife's friends make his life miserable with their gossip. A small ceremony at John Jacob's mother's house in the country, all done quickly. Which was why they'd run away for a six-month trip abroad, but still she'd had to be so careful to stay out of the papers . . .

"I need your help on a very serious matter," she said, clasping her hands together.

The blond man blanched. "My dear Mrs. Astor, surely you don't need my services. I can't imagine—"

It was bad enough that she was driven to consult him at this event, in front of Helen and Mabel and who knew how many other people— did he have to haggle? And Jack would be here any second—there was no time to argue. He was making her angry. "I *do* require your services, Mr. Williams. Isn't that what you *do*? For money? I can pay you, of course. Money isn't a problem." She carried a little spending money on her at all times. She reached into her little beaded evening bag, pulled out a hundred-dollar bill, and shoved it into his hand. "There? See? You've taken my money. I insist you give me a reading."

He was flustered, looking over his shoulder to see who was watching. He took her elbow and escorted her to an alleyway, a passage for crew that led to a pantry. "I didn't mean to make you upset, Mrs. Astor. I had no idea you were such a strong believer in . . . the spiritual."

Was she? "I don't know that I *am*, really . . . but I am in desperate need of your help."

He stroked the corners of his mouth. "Well, what seems to be the matter?"

How much to tell him? Oughtn't he be able to guess if he were a psychic? She pursed her lips, trying to think of the right way to pose the question. "As silly as this may sound, I believe I might be cursed. I heard . . . from a trusted source . . . that someone has paid to have a curse placed on me. I know how that sounds. I was disinclined to believe it myself—at first. Yet, since I found out, bad things have been happening to me. . . . Terrible things."

He grew quieter. He was listening. Someone, at last, was listening to her.

"They said whoever I loved would die. That was a few months ago." Her chin wobbled. "And now Teddy—"

"Most unfortunate, Mrs. Astor, but—children *die*. They're weak and vulnerable. Back where I come from, nearly as many children die as see their twelfth birthday."

She knew this was true, but she also knew that Teddy had been in good health. He'd been a champ all throughout the great long trip. Sure, he'd developed a few sniffles before they boarded the ship in Southampton, but it was only a tiny cold. Children got colds all the time. "The circumstances surrounding his death are . . . *unexplainable*. Something very bad is afoot . . . I can tell. In any case, I can't risk it. I have another child to think of." Her hand went to her belly.

The man's expression went dark, very dark. He stroked his chin for a long while before he finally spoke. "I'm inclined to agree with you on that. I've had a bad feeling since stepping on board this ship. There's something evil here. Is it what got your little servant boy? I can't claim to know. Now, there is something I may be able to do to help you . . . but it's quite dangerous. I can try to make contact with this malevolent spirit. For me to take on such a risk, I would need to be appropriately compensated, if you see my position."

"I do."

"Now, I have a serious question for you." He dropped his chin, looking at her from under hooded lids. "If you don't mind my asking, Mrs. Astor, does your husband share your attitude? That is, is he spiritual, too?"

My husband is a believer in a jolly good time, and little else. "Not exactly, no."

"Then—and I don't mean to be indelicate, but I must ask in order not to waste everyone's time, yours and mine—Is it likely that he'd agree to the additional compensation I would require for such a risky undertaking? I think not."

Is this man going to quibble over money when my safety, and the safety of my unborn child, is at stake? She wanted to grab him up the shoulders and shake him. "Don't worry about money. I have more than enough to pay you at my disposal, right here on this ship. How much would you charge? One thousand? Two? I can lay my hands on that in an instant. My husband never travels with less than twenty-five thousand dollars on him at all times."

That, at least, seemed to give him pause. "But surely he'll know if you avail yourself of this . . . he'll realize it's missing."

"He won't know! He keeps it in storage. He won't even look at it before we arrive in New York and then it will go straight into the safe in our house."

He rubbed his jaw again. "I tell you what, Mrs. Astor—let me think about your predicament. I want to be absolutely sure that I'll be able to help you before we take another step. Give me time to think about it."

"But my child—"

"I won't take long, I assure you. And I can tell you're safe for now. I don't feel anything bad hovering over you at the present time." He had taken her by the elbow and was escorting her back to the ball, as though she could think about dancing at a time like this.

"But, Mr. Williams . . ." She tried to get him to stop, to talk to her, but to no avail. It was like a mad carousel all around her, a kaleidoscope of color and light. The swell and swirl and sparkle of gemstones and light glinting off silk and satin, the deep black of men's dinner jackets. Aromas, too. The smell of perfume and pomades, roses in flower arrangements, shrimp and lobster in champagne sauce, good prime rib. The sweet sound of violins; a swell in the background like a buzzing hive; deep male voices swooping in and out; the high, bright tinkle of female laughter cutting through it all like a knife.

Jack. She practically ran into him, his green velvet–clad chest suddenly in front of her like a wall of embroidered moss. She felt the boxer release her elbow abruptly, as though they'd been caught doing something wrong together. Perhaps they had.

Her husband was frowning. Why was he displeased with her? Was it the hand on her arm? Was it because he knew who this man was? Of course he did; he went to watch him almost every day in the gymnasium.

"Come, Madeleine," he said coldly, taking her arm now. Scuttling away on tiptoe, she tried to look over her shoulder. *We'll talk again*; she tried to convey this with her expression. *Don't forget.*

Chapter Thirty

Mark would never forget the first time he met Caroline. It had been shortly after the terrible fire at the factory where Lillian worked. The only reason Lillian hadn't perished in the fire, too, was because she had been sent to take care of a customer: Caroline.

Caroline summoned him to her London apartment, a move he thought rather imperious, but he complied because she had, in a way, saved his beloved's life. He had been suspicious, too, of the woman who had so quickly become as close as a sister to Lillian. He wanted to see what this was about for himself.

But he understood from the minute he met her. She was forthright but also charming, as radiant as sunshine in that way Americans have. It was apparent that she genuinely adored Lillian, the same as he.

Before long, he came to appreciate Caroline in the same way that Lillian did. He loved her because she loved Lillian. The two women became bound together in his mind. He could almost not think of one without automatically thinking of the other. But after a time, things began to change, imperceptibly at first and then with sudden swiftness. Lillian became stormy, envious, rageful. Caroline became his solace—and he hers. Alliances had shifted with an inevitability that felt beyond what he could control.

By the end, he sometimes wondered if he didn't hate Lillian, almost with the same ferocity he had loved her. If Caroline hadn't prayed for Lillian to disappear—as he had.

Or if something far worse had happened. If Caroline had *made* her disappear. If he'd been deluded in trusting and falling for her. She had always seemed so bright and strong to him—her presence made his fear and doubts fall away. But when she wasn't around, the questions returned, dark and menacing. Dogged and brutal.

And so it was with an odd and overwhelming sense of relief—joy even—that he realized the sight of Caroline could still take his breath away, still bring him out of his dark mood, as he watched her arrive at the captain's ball that evening. He wasn't sure why he'd come to the ball at all except that after their argument this morning over Miss Hebbley, and his disturbing conversation with Stead about anchors, about Lillian—*What did the old man know?*—Mark didn't want to be alone. Couldn't stand the snakelike thoughts that slithered through him.

The police had deemed Lillian's death a suicide though there'd never been any proof.

Female jealousy was a powerful thing. It could take many forms. He'd seen so himself.

But now, here Caroline was, walking into the reception room, and the crowd seemed to part before her like she was a queen. His mind, too, parted ways with its former broodings. She was too dazzling to be false, too warm to be deceiving. It was his own guilt at work, projecting fears onto her that weren't true, weren't possible.

She wore a gown made of gold satin, a tall column of a dress that made her look like a wand of the most precious metal, a king's scepter. Her dark hair was pinned up with topaz, flashes of a beautiful deep orange winking like daubs of fire. He was reminded how lucky he was to be married to this beautiful, intelligent woman, especially when just before, everything in his life had gone to ash.

She had been a kind of divine intervention.

She spotted him through the crowd and started in his direction.

How graceful she was. He took her dainty hand, light as a butterfly in his.

"The music sounds wonderful. I would like to dance, Mark."

"Of course." He didn't bother to explain that he'd been about to ask but had been dumbstruck by the sight of her. He didn't want to say anything that could break the spell, could make her grow angry and cold again, like she had this morning.

She was a superb dancer. Confident. Responsive. Far more graceful than Lillian, who'd bounded about too enthusiastically, always tending to lead rather than follow.

The touch of the satin of Caroline's dress under his hand at her back felt so intimate, more intimate than skin. It made him giddy with, if not happiness, something close to it. Relief and wonder and, most of all, gratitude. *This marvelous creature is my wife.*

Despite everything.

And then, the shadow thought that always followed it—that he'd lose her, too.

But no: she was in his arms now, wasn't she? Everything else fell away. The anger of their fight earlier, their suspicions, the worries about Ondine. All of it melted. He wheeled her effortlessly through the crowd of dancers. They were both so light. It was like being a leaf carried on the wind. As though they could fly, but only when they were a pair. A burble of laughter escaped from his mouth and she laughed in reply. How well they fit together, her body to his.

They were meant to be together. If only the rest of the world would go away.

Moving to America was a good idea—and Caroline's, of course. In America, Mark would not be constantly reminded of Lillian. There would be no relatives or friends to ask awkward questions. His past would fade away, immaterial to people who knew him only as Caroline's husband. He'd be a man with no life before, who existed only in relationship to Caroline. It was humbling but necessary. His gambling indiscretions would soon be forgotten. As little as he cared to say goodbye to England, he had to admit it was for the best.

Best for Ondine, too. They'll have a fresh new start, the three of them together.

"This is nice," Caroline said dreamily. "We should go dancing more often."

"We shall, in the future. We'll have a whole new life full of brand-new things."

She tilted her head the other way, following his lead, anticipating his moves. "Sorry it took so long to get away. I had the most difficult time with Miss Flatley. I tell you, *sacking* her cannot come a moment too soon."

He made a noncommittal sound, but something niggled at the back of his mind. *Sacking her.* There was something he'd forgotten to do . . . something important. He'd been too focused on other things. . . .

He remembered the split second Caroline spoke. "Have you spoken to the stewardess Miss Hebbley? Have you had a chance to tell her we'll no longer be needing her services?"

His stomach dropped to his feet. He stumbled, nearly bringing them both down on the dance floor.

She stopped dancing; luckily, they were at the edge of the floor and out of the way of the other dancers. It felt like the whole world continued to move without them, leaving them behind. It was dizzying. "You didn't, did you?" she said quietly.

Lying would only make things worse; he knew that much. "I'm afraid not. I didn't see her, and it slipped my mind—"

"How could you? She could drop in to see the baby anytime, even tonight while we are away from the room. I don't want to think of what she might do if we're not there."

"Oh, surely you're worrying over nothing." He thought he could make her see how silly she was being; he didn't realize that this was the worst thing to say until the words were out of his mouth.

The warm, golden glow had vanished—if it had ever existed.

Caroline froze. "This *is our child*. I thought we agreed that there is something wrong with Miss Hebbley and we don't want her around Ondine."

"I don't think *I* agreed there was something *wrong* with her—"

She pulled away from him, and his hands and the side of his face, which had been pressed to her cheek, suddenly felt cold and empty. "Mark, how could you? You did agree! I feel *betrayed*."

The words went through him like a dagger. He stood senseless while she hurried off, pushing her way through the crowd.

And ran into Guggenheim. He could just see her through the sea of people. His wife, just out of his reach. Her head bobbed furiously as she spoke. Guggenheim's hand fell on her shoulder. *There, there.* There was something possessive about that hand. Like they were already familiar. Had she known Guggenheim before they'd married?

I feel betrayed.

He'd be damned if he would run after her. He turned, looking for the bar. It was thick with men for whom the trays of champagne punch, circulating around the room, were no better than lemonade. He resolved to join them. He picked the thinnest part of the mass and waited his turn. He knew no one in the pack of dour, unhappy faces. He recognized some from the card tables but had not made their acquaintance. No one was inclined to make small talk with his neighbors; some even looked at their watches. Did even one man want to be here tonight?

A hand fell on his shoulder, firm and deliberate. Turning to confront whoever it was, Mark came face-to-face with a smiling blond man he'd seen with Dai Bowen.

"Do we know each other?" Mark asked.

Williams chortled. "Leslie Williams. I need you to come with me, Mr. Fletcher. Trust me: it's in your best interest."

It didn't seem a good idea, but he obeyed, even as the champagne he'd drunk burbled up in his stomach with curiosity. With dread. What did this man want?

Williams led him away from the crowd and down an alleyway that only the waiters seemed to be using. He found an empty closet and they stepped inside.

"What is this about?" Mark asked. He couldn't help but feel belligerent, didn't like standing in a dark closet with this man, breathing in his pomade, his breath reeking of liquor.

"David Bowen is me mate and he told me *all* about you. Everything. You'll be needing to keep me on your good side, that is if you don't want your wife to find out how you've been paying for your little habit." He paused for Mark's shock of recognition. "I have a proposition for you."

Mark thought about arguing with him. *I know how it looks, but it's not what you think. It's just that I'm low on cash here on the ship. . . . Your friend got it all wrong. Caroline knows what I'm doing. . . .* One look at the man's face and he knew he could save his breath.

"Why the glum face—it's not as bad as you think. You'll only have to do one thing for me and then you're off the hook."

Mark had to admit, it sounded pretty good. He'd needed something good tonight. For a wild second, Mark thought that maybe he was not terribly unlucky but terribly blessed—always falling down on his own mistakes, always receiving a miracle to lift him back up.

Williams took his silence for agreement. "I need you to get something out of storage for me. That's all. And you get to keep half. Half for you, half for me."

Williams wanted him to steal something. Not blessed, then. Going from bad to worse. "I'm not a thief."

"I beg to differ."

There was a time when he'd have fought a man for saying that about him, but it wasn't a dirty lie anymore.

Williams was grim faced. "You do this for me or your wife learns everything. Trust me, it's easy as falling down. And you'll walk away with good money, enough to buy your wife some new baubles."

There was no such thing as easy money. Hadn't he represented enough criminals to know this? "What is it?"

"I have it on good authority that Astor keeps a box of money down in storage."

"That's ridiculous. Why wouldn't the man keep it in the ship's safe with the rest of the valuables?"

Williams shrugged. "Who knows why rich people do anything? He may very well have another stash in the safe—all I know is I was told he keeps large sums of cash on hand. You find it. But don't damage the box: it's got to look like nothing's been done to it so they don't have any reason to look inside."

Mark looked befuddled. "That's it?"

"The Astors' luggage is in storage on the G deck, by the squash court. You'll need this." He passed a brass key to Mark.

He held it up to catch the light. A plain brass key, like the ones he'd seen used by the ship's staff. "Where'd you get this?"

"Never mind. Just get it back to me tonight."

"You want me to do this *now*?"

"There'll not be a better time. They've been moving luggage in and out of storage all day due to this ridiculous event—so many ladies requiring dresses they'd been saving for America. So many people coming and going, they can't keep track of them all. And now, everyone's up here enjoying themselves. No one will be on the squash court or down at the Turkish baths enjoying themselves. The place will be empty." The boxer had obviously thought this through.

Mark fingered the key. It was weighty. It felt like a sure thing. "How much money are we talking about?"

Mark tried to put everything else out of his head. Caroline, the argument, firing Miss Hebbley. The first order of business was going back to his cabin for an empty suitcase. He moved in that absent kind of way he was used to now, the way things were the morning after a bad night of gambling. How he'd stumble home, his mind straining to focus, his body fighting toward sobriety. How he'd mask the scent of alcohol with a stinging face tonic and a fresh suit; how he'd march through his workday thinking only of the feel of the cards in his hands, and how things would go differently the next night. Mark was very familiar with allowing his body to go through the motions of life while his mind followed the smoky, half-lit fantasies in his head, what he hoped for the future, or memories of a happier past.

Miss Flatley was there with a sleeping Ondine, but it was easy enough to throw her off the scent with a little white lie. Then he went straight down to the G deck, taking one of the back stairwells. Williams had been right: it was quiet as a tomb down there, his footsteps echoing up and down the empty alleyways.

Being away from the throng upstairs was calming. It was tranquil.

He wondered if he would run into any stewards in the storage room trying to bring organization back to the day's chaos. If he did, he figured he would pretend he'd come down to get something out of his luggage and leave it at that. However, he was rewarded with a room as still as a crypt. Sure enough, it was a mess, trunks and chests as big as pony carts left in heaps in the aisles. Suitcases were stacked haphazardly to the rafters. From the corners of the room, he heard the squeak of rats and tried not to think about them scurrying in the walls or weaseling their way into the suitcases, ready to spring out at him.

He clambered up and down the tight, twisty aisles, trying to figure out how the room was organized. By stateroom, it turned out. Logically, the Astors' baggage should be somewhere near his own. He had worked his way through the cavern for about thirty minutes when he found the Duff-Gordons' luggage, a veritable train. That meant the Astors' couldn't be far away.

And it wasn't. He found it, a mountain of boxes and suitcases taking up three whole compartments. They were the finest suitcases Mark had ever seen: oxblood leather trimmed with piping and mono-grammed *JJA*. Madeleine's appeared to be shagreen dyed a delicate shade of pear, and came in all sorts of odd sizes, ostensibly for hats and petticoats and other feminine accessories. Both husband's and wife's sets had matching trunks. Curiously, most were unlocked. Perhaps the Astors' staff thought the cases were safe behind the locked doors of the storage room.

It was all too easy, wasn't it? They were all the same, these people. They were like his wife—open, vulnerable, as if they believed that since the world fell to their feet, that things came easily to them, it must be that way for everyone. Ease. Freedom. Open windows. Un-locked doors.

Mark paused, hands hovering over the brass clasps. *Is this what I am now, a thief?* No, he refused to lie to himself: he'd been a thief for some time now, like Leslie Williams had said, a cowardly one. A thief who only dared steal from women who'd trusted him, who would never press charges if they found out. Once he stole from the Astors, he would graduate to the ranks of professional thief and there was no question that he'd be subjected to the full weight of the law if he was found out.

He'd been a barrister himself. He should know.

He started, trying hard to concentrate and remember how the suitcases had been arranged in the compartments so he could put them back without arousing suspicion. Many were filled with clothing—so much clothing, especially Jack's—but just as many con-tained bric-a-brac the Astors had picked up on their travels. Though after a minute, Mark realized it probably wasn't bric-a-brac at all but expensive artwork and antiquities. He poked through the swaddled objects just enough to satisfy himself that the money wasn't there. The locked cases he shook like wrapped Christmas presents to get a sense of what might be inside. He figured he could probably smash the lock or even cut through leather if he came across one that might be hold-ing the money.

Eventually, he found what he was looking for in the bottom of a trunk, hidden beneath some ancient pottery wrapped in butcher paper. A plain wooden chest. Under the lid was a shallow tray containing papers (probably important but summarily dismissed) and, under the tray, he found what he'd been looking for: eight-inch-high stacks of American paper bills. All denominations.

He tried to estimate the haul as he filled his empty suitcase. Twenty thousand dollars? More, easily. Giddy laughter nearly erupted from his mouth. He'd never felt like this before, like he could walk on air. Like he was no longer mortal. He was untouchable. He would never be unhappy again. He hadn't earned this money or won it, and so laying his hands on it was oddly unreal, as though it wasn't real money.

But real or imaginary, it made him delirious nonetheless. He wanted to laugh until he cried, though the thought also terrified him. He didn't want to know what would be at the end of the long tunnel of laughter.

He was halfway back to his stateroom, his mind dancing a jagged reel the entire time, half thrilled, half panicked, before he realized where he was and what he was doing. In a few minutes, he'd be back in his stateroom, hiding this suitcase from his wife. It occurred to him that he didn't *have* to tell Williams the truth. He could take out half the cash first and split the remainder with the boxer. Or he could give the boxer a measly thousand dollars, tell him that's all he could find—How would Williams know otherwise? The feeling of being in control—for once—left his head spinning.

This was how a professional thief thought.

He might as well get used to it.

He had to think like one, then. A professional would not keep the evidence on him, in his own room, where anyone might discover it, particularly Caroline. He couldn't carry it with him while he looked for the boxer; what if it were discovered on him, a suitcase full of evidence? No, he'd have to hide it, the way men buried treasure in walls and hidden patches of forest floor, unconnected to him should it be discovered, deniable but safely tucked away where only he knew where it was.

The ship was vast and likely full of hiding places, but unfortunately these weren't known to him. He simply hadn't spent any time exploring. How awful it would be if the suitcase were discovered, say by a child from third class hiding from his parents? Imagine the hue and cry then. No, he had to think of someplace foolproof. Someplace not too far from his cabin so he could get the case quickly and without raising suspicion.

His mind went to the fire in the smoking room. It had been a funny little alcove in the room, fitted to make the most of the ship's peculiar architecture, no doubt, but it had been deserted then—no one realized the room had been on fire, for god's sake. It might be deserted now.

He fairly jogged down the alleyway, going as fast as he dared without drawing attention to himself. When he entered the smoking room through the side entrance, however, he was surprised to see Annie Hebbley sitting in one of the chairs.

That was odd. He never saw the crew sitting—never. It might even be a rule, now that he thought about it. Passengers were never to see the crew relaxing.

Her position was quite funny, as though she were awake, but clearly she was asleep. Poor thing. She must've been run ragged getting her passengers ready for the ball. He'd overheard a steward saying this very thing to Miss Flatley. "Worst day in all my time at sea," he said, their heads bowed together so none of the passengers would overhear. It was probably all right to complain to one of the servants.

He was going to let her sleep so he could attend to the bag, when she suddenly stirred. Her eyelids fluttered. "Mark, is that you?"

It sent an icy finger down his spine. She had never called him by his given name before. Everything about her was different, her tone, the way she held herself. So much more casual, as though she were dealing with an equal. An intimate friend.

At the same time, there was clearly something wrong. Her words were slurred and mumbled. She rose but shakily, as though she had had too much to drink. Could she possibly be drunk? Drunk or not, she might see the suitcase. If questions came up later, she could testify as to having seen him with it. Panic began to fill his chest, flood his arms and legs. *Run. Run.* Leave it all, let someone else deal with the mess.

No, he had to keep his head.

He dropped the suitcase to his feet and took a step forward. "Miss Hebbley, are you all right? Do you need assistance?" He started toward her, arms outstretched, when she swooned, falling forward. It was all he could do to catch her before she fell. Holding her close, trying to bring her back to the chair, their heads drew near and he could not help but notice the scent of her hair—it was just like Lillian's. An oil she'd mixed herself to smooth tangles, and left her smelling like lavender and oranges. He'd never smelled the like of it on another woman and certainly did not recall smelling it on Miss Hebbley before.

The way Miss Hebbley felt in his arms just now. Her precise weight. Her precise warmth. The gentle give of her flesh. The softness of her skin. Lillian.

She looked nothing like her. And yet, in this moment, she was so like Lillian that, if he closed his eyes, he would swear she was with him.

He did close his eyes, to keep his tears from falling on the stewardess's face. He was hallucinating, he had to be. This damned ship, the damned journey. The stress of the robbery. The argument with Caroline. It was all driving him insane. Lillian was gone—and all the wishing in the world would not bring her back.

But for this moment, this one moment alone, the two of them without another soul nearby, he could have her back.

Chapter Thirty-One

Dai Bowen moved down the alleyway stiffly, feeling conspicuous as the sounds from the improvised ballroom fell away behind him. He was now three decks above the one where he should be, the noisy, stuffy cavern assigned to third-class passengers. Here, among the first-class cabins, everything was quiet and serene. Below, the walls were painted white and floors were barely varnished planks, well marked with spilled food and beer a scant few days into the maiden voyage. Here, the walls were polished mahogany, the floors carpeted. So heavy and rich, he could imagine being crushed beneath the weight of it all if the ocean should decide to have its revenge on these rich devils, pinned under an avalanche of luxury, helpless as he was dragged under the cold, unforgiving waves.

Every nerve in his body screamed out that he should not be here. *Go before someone discovers you.* His panic wasn't justified; he knew enough passengers in first class to come up with an excuse if questioned, and besides, they were having a good time still at the fancy party; but he couldn't shake the feeling that he didn't belong there and that this excursion would get him into trouble.

When he and Les had come up here the other night with Violet, it had all seemed frivolous, exciting even. Sure, he'd been nervous then, too. But this was different. He knew now what a loose cannon Les had become.

He knew now that he had to stop him from going any further.

Trouble was, Les had disappeared on him. Which was what had set him into a panic to begin with.

The only thing Dai could think was that he'd gone in search of another mark. He was doubtless behind one of these doors, but the doors were silent. He couldn't knock, hoping Les would answer. How would he find him? But he couldn't wait; he had to talk to Les. Worry ate at him like acid. He wouldn't last the rest of the journey at this rate; he'd climb the rails and throw himself into the ocean.

He started crooning in Welsh, a lullaby his mam had sung to him in the cradle.

Ni chaiff dim amharu'th gyntum
Ni wna undyn â thi gam
Nothing will disturb your slumber
Nobody will do you harm

Leslie would hear it, and know it was Dai.

But instead of finding Les behind one of the doors, Dai was surprised to find Les come around the corner a minute later, whistling, hands in his pockets.

"What are you doing, just taking a stroll?" Dai asked, alarmed.

Les looked just as surprised to see him. "As a matter of fact, I'm waiting for someone. Why are you here?"

"I was looking for you. To try one more time to talk you out of this crazy scheme of yours." Dai clasped Les's shoulders. "You have to stop this. Now. Before you're found out and arrested."

Les held a finger to his lips—*ssh*—and broke away, pulling Dai by the sleeve after him. He shoved Dai into the dark vestibule of a stairwell, where they would have privacy. "Are you mad? This is the most lucrative con I've ever done, and we'll not see the likes of it again. It's just a few more days, Dai. Then we're off this ship and we'll never cross paths with any of them again. Where's your nerve?"

262 | ALMA KATSU

"What's gotten into you, Les? We don't need the money. We have enough to get us to New York. . . ."

Les's laugh was grim. "Have enough money? You're fooling yourself, Dai. Look around you. Are we staying here in first class with these swells? No—we're crammed four to a room down in steerage. These people look down on us, Dai, though they've no right to. Aren't we as good as them? Of course, we are. But you'd never convince them of it."

"You're pulling a con on them. We're *not* as good as them."

"Don't be a fool. You don't think they got to where they are by conning the rest of us?"

"These people never hurt you. They don't deserve what you're doing to them."

"Oh, they deserve it all right. Maybe they haven't hurt us, Dai, but they've hurt someone like us."

"What if you get caught? You'll go off to jail, in a foreign country, where we have no idea what will happen to you. You've gotten too reckless. I can't take it anymore. I need answers from you, and I deserve them. Haven't I given up everything for you? Left my family behind, my career? Willing to risk it all for your sake—"

"Don't say it," Les cut him off. "You don't have to say it."

An ache formed in Dai's throat. "Is that because you don't feel it, too?"

"Don't be daft. I'm here with you."

Dai felt a chill run through him, like the ague. He was feverish and raw and ready to be sick. "Are you though? Here with me? One minute you are, and then you're gone again. Anything might happen. You could toss me over for that stewardess, or the first rich old lady who bats her eyes at you—"

A groan escaped from Les. He pivoted on his heel to face Dai. "You're being stupid, Dai. We're together, aren't we? I'm with you now. Why does anything else have to matter?"

Because it did. It always mattered. He wanted to believe Les,

but— "Everything's a con with you. You say one thing and do another. You told me tonight what you were going to do—but I find
you here, walking around first class whistling a happy tune! What's
that about, eh? Who are you conning, Les? Am I just another mark?"

Les wanted to get mad and yell in his face—Dai knew him well
enough to know that, could see it in the flex of his muscles beneath
his fancy new suit—but he held in his anger, somehow. "I found a
better con. A bigger one. And it's going off right now. That's what I'm
doing here, David Bowen. You've got to learn to trust me. You say
you care for me, but how can you, if you don't even trust me?"

"Do you really think I should trust you, Les?" Dai asked, his voice
wavering. It was a true question, one he didn't know the answer to.

"I can't say what you *should* do, Dai. Probably, you should run far,
far away from me. All I can answer is what I *want*."

Dai held his breath. "And what do you want, then?" His voice
came out a jagged whisper. Les's hands were on his arms.

Les pushed him, gently, until his back hit the wall of the vestibule.
His mouth was at Dai's ear. "You." The word brushed against his jaw,
featherlight—a chill. Les's lips found the spot just at the edge of his
jaw where his face had been punched so hard once he hadn't been
able to eat anything but broth for three weeks. And his lips found
their way to Dai's.

The hunger of it was almost too much. Both their bodies shook
with it. The scuffle was intense—the pulling at the wretched, strangling bow ties, the buttons. Dai swung him around so that Les was
now the one against the wall. Dai was the stronger one, after all. Always had been, even if he didn't always show it.

Just like Les didn't always show what he was showing now—the
baring of his soul. The insane connection they had; the way, in these
private moments, he seemed to worship Dai, worship his body, crave
it, become one with him. The way he'd get tears in his eyes. Dai
knew no one ever saw Les like this. No one but him. This was the real
Leslie Williams, and he was *his*—at least in the rushed, heated span of

these minutes in the stairwell. *He's mine*, Dai thought, tugging at Leslie's hands, at his clothes, his teeth scraping Les's tongue.

The heart wanted what it wanted. There was no arguing with it.

He leaned against the wall afterward, panting as Les arranged his clothing, making himself presentable again. Dai tucked his shirttails in, breathing hard, his whole body flushed. He was pulling on his jacket when he heard the clop-clop of a woman's shoes on the metal treads, and looked up just in time to see that they'd been caught.

~elle~

Chapter Thirty-Two

Lucy Duff-Gordon had left the ball early. It was pleasant enough, but what could you expect on a ship, even one as nice as the *Titanic*? The room was beautifully appointed, true, but there was no formal ballroom. There was too much carpeting for a proper dance floor. The ceilings, while high for a ship, were too low to create the right dynamics for sound, and there wasn't a full orchestra. The food had been good, lovely canapés, and the champagne passable, though diluted in a punch. She didn't mean to be critical, but it came naturally to her, a businesswoman, always looking for ways to make things better. She would never say a word to J. Bruce Ismay, the chairman of the White Star Line, who had overseen the arrangements tonight, but it had been more like a dance held in a country vicarage than a proper ball.

Cosmo was having a grand time, however, and so she hadn't bothered to try to pry him away. It wasn't every day he got to shoot the breeze with the likes of John Jacob Astor and Benjamin Guggenheim. The company of those silly American society people set her on edge. Even Astor—he was a strange bird. Always dressed so fantastically, so showy. And wed to that girl, practically the same age as Astor's own children. He was a man with no shame. It rubbed her the wrong way that her husband should be so fond of Astor, but then, her husband did a great many things that she couldn't see the sense of.

To each their own. That was the unspoken agreement between them.

Lucy took the stairs slowly, preferring a back stairwell to the grand central staircase. On the grand staircase, she always felt rushed, worried she'd catch a heel on the carpeting and go for a tumble. On these back stairwells, you could take as much time as you wanted. No one was watching.

She couldn't wait to get to her stateroom, to wrench off her shoes and put her feet up. She knew what was going on now, after stumbling across those two boxers in the stairwell, and it always made her happy to know things that no one else did. There had been no robberies. The big boxer, red-faced, had confessed it all to her. He had been ridiculously helpless for such a strong man, barely able to get the words out. They were working a con, he'd explained, but no thievery—just a few stints at fortune-telling. They didn't mean anyone harm, they were just trying to make a little extra money to start a new life in New York City.

It was disappointing to learn he wasn't so heroic after all, after she'd touted him to the others. She'd like to expose the deception to her fellow voyagers. Throw it in their faces. They had been so worried about their valuables despite the fact that no one could prove that anything actually had been stolen. Guggenheim had been particularly vocal, but her husband suspected Guggenheim was just afraid of what the "burglars" might find in his cabin. And now this boxer confirmed they'd taken nothing but secrets.

Only a very stupid person would be so careless as to keep her secrets somewhere they could be easily found, like in a valise or hatbox or tucked in with their silk unmentionables. A valet or ladies' maid could blackmail you just as effectively as a thief. Lucy knew these things, as one who had spent most of her adult life making sure her own secrets were well hidden.

There had been real fear in the boxer's eyes when he asked if she was going to turn them in. She couldn't, not two boys who shared the same secret as she. He hadn't admitted this to her, but she could read it on his face. The way his eyes softened every time he glanced in the other boxer's direction.

"You're playing a dangerous game," she told him before taking her leave of them, though she failed to say exactly *which* game she meant.

She could feel the pain of his circumstances, as if they'd been splashed over her as she passed him by. She could feel it because it had been her own, too. She still remembered the first woman who had broken her heart. Still remembered the terrifying urgency of the way they had kissed, the secrecy of every touch, of every *thought*.

It was surreally cruel—or it could be. You had to learn to navigate it. To sail slightly above it. To use men—husbands, business owners, the true controllers of society—to your benefit, to rise high enough that they couldn't hurt you there. Once you were high enough in it, you were safe. And then you could worry about your secrets in peace.

But there were other secrets she had to protect now, ones that made her past heartaches seem juvenile and sweet. Harmless. No— what she had to hide now was black as a starless city night and carried the scent of ash on its breath.

As soon as she got to her cabin, the first thing she would do, she resolved, would be to go through the sheaf of letters waiting for her review, letters from a solicitor who was helping her locate a new factory. He was to meet her at the hotel the day after they arrived in New York to start showing her properties.

She'd chosen to see the fire that had destroyed her business in London as an omen. Rather than let the tragedy ruin her—she'd lost not only her supplies and stock but all the seamstresses and pattern cutters trapped inside—she decided to view it as an opportunity. Fate's way of telling her to look to America. It certainly was a bigger market than England. Word was there was a surplus of talented seamstresses there, immigrants flooding into the country not only from Ireland

and England but Italy and Poland, too. More coming each week. Labor to replace all the workers she'd lost.

Plus, she could put all the bad press behind her. Let the solicitors and insurance men sort it out. Lucile Ltd. would carry a certain panache in New York City, rather than the taint of scandal.

Not that she was being blamed in London for the fire. There had not even been a hint of such a thing at the inquiry. It had been an old building but not decrepit. Not a firetrap. It had not been a workhouse, for goodness' sake.

The factory was where the sewing was done. Lady Duff-Gordon, when she went to work at all, went to the salon on Hanover Square where she met clients, her rich and titled friends. She chatted with them while mannequins walked about, wearing the current line. She could barely remember setting foot in the factory, though she was sure she had at some point.

That was why the incident haunted her. Guilt. Had she been negligent? She should've been there more frequently. If she had, who knows . . . maybe she would've noticed *something*. Not that she blamed the factory's manager: an overseer would never suggest to an owner that she ought to spend good money to spruce up a factory or warehouse. If she'd been more involved, she might've made a difference.

Then all those sweet girls wouldn't have died.

The memorial services had been written up in the papers for days, followed by angry letters about the shameful treatment of the working poor. Soapbox anarchists railed against the upper classes and exploitation of the masses. People in the streets wore black armbands in solidarity with the families.

She pushed these thoughts away.

One girl had survived, the *only* one to survive. Lillian Notting. She would've died that day if Lady Duff-Gordon herself hadn't sent her to deliver a dress to a client. She liked the women who did the final fitting with customers to be pretty. It made the right impression. Only the prettiest women were selected for the job. Lady

Duff-Gordon had spied Lillian Notting at the salon one day, sent from the factory to deliver a sample dress for a particularly demanding client. The girl had shown up, hugging the dress box to her chest, all out of breath, disheveled black hair falling out from her hat, the apples of color bright on her cheeks, and Lady Duff-Gordon knew right away that the girl was wasted in the factory, no matter how good her needlework. She remembered, too, the slight pang of desire for the pretty young girl. Maybe she would invite her to the house one day for tea to ask about her aspirations. Lady Duff-Gordon did that some-times, in order to make a harmless offer. *Come work more closely with me. You may see your fortunes rise.* Sometimes it led to good things—for both Lucy and the girl. And Cosmo never minded.

To each their own.

Lady Duff-Gordon recalled with a jolt that Lillian Notting had been delivering a dress to Caroline Fletcher that day, the same Caroline Fletcher who was on this ship. Lady Duff-Gordon forgave herself the slip: it had been Caroline Sinclair at the time, the young widow not yet remarried. She even remembered the dress: blue silk, a pecu-liar shade of hyacinth that Caroline had insisted on. Why had she not remembered Caroline earlier? Caroline hadn't mentioned it, perhaps not knowing that Lady Duff-Gordon was the Lucy of Lucile Ltd. A shiver ran through her, like someone had walked on her grave. It was not a good coincidence, a favorable coincidence. Stead, the old fool, was right about one thing: there *were* spirits of the dead, and they were everywhere. They hung about, an invisible smoke.

A draft slithered over her shoulders and through the silk of her dress. Her thoughts had made her cold. As soon as she was settled, she'd order chamomile tea to warm her up—and calm her down.

The ship lurched suddenly underfoot, and she almost slipped. She had gotten used to the ship's lumbering rhythm after the first day and almost didn't notice anymore. Only when the sea got a little rougher, like tonight.

Lady Duff-Gordon was surprised to see a silhouette in the window of the door at the end of the alleyway, a door that led to the promenade. It looked like a woman was out on the deck. At this hour in the evening, however, that was impossible. Besides, it was freezing outside, the temperature dropping steadily all day.

Lady Duff-Gordon passed her stateroom and continued toward the door. Perhaps the door had jammed and the poor woman couldn't get back inside . . . Maybe she'd panicked and didn't think to look for another way in. She would freeze in no time out there. Lady Duff-Gordon couldn't bear the thought of another woman dying, not if she could do something about it *this time*. She started jogging, lifting the hem of her gown to keep from tripping.

She got to the door, reached for the handle—and froze.

It was dark and the lights in the hall were dim, but now that she was close, Lucy could see the woman and she didn't look like she belonged in first class. This woman was disfigured. She was a ghastly sight. She looked as though she had been clawing at her own face. A gash, a wicked thing made by a knife or razor, ran diagonally from one eyebrow and over the bridge of her nose and on to open one cheek. With growing horror, Lady Duff-Gordon realized she looked like an escapee from an asylum. Her head was shorn, the hair raggedly hacked off. Her eyes smoldered like burning embers.

Most disturbing, she looked slightly familiar.

Lady Duff-Gordon pulled her hand back. She couldn't let a madwoman—if that's what she was—loose in first class. Maybe the poor thing had wandered above deck from steerage—what other explanation could there be?—but that didn't mean Lady Duff-Gordon could allow her access to the first-class cabins.

Still . . . mad or not, the woman would freeze if Lady Duff-Gordon didn't let her in.

She wished there was someone else in the hall, someone she could ask for help, but she was alone.

No—she couldn't let this woman die. Her conscience throbbed like an open wound.

After one more second's hesitation, Lady Duff-Gordon pushed the door open (noticing not the slightest sign of sticking) and stepped onto the deck.

But where had she gone? The woman had vanished. Lady Duff-Gordon looked left, then right, her vision not going far in the blackness. Her breath rose in a ghostly white plume before her face.

Without warning, a hand clamped over her mouth.

She started, but another hand dug into her upper arm.

"Shush," a man whispered in her ear. "Don't move. You'll scare her away."

It was Mr. Stead, the strange old man, the occultist. She nodded and Stead removed his hand from her mouth. His hand was covered with ink stains as though he'd been scribbling for hours. "You see her, too?"

"The spirit."

Lucy felt herself shaking.

"Bah. She's gone now," he said, looking bewildered and upset—sad, even.

She glanced around them, but there was nothing but the darkness, the rush of wind, the night wrapping around their great ship, and the pinpricks of stars, far above it all, blinking and cold.

The water was a froth around her head, a swirl of bubbles, rushing and flowing all around her. Water buffeted her in all directions. Water never stood still, was never dormant, was never satisfied. Water was always rushing somewhere and everywhere.

With the water came the voices, carried far and wide.

You don't understand, dear: he lost the business. He says he was forced out by those terrible Standard Oil fellows. How could you not have heard about it? It's been in all the papers. . . .

She's gone and gotten herself pregnant. Ruined her life, and for what? Anyone could see his intentions were not honorable. I don't know what we'll do if the neighbors ever find out. . . .

His prospects are better in America, he says. There's no work here. He'll send for us when he's gotten established. No, I don't like it, but what can I do. . . .

Bubbles brushed her cheeks, lifted her hair, carried it—long and black and flowing, like seaweed—on the tide. She turned her head away, but she could still hear them. You could never escape the voices.

I don't want to spend the rest of my life as a maid. . . .

You're fooling yourself if you think it'll be any better. . . .

They never learned, it seemed. Never changed. You couldn't save them from themselves. The best you could hope for was to save a few—the young, the willing. The innocent.

1916

Chapter Thirty-Three

19 November 1916
HMHS *Britannic*

Even at night, the ward is no place for a man to think.

The beds are mostly empty as *Britannic* is steaming toward Mudros, where—he has been told—it will take on the majority of its patients. The patients who came aboard with Mark in Naples have been situated together to make it easier for the nurses and orderlies, and when he'd been placed among them, Mark found he was surrounded by men for whom sleep is painful. He'd lain on his cot, listening to them whimper and gnash their teeth, plagued by bad dreams. Some mumbled as though in conversation. Others thrashed, fighting enemies left behind on distant shores. Now, in the smaller, more private room, there are only the cries of one lone patient to contend with.

Beside his own.

It's the exhaustion that has mostly kept him bedbound. He's mobile, though, capable of walking about with the use of a cane, though Nurse Jennings prefers he not do it alone. He cannot lie still any longer, not when every time he closes his eyes, he fears opening them again, fears seeing that eerily familiar pale face hovering above his. Those strangely vacant, searching eyes. No matter that it is night—night and day have become the same to him anyway. He rises, puts on his drab, military-issue dressing gown, and reaches for his cane, the feel of it glossy and foreign in his hand.

The dining hall is sparsely populated with others who have also given up on sleep, mostly men sitting by themselves in the dark. One man reads under an electric light, the single bulb casting him in a shaft of light. A quartet plays a serious hand of cards at a far table. In the old days, he would've itched to join them, but nowadays the sight of a deck of cards turns his stomach.

He chooses a chair and sits in the dark, fingering the top of his cane like he's nursing an old grievance. *Annie Hebbley is still alive.* Seeing her has released a flood of memories that he had painstakingly packed away. He had woken up in that hospital in New York after the *Titanic*'s sinking to be told that he'd lost the only two people in the world who mattered to him: Caroline and Ondine. It had taken months—years, really—to claw his way back from that. At first, he didn't want to bother. Madness or suicide seemed infinitely easier and less painful than trying to find a way to go on.

It was only after nearly half a year of distance that he could face the *Titanic*'s list of the dead, checking to see who among the people he'd met on board were no more. He was shocked at how many had perished—especially the wealthy Americans, clinging to some notion of chivalry that seemed to have escaped the British aristocrats who'd managed to find a seat in a lifeboat, like Sir Duff-Gordon and J. Bruce Ismay. Cosmo Duff-Gordon appeared to be in trouble for escaping in one of the lifeboats, and subsequently offering the crewman bribes to row away from the foundering wreck. *Serves him right*, Mark thought. Better men—Astor, Guggenheim, Stead—were missing and presumed dead. Months and years of inquiries and lawsuits were still to come.

He counted himself among this unholy lot of cowards. He heard the story of his rescue after he'd regained consciousness, how he'd been fished out of the frigid waters adrift, his life belt not yet waterlogged. He'd bobbled close to one of the lifeboats that had been sent off not close to full, and one of the occupants harangued the others into bringing him in. His life since the sinking has been one long nightmare, starting when he woke in a New York City hospital. They'd had to amputate several of his toes, but he was told he was extraordinarily lucky: few men had been pulled out of those frigid waters alive. He'd been unconscious for days. By the time he woke, the entire world had learned about the great tragedy at sea. *Titanic* survivors were being feted around town, made to give speeches, written up in the newspapers.

He wished he could track down that good Samaritan and tell her she shouldn't have bothered: there wasn't a less deserving man on that ship. She should've saved her good deed for old man Stead, or somebody who'd done an ounce of good in his life. She'd wasted it on him.

Finding out that he'd lived when his wife and child had died only made it worse.

He had one thing to be grateful for: Lillian's journal had survived. His hand went to his breast pocket, where he always kept it. Somehow it survived the hours in the sea after the *Titanic*, as though it was meant to be. As though Lillian's memory was meant to survive long after everything else fell away. The dried pages of the journal crinkled softly under the press of his hand. *There, there.*

For a long time, he hadn't been able to accept the news, especially concerning Ondine. He wanted to believe that she was still alive, that she had been rescued but that the authorities, with no clue to her identity, handed her over to a foundlings' society or orphanage. She might still be in some cheerless institution, raised without love, like a child in one of Mr. Dickens's sad stories. Or maybe she had been adopted, raised to believe she was someone else, never told about the *Titanic* connection, the adoptive parents waiting until she was grown and better equipped to handle the tragic truth. If she were alive, she would be four now. After a time, he started to realize that when he imagined his daughter alive, he pictured her like Lillian, a gorgeous child as radiant as the sun, but with hair dark and reckless, tangled and wild.

He had become an imposter in his own life, in his own skin. His former self had died a long time ago—perhaps before he'd even set foot on the ship. He didn't know who he'd become. Maybe he was a ghost, and this was all a version of purgatory.

He didn't bother informing Caroline's family of their marriage. What would have been the point? When the ship's manifest was questioned—after all, he and Caroline had been registered as man and wife—Mark swore to Caroline's grieving father than it was a clerical error, that he'd never met his daughter. Mark wanted no part of Caroline's fortune and had no interest in ruining a father's memories of his beloved dead daughter. She belonged to her father; Mark wasn't sure, in retrospect, that he'd ever really known her at all.

Eventually, Mark stomached the overseas journey so he could come home to London, where he hid in his dark little apartment until the war broke out. It had, strangely, been a kind of relief. The idea of the world ripping itself apart—as if everyone had gone mad. It made him feel less alone. Perhaps the world had always been a cruel, savage place, and now, at least, the truth was out in the open. It no longer needed to be his own private misery, a dark secret eating him from the inside.

Besides, the idea of joining the war effort appealed to him: he'd just as soon die on a battlefield as go slowly mad in his bitterness and solitude. Maybe on the muddy fields of the Balkans or in the hills of Gallipoli, he could reclaim his honor.

In the four years since the *Titanic*, Mark had managed to whittle his life down to almost nothing: a two-room flat, days spent as a clerk in an accounting house, nights pacing the floor or out walking until he was exhausted and could fall asleep. Sundays were his day of penance, when he would go to various cemeteries and sit before graves that served as substitutes for the watery resting places of Lillian, Caroline, and Ondine.

How did his life come to this, a near hermit, miserable and alone? He thinks back to the happiest time of his life, the months after Ondine's birth when he and Lillian lived with Caroline. An unconventional life to be sure, and constrained: he could tell no one about it at the time. But he'd trade anything to have those days back again.

He makes his way around the ship, heading back to his hard, narrow cot. His progress is slowed by the cane, especially on the steep stairwells. The sound of his footsteps and the thump of the cane seem disproportionately loud in the still of night, and he feels like a monster in a nightmare chasing down a frightened child. He looks into the patients' ward, expecting to see Annie. He hasn't seen her anywhere: not in the halls, not in the wards. She is nowhere to be found, a thought that is hauntingly familiar. He's been in this very position once.

He pushed her away. He saw the look of confusion and hurt in her eyes. He knew, without understanding why, how intense the knife of betrayal had been. How she seemed to crumple inward at it, at his insistence that they stay apart.

What have you done, Annie?

Could she have thrown herself overboard? *Get a hold of yourself, man.*

Doesn't she know that he is cursed, that loving him is a curse? He's responsible for the deaths of two women. Wonderfully smart and vibrant women whom he did not deserve. They didn't just die after falling in love with him, either—they died after he'd broken them, made their hearts bleed in pain.

He won't be responsible for yet another.

It's clear there will be no going to sleep tonight—not without drink. Back at his cot, he eases open the tiny locker at the foot of his bed for his gentleman's flask. He rattles it: about a quarter full. The nurse on duty won't like it if she catches him drinking, though many of the men do it.

He downs swig after swig, not bothering to pause long enough to taste it. He just wants to knock himself out. But it isn't worry over

Annie that makes him so desperate. It's what he can't forget or forgive: what he did to Lillian.

And what he did after, too—days after Lillian's body was found, pulled from the Thames. The memory of it replays in his head, again and again, as he drifts into a thick sleep:

How he got down on his knee and proposed to Caroline.

Chapter Thirty-Four

"You don't have to say anything," Annie whispers.

Mark startles awake.

She can smell whiskey on his breath.

He is afraid to see her again—his eyes are full of hatred. But this time she is prepared. While he slept, she gently strapped his arms down to the bed so that he could not protest or push her away.

"Shh," Annie says calmly. "I understand, Mark. I really do. I understand that you don't want to relive the past and, though it hurts me, I forgive you. But—let me speak. I've come for another reason: I'd like to help you restore your life. Because you said you were alone in the world—but you're not, Mark. Ondine is still alive. She survived the sinking. Didn't they tell you?"

It's as though a switch has been thrown and the deadened, resigned man comes alive in front of her. "What are you talking about?"

She is happy to be the one to tell him this, to be the one to bring joy back into his life. He obviously has been suffering since the sinking. Now his life will be better and he will have her to thank for it. "I was there when Caroline . . . drowned. I dove into the water after her. I helped save the baby. Only I was injured and lost consciousness. I don't know what happened to her afterward, but I know Ondine is alive, Mark."

He stares at her in disbelief. "Why are you telling me this now? Why didn't you try to get in touch with me after the accident?"

She feels attacked. "I didn't know you survived that night, did I? I told you: I was injured. I've been ill, and only recently got better." She doesn't want to go into details, to tell him about Morninggate, the lost years, the voices, the uncertainty. The past is the past. She resolved to put it all behind her as though it had never happened.

She tries to take his hand, but it is still strapped down. "I can help you find her, Mark. The first thing is that we must go to New York. They'll have records of the survivors there. They'll be able to tell you what happened to your daughter, where they sent her. I'll go with you. You won't have to find her on your own."

But he doesn't look comforted. He is still angry with her.

Worried, Annie tries again. "You must believe me, Mark: I only want what's best for Ondine. That's all I've ever wanted. I'm terribly sorry to have to tell you this, Mark, but it is the truth: there's something else, something you didn't know about."

He's not paying attention to what she's trying to tell him, however. "Where did you get that?" He is looking at her brooch. Tries to point at it but realizes he's bound to the bed. "Did you steal that from my wife?"

She persists. "Your wife is *dead*, Mark." She lets him absorb those words, feel the weight of them. "Those terrible things happening on the *Titanic*? It was exactly as Mr. Stead told us. A spirit was behind them."

"Enough, Annie! Stop," Mark barks at her, yanking his wrists out of their bindings. His tone is sharp and abrupt, like a slap. She pulls back, stunned.

He rubs his face, which has gone as dark as a thundercloud. "I can't listen to this nonsense anymore." Is it her imagination or does he look guilty? "You know nothing about it. I can see you're out of your wits. The trouble on the *Titanic* obviously had its effects on you."

Annie feels herself shaking, crying. It's mortifying. But he's pushing her away *again,* and she doesn't think she can bear it.

"No, now don't cry. I'm not angry. Only worried for you."

But it's too much, his pity. It only makes everything worse.

She flees, feeling more desperate and disoriented than ever. She thought the story of Ondine, above all, would change him. Would make him see.

But something—or someone—has clearly turned him against her from the start.

She reaches into her pocket, for the item that she had discovered after tying his wrists, while patting down his bed. A notebook of some kind. She'd slipped it away to look at later; he'd woken up before she'd had a chance to open it.

But now she pulls it out and sees that it's a small journal. She had seen Mark carrying it close to his chest on the *Titanic*—opening it here and there in the smoking room when he thought no one was watching. When no one *was* watching . . . except for her.

She opens it to the first page, and a chill runs through her at the name inscribed, even though she had known, had suspected all this time, what she would see written there.

Lillian Notting.

1912

WESTERN UNION, April 14, 1912

FROM SS *CARONIA*
7:10 a.m.

Captain, 'Titanic.' Westbound steamers report bergs, growlers, and field ice in 42N from 49 to 51W April 12th.—Compts. Barr.

FROM SS *BALTIC*
11:55 a.m.

To Captain Smith, Titanic, Have had moderate variable winds and clear fine weather since leaving. Greek steamer Athenai reports passing icebergs and large quantities of field ice today in lat 41.51N long 49.52W. . . . Wish you and Titanic all success.—Commander.

FROM SS *CALIFORNIAN*
6:30 p.m.

For Captain Smith, Titanic: Ice sighted at 42.3N, 49.9W.—Compliments, Captain Lord.

Chapter Thirty-Five

14 April 1912
Titanic

Caroline woke to a scream.

A woman's scream.

It took a moment before she could place that it had come *from* her dream, from her own past. She had been with Mark that night. She would remember it always, every second of it: how they'd stolen off to a small room in the attic where there was no chance of being discovered. How they rushed, not even taking off all their clothes. Shushing each other, so afraid of being overheard. They couldn't let Lillian know.

Caroline opened her eyes, letting them adjust to the darkness in their stateroom. The *Titanic* swayed gently beneath her bed.

Her hand felt around for Mark's reassuring presence, but he wasn't there. Instead, there was a warm hollow in the mattress. A depression, too, on the pillow. Despite these discoveries, she couldn't shake the feeling that it was all wrong. This was not the shape Mark usually left behind in their bed, the scent lingering on the air—of a heavy citrus and musk cologne—was not Mark's. This didn't even feel like the blanket that was on their bed: this one was woven silk, rich as anything she'd ever felt in her life.

Where was she?

She sat up too fast and felt the room spin. She clasped a hand over her mouth, afraid that she was going to be sick. After a few morbid wobbles, the spinning stopped.

The scream was now only a distant echo in her mind. It had been replaced by the sound of water running. Water sloshing in a tub. The occasional low rumble of a man's voice. A man talking to himself while he bathed.

It was not Mark's voice.

Her stomach lurched again. Tiny snippets of scenes played in her head. The dream had dissipated; reality was taking its place. The last thing she remembered was the ball. The chandeliers, too bright. The crowds of women and men in evening dress. Candlelight glinting off silk and satin, jewels and gold. Music and conversation.

The fight with Mark. The suspicion, tangling itself around her heart. Not really that he'd dallied with Annie, or wanted to. Only that he didn't love *her,* Caroline, that he was incapable of it, after everything that had happened.

Then she remembered: leaving the dance floor. On someone else's arm.

She knew where she was: Benjamin Guggenheim's room.

In a flash, she bolted out of the bed and stood on uncertain legs in the center of the ruby-red Axminster rug. How had this happened?

She pressed a hand over her eyes. She remembered taking a bit too much of her medication. She would've preferred to stay in that night with Ondine, but Mark had already left for the ball, she recalled now, and she was afraid of making him even madder by standing him up. She remembered Mark taking her hand and leading her onto the dance floor—and it had been heavenly dancing with her husband, something they hadn't done in a long time. It had felt so good, as good as the best times they'd ever had. And then they were arguing over that stewardess. And then Mark disappeared.

Her gown was draped over a chair in a way that told her it had been done by a valet. *Someone had seen her here, in another man's bed.* Shame crested high in her chest. She thought she might faint.

I've made a terrible mistake.

Last night, she'd been upset after Mark had left. She'd told Guggenheim she needed air, expecting the millionaire to bow courteously and leave, but he had followed her outside. They'd stood at the railing. The night air had felt delicious at first, washing away her overheated anger. He'd said he could tell she was upset and encouraged her to tell him what was troubling her—and God help her, she did. He listened as she spoke, and the way he watched her made her feel she was the only woman on earth. He made no attempt to interrupt or to tell her what he thought, or explain why Mark did the things he had. He merely listened, which Caroline noted with the greatest relief.

Eventually, the conversation turned to other things. She spoke of her father in Pennsylvania and how she looked forward to seeing him again and to simply being in America, where she knew what was expected of her. What to say, how to act.

"You were quite brave to have your child overseas," Guggenheim remarked as they stared over the great black expanse.

Her cheeks warmed—the task she most dreaded was explaining Ondine to her father. Though Caroline *had* written to tell him she was bringing Mark; still, the marriage would be a surprise. Better for her father to have met Mark before she broke the news to them. He'd like Mark's levelheadedness, his intellect, his manners.

Or so she had thought. Now, she wasn't sure what to do.

"You're cold," Benjamin had said, running a finger over the goose bumps on her arm. The blessed relief had turned to chill and set her teeth to chattering. People strolled by in furs and heavy coats, eyeing her with curiosity—or perhaps it was disdain. They might've recognized Guggenheim and knew of his reputation. "Let's go to my rooms for a drink. I have something that will warm you up."

Guggenheim sent his servants away and poured cognac himself. Caroline took in his stateroom as he made the drinks. It gave the impression of being different from hers, but certainly that couldn't be. Nevertheless, it seemed warmer. Richer. The chairs were draped with ornate tapestries. A beautiful chess set, the pieces cut from stone, waited on the table, midplay. A heavy perfume hung in the air, spicy and musky. Through the door, she saw into the bedroom, a burgundy silk dressing gown hanging from a hook on the wall. It was, in every respect, a man's room, more so than any study or billiard room or hunting lodge she'd ever been in, Guggenheim's own stamp all over it.

As they sipped, he'd talked about himself. He had to be her father's age, but Caroline found him easy to be with. Every conversation with Mark had gotten so fraught. Ondine, money, where to live, how to spend their lives—every subject was a problem, likely to set off a confrontation. She was tired of walking on eggshells around him. Of feeling like she always had to defend herself or apologize for her wishes.

It was easy being with Guggenheim. Perhaps because they both had money—his fortune was ridiculously greater, of course, but the principle was the same. They both had the same way of looking at life.

"I hate to see you suffer for making one bad decision," Guggenheim said, caressing the back of her hand very lightly with his index finger. They had swung around back to talking about her marriage. "One bad, hasty decision. I've made bad decisions, too. Hasn't everyone? Should we be made to suffer for it for the rest of our lives?"

That was what she'd done with Mark—acted hastily. She'd only gotten close to him because of Lillian. Maybe it was Lillian she had loved all along, and never Mark. Mark had been a handsome distraction, a conduit to Lillian. But it was Lillian who'd held her heart, whom she mourned deeply.

The thought brought her to the brink of tears.

What was Guggenheim saying now? Minutes slipped by in a honeyed haze. They were sitting side by side on the settee now, Guggenheim's arm on her shoulders, weighing her down, drawing her close. The smell of spice and musk was intense now, filling her lungs and her head. The cognac had numbed her lips, making it hard to speak. He explained how things were, what she could expect. That he had a wife with whom he had not been close for years but could not leave. Children who were taught to care little for their father and would inherit everything. But he still needed companionship.

"I sense that we are unusually compatible, Caroline. I would like to find out. Would you like that, too?" His breath smelled of cigars and cognac and was warm in her ear. He brushed her cheek.

She turned her head and found his mouth on hers. It was a gentlemanly kiss, not opportuning. Not strong either, like Mark's. Mark's kisses were always hungry. Guggenheim was testing her—gentle, almost teasing in its hesitance. She kissed him back, drawing courage from the cognac. She cupped his smooth cheek, stroked it. *This is the sort of man I should be with*. She remembered thinking that if she said it to herself enough times, she would come to believe it.

She felt safe with him, she told herself.

Or at least, she felt safe in her loneliness. Felt it was, somehow, matched.

Now, as she moved through the empty hallways, past the quiet bustle of the few stewards who were awake this early, preparing for the day, she saw the truth in the darkness: she had done a terrible thing. Her life was turning to ash, crumbling around her.

She slipped into their stateroom, noticing with some concern that the door seemed to have been left open by a tiny sliver—perhaps it hadn't been shut firmly in the night and had drifted open with the movement and sway of the ship, though the detail gave her an eerie sense of misgiving. She closed it soundlessly behind her. By some miracle, Mark was in bed. She expected to find him awake, in his dressing gown, arms crossed, a storm brewing on his face, ready to fly at her. *Where were you? Where have you been all this time?* But his gentle snores drifted in from the other room.

She eased out of her gown—a hideous thing to her now, a reminder of her perfidy, fit only for burning—and into a dressing gown. Standing over her dressing table, her fingers found the packet of cocaine Dr. Leader had prescribed for her. She was so eager for the medicine that she almost spilled the contents of the glassine envelope all over her vanity set, but she managed to tap powder into the water glass and add water as she'd been instructed. It was more powder than she was supposed to take in one dose, but she gulped it down anyway. A little more now and then, what difference did it make?

She stood over the crib to look at Ondine. It always soothed her to look on the baby while she was sleeping. So peaceful, so blissfully unaware of life's tribulations. Sometimes, it frightened Caroline to think that she was responsible for another life now, but usually it made her happy. Happy to have someone who would love her without reservation. Someone to raise, to protect. Someone who would be with her always. Tonight, she felt guilty looking down on the sleeping baby. She'd betrayed Ondine's father. The future was now suddenly very uncertain. Very unclear.

Without any warning, the baby started to cry. Or not cry, not exactly. It was like no sound Ondine had ever made before. It was more like choking, a strangled, muffled sound. It was a sound designed to fill a parent with sheer, unadulterated panic. Caroline snatched her up but then could not think what to do as the child blinked her eyes open, crying and—no, choking. What in the world could Ondine be choking on? Without thinking, she flipped her over her arm, patting her roughly on the back. It didn't seem to help. Panic overwhelmed her. And irrational, confusing questions flooded her mind in outrage. What would fit in that tiny mouth of hers? Could that terrible Miss Flatley have left something in the crib? Caroline lifted the baby, trying to see into her mouth. As the seconds ticked by and the strange gargling sound continued, Ondine turning redder in the face, beginning to gasp, Caroline—not knowing what else to do—jabbed her fingers straight into the back of Ondine's throat.

There. *There.* She felt it, whatever it was. Something solid and metallic. She began to pull.

A hand gripped her shoulder. She almost dropped the baby as she spun around. It was Mark, his eyes blazing. "What are you doing? Give her to me." He didn't wait for Caroline to surrender Ondine, ripping her out of his wife's hands.

Caroline stood trembling, nerves fluttering. What had just happened? The crying had stopped. Mark was across the sitting room with Ondine lying over his shoulder. The baby was cooing at him, as she always seemed to do with Mark, and he was making soothing noises in return. . . . *There, there, it's all right now.* . . .

"There was something wrong with the baby," Caroline said. Her voice sounded frightened and apologetic. "I was trying to help—"

"I don't know what you're talking about. She's fine," Mark said over his shoulder at her. Why was he keeping Ondine so far away? She wanted to hold her daughter, to reassure herself that everything was all right.

"Didn't you hear? She was making this awful noise—"

"The only thing I heard was *you*," Mark said. His voice dripped with recrimination. "You're off your head—as usual, lately. You've taken more of your *medicine*, haven't you, Caroline? Too much, I'd say."

"What are you going on about?"

"It's almost morning—do you really need to be taking that stuff at this hour?"

So, it was. Outside the porthole, the sky was lightening. She hadn't thought about it. Taking the medicine was reflex now.

Mark nodded in her direction. "I've heard that some people have gotten really sick on cocaine . . . And it can make you dependent on it, like opium. You ought to take it easy—"

She slammed a hand on the dressing table. "I'm following the doctor's instructions. . . . This is medicine."

She waited for him to say something soothing. *There, there, my poor dear, you've been through so much.* To stroke her back, fetch her some water. But he didn't. He turned away, still dandling the baby.

She sucked in a breath and held it. Everything felt wrong. She couldn't be sure guilt wasn't warping her perception. The air was chillier, the silence more ominous. But something was definitely wrong with Mark. The way he was looking at her, as though he wished she would disappear. As though he *hated* her. And he hadn't asked where she'd been. Did he not care? Had he guessed? Could he smell another man on her or figure it out from the sad set of her mouth?

"I'm going to lie down with Ondine to get her to go back to sleep," Mark said wearily, crossing to the bedroom. He closed the door behind him.

Caroline leaned over the crib, her tired gaze settling on the empty spot where her baby had been. Maybe Mark was right; maybe the medicine was to blame for what was happening to her. She seemed to be slowly losing her mind. He was right that she had been taking a lot of it lately; every time something upset her, she went for more powder. The envelope was almost empty and she was dreading going to Dr. Leader to ask for more. Maybe it was a blessing in disguise. Time to taper off.

And what of Ondine? If Mark had decided that she was dependent on this medicine, he might take the baby away from her. They were married, it would be within his legal rights. That idea put a chill down her spine. She could lose Ondine forever.

She reached into the empty space of the crib, as though she would be able to feel Ondine there still.

What was this, tucked in one of the blanket's folds? Her hand found something hard and cold and metallic. And damp.

And she knew—it was the object she'd felt in Ondine's throat. She *had* been choking. Caroline had saved her.

She pulled it from the tangle of blanket, like a ribbon laced through a grommet. What was this, lying in the crib with Ondine like a serpent in the garden?

It was a crucifix on a chain. A tiny gold crucifix.

Chapter Thirty-Six

The world came at Annie all at once with a jolt. It shook beneath her, like that time in Ballintoy when she stood on the cliff as a great wall of dirt and stone sheared off and fell into the ocean.

But the world kept shaking. Her mind scrambled to try to make sense of it. She was on a ship, the glorious *Titanic*. Why would it be shaking?

Her eyes finally were able to focus and she saw Violet leaning over her, jostling her, her loose hair dangling in Annie's face. Her look of fright gave Annie a fright, too.

Violet released Annie's shoulders. "Thank Jesus you're awake. I was afraid there was something wrong with you. You were having a seizure, your eyes rolling in your head and lips pulled back from your teeth. I never seen anyone in such a state. I thought you might be possessed by a demon, like the priests warned us about in school."

Annie stared up at Violet. She wished her friend was playing a joke on her, but it was plain that she wasn't. A shudder ran through her.

"Have you ever had seizures before?" Violet asked.

Annie rubbed her face. "Never." The last she'd heard of a seizure was the little boy—the Astors' servant.

"Maybe you should go see the ship's surgeon. Make sure you're all right."

Annie rubbed her upper arms. Cold. So, so cold. How could this ship be so cold, with its big, roaring engines and fires going all day and all night? The tiny cabin was freezing. Her cheeks were cold, as were the tips of her nose and ears. Her fingers and toes.

She heard murmurs and other noises in the cabins to her left and right. That meant the rest of the staff was rising. "No, no. I'd better get to work." Mustering her resolve, Annie sat up in bed, sucking in breath as cold slipped over her bare head and arms like a garment. She scrambled out of bed and started dressing quickly. Her clothing was icy to the touch, as though it'd been left outdoors. Gritting her teeth, she pulled on her petticoats as quickly as her numb fingers would let her. Lastly, she splashed water sparingly on her face. It was ice-cold, like it had come straight from a frozen creek.

Violet stood watching her dress. "What happened to you, Annie?"

Annie stopped, her dress dangling in her hands. "What do you mean?"

Violet gestured to Annie's arms, where she looked down to see bruises the size of fingers. There was a nasty one on her ankle, too, and another on her upper thigh. She had no recollection of how she might've gotten them. Possibly it was in the course of her duties. The ship could buck like a wild horse when the weather turned bad and you could find yourself suddenly thrown into a railing or tossed against a wall, especially if you were frequently hurrying about the narrow servants' halls carrying heavy trays.

And then she realized they were from Madeleine Astor.

"It's nothing. They don't hurt," she said, hoping to deflect Violet's curiosity.

Violet shrugged and finished readying herself, prattling on about scuttlebutt she'd heard over breakfast that morning, the first officer warning that it was so cold there might be ice in the water. Annie only half listened as she put on her dress and shoes, trying not to let fear creep into her—fear of what William Stead had told her: that there very well might be an evil spirit on this ship. And that she could be one of its victims.

She hurried to straighten the bed and begin her day, but when she pulled at the blue and white blankets to tuck them in, she felt something silky at the tips of her fingers. Curious but slowly, as if afraid a snake might emerge, she turned down a corner of the blanket, and saw it—a flash of satiny blue with a dainty pattern.

A man's necktie.

Heat flushed through her and she glanced over her shoulder, but Violet had already hustled out of the room, leaving her alone.

Carefully, she pulled the strange object out of the bed and held it in the light. It was definitely a man's tie, a formal one, and she'd seen it before. Last night, the men had been dressed up for the ball, wearing ties just like this. As soon as she laid her hand over it, she knew that it belonged to Mark. A tiny gasp slipped from her lips.

What had happened last night, after the ball? She could remember it but dimly, illuminated only by flickering touches of light, as if it'd been another one of her dreams. Standing in the smoking room. Why had she been in there? Staring at the smoldering flames. Thinking of hurling herself into them. And then—he appeared. Raggedly breathing, an urgency in his eyes. She remembered flashes of it perfectly and yet it also felt distant, like it had happened to another person. The way his name had fled from her throat, the way she'd gasped, grasping his neck, wanting to be closer. It had all happened, the thing she'd dreamed of, hadn't it?

But it was too much, and she couldn't quite believe it. Her heart swelled with the idea that finally they both knew how the other felt. She loved Mark. It seemed it had been months, or even years, not mere days, that she'd known him—that she'd longed for him. As if they'd been souls parted in another lifetime and here they were, now, finding each other again. Beautiful stories she'd read in books, books the village priest had frowned on.

What have you done, Annie?

Her hand trembled. She felt afraid all of a sudden. Ashamed. Out of control of her own body, as if every touch of skin against skin had singed her and now here she was, a burn victim, exposed and wounded. And the memories of last night—they were waves folding over her, tasting of salt and pushing down her lungs, drowning her.

Footsteps passed her door. In a hot flush, she stuffed the tie into her pocket, where it sat nestled near the brooch.

Her first duty of the day was to help with the breakfast service, but before that, she had to prepare Ondine's warm milk. The Fletchers would be expecting it—though the thought of being near Mark again made her knees feel as if they'd crumple beneath her. She hurried up the stairs to the kitchen, heading back where the cooks were heating up huge pots of milk to make oatmeal. They were used to her now, dipping one of the little metal pots into the cauldron for a small amount of milk, and the big cook in charge of the day's porridge stepped out of her way so she could be about her business.

She finished her preparations in the pantry. She dropped a cozy over the pot, resting her hands momentarily on the cozy for the heat coming up through the quilted flannel. Then she slipped a hand into the pocket of her apron, where she kept Caroline Fletcher's brooch. She liked to stroke it throughout the day: it calmed her, for some reason. Like petting a cat. She knew she should return it to Caroline, but she couldn't make herself do it. It was so pretty. Something about it went straight to her heart, like it was meant to be hers. It was wrong to keep it, though, and for a minute she wondered if this had something to do with the evil that seemed to follow her around the ship. She had stolen it, which was bad, and didn't bad things happen to bad people? All the more reason to give the brooch back.

She used her passkey to let herself into the Fletchers' stateroom.

Strange, the curtains were still drawn; she'd expected them to be open. The room was dark as a tomb. After depositing the tray on the table, she went to the porthole, reaching up to push the heavy curtain back to let some of the morning light in.

She nearly screamed when she saw Caroline in a chair. For one brief moment, the woman had seemed a ghost, a pale figure lying back in the chair as though in a faint. What was Caroline doing sitting by herself in the dark? And where was the baby?

Caroline bolted upright, a hand going to her throat. "Miss Hebbley! What are you doing in my cabin?" Annie realized with a sinking heart that she'd startled Caroline awake. Caroline had already developed a dislike of her, and now she'd only made matters worse.

Annie turned, hoping to slink out. "The milk, ma'am. I brought the milk." As she reached for the doorknob, however, she caught a glint of gold in the corner of her eye. Her crucifix! Sitting on a corner of the dresser. Perhaps it had come undone one of those times she'd been in this room, fallen to the floor, and someone had found it— Miss Flatley?

She covered it with her hand as she passed and slipped it into her pocket quietly.

Caroline's voice rang out immediately, accusing. Like an arrow into her back. "I saw what you did! You're the thief! The one who's been stealing jewelry."

Annie's stomach dropped. This was a nightmare. She turned to face Caroline, even though she feared her. "But it's mine. I lost it a few days ago—"

"You're lying. I only just found it. You're a liar as well as a thief." Why wouldn't Caroline stop saying that? She was pointing a finger at Annie, shaking it in her face. "You were in here last night. That's when you left your necklace. You came in last night and you left the door open when you'd gone."

Annie's knees trembled. What was happening? What did Caroline Fletcher think had happened? Annie had no recollection of being in this cabin last night. But there was the necktie, Mark's necktie . . . It was in her pocket at that very moment, a mute witness.

Even with the curtain pushed back, the room was still dark. Annie reached for the switch, but there seemed to be a problem with the electric sconce (the stewards had been complaining about them on this end of the passage) so she reached into her pocket for a candle, and lit it. She lifted the candle so she could see Caroline better—and for Caroline to see her, to see how upset she was to be accused unjustly—and was shocked by what she saw. The woman's pupils were open, her eyes as dark as licorice, her face damp with perspiration. She looked as though she'd barely slept, her dressing gown twisted oddly around her body.

Something very strange was going on.

"Where's Ondine, Mrs. Fletcher?" Annie turned to the cradle, lifting the candle.

Empty.

Caroline rushed toward her. "You stay away from there! You leave my baby alone! You're to have nothing to do with her ever again, do you understand—" Anne felt the hands against her ribs, pushing her back. She stumbled and fell against the wall.

The lit candle rolled across the floor, aided in that moment by the lift of the ship on the waves.

Annie could only watch in horror as the edge of Caroline's dressing gown caught fire, a long lick of orange flame rising as quick as the blink of an eye. Caroline reared back, screaming. There was nothing at hand to put it out, no blanket. Annie backed against the door, her mind frozen, trying to think of what to do.

"Dear God, what's going on here?" It was Mark's voice, Mark suddenly appearing in his pajamas, his face lit up by flame. Then he was gone—and back again, the basin from the washstand in his hands. A wave hung suspended in midair, then washed over Caroline, followed by the smell of smoke.

The last thing Annie saw, as she hurried out of the room, was

Mark's face: shock, anger, disbelief. Caroline's words ringing in her ears: "There's something wrong with her, Mark. . . . She tried to kill me just now!"

Then Mark. Words that broke her heart. "You stay away from us, Annie Hebbley! Stay away from my family! Just leave us alone."

Chapter Thirty-Seven

The suitcase filled with stacks of Astor's cash hung lightly in Mark Fletcher's hand. Just being close to so much money made Mark giddy, light-headed. But determined. He'd gone to the smoking room to retrieve the suitcase and then make the planned handoff to Williams.

The fresh light of morning stung his eyes as he made his way past a series of portholes in the first-class entrance of the grand staircase. With his free hand, he rubbed at his eyes. It had been a restless, sleepless night, the suitcase ever present in his mind, guilt and excitement like two scorpions scuttling at the edges of his vision. Had a passing steward seen him in his frenzy last night? Would someone stumble on his hiding spot while he slept?

On the other hand, there was his future ahead of him, the suitcase and its stolen fortune, the most money he'd ever had all at once. It made his blood run wild, the risk of it, the possibility. He kept imagining what he could do with so much cash. He'd heard the gambling in America was epic: riverboat casinos, gaming cars on trains traversing the wide, lonely western plains, infamous pleasure dens in New Orleans. With this kind of money, he could go anywhere he wished, sample delights that were unheard of in England. But then: What had Annie seen last night? It had seemed eerily as though she'd been lying in wait, just to catch him in the act. And then that strange scene in the stateroom just now. Had she tried to kill Caroline, as Caroline insisted? He could not think about it now. . . . Later, after the handoff was complete and he could rest at ease, he could return to himself. But until then, he felt off-balance, and Hebbley's big, prying eyes seemed to say she knew more than she let on. Last night, she'd been, well, not in her right mind. Gone had been the timid maid he'd met only three days ago—in her place appeared someone aggressive and distraught, desperate, determined. Familiar, somehow, too, in a way that irked him to no end, left him feeling as though he was missing something, as though he'd stepped in the middle of a play.

It had been a terrible night, terrible. He'd spent it sweating, nervous and ecstatic by turns. He felt as though he would burst out of his skin at any moment. He was angry that Caroline had disappeared on him—still furious, no doubt—but relieved, too, because it meant he didn't have to explain why he was acting so oddly.

But now, making his way to meet up with Williams, a strange feeling came over Mark. The madness had worn off overnight and his conscience had returned in the cold light of morning. After what he'd done last night, he could no longer pretend that he wasn't a thief. He'd done a serious thing—and he didn't like it. He was no better than the men he'd met on his many visits to the courts. Men who'd gambled away the last of their money when they could've paid the rent or put food on the dinner table for their children. Men who lied to themselves about the terrible things they did, so they could continue to gamble. He despised those men, and now he was one of them.

He couldn't keep any of this money. Not one crisp bill. If he did, it would be easier the next time—and if he kept the money, there *would* be a next time. Once you'd known what it was like to have money, it would become like an addiction, a right, an entitlement. He would rationalize his thieving, just like the men he'd met in jail. And he would be one of them one day; that's how it always ended. To go from being a barrister to a convict: he didn't think he could face the shame. It terrified him, how tantalizingly easy it all was. To slip.

To fall.

He followed the stairs down to G deck, where some of the third-class passengers were quartered. A good deal of the space on this deck was given over to gigantic boilers, with their god-awful noise, all that rumbling and groaning. It was the closest he'd gotten to the inner workings of the engines and he wondered how these people could stand it. One end of the long, long passageway housed machine rooms full of turbines, great whirling pieces of machinery that could crush a man with no difficulty whatsoever. Mark thought briefly about throwing the suitcase into one of those, letting the gears grind the money into meaningless tatters, but while it would be emotionally satisfying, it wouldn't achieve any useful end. It wouldn't prevent Williams from blackmailing him. So, he continued to the bow of the ship, toward the mail and parcel rooms, and second-class baggage, where he was to meet Williams.

The third-class passengers were waking up. They eyed him curiously as he passed, women in cheap straw hats or with kerchiefs tied over their hair, men in coarse woolen trousers and work boots. They were making their way to the third-class dining room—long tables and benches, the way field hands and servants were fed—from which came the aroma of porridge and fried kippers and kidney pie. His own stomach growled; he couldn't wait to get this damned transaction over with so he could return to the upper decks and the things he was accustomed to.

He glanced into room after room, anywhere there was an open door. So many people crammed down here, four or more to a room. Eyes stared back at him, some frightened, some suspicious. He began to feel a little intimidated; what would he say if someone asked me why he was there? Or tried to take the case away from him? Had he gotten turned around? Finally, he decided to take the initiative and ask if anyone knew where he could find the boxers. He chose a meek-looking older gentleman wearing a cleric's collar.

"I think I heard they were staying by the squash court," he said, pointing vaguely forward.

Luckily, there were fewer rooms in that section of the ship—a seeming afterthought, rooms shoved in wherever they fit—and he found the right room before long. The door was open, but there was only Dai Bowen inside, with no signs of his extortionist.

Bowen seemed surprised and slightly embarrassed. "Mr. Fletcher, what are you doing here?"

"I'm looking for your friend, Mr. Williams."

Bowen rubbed the back of his head. "He's not here, I'm afraid. I haven't seen him since last night."

A man like that undoubtedly found himself a woman last night willing to take him in. It was a disappointment: now he wouldn't be able to unburden himself of this damned anchor, this chain to his old ways and his old troubles. As much as he wanted to be rid of it—and of the temptation, too.

Mark started to turn away but Bowen reached for his arm. "What is it? Something I can help you with?"

Mark shook his head. "No, it's nothing."

But Bowen didn't release his hand. "Any business of Les's is my concern, too."

Mark was about to object a second time when he realized what the big man said was true. If anyone had told Williams that he'd stolen Caroline's jewelry, it was Bowen. He was no innocent. He shoved the suitcase at Bowen. "All right then—here. Take it. I'm sick of the damned thing. Tell your friend that's all the money I could find. And it's all his. I don't want a damned penny of it." Mark stepped back before Bowen could say or do anything, anxious to say his piece. "You tell your friend it's over. My debt to him is paid. I don't want any part of this anymore—and he better remember this, if he gets caught. It's all on his head. I wash my hands of it."

"What are you talking about?" He shook the suitcase at him. "What's this?"

All the emotions that had been whirling inside him—indignation, anger, fear—crashed, leaving Mark oddly embarrassed, even though Bowen probably knew everything Williams had on him. Even though the two men were partners, Mark felt—Was he only fooling himself?—that Bowen was different. You could tell that he was more honest, in his way. Mark shut the door to the tiny, tight space and, in low tones, barely above a mumble in case someone walked by, explained Williams's plan to the boxer, took him through every step, down to finding the box that had held the money, and was gratified to see the look of horror spread over the man's face.

Bowen held the suitcase away from him like it contained something repulsive. "And this is the money, here?"

"Every last bit. I've done what he asked. Now I demand he leave me and Caroline alone. I—I know I haven't been the best of husbands, but that's in the past. I'm going to try to patch things up with Caroline. We're going to America to start a new life together—and I'm going to give it a proper go." He realized, as he said it, that this was what he wanted most of all. Some demon had been exorcised.

Bowen leaned against the bunk bed behind him, his head just shy of the ceiling. "I'm glad to hear that. I wouldn't blame you if you told me to mind my own business, but if you don't mind my saying, your wife seems like a wonderful woman and—"

"And I shouldn't be doing this sort of thing to her?" Mark said, his tone bitter. "You're right: she is a singularly remarkable woman, not the least for taking on a failure like me. This isn't the first time I've courted ruination."

"Cards?" Dai asked.

It wasn't only cards. He'd haunted country horse meets, dogfights and cockfights held in London back alleys, ferrets pitted against rats in the basements of corner pubs. At his worst, he'd bet on which man could down a pint of ale quickest. But he could admit only to cards;

gentlemen played cards. And they were his special weakness. Mark found himself describing to the boxer the worst of the nights—the night he'd lost Lillian's savings. He could still feel the terror of free fall, the bottomless pit open beneath him as, hand after hand, his pile of money dwindled. How he kept playing and betting, thinking his luck had to turn, but it never did. At the end of the evening, he'd had only pence to his name and the gent who had cleaned him out seemingly vanished into thin air.

The boxer listened politely at first, then with increasing concern. "And the dealer, how was his luck?"

"Nearly as bad as mine. He lost the house a goodly amount that night."

"And he did nothing to stop his losses? Didn't call in a new dealer, send the gent to another table?"

"It happened so fast, I suppose there wasn't time."

Dai let out air through his teeth and shook his head.

"What?"

"It's got the sound of a con all over it, Mr. Fletcher."

"What do you mean?"

"The gent and the dealer—my bet is they were in on it together," he explained softly. "For the gent to have cleaned you out so quickly. He gets the dealer to lose, too, ya see, so it seems natural like. It's called 'dumping.'"

"No, no, nothing like it— That's not— It couldn't have. I'd have known it," Mark stammered, though even as he protested, he felt the truth of it wash over him in a wave of heat. "And how do *you* know of such a thing? Has that happened to you?" But Mark didn't need the answer. He could see from the red shame on Dai's face, in the way he chewed the inside of his cheek. Dai hadn't been the victim of a con— he'd been in on it. Maybe plenty of times. He and Leslie, both of them con artists. And yet this one cared enough to let Mark in on the truth.

Mark felt himself getting hot all over, as he had done that night, a tingling spreading down his arms to his fingers. His mind raced back to that night, the night that changed his life forever, that had set everything that had come after in motion like a wound clock: his and Lillian's ragged, horrible arguments—weeks of it—and the hideous, seething resentment. Then, the forgiveness, frantic and urgent and full of hot kisses and tears, as was Lillian's way. Begging his family for help. The rejections and denials. The humiliation. Finally, the boon: Lillian's promotion. She'd advanced from the sewing floor to deliveries and tailoring. The hope that it was all going to get better now that they were on the straight and narrow.

And that's how she'd met Caroline.

But there was nothing he could do to change what had happened. He'd been over that a thousand times in his head. The past was immutable. The only thing that he could change was the future. Lillian was gone. He would never get her back and wishing would only make him miserable—and steal what he did have from him, through bitterness and resentment. He had Caroline and Ondine. This was the situation he found himself in. He owed it to them to try to make it work. He might not be able to control what happened next, but he could try.

"Are you all right, Mr. Fletcher?" It was the boxer snapping him out of his despair, his voice ripe with concern. Mark opened his eyes. "Have you come over ill?"

"No. Quite the contrary. I feel better than I have in a long, long time."

He breathed a sigh of relief when he saw Caroline alone at one of the small tables, a teacup at her lips. Before she noticed him, he took a moment to observe her that way. You wouldn't suspect the terrible scene in their cabin this morning, the fire, or their row last night.

Though he knew her well enough to sense there was sadness in the arch of her neck, in the slight downturn of her pretty lips. She would never show her troubles to the world.

She was the kind of person who could survive any misery the world might throw at her. Look at how she'd bounced back after the death of her husband, crossing the ocean to find a sisterhood with Lillian. It made him want to weep, that she'd chosen him, with his weaknesses and flaws. He couldn't fathom why.

Lillian had always been a storm—one that stirred you, took you by the lapels and made you helpless to it. Thrilling. But Caroline: she was a lighthouse. The first sight of her after days at sea, days spent away from her side, left you with a simultaneous feeling of gratitude and the deep satisfying comfort of home.

He pulled out the chair opposite her before he lost his nerve. "There you are. I was afraid I wouldn't be able to find you—"

She sat back. "I would've waited for you, Mark, but when you dashed out of the stateroom, I wasn't sure when you might be back . . ."

He'd told her so many lies. He took her hand. Was it his hand that was trembling, or hers? "You have every right to tell me to go away, Caroline, but I hope you come with me, someplace where we can speak in private, and I'll explain everything."

It nearly broke his heart to see his wife look at him that warily, as though he'd lied to her so often that she'd never trust him again. But she nodded, dabbing her lips with her napkin. She let him lead her out of the café, through the doors, and onto the promenade. It was windy, even with overhead shelter from the deck above, so he took off his coat for her to wear over her shoulders. They were still surrounded, couples and groups strolling by, mostly moving in the same direction. It reminded him of skaters taking laps on a pond in the wintertime.

The rail at the very back of the ship was mostly deserted—too windy to linger for very long, he supposed. They stood looking at the ship's wake, twin curls of white cutting into the gray-green water. It was mesmerizing, like watching a magician pull an unending spool of white handkerchiefs from his sleeve. The wind teased long strands of Caroline's hair out of its upsweep and whipped them around her face, made her pale lavender dress billow around her like sheets caught drying on the line. When she looked around uneasily, as though afraid the wind would swoop down and carry her over the railing to her death, he drew her closer.

"I have to make a confession." She opened her mouth to cut him off—she was always making excuses for him, but no more. He overrode her objections. "This is a real confession, and it's serious. Hear me out."

"Mark, you needn't confess to me—" The look on her face was so sad, Mark was sure he knew what she was thinking: that she'd been turning it over all night and come to the conclusion that they should part. That they were wrong for each other. That there was too much distance between them.

"I do—you don't know how much I do."

Her brows pinched and her mouth started to crumple, ready to burst into tears. "Mark, you must listen to me. You're not the only one at fault."

She was only saying this because it was what he wanted to hear, he was sure of it. "Don't say that. I'd never believe it of you. The truth is you are too good for me, Caroline, and I was too proud to admit it. But I see it all now, and I need you to hear me out. Please." He squeezed her hands in his, and didn't stop squeezing until she bowed her head in acquiescence.

It was the scariest thing he'd ever done. Scarier than stealing Astor's money, scarier than telling Lillian he'd lost all her hard-earned savings. After all, he didn't think he'd be caught breaking into the luggage room and even if he had, he knew he could explain it all away: he was a first-class passenger, after all, and they would be reluctant to accuse a first-class passenger of committing a crime. They'd be grateful for anything that would make such unpleasantness go away. As for Lillian, he'd known she'd be disappointed with him, but she wouldn't leave him over it.

The situation was completely different with Caroline. He had everything to lose by telling her the truth, but he knew that if he didn't confess, it was only a matter of time before the marriage failed. The only way she could respect him—the only way he could respect himself—was if he told her what he had done. And he *needed* that, he saw now. Needed her respect, her forgiveness, her acceptance. Her love. Sometimes he didn't know what it was he wanted, but what he needed was obvious. Without Caroline, he had nothing. Without Caroline, he *was* nothing. Maybe this was the truest definition of love he'd ever experienced. Not the kind he'd experienced with Lillian, the kind that unhinged him, made him wild. But the kind that had the power to anchor and secure him, to make him become the man he ought to have been all along.

And so he poured out his heart to her. He told her about his gambling, about stealing her jewelry (how her face paled at that—not even in anger but something far worse: pity). About losing Lillian's savings, too. He told her that he still thought of Lillian and that he loved her, but that he loved Caroline as much if not more. He told her how he'd doubted their marriage but realized now that was only insecurity because he couldn't believe a woman like Caroline could love a man like him.

She cupped his cheek. Her fingers were like ice, so he took them in his hands and blew on them. "Oh, Mark, I—I knew something was bothering you. . . . I thought you were having misgivings. I was afraid you thought you'd made a mistake marrying me." She was really crying now.

He dabbed at her tears. "Please, darling, don't cry. I hope you can forgive me."

She pressed the back of her hand to her cheek. "We all sin and we all deserve forgiveness, isn't that what the preachers say? If you say that

from this moment forward, you are a changed man, I believe you—
and I will do the same. From this moment forward." She let out a
breath, as though she'd been holding it in. She stared over the ocean,
as if willing herself to calm. "It will be better once we're in America.
When you've had a chance to meet my family and we move into our
new home, we'll be able to put everything behind us." *And never, ever*
think of it again, he promised himself. Even Lillian: Mark would put
away his every thought and memory of Lillian, if it would save his
marriage.

The wind suddenly swooped down and plucked the hat from Caroline's head, flinging it into the ocean. It disappeared in the frothy
wake of the ship, pulling it under the frozen water.

Before Caroline could say another word, Mark got down on one
knee, still holding her hands. From the corner of his eye, he saw pass-
ersby ducking their heads together to whisper—*Oh look, he's proposing.*
"Caroline, if you will do me the honor of remaining my wife, I
promise I will always strive to be the man you deserve."

She pulled him to his feet and kissed him hard. Her tears fell on his
cheek, as cold as tiny pellets of hail. "Oh, you silly fool, of course I
will. Now, let's go inside, before we freeze to death!"

He wrapped his arms around her and held her close as they made
their way across the promenade and into the warmth of the ship. It
made no sense that he should land on his feet with Caroline. All he
knew was that this marvelous woman had forgiven him. Their whole
lives stretched before them now, the past swept clean, the future shiny
and new.

Chapter Thirty-Eight

Fury simmered like stars in the darkness of Dai's thoughts, drove him to search the ship up and down until he finally found Les in the third-class stairway, trying to talk two men into a game of cards at ten o'clock in the morning. He extended no greeting, no *If you don't mind, I need to talk to my friend*. He simply grabbed Les by the arm and dragged him away.

They ducked into a steward's closet, tight as a coffin. Dai found a light pull. Leslie Williams's face was white as a ghost: he knew he was about to get his comeuppance.

"What the hell's the matter with you?" Les snapped.

"I could be asking you the same thing." Dai held up the suitcase and shook it in Les's face. "I ran into Mark Fletcher. This is the con you were so proud of? When were you going to tell me, Les? When?" He was angry with himself, really. How could you love someone so terribly, so mercilessly, that you let him lie to you again and again? No matter how worthless it made you feel.

Les kept his composure, eyeing the small tan valise coolly. "To be honest, I didn't think you needed to know."

It stung worse than a punch to the gut. He felt breathless.

"So, what? You were going to take the money and run off on me?"

And why shouldn't he? Why keep Dai around, with his morals and complaints, his constant questions, his neediness? Because that was it, wasn't it? It didn't have to do with love, but *need*. Dai needed Les and it just wasn't the same the other way around.

"Don't be an idiot. I was going to tell you that I made a killing at the tables is all. Found some rich old sod who was monumentally bad at poker."

Dai threw his hands up in the air to keep from strangling him. "Lies, that's all you're about, Leslie Williams. Have you ever told me the truth, even once?"

Les leaned back in the tight space and awkwardly crossed his arms. "I don't see why you prize the truth so much, Dai. The truth can kill ya. Not everyone's strong enough for it."

"What's that supposed to mean?" Dai could feel the tips of his ears going hot.

Les sighed. "I don't see why you're upset. It worked, didn't it? It looks like Mark Fletcher pulled it off, and no one's the wiser."

When he started to reach for the case, however, Dai pulled it back. "No, Les. You're not keeping this money. It's too dangerous."

"Are you mad?"

"No, it's you who's gone mad. What do you think's going to happen when Astor discovers his money's missing? Who else knows he had this money in his luggage?"

Les frowned. "You're worrying for nothing. His missus could've told everyone she met, for all I know. She told me readily enough."

"Do you really think the authorities are going to question all of her society friends? They have no reason to rob one of their own. But a penniless boxer . . ."

Les scowled back at him, but didn't say another word.

"I'm going to return this—and I don't want to hear another word of argument, do you understand? And no more wild schemes while we're on board this ship," Dai said. When Les tried to lunge for the valise, Dai pushed him back. "Don't try me, Les." The words came out of him in a low growl, and he could see the flicker of fear cross Les's face. It gave him brief satisfaction.

"You can't be serious. We have the money *right here*. We're free and clear—"

"No, Les. We don't know that. Someone could've seen Fletcher, could be talking to the captain about it as we speak. Once again, you've put us both in danger, and for what? We don't need this"—he wasn't going to listen to Les's objections, not this time—"and I'm going to take it back before someone discovers it's gone."

Les's eyes bugged and his face got red, like someone was choking him. "You can't do that, Dai. It doesn't belong to you. It belongs to me—"

The laugh came out fast. "Listen to yourself, will you? It doesn't belong to you, either, and you know it. You want me to say it, Leslie Williams? To put it to you plainly? Then I will: it's this money or me. You have to choose right now. If you take this valise, this is where we part ways."

He was afraid that Les would choose the money because he knew how deep that ran in him. And with good measure: there had been many times in both their lives when there had been no food and no heat, and no clothes except what the church gave. They took a beating to put bread on their table, and every bit of labor they'd ever done had benefited a bloke like Astor a lot more than it had benefited them. It barely felt like stealing; it was more like finally getting a piece of what was owed them, but the law wouldn't see it that way.

Les huffed, his cheeks puffing in and out so hard Dai was afraid he might blow a hole right through them, but in the end, he held out the brass key to Dai.

Dai was pretty sure he remembered where Mark had said the Astors' luggage was located down in that cavernous hold. Even which trunk he'd found it in. Dai had a strong and detailed memory, which aided him in studying his opponents in the ring. It didn't occur to him until this moment that he should've had Mark bring it back, but who knew if Mark could be trusted, in the end. He didn't want to dangle this kind of temptation in front of him, not when the poor man had come this far.

Finally, after making a discreet inquiry of a harried steward, he located it. At least it was still early enough in the day that there were few people milling about this end of the deck. It was the morning after the ball, and Dai worried that some of the partygoers would be dispatching stewards to take their finery back down to storage. He picked up his pace.

The luggage room was a mess, no longer corresponding with the description Mark had given him. There were trunks and chests everywhere, great dangerous piles blocking the aisles. Suitcases and valises thrown around like a tornado had touched down. Maybe Les was right; if luggage turned up missing at the end of the journey, there would be no way to track it down. Anyone could've come in there and helped themselves to another passenger's things. For the first moment since he'd run into Mark, Dai felt a tiny bit better.

He was just about to abandon the suitcase where he stood and hope for the best when he saw the Astors' storage area. This was the messiest corner by far. Had Mark left it in this state, he wondered, or had the Astors' servants been down since then, milling about? If that was the case, then someone might have noticed the missing money. . . . Sweat started to bead on his forehead. How would he find the right trunk in all this mess? One trunk looked pretty much like the next; how would he figure out which one had held the money?

Dai climbed over the mountain of luggage to the back of the compartment, moving suitcases aside to get to a large trunk that matched the description Mark had given him: oxblood leather, straps with brass buckles. It was unlocked. He had just thrown the lid back and had started to poke through the contents when he heard the sound of low voices heading his way. He went into a panic; he knew how to think quickly in the ring—how to think with his body—but in situations like these, his mind went flat.

He was trying to jam Mark's suitcase into the trunk when a man popped around the corner, holding an oil lamp. He shone the light right at Dai.

"Hey—would you look who's here. It's that boxer, I tell you! I can't believe it's that boxer." The man—a steward, to judge by his uniform—beamed at Dai.

Dai would've paid him cash money to shut up. This was the worst day of his life and the fewer people who knew, the better.

They were quickly joined by two other men who didn't look as pleased to see Dai. The oldest man gave Dai a sharp look up and down. "What are you doing here? This area is off-limits to passengers."

"You're not even a first-class passenger, if I'm not mistaken," the last man said. "And I'd bet anything that you're not one of the Astors, so what are you doing in their compartment?"

Because Dai had no answer for this, they escorted him up to the boat deck, to the bridge where, the stewards argued, they knew they would find at least one officer standing watch. Dai hadn't liked being marched through the entire ship, the eyes of every passenger on him, knowing that he had done something bad—or so it seemed.

"I found it, I tell you, and I was returning it. It's not even my suitcase," he said to the first officer, Lieutenant William McMaster Murdoch, once they'd gotten to the bridge. Murdoch seemed unimpressed by Dai's denials. He stood with his hands behind his back, rocking on his heels. They'd looked the suitcase over and luckily there was nothing on it—no monograms or stray receipts—that led back to Mark Fletcher. At least that part of the whole sorry operation was safe.

"If you don't know anything about it, how did you know to return it to the Astors' storage?" Murdoch asked.

Dai had no answer for this. He could hardly argue that he'd deduced it, that no one else on board could've had that kind of money except the Astors. There were so many millionaires on this ship that it seemed almost blasphemous. During the interrogation, Dai learned that Astor did have money in the safe-deposit box, so much that they'd run out of space and that was why he'd been forced to keep the rest down in storage.

"Where did you find the suitcase? Did someone give it to you?" Murdoch asked. He was clearly running out of patience, but the more he pushed, the more jumbled Dai's mind became. He wasn't used to being questioned like this. His was a simple life: someone took a swing at him, he punched back.

"I found it by the engine room. I thought I recognized the suitcase as belonging to the Astors. I was just trying to return it," Dai said, trying to keep his voice steady.

"If you thought it was the Astors', why didn't you bring it to their room?" Murdoch had been joined by another officer now, the second officer, Charles Lightoller. A nervous man, clearly trying to impress his superior. Murdoch paced around them, stroking his mustache.

"I don't know. I—I didn't want to disturb them."

There was a sudden squabble outside the door, the sound of pushing and shoving, and voices raised sharply. Dai recognized one of them by the Welsh lilt. Les must've seen him being paraded through the ship or heard the rumors. A second later, the door flew open and Les stumbled inside. His clothes were disheveled and his hair mussed, as though he'd had to fight his way in.

"You've got to let this man go. He hasn't done anything," Les said, pointing at Dai. "It's all my fault. I'm the guilty one. It's all my doing."

Murdoch's and Lightoller's heads snapped in Les's direction. Dai knew what they were thinking, these London boys: of course it would be the Welsh making trouble. Stealing. Fighting. What do you expect from country trash?

"Dai didn't take the money—he's returning it, for Christ's sake! Do you ever see a thief trying to return what he stole? It was me: I stole the money." Dai could only stand dumbstruck as Les explained the whole thing, every bit of it, how he'd sneaked into first-class staterooms—leaving Violet out of it, of course—to plan his cons. Surely the officers had heard the first-class passengers talking about the man who told their fortunes—for a hefty sum? Then, he further explained, he learned of Astor's cache in storage when he'd been prowling through their rooms. He even claimed to have stolen the suitcase from another passenger to throw authorities off the scent should the whole thing be discovered. He avoided looking at Dai the entire time, his red-rimmed eyes trained on the floor or imploringly on the officers' faces. Anywhere but at Dai, and Dai knew why. Les would break if he looked at him.

"You can't pin this on Dai. He was trying to get me to do the right thing. He's an altar boy. He's a good man. Too good to be friends with the likes of me."

This whole time, Dai could say nothing. Words choked in his throat. He never thought he'd see the day when Les would do something like *this*. He'd seen Les do so many objectionable things. He'd taken coins out of a blind beggar's cup, taken a simpleton's last shilling and left him to starve in the street. And they'd been caught a couple of times before by local police. Les always got them out with some sly excuse, a quick promise or a bit of change or the knowledge of some secret about this one's sister or that one's cousin. Where they came from, it was different—everyone knew everyone. You had to do something *really* awful to get put away.

But here they were on the great *Titanic*, and here was Les, willingly turning himself in to unknown enforcers. Who knew what the punishment would be? It made no sense—Dai felt the world had turned upside down. He didn't know whether to be grateful or horrified. He couldn't let Les take the fall. But that made no sense either—it *was* all Leslie's doing. And yet—

The boat bucked at an unexpected wave, and Dai lurched out of his thoughts.

"This whole thing stinks," Lightoller said to Murdoch, as the first officer rubbed his chin. "I think we should lock them both up until we can hand them over to the authorities in New York."

Les wailed. "It would be a great miscarriage of justice. David Bowen is innocent. You can't lock up an innocent man. Ask anybody on this ship. He saved a kid from falling overboard the first day! He's a hero. You can't go locking him up."

The officers huddled quickly. Dai didn't like the sound of their voices, angry and growling, like wasps in a rattled nest. In the end, Murdoch called for the men who had been waiting outside the door, and pointed to Les. "Take this man and secure him in the chain locker." He turned to Les. "We don't have a brig on this ship—we didn't envision *needing* one," he added with disdain. "We'll keep you in the chain locker until we can find a more suitable place. We'll wire the authorities in New York and let them know what's happened. They'll take custody once we've arrived."

"You can't—" Dai started, but no one was paying attention to him. He lunged after one of the crew members, but the look the man gave him when he grabbed his arm was enough to make him drop it immediately. He knew what would happen if he got out of control, if he acted out. They'd take him, too. And then there'd really be no hope. Still, it took all his force of will not to take the door right off its hinges in anger as he watched the crew members drag Les by his arms—as though he might try to run away, as though he could somehow escape while he was trapped aboard this ship—and haul him away before Dai could even say goodbye.

Chapter Thirty-Nine

Annie stood outside the Fletchers' stateroom. The hall up here was hushed. But no—another steward walked by, listing slightly with the rise and fall of the ship. He gave Annie a nod as he passed.

Annie waited until he was out of earshot before she knocked at the door.

No answer. No sounds within, either.

She used her passkey to let herself in. There was no murmur of voices from the other room, no high squeal of Ondine's laughter. The suite was as still as a crypt, dust motes the only movement. Everyone was out—including Mark.

She would wait for him. She had to speak to him.

She paced between the rooms, all the while listening for the sound of Mark's footsteps outside the door. Time had crept all day. Every chore seemed to be over within minutes, and then she had to think of something else to do to keep her busy. All she could think about was the scene this morning. Caroline lunging at her out of the gloom like a ghost. Caroline accusing her of theft, trying to make Mark think Annie was the villain, that the bad things happening on the ship were her fault.

She needed to make him understand that it wasn't her fault.

Caroline had a vendetta against her. Anyone could tell by looking at Caroline that she had a problem. Mark needed to face the truth, needed to see it. Needed to see that he could trust Annie. That Ondine's safety could be at risk.

She'd been in these rooms a dozen times bringing Ondine's milk but never had the chance to really look around, she realized. She took a slow turn, her gazing settling like a chill over all the Fletchers' possessions. Hats. Shawls. Books. A parasol. Ondine's baby things, the crib and stacks of baby clothes, glass bottles and rubber nipples. *This could be mine*: The thought popped into her head as natural as could be. *If I were married to Mark, this would be my room. My things. My baby.*

My life.

It was a silly, impossible fantasy, and yet in just this moment, alone with his things, it didn't feel so far away.

There was Caroline's jewelry scattered across her dressing table. Having just been accused of stealing, Annie's instinct was to give it wide berth—but then her eye fell on a locket, a plain, simple silver locket. Her hand went to it as naturally as if it were her own. She opened it to find pictures of two women: Caroline, and one she didn't recognize. So beautiful that it could've been from an advertisement for soap or perfume, but Caroline Fletcher was not the type to save pretty pictures from magazines. Carefully, Annie slipped the photo from its frame, flipped it over. Nothing, no inscription.

She opened the clothes trunk and skimmed through the jackets and trousers on their hangers. She didn't recognize the labels— London tailors, no doubt—but could tell that the clothes weren't of the best quality, and much of it showed signs of strain and wear. Darning, patching, loose buttons. Same with his shoes. Several pairs had been resoled. There was only one suit of new clothes, the things Mark had worn the day he boarded. On the other hand, Caroline's clothes looked to be mostly new, far more abundant than her husband's, and of very good quality. She recalled what Mark had said to her on the promenade that first time they'd really spoken. How he didn't feel he belonged, that these weren't "his people." That had been the first sign, the first clue that he wasn't happy. That he longed for something else.

She stood over the dressing table, her fingers itching to pick through the jewelry and cosmetics and toiletries, brushes and combs. Caroline's things took up almost every inch, while Mark's fit into a square leather tray: collar stays; two pairs of studs for his cuffs; a signet ring; and a fob for his watch, a tab of worn leather with an insignia she couldn't make out.

On the tiny stand by his bed, a book, a collection of stories. It fell open at the bookmark: "The Man Who Would Be King," by Rudyard Kipling. Annie had heard of the author but not the story. She picked up the tome for no other reason than Mark had held it in his hands. She flipped through the pages, their words flowing over her. She'd been taught, growing up, that reading novels was a sin. *The Lord favors good girls, Annie.* A flash of darkness at the corners of her vision. No, it was too late for those thoughts.

She put the book down. Beside it lay a few pieces of paper, folded— receipts for their luggage in storage, a note scribbled in an unfamiliar hand.

The bed was made up, the sheets drawn tightly over the mattress, but she couldn't resist lying down on it. Something more than curiosity had taken hold of her. Something like need. She had the sensation that she'd experienced every morning on this ship—like she hadn't existed before that moment. She snuggled her head on his pillow, fragrant with his hair oil. She burrowed her nose in deeper. She folded back the blanket. *This is where he sleeps.* She pictured his body in this very bed, drank in the lingering scent of his powder and soap. The smell of it made her want to weep. It wasn't *enough.* Unable to resist any longer, she lay down in the place where his body would be, in the exact spot, so she could feel the indentation in the mattress. Pressed her head back into his pillow, reached beneath it to draw it around and envelop her fully.

On the tiny nightstand, a shiny wooden box. She tilted the lid up: it was filled with the usual sentimental mementos. A dried corsage. A snippet of faded ribbon tied around a dance card. More photographs, curled at the corners, browning. She looked through them quickly; no one who bore a resemblance to Mark, probably all from Caroline's side of the family.

Wait, here was that woman again, the woman whose face was in the locket. She was sitting in a chair, wearing a stiff black dress, holding a baby. Not any baby: Ondine. It was unmistakably Ondine as a newborn.

Annie lifted the photo to her face to get a better look. The woman wasn't just holding the baby: she was breastfeeding her.

The room tilted suddenly, like someone had crept in behind her and tapped her on the shoulder. Who would breastfeed Ondine except Caroline?

No, silly. Caroline wasn't breastfeeding. Annie brought the milk herself, several times a day.

What a strange picture. But Annie had heard of this craze, this fad of taking pictures while breastfeeding, heard her mother and the Ballintoy crones talk about it—*Silly Londoners, whatever will they do next.*

She flipped the photo over. This time there was a name. Two names.

Lillian Notting. Ondine.

She thought she heard a scratch at the door, though how she heard it over the thudding of her heart, she wasn't sure. Was it a key turning in the lock? She threw the photo in the wooden box and slammed down the lid, guiltily. She didn't want Mark to catch her snooping.

But the door did not open. Whatever made the sound, it didn't happen again. Once again, the rooms fell still as a tomb.

She left the room in a hurry. She couldn't stay there any longer. It felt, suddenly, like a stranger's room, like she had no business being there.

So many confusing facts—what could it all mean? Caroline was *not* the baby's mother. The truth of it thudded through her. That other woman was the mother. That Lillian Notting. So, why did Caroline have the baby now, and why was Mark with her, and why were they on this ship?

And then it came to her: they were running away.

Maybe Caroline Fletcher had something to do with the bad things that had been happening on the ship. Caroline changing overnight from sweet and warm to cold and distant. Mark confessing that he was afraid his wife was guilty of something—of what? Caroline somehow luring the servant boy away with her dazzling brooch, and then . . . ? Annie didn't know, but she couldn't rule it out. Maybe Caroline had charmed and stolen Mark, too, stolen him away from Lillian.

She could think of no other explanation.

Annie shivered as she raced down the hall, past stewards who gave her an odd look over the shoulder. She paid them no mind. She felt feverish and dizzy. This was all too terrible. Did Mark even know?

They had to track down this Lillian woman, or her relatives—someone, anyone—and let them know the baby was safe and that they'd bring her back as soon as possible. Even as she had this thought, there was a second, darker, more horrible one lurking in the back of her mind.

No woman leaves her baby behind willingly. Annie felt this with a terrible, cold certainty in the marrow of her bones, as certain as she'd known anything in her life. The woman in that photograph, the one with the look of steel and fire in her eye, would not give up her baby to another woman without a struggle. Annie was sure of it—that she would, in fact, do everything in her power to keep Ondine with her. Use her last ounce of strength to hold on to her.

She'd go to the wireless room and get the operators to send a telegram to the London police. And prepare herself should the word come back that Lillian Notting, the true and rightful mother, was no longer with them. That Lillian Notting, in fact, had been murdered.

———

Annie ran to the wireless room on the top deck. Past passengers who muttered under their breath at the reckless girl. Past stewards and crew members, who gave her quizzical looks. If someone tried to stop her, she darted around them. She had no time to explain.

Finally on the boat deck, she stood at the top of the stairs to catch her breath. She'd run so she wouldn't have time to think about what she was doing, but now she couldn't catch her breath. She doubled over, head practically tucked between her knees, as she gulped big swallows of air.

She had never been this close to the bridge. She knew it was where the officers were, where navigation took place and the important decisions were made. But she'd only seen the captain from a distance and wasn't sure she'd recognize any of the ship's officers if they weren't in uniform, wearing their double-breasted reefer jackets with eight brass buttons. Mr. Latimer, the chief steward, had warned them all to stay away from the officers. "You've no reason to be on the boat deck forward of the grand staircase," he'd told them once at a steward's meeting. "And if I get word that you've been seen up there, you'd better have a damn good reason for it."

Was this a good reason? Annie wasn't at all sure. But a baby's future was at stake. Annie knew in her heart that she had to follow through. The urgency of it made her dizzy. She could almost feel Lillian's outrage, her devastation and desire, from across the sea, from the grave.

Besides, she had to do what was right—now more than ever.

The Lord favors good girls, Annie.

No one ever went to the radio room, small and closet-sized, behind the first funnel. The radio operators scurried in and out to deliver messages to passengers. Annie had heard it was painstaking work, listening to strange dots and dashes, writing it all down. She'd heard the two radio operators subsisted on black coffee and cigarettes and were as jittery and foul tempered as addicts. Standing outside the door in the dim alleyway, she could just make out bursts of scratchy noise. She felt as though she were being swarmed by fleas.

Annie nudged the door open a crack. "Hello?"

The room was kept very dim with just one bare bulb shining down on a table in the center of the room. It was a mess in there, as though a tornado had hit: an entire shelf of books tipped on their sides; papers stacked everywhere, in no seeming order; cups and saucers piled three high, like someone was playing a child's game with them. She recognized the man on duty as Jack Phillips, the senior wireless operator. Annie's heart sank a little, for she would've preferred Harold Bride, the junior operator. It wasn't that Phillips was so very old—he was only twenty-five—but he was the nervous sort, and difficult, and he made everyone who came in contact with him nervous, too.

He barely looked up from his work. "What are you doing here?"

She froze.

"Who are you?" He was giving her a good looking over now. He would remember her face. "You shouldn't be in here."

"I need you to send a wire for me. It's very important."

He gestured at the piles of papers. "Just drop it off here. You'll have to wait your turn. The machine was down yesterday and there's a tremendous backlog. You'd think these people had never sent a telegram to their friends before, but no, they've all got to send one from the *Titanic*. We're just now coming into range of Cape Race and there's only this short window to get all these messages sent. So off with you and let me do my work."

"I'm sure none of these are as important as this." As soon as she'd said the words, however, she heard a tiny scritch, scritch, scritch, as though a mouse were scratching at the pile of telegrams. The insistent noise needling her. *Look here.* She felt drawn to skim over the sheets on top.

Ice sighted in the water . . .

A string of numbers that meant nothing to her but made her pulse race all the same. Coordinates, perhaps.

SS California *stopped by ice field . . .*

She'd overheard a couple of passengers talking about ice the previous day, hadn't she? Two white-haired men coming in from the promenade. *The only real danger to a ship this big is ice,* one of them had said. *Ice and the Germans,* the other had replied, *one we're as likely to see as the other.* "These are incoming messages, aren't they? Shouldn't they have been delivered to the bridge?" Her hands itched for them—*Look here, this is important*—but the tingling stopped once she picked them up.

"Are you daft? Get away from those. They're confidential." He swatted at her. "You telling me how to do my job? I've already told you: there's only a short window to get through to the Cape Race station and I've all these wires to send. Bride will take those messages up to the captain before he starts his shift."

No, no, no. Annie danced back out of Phillips's reach, the messages still in her grasp. The scritching was joined by buzzing in her head, as urgent as the clanging of alarm bells. *Danger, danger. Someone must pay attention.* Annie, *they need you. All those innocent people on this ship, they need you.* That was why her attention had been drawn to the weather reports, which she'd normally not pay attention to. It was up to her to save them. Her initial mission was forgotten for the moment. "And when's that?"

"Be quiet now. I can barely hear Cape Race as it is . . . Where do you think you're going with those? I said—"

"But—but these are important. It says there is ice! I heard that's a special danger on this run. . . ." Her hands skittered over the papers, sending them in a blizzard to the floor. "You mustn't ignore them. . . ." She had to make him understand, to see what she knew. "But don't forget my message—my message is important, too. There's a missing baby. Well, what I mean is, a *stolen* baby." Her voice rose uncontrollably.

"What are you on about? Stolen babies," he huffed.

"No, I'm just explaining it wrong. It's a private matter of great urgency. There's a woman— Can't you feel it?" Annie could, now, feel Lillian's fear and anger, her need, wrapping around her, reaching across the waves. . . .

"Calm down, miss. I need you to calm down."

"No, don't you see? I heard her voice. I mean, I saw her face, it was there, plain and simple and it's wrong, don't you see?"

"I can't make sense one way or the other of what you're saying, but I'm going to ask you one more time to vacate the area or I'm going to have to call for help—"

"But—" Annie lunged for the floor, reaching for the messages about the ice. *The only real danger is from the ice.* Even as she was rambling, she knew she wasn't making sense, at least not out loud. And what's more, the urgency had brought about a new tremor of fear in her. A voice that frightened her, yet was familiar.

You know what I want.

You know what I need.

Through the window, Annie saw the officer's promenade, the open-air deck they used to observe the condition of the sea or get some fresh air. It was deserted. If she could make it to the promenade, she'd have a clear path to the captain's bridge. It was her best chance to get these messages to Captain Smith.

Yes, yes, yes. She felt a bleat of reassurance within her jangled nerves. This was what she must do: take the messages to the captain, make him see that they were about to sail into danger. He would understand. She would have saved the day, and then they would listen to her about Caroline Fletcher.

"I'm so sorry," she whispered. "I must have gotten carried away." She pretended to slip out the door, while Phillips, with a disgusted shake of his head, went right back to transcribing outbound messages. As he busied himself, however, she clutched the stack of important messages to her chest, then darted around him and was through the door before he had left his seat.

Wind whipped down the open deck, striking her full force in the face. It was so cold it nearly paralyzed her. Her uniform was no protection at all. With the air so frigid, she could easily believe the inky waters below were choked with ice. They'd been told—they'd all been warned—about the special danger from ice on this course. What was the matter with Phillips? Why hadn't he taken the warnings more seriously; why had he felt it was more important to send telegrams for foolish rich people? People who made silly demands, who had no idea of the danger. The captain had to see these messages right away. Too much time had passed as it was. . . .

A force hit her from the side, knocking her to the deck. Her head made contact with the cold, wet boards hard and fast.

Squares of white slipped out of her hands and danced up on the wind, out of her reach. The messages. They fluttered on the air, swooped over the railing, and then—turning and twisting on the wind—drifted out over the open water. They shrank smaller and smaller until they were mere dots of white in the darkness, the sound of their fluttering lost in the roar of the ocean. Until they disappeared.

The warnings with the location of the ice were lost.

"I got her, Mr. Phillips." A hand jerked her to her feet like a rabbit caught in the vegetable garden. Harold Bride grinned at having brought her down. The hound that caught the rabbit.

She pulled away. "Let go of me! Don't you see what you've done? The messages—"

"They were never your concern to begin with."

"They were warnings! There's ice ahead—"

"That just goes to show what you know." Bride puffed up, happy for the chance to show off in front of a member of the fairer sex. "This ship's got nothing to fear from a little ice. It's unsinkable, or haven't you heard?"

"You're in trouble now," Phillips said as Bride wrestled Annie back into the radio room. The room was far too small to hold three people at once and the two men pressed against her. She felt they enjoyed her distress. Small pleasures for small men. "I've sent for Mr. Latimer."

Latimer, the chief steward, was a big bearlike man who could barely fit into his White Star uniform. She'd seen him angry before— seen how he grew silent, wore an icy white stare that implied terrible consequences to come. It tied her stomach in knots, even though she knew there was nothing Andrew Latimer could do to her worse than what she'd already done to herself once.

"What in the world possessed you to steal them telegrams?" Now there were four of them in the radio room, Latimer looming over An- nie. It was so hot and stuffy, she was afraid she would faint.

"It's female hysteria," Bride said with confidence beyond his years. "I've seen it before. Sometimes they get ship fever. Not meant for the sea, some women."

"No, I—" But the men weren't listening to her.

"I knew there was something wrong with this one from the min- ute she stepped on board," Latimer said as though Annie wasn't stand- ing beside him. He lifted his cap to wipe sweat from his forehead; Annie watched it trickle down his face.

He gripped her upper arm—just like Bride. She'd been grabbed and pulled so much as a child, the sensation was strangely numbing. When you were treated like an object, a wild animal, sometimes the easiest thing was to let your mind go dead. It was a version of the Van- ishing Game, and it made it like they weren't touching you, not the real you. "You're confined to the crews' quarters," he was saying, "un- til I get a word with the captain and he decides what to do with you."

She thought he meant for her to stay in her own cabin, the one she shared with Violet, and so she went meekly, but, no. He brought her to a different room, this one as small as a broom closet and without a bed, just a hammock hanging from a hook on the wall. There wasn't an electric light or candle, and being an interior room, there was no light from outside. She told him in a faltering voice that she was afraid of the dark and asked if she might not stay in her own cabin—she promised not to leave, not until they told her she could—but he didn't react in the least, as though she hadn't said a word.

Maybe the Vanishing Game had worked too well.

She sat on the floor, knees tucked to her chest. It was cold, even though the cabin had to be close to the engine rooms. Could Bride be right? Was she hysterical? What did that mean—female hysteria? Was it different from when men got upset, yelled and stomped and slammed things about, like her father when he was at his worst? Maybe she was more like her father than she wanted to think. She tried to remember what had happened on the officer's promenade. That wasn't like her, not at all. She'd always been a quiet, meek girl. What in the world had possessed her to take those telegrams and run out on the officer's deck? She could picture it all, as though she'd been watching another girl. Maybe she *was* going mad.

Her thoughts wound round and round the sequence of events, and what she'd learned. There was so much she still didn't understand. The eerie note, like some kind of frantic warning—*you know me*—haunted her now. Stead had given credence to the idea it might be a prank . . . or it might be a spirit.

Oh, Lord.

She was shaking so hard she could barely think. Tears were streaking her face uncontrollably. The pieces slotted and pieced together in her mind. She thought she knew now what was happening.

Caroline had stolen Lillian's baby. . . .

And Lillian Notting was dead.

Lillian was the spirit. The spirit that had shaken the table and blown out the lights at Stead's séance. Who was responsible for the note under her door and maybe even the seizures.

Lillian. Enraged. Despairing.

Annie didn't know how long she'd been curled, silent and alone, in the dark room. She'd begun to feel as if she'd been buried alive, and, disturbingly, a part of her didn't mind. It wasn't a land burial but one at sea, like Teddy's. She was wrapped in gauze, floating in the deep, weightless. Peaceful. For the first time in a long time, she knew exactly where she was going, where this journey of pain and loneliness was leading. She knew the destination.

When she awoke, however, she was still in this room. The ordeal of the past few days wasn't over. There was still a mystery to be solved, a spirit to be exorcised. She had to get out of here somehow and to let Stead know that she'd figured it out. Someone had been possessed by the spirit of Lillian; and, whoever it was, they were doing terrible things on board this ship, all in the name of getting Ondine back. But how could you take back your child if you were already dead?

She couldn't panic. She had to get hold of herself. To remain in control. Even if she got out of here soon, no one would ever take her seriously if they thought her mad. She had to behave, had to soothe herself, had to think.

She reached into her apron pocket and, out of what had become a new habit, drew out the brooch. Ran her fingers over it. She'd looked at it so many times that she'd memorized the design, the curves and whorls cut into the metal. By now, it was almost like it was her own. It made her feel better somehow, like she wasn't so alone, so lost, so trapped.

Her fingers found the latch instinctively.

Latch?

She hadn't known there was a latch.

And yet . . .

The heart popped open with a satisfying little snap. It was a miniature snuff box.

And there was something in it—or there had been.

She breathed in the scent of the powder. She knew what it was: Caroline's "medicine," the medicine she privately indulged in when she thought no one was looking. Afterward, she would be steadier, calmer.

There wasn't much left, just a rim of compacted powder. Annie licked her finger and ran it around the edge. She could feel the dust wick moisture off her fingertip. Before she could stop herself, Annie stuck her finger in her mouth and sucked the powder from it.

Nothing.

She chipped at the ridge of powder with a fingernail, breaking off a sliver no bigger than a splinter. She swallowed it.

Nothing.

She worked the remaining bits of compacted powder loose, yielding four more little slivers. They were bitter as bicarbonate.

They melted onto her tongue, now like tiny icicles.

Ice.

Ice floating in the water, lying in wait for the ship.

The child, floating in the water. Blue as a corpse.

Ondine.

She knew the name, now that she thought about it. Ondine was the name of a mermaid in one of her grandmother's stories. It was a myth, wasn't it? Annie wasn't supposed to know about myths. Like novels, like fairy stories, they were full of sin.

The Lord favors good girls, Annie.

She wanted to weep. She had to do something, but how could she, trapped in this frigid cell in the bottom of the ship? When she was frozen herself, like a sleeping princess in a fairy tale, locked in her casket, staring out of it forever.

Waiting for her prince. Waiting to be freed.

Why was she here again? She touched her head, as though her touch might release something. Yes, she remembered it was because of the messages, yes. The ice. No, because of Lillian.

No, because of Caroline and this brooch. This empty brooch that had once held a very powerful medication. And had been in the hands of the Astor boy when he went into a seizure.

She saw the truth now: it wasn't Caroline, or any evil, calculating spirit who'd killed the boy. The brooch itself had killed him. Or what had been inside it.

With aching surety, Annie saw now what had been happening.

She looked at the brooch in her hand like it was a hissing cobra, waiting to strike at her.

Caroline *was* responsible for Ondine's wasting away. Caroline had been making Ondine sick. On purpose. The brooch hissed the truth to her. Caroline had been poisoning her child this entire time, right under everyone's noses.

But Caroline *wanted* Ondine. Why would Caroline have gone to so much trouble to make Ondine hers, only to try to kill her?

There'd been a fisherman's wife outside of Ballintoy caught poisoning her own children with arsenic. She claimed it drove out the evil spirits and she was doing it to save their souls, but her own sister had said the woman had grown weary of raising them by herself, the husband out at sea, leaving her alone in her misery. Said motherhood could be its own kind of grave. There was no escaping it, except in one hideous way or the other—their deaths or the mother's.

And, too, Annie's grandmother Aisling had told her of a woman who had abused her children for the sympathy it brought her—not to mention the parish alms. Women did mad things, didn't they? Hysterical things.

Hysteria.

The stories flitted through her mind now, a dizzying cycle. Stories she'd heard or read, stories she'd perhaps only dreamed.

Annie snapped the brooch's lid shut, regretting she'd used up all the powder. She had no proof, only suspicions. No way to prove that *she* wasn't the mad one after all.

Chapter Forty

It had to be near midnight, but William Stead resisted the urge to dig out his watch. It was buried in his vest pocket, hidden beneath several layers of wool. He was buttoned up tight against the cold winter night. He had to have been out here close to an hour—in near-arctic conditions. The ship had to be at one of its northernmost points on the journey and the spring weather had taken a turn for the frigid tonight. His nose and cheeks were stiff, his lips tight and uncomfortable. He stamped his feet to ward off the cold, wishing he'd brought a flask of hot tea with him.

What they—Guggenheim, the Duff-Gordons, the captain—must think of me out here by myself in this weather. Crazy old man, they're probably saying right now. The captain had already sent a crewman to check on him. "Might you be more comfortable indoors, sir?" he'd asked politely, nudging Stead toward the door like a border collie. He finally gave up when Stead made it clear he'd go inside when he was good and ready. Maybe this was how his public career would end, he thought stoically. As a joke. The speaking events were already starting to dwindle; invitations to holidays in the country, even dinner parties, drying up. It was bad enough being infamous; he couldn't afford to be known as a crackpot, too.

"Who are you? What do you want from us?" He spoke softly, saying the same words over and over and as he made slow circuits of the promenade. Normally the deck saw its share of passengers, even at this hour, but the freezing temperatures had driven everyone else indoors. As cold and tired as he was, he continued because he was sure there was *something* lurking aboard this ship, and what's more, that something was going to happen soon, perhaps tonight. There was an electric charge crackling through the air, a special charge that only certain people could feel. People who were attuned to the other plane. People like himself.

If the spirit was malevolent . . . if something terrible were to happen, Stead would not be able to live with himself. He felt sickened over the death of the servant boy (though of course the blame lay with the Astors, treating the child as though he were a pet). Just as he felt gutted about what had happened to Eliza Armstrong.

He would not let another innocent suffer.

He made another slow lap of the promenade, his legs stiffening up as the temperature continued to drop. He called to the spirit under his breath and with his heart and mind. He could feel something in the air just beyond his reach. Something tantalizingly real, absolute.

It wasn't until he'd returned to his starting point near the smoking room that he noticed a thickening of the mist over the water. It hung like a figure in the air, suspended over the black lapping waves. It wasn't fog, Stead was sure of it. He knew what it was. He'd seen it before. The spirit was trying to answer him. It was attempting to materialize, to become the corporeal body it once was. Stead's heart swelled with hope and amazement—and fear, too, for how could he not be afraid? As much as he wanted to witness a materialization, it was as frightening as seeing a corpse claw its way out of the grave.

As he waited, he became aware of the tremendous cold pressing down on him as though it had weight. As though the cold were a presence. He felt like nothing, a mere insect, confronted by this huge, annihilating manifestation. He felt the weight of the other world, the gravity greatest because the two worlds were so close. It was a feeling he'd never known before.

But as the mist took shape, it was no figure, no person coming closer, but something vaster, amorphous. These were not limbs being made from crystalized breath. The presence grew larger and larger, and whiter. Until there was no mistaking what was coming at him, what had emerged from the clouds hovering just over the surface of the ocean.

As tall as any building in London. And as massive.

An iceberg.

Chapter Forty-One

Mark and Annie lay side by side in a field beneath a flowering cherry tree, pink blossoms raining down on them like snow. His gaze was soft, his mouth tense. There was no question in her mind that he was about to kiss her.

The anticipation was almost as sweet as its realization.

His hand met her cheek and she shivered. . . .

As their lips met, she felt his breath against hers, felt them breathing as one. His mouth parted hers, hesitant. Then he pulled back.

"We shouldn't . . ." he whispered.

Only he wasn't Mark.

He was Des.

Desmond Flannery. The boy she loved. The boy she was not allowed to love. Because he was already sworn to God.

But the Lord couldn't truly deem it a sin to do this—not when it felt like heaven. Could He? In that moment, it just didn't seem possible. In all the earth, there was only the two of them: Annie and Des. Intertwined in the field. Waves crashing beyond the cliffs in the distance. Where nothing, not even God's wrath, could touch them. Des holding her hand over his heart. Des saying, "Why do you do this to me?" Des murmuring, "Lord forgive us," over and over and over again. A cry and a prayer together.

Annie snapped awake, feeling as if a scream had wrenched her in half. She'd been sobbing in her sleep, and now she shook as the terrible noise continued echoing *outside* her, everywhere, overhead and around.

The sound was indescribable—a deep, reverberating groan beneath an avalanche of glass. A roar and a screech, like a sheet of old metal wrenched backward against its will.

Then came the juddering, as if the vessel itself were seizing.

Overhead, it seemed as though the entire ship had awakened—she could hear a commotion of voices and screams. Instinctively, she lunged for the door. She tried the handle, but the door was still locked. She pressed her ear against the wood, listening. Of all the noises—crying, shouting, footsteps on stairs, running through the alleyways—which were closer? In which direction was the running headed? The voices were muffled so the words were indistinct—what were they saying?

Her mind felt fractured, slowed by the weight of her dreams, the fear of the spirit, of Lillian's photograph, and the strange spell that white powder had put on her. How much time had passed?

And then she remembered everything: Caroline, poisoning the baby.

The sound of bells broke into her thoughts. This was how they communicated with the staff. Bells told the stewards—spread throughout the ship—if there was a problem and if they were to report for orders. When Mr. Latimer had gone over emergency procedures in orientation that first day, Annie had panicked, but Violet had assured her not to worry. "We'll never need them," she had cooed, patting Annie's arm. "Only if there was a really bad storm and the ship was taking on water." Annie had trusted her. Violet was wise to life on the sea.

Violet—did she guess where they'd put Annie? Would she come to rescue her now?

She began to bang on the door—frantically and so hard her fist hurt in seconds. She screamed out, but no one seemed to hear.

The bells drowned out everything else.

She tried to calm her mind and focus. Focus on the chimes. Judging by the pattern, the stewards were being recalled. That meant it was an emergency. That would never happen unless it was something bad.

And then she remembered: the telegrams. From other ships, telegrams containing coordinates and warnings: *Ice sighted.* The messages that had flown from her hands when she'd tried to report them to the captain.

The panic—as cold and impenetrable as a block of ice—closed in on her from all sides.

Oh God. What had she done?

She resumed her pounding until her fists bled against the door. Footsteps sprinted by. Still no one stopped.

The locks on the lower levels, crew's quarters and in third class, were known to be flimsy; maybe she could make it pop open. She began pulling on the doorknob with all her might, but it quickly became obvious that her shoulder would dislocate before the door opened.

She kicked at it, threw her weight against it, screamed for help. The seconds ticked by, faster and faster, then whole minutes, and her calls were still drowned out by the sounds of people running on the stairs and down the halls, the shouts of stewards shepherding their passengers. In their panic and fear for their own lives, had everyone forgotten about her?

Then she heard feet scuffling in the alleyway. Right outside. She was sure of it. She pounded her fists against the door once more. "Is someone there? Help me, please! I'm trapped in here. Help!"

The doorknob rattled. "It's locked."

She gasped. A man's voice. She couldn't place it.

"Mr. Latimer has the key," she yelled out. "The chief steward."

"No time," the man grunted, his voice strangely muffled through the thickness of the closed door. "Stand back." Annie had barely stepped to the back of the cramped space when she heard a weight slam into the door. The door shuddered but held. The man threw himself against the door again and again, until finally, the frame splintered and the door swung open.

It was one of the boxers, the bigger and kinder one. He reached for her hand. "What are you doing down here, miss? Don't you know there's an emergency—"

"A—a misunderstanding," she stammered. No time to explain. She could hardly tell him what she'd done anyway or that they thought she'd lost her mind. "What's going on?"

"We hit an iceberg."

She pictured the white slips of paper flitting from her fists, flying through the air, sinking into the black water. The wireless operators had been wrong not to tell the captain sooner. It was their fault, not hers. Wasn't it?

The man was pulling her along, practically dragging her through the narrow hallway toward the stairs. Strangely pounding at other closed doors as they passed. "They've told passengers to put on life belts and wait for further instructions, but not everyone is listening to them. They're clinging to the hope that the ship is unsinkable, but I'd just as soon not find out." He craned his neck to look down the sparsely lit alleyway. "Is this where they keep the prisoners? You don't know if there's another person locked up on this hall, do you?"

"Are you looking for someone?"

"My pal Les. He had a, uh, misunderstanding, too. They said they would keep him in the chain locker— Do you know where that is?"

He cared for his friend very much—she could hear it in the thin strain of his voice. "I'm sorry, but I don't know where that is. From the sound of it, I'd say it's probably on the very lowest deck."

The boxer rubbed his upper arm, the one he'd used as a battering ram. "I'll keep looking, then," he said, nudging her up the steps. "You'd better get above deck in case they start evacuating the ship."

"I thank you." She wondered if she should offer to help him look for his friend, but at that moment, all she cared about was Ondine. It might be that no one was looking after the baby. A cold terror gripped Annie by the throat: if anything happened to Ondine, she would never forgive herself.

She raced up the stairs, past passengers stumbling about in confusion, crying, searching for family members, many of them in their sleeping clothes. She wanted to help them—to help them all—but the captain could lock her again in the bowels of the ship when the emergency was over.

She moved in the opposite direction of the thickening crowd. They were straining to get up to the deck, bulkily padded with life belts, losing their tempers. A few froze where they stood, refusing to take another step. But Annie pressed on. Past a pair of women from third class who smelled of sardines and cheese, their fleshy arms linked to keep from being separated by the crowds. Around a trio of white-haired men in funereal garb moving slowly up the stairs, huffing and puffing every third step. She practically knocked aside a pair of crying children trailing behind their mother and father, and paid no heed to the string of epithets the father hurled in her wake. It didn't matter. None of it mattered right now.

As she scratched and clawed and struggled past the others, she could not shake the growing feeling that every one of these people was going to die. For all that was said about the *Titanic*, how superior it was, how well designed, how glorious and noble—as though it were a person, with a person's traits—it would do nothing to save them. The *Titanic* was indifferent to the humans crawling on its decks and would willingly sacrifice them to the sea.

She could feel the ocean's cold reaching up through the ship, rising like morning mist over a battlefield, creeping slowly upward deck by deck. Then would come the icy-cold black water. Hungry, greedy water wanting its due. One by one, the water would take them, swallowing them whole. They would die with startled looks on their faces, sentenced to an eternity of surprise: none of them thought they'd die this way.

She observed them in a detached way as they fought to get by her. The old man hobbling with canes up the alleyway, aged daughter a step behind, smothering her own panic to remain at his side. The poor woman with a tattered shawl wrapped around her infant, afraid she will be turned away at the lifeboats because she has a steerage ticket. The asthmatic woman collapsed on a deck chair, fighting for each breath. Their struggling, their sacrifice, their fear—Annie saw them now as if they were all just drifting phantoms from another life. Caught frozen in time.

But when the moment thawed, they'd see that they were all, already, long since gone.

Chapter Forty-Two

The night was dark and frigid, but torches and electric lights blazed across all the decks, and the hubbub of passengers almost made it feel like broad daylight. Only instead of the optimistic bustle of travelers boarding the ship for the first time, there was only chaos, disordered panic, and a series of contradictions. Here, a steward helping an elderly lady. There, a child lost and crying. Here, a musician opening his case. There, a man lighting a cigar as if on a leisurely after-dinner stroll. Some passengers had clearly decided to mock the situation, insisting an emergency was just a good excuse for a story to later write home about—or a bad excuse to be awake so late. Others were openly weeping, praying, acting as if their lives were over, as if their gods had abandoned them.

Caroline stood in a loose crowd of people, clutching Ondine to her chest. She'd found Miss Flatley at the usual spot she liked to take the baby, a sheltered area under an awning, and the nanny handed the baby over almost with relief. Caroline couldn't blame her under the circumstances.

Mark was nowhere to be seen. An officer had come around looking for volunteers to help ready lifeboats and Mark—after getting assurances from Caroline that she was fine—had gone to help. She promised to stay right where she was until he returned.

She looked down at the baby in her arms. Her sweet face, cheeks reddening from the ocean wind. Ondine wailed and Caroline shifted her, patted her back, but as the wailing increased, so did Caroline's terror. Of the writhing crowds. And beyond them, the sea, black and icy and roiling.

A reckoning was going to take place. She felt it in her bones.

"Lillian," she whispered, feeling tears streak her skin, turning to ice.

But there was no undoing the past. Caroline knew that.

"I loved you," she whispered. Was she trying to appease the spirit, the wild, reckless spirit that was undoubtedly here, with her?

She had tried to take care of her friend. Lillian had been so stubborn. It had been hard to convince her to see Caroline's physician. "What right do I have to complain about a little ache or pain—at least I'm alive, not like the women I worked with in the factory," Lillian had said whenever Caroline brought it up. But the pangs persisted, sometimes shaking Lillian's entire body, and Caroline grew worried for her friend. Eventually, Lillian relented.

Caroline had waited in the doctor's office while Lillian dressed afterward, old Dr. Braithwaite returning from the examination room with a smile. "I can see why you'd be concerned for your friend. It can be a great shock to the body, narrowly surviving a tragedy like that. The young lady is lucky to have such a devoted friend." He was wiping his hands on the linen towel with his back to Caroline, prattling on about the nervous disorders women were prone to. "You can rest assured that your friend is in perfect health."

Caroline had let out a tight breath.

"Cramping is perfectly normal in pregnancy," the doctor added.

And that had been how Caroline had found out.

Henry, Caroline's first husband, had never truly understood how badly Caroline wanted a child. How could she have expressed it to him? She'd spent her life craving love—every expression of it. But once she had married, she'd felt it: the inevitable disappointment, hidden there between the sweetness, lurking in the quiet moments. With a child, though, she'd been sure: she'd finally feel it. She was meant to be a mother, knew it as sure as she knew anything.

But the doctors had said it was impossible.

And so, in that moment, Caroline had done what she always did. She opened the doors, and took Lillian into her home, into her life, and into her heart. She had not known then that she would fall in love with Mark, too. She hadn't met him yet. She'd only known him through Lillian's words. How could she have known how it would all go?

The cold biting wind reminded her where she was: standing on the deck of a sinking ship. She'd always believed you could rise above your troubles in life, but now she wondered if she'd been fooling herself. If everything she had ever done—horseback competitions and singing lessons, holding Henry's hand as he passed into the sweet hereafter—was just a prelude to this moment.

Looking down at Ondine, all she had left of her friend Lillian, Caroline saw how sick the baby was. Gray and listless and barely breathing, it seemed. Horror spiked through her: she had been so preoccupied with Annie Hebbley, her anger with Mark, her fascination with Guggenheim, she had neglected Ondine. What kind of mother was she?

Just then, a steward was in her face, his eyes wide, his hair in disarray. "What are you doing, just standing there!?" he was shouting. "Where are your life vests?"

She looked around. It was true: everyone milling around her was wearing one, clunky canvas and cork vests thrown over their clothing. Why didn't she know this?

"Never mind, take this one," he barked, forcing a clunky life vest at her with a not-so-gentle shove. "Onto a lifeboat with you, now."

She balked even as his hand pressed hard into her back. "I can't go yet. I'm waiting for my husband—I—"

The steward only shook his head, frowning firmly at her. "Only women and children, didncha hear? You and the baby—into a boat! Now!"

Chapter Forty-Three

Lucy Duff-Gordon didn't feel any fear, only annoyance. Perhaps she ought to be grateful to her upbringing for that—not much could unsettle her. She knew, without knowing how she knew, that she'd come out on top. Surviving, fighting, clawing, studiously planning, strategizing—doing that all your life made you incapable of failure. There was no falling, only climbing. No sinking, only swimming. You kept yourself just a little bit separate from the masses. You just kept going. Empires fell. Enormous ships sank. But people like Lucy soldiered on.

"You must put yourself first, Lucy," her mother had once told her. "You can't assume someone else will take care of you, even your husband. *Especially* your husband. As a woman, you must fight for yourself, if you expect to survive in this world."

She had left her first husband—a drinker, and not a nice one, after that. She'd taken her mother's advice to heart and learned to respect herself, to wear an invisible shield—her greatest fashion design and one no one would ever see. To let expectations slip off her like silk and fall to the floor.

And now: she would be damned if she had come all this way in her life to die in the middle of the ocean.

They stood near the lifeboats, watching as one was being loaded. That stodgy officer, Lieutenant Lightoller, was supervising. He personally helped each woman over the side into the waiting boat. The going was slow but more orderly than she would've thought possible.

Cosmo was an important part of her life. A woman without a husband was a suspect character in some circles, and vulnerable to legal chicanery by those who might fancy her an easy target.

She turned to him. "Cosmo, get in the boat with me."

He gave her a weary look. "You know me, Lucy: I'm not a hero. I'd just as soon save my neck than freeze to death in those waters. But you heard the officers. It's women and children first. Lightoller won't let me aboard."

"You'll get on the lifeboat with me if we have to put you in a dress and feather boa," she said through gritted teeth.

Passengers had still been skeptical when they'd begun loading the first two lifeboats, but word of water belowdecks had traveled through the ship. Women who had vowed not to leave husbands behind were beginning to rethink their position. A few men were starting to argue that they should be allowed on the lifeboats as well, and in at least one instance a pistol had been drawn. There were rumors of violence below and of women and children in third class locked in their compartments to keep them from claiming space in the lifeboats. Things could spin out of control very quickly, Lady Duff-Gordon sensed. It took so little to turn a crowd ugly.

Then she saw her chance. Lieutenant Lightoller seemed to be called away, leaving another office in charge, a Lieutenant Moody, the sixth officer. The junior-most officer.

How frightened he looked. He seemed to realize that he was going to die soon and didn't embrace the prospect of dying a hero, like Lightoller. He watched, his eyes glazed, as the sailors helped the assembled women over the side of the boat, others steadied the largely empty vessel.

"Take off your hat and cover your head with this," she said to her husband as she handed him her shawl. It was huge and diaphanous. She pulled the edge up to his nose, covering his mustache. "Don't speak to anyone. Just follow me."

She went up to Moody and showed him the ring on her right hand, the huge opal-and-diamond ring that she'd thought she'd lost earlier. The ring given to her by her first and only *true* love. That ring meant more to her than any of the rest of her jewels, and now it was going to save Cosmo's life. "Might I have a word, Officer Moody?" she asked.

He seemed to break off his reverie and remember where he was and what they faced. "As you see, I am very busy, madam, and have no time to—"

Be straightforward. Pull no punches. Show him that he can trust you. "Look, Officer Moody, it's very likely that you're going to die tonight. And what will your family get? A nice letter from the directors of the White Star Line and a few extra pounds in your last paycheck? Do you see this?" She shoved the ring under his nose, so close he could've licked it. "This ring is worth a fortune. If you get me and my husband"—she nodded in Cosmo's direction, the shawl cascading over his shoulders disguising his gender somewhat—"on that lifeboat and safely off this ship, I'll make sure that your family gets it. You can make sure they'll be provided for."

His eyes brightened for the first time. But there was hesitation, too. The circumstances didn't lend themselves to trust.

"I wouldn't cheat a dead man, Officer Moody. You have my word on it."

He helped Cosmo over the side as though he was an infirm old lady, giving a convincing performance. Lady Duff-Gordon hustled her husband to the furthermost seats, by the bow, and sat to his outside so that he was segregated from the others.

"Lucy, I don't know if I can do this," Cosmo whispered to her. But just then, there was a huge roar to their right. One of the davits supporting the lifeboat just beside theirs began to crumple, the metal

failing. The vessel began to plunge toward the sea, only to be jerked
short by rigging to the davit on the other side. The mishap had a
strange effect on the passengers waiting on the deck: they swarmed the
boat, afraid of being left behind. Several were pushed from behind over
the deck and plunged into the ocean, screaming as they fell. People on
the lifeboat were screaming, too, as they dangled at a precarious angle
from the rope lines. A few threw themselves at the rigging, trying to
slide into the lifeboat, but most were too weak and were shaken off as
the boat swung. All was pandemonium in a matter of seconds. Cosmo
watched agape and several of the women turned their heads or wept or
began to pray, but not Lady Duff-Gordon. She clambered over the
empty benches until she was at the side of the boat.

She shouted up to Officer Moody. "Remember our deal. If you
want your family to receive this ring, you will lower this boat into the
water immediately."

"But half the seats are empty—"

"And we need a couple of your men to row." She wanted to tell
him to save his breath; she knew what was needed and would make
sure that it got done. Nothing mattered except that she survived.
Honor didn't matter, nor chivalry. The story would be written by the
survivors, in any case.

Stories always were.

Moody hesitated again.

"Do you want the ring or not?" she demanded.

Moody put four crewmen in the boat and ordered the lifeboat
lowered into the water. There was grumbling among the women:
Why hadn't they filled all the seats? Surely, they could fit more. And
why had they given seats to sailors—shouldn't male passengers have
been given the option of rowing, if they wanted to save their lives?
Lady Duff-Gordon wouldn't let the crewmen listen to the crying,
hysterical women. Let them glare. She was in charge now.

She grabbed an oar and thrust it into the nearest one's hands.
"Row," she said.

Chapter Forty-Four

Les had been in plenty of scrapes in his lifetime—it took a lot to scare him.

But just now, as he banged fruitlessly on the locked door in his dank cell, the fear started to get to him, wrapping itself up around his neck like the massive pile of anchor chain that sat gleaming in the wet darkness of the room behind him. He was well and truly in the shite this time.

"What if they drop the anchor?" Les had asked the crewman who'd taken him down here earlier, his voice hoarse with apprehension, but the crewman had only laughed at him. "That's not likely to happen until we reach New York, and we're still a few days out at that."

The crewman had given him a small lantern, but with the shuddering scream of the ship minutes ago—the great metallic shearing sound, followed by the panic and chaos of footsteps above—the light had splashed down onto the floor's inch of icy seawater and snuffed out, leaving a faint whiff of smoke in the dark.

He tried to save himself. He pummeled the doors, kicked, and yelled till his throat gave out, but he knew there was no one around to hear him. Dai would be looking for him for all the good it would do:

no one was going to give him the key and even that great sweet lummox would not be able to tear that metal door off its hinges.

He slumped against the door, letting the cold seawater seep into his bones, thinking to himself that this was it, that maybe he'd known it all along instinctively, ever since they'd stepped on board. There'd been something really wrong with this ship: a born troublemaker knows when there's trouble. He'd known it just as he knew now that no one would worry about him; if there was a serious problem, he would be the last thing on the mind of those officers and crewmen. They wouldn't remember him until the crow's nest was sinking below the waves.

Was it his imagination, or were there now *two* inches of water sloshing around the floor?

He had just climbed to the top of the pile of chain when he heard a noise at the door. A rattle of the handle, a scraping of metal in the keyhole. Was he hallucinating? This couldn't be. Miracles didn't happen to men like him.

Nor should they, unless the angels had no idea what they were doing.

The door swung open to reveal Madeleine Astor, preposterous in her fur coat with a life belt strung over it, wearing a broad-brimmed hat with ostrich feathers. Fingers pinching at her skirts to keep the hem from getting wet. She turned her little girl's face up to him. "Mr. Williams? Is that you, up there? I've come for you. Don't dawdle."

She didn't need to ask twice; he scrambled down before she could come to her senses. He had no idea what had possessed her to come to his aid—Did she not know why he'd been taken into custody? Had no one told her?—but he wouldn't bother to set her straight. "Mrs. Astor! You, dear lady, are my savior, my guardian angel—" He landed in the water next to her, splashing noisily. "How did you get the key?"

"You'd be surprised what you can get for a hundred dollars," she said, handing the key to him, as though he wanted to keep it as a souvenir. "You may not have heard, but there's an emergency. The ship appears to be sinking—"

He looked down at the water at his feet, now above his ankles—and hers, too. He could see currents pull through the water: it was rising fast. "Then we should get above deck as soon as possible."

She let him take her hand, touch his other hand lightly to the small of her back, escort her down the narrow alleyway, her skirt sloshing. The whole thing seemed surreal to him. Why had she saved him? Since when had a rich bloke cared a whit for the poor? What did Mrs. John Jacob Astor care what happened to him?

"I came for you for a reason," she said over her shoulder, as he hurried her along.

"Yes? And why is that—no, don't stop. Keep moving," he said, trying not to show panic in his voice.

"Because you have a gift, Mr. Williams. A gift that I need. I really can't do this with my back to you. Can't we stop for a second—"

Another gentle push. "No, we can't. I can hear you fine, Mrs. Astor. Please tell me—What can I do for you?"

Her voice turned thin and pleading. "I need to know what is going to happen to me, Mr. Williams. I can't die here, tonight." He saw her hand dart to her belly momentarily, as though she was comforting the child inside.

It was that gesture, her fine little girl's hand going to her stomach that did it. Until then, he was thinking of asking for money—God help him, hadn't the woman just set him free?—but she was giving out hundred-dollar bills. She'd said as much just now. And old habits die hard.

But now, he couldn't. Even if she was rich and deserved it.

"And what of Jack? The captain has said women and children only in the lifeboats. Jack insists that he will remain on the ship. He won't be seen a coward." Her voice trembled.

"Your husband's a brave man," Les said. *Me, I'm on one of those lifeboats if I have to dress in me grandmother's Sunday best.*

They were going up the stairs now, narrow metal stairs, mean and plain, meant for the crew who shoveled coal and stoked the engines and the stewards with their trays of tea things and extra blankets. Her skirts caught on the metal edges, her heels in the grates, and Les grabbed her elbow more than once to keep her from falling on her belly.

"I—I can't go to New York without my husband," she said. Her voice was so frightened now, indistinguishable from a girl's. "They hate me. I'm a pariah to them. They'll eat me alive."

They were on the upper decks now, Les reasoned, judging from their surroundings outside the stairwell. They were maybe one flight down from the boat deck where they'd be loading the lifeboats. He could tell by the great swarms of people rushing this way and that, the frightened burble of the crowds. He did his best to protect Maddie Astor, holding her up by her arm, shoving people out of their way. He wore no coat and was freezing, his teeth chattering and the tendons in his neck straining. But he couldn't stop moving.

"We're going to get you to a boat, Mrs. Astor. You're going to be all right. . . . You're going to be fine because you *have* to be, don't you?" They stopped now, close to where they were loading one of the lifeboats. He took her hands in his—she wore gloves, finest calfskin, whereas his hands were bare and near ice—and gave them a squeeze. "Listen to me, now. Trust me. You owe it to this baby to survive. You have no choice. Only you can save it. Your husband wants you to do this. You must do it—for him."

She was crying. Looking into his eyes and crying.

"It's going to be hard, but you're going to be fine. I can't see all of the future, but I can see that. You have to be tough for your baby and your husband. They're both depending on you. Now, get into this lifeboat. Here you go." He held her hand as she climbed awkwardly into the swaying, dangling boat, handing her off to the crewman inside like the father of the bride at the altar handing his daughter to the man she will marry. Handing her off to the future. Funny, in that moment, he wasn't cold anymore. He felt much, much better. He wasn't even afraid.

He felt a jostle beside him and there was Dai, dazed to see him but shocked, too. He'd seen that look before on the boys who stumbled into the ring for the first time, thinking they were tough enough because they'd had a scrap or two in the schoolyard. Dai must've been scared out of his mind for him, Les realized, and was overcome by the sheer luck of finding him free and standing on the boat deck, the two of them together—for what looked increasingly like the end. The very end.

They had started to lower the lifeboat with Mrs. Astor and a group of other women into the water but then stopped for some unfathomable reason. They were shouting at him, but he couldn't hear them over the crowd. Madeleine Astor was waving her arm at him, beckoning him. "We need a man to row," the crewman called through cupped hands. "Jump down, jump down. You saved her life, she says. We can take you."

Les peered into the crowded lifeboat. There was only one tiny square of wood visible, next to the oarlock. Room for one man, and one man only.

He remembered the day he met Dai at a squalid little training room set up in an empty warehouse in Pontypridd. It seemed like a lifetime ago. There was this big, strapping young fellow punching a sack filled with sawdust strung from the rafters, hitting it with so much power and might that the building shook with each blow. The sack split open in no time, spilling sawdust all over the floor. You knew Dai Bowen was going places, that Pontypridd wasn't going to contain him for long.

And it wouldn't have, if Leslie hadn't taken up with him.

Leslie couldn't stay out of trouble. Life was one scrape after another, whether with the authorities or the bookies. Dai had stood by him throughout it all. He never moved on to London, despite all the promises from fight promoters and rich would-be patrons. Dai just shook his head and told them he couldn't leave, not yet, but he never explained why.

America was supposed to have been their chance to start over.

Their last chance.

They stood together at the edge of the deck. The railing had been removed so that the lifeboats could be swung out over the water. The boat hung six feet lower than where they stood. Men were vying for Lieutenant Moody's attention, both passengers and crewmen, begging to take that last seat. There was no time to argue.

It was his last chance to make things right.

He leaned close to Dai's ear, close enough to kiss. "Never doubt that I chose you."

Then he gave him a shove, knocking him into the lifeboat.

Chapter Forty-Five

A hand grabbed Annie's arm as she attempted to rush by. It was Lieutenant Lightoller. "Stewardess, there's room for you in this boat."

The vessel was packed tight with older women dressed in a mishmash of overcoats and furs, life belts strapped over everything awkwardly, some outlandish dress hat perched on messy hair to top it all. Each and every one of them was frightened, a few were crying. Annie recognized the face of the man put in charge of the rudder—a nodding acquaintance—but not the two sailors at the oars.

She drew back from him. "But I don't want to go. . . . I'm looking for someone."

He frowned at her as he would a child. "That's an order, miss. I need a stewardess aboard to take care of those two elderly passengers— Do you see them?" He nodded discreetly in the direction of two frail women sitting in the middle of the boat. They looked like wraiths, their nightgowns peeking out from their life belts, diaphanous white skirts and sleeves flapping in the wind. The two old women held hands like lost schoolchildren. As though holding hands would save them.

They're dead already, she wanted to tell Lightoller.

He wrestled Annie over the side and into the boat before she had a chance to break away; and before she knew it, the lifeboat was being lowered. The man at the rudder looked terrified, his knuckles white on the tiller, but he scowled at her to hide his fear. "You heard Mr. Lightoller: take the seat next to those passengers and do as you're told."

But Annie stood where she was and scanned the decks for Mark or Ondine. Her heart sank with every second that ticked by: there were so many people on the ship, more than she'd realized. She'd never seen most of them before, confined to the first-class section. She started to understand that she would probably never see either Mark or the baby again.

She turned away, resigned to taking her seat, when a miracle occurred. There was Caroline on the other side of the lifeboat, holding Ondine in her arms. The baby was crying and flailing, as though fighting to be free of her mother. And there was a look of fright on Caroline's face, almost indescribable—as though she was seeing a ghost. *It's me*, Annie realized with a jolt: *she's frightened of* me.

Because she knew, didn't she? Annie knew her secret. She was guilty—it was plain to see now. Annie lunged toward her—but as she did, Caroline panicked, turning too abruptly in her spot. She stumbled against the side. The vessel rocked with the sudden shifting of weight.

Annie gripped her seat as everyone on board seemed to shuffle and shift like dominoes, causing the boat to buckle a second time (maybe helped from above, one of the seamen mishandling the ropes, the lifeboat bobbling) and in the blink of an eye, Caroline stumbled—

She hit the inner lip of the boat and fell backward over the edge.

Ondine still in her arms.

Without taking a moment to breathe, Annie threw herself at the side just in time to see the froth of white where Caroline had fallen into the black water. The smell of brine mushroomed into the air, like a gasp from the sea.

Ondine.

There was no hesitation, not an instant of thought. Annie leapt over the side after them.

Frigidly cold. Bubbles teased her, as though someone was breathing down her neck. The taste of salt and filth filled her mouth, like a deep-held memory.

For a whole moment, the water wrapped around her, dark and womblike. Then she burst above the surface.

Still, it was completely black; Annie flailed out her hands, waves continuing to slosh over her, rising all around in the darkness of the night. She listened to the sound of panicked thrashing and tried to pinpoint the direction it was coming from, but there was noise everywhere: the movement of other lifeboats splashing in the sea, items being pitched off the *Titanic*'s upper decks. People jumping to have it over with, because they couldn't live with their fear for another minute.

And beneath it all, a kind of low, slurping hiss—terrifying and everywhere. The sound of the ship itself, taking on weight. Succumbing to the hard suck of the deep.

She treaded water as she swiveled in a slow, cold circle. Caroline could not be far—unless she'd gone under already.

Then she heard it, the most discernible noise in the cacophony: a baby's cry. It was straight ahead. She swam toward the noise confidently: she was as good as a seal in water. The water was her element, always had been. There was Caroline, bobbing straight ahead, her blue hands holding the baby above lapping waves even though she herself was sinking.

Annie had a choice. Reach out and Ondine would be in her arms in a moment, the struggling Caroline lost to the waves. Or—

She pulled Caroline up from the water, able to keep her face just bobbing above the surface.

"Hang on to Ondine, Mrs. Fletcher, and I'll keep you afloat—"

She would save them both.

No matter what Caroline had done, it didn't mean she deserved to die. Or if it did, it was not Annie's judgment to make but that of God and the law.

But Caroline gargled and cried out, barely able to balance herself. She heaved the baby at Annie. "You won't be able to. I'm not wearing a life belt . . ."

Through the churning darkness, Annie saw the swirl of heavy coats, their pastel colors wavering, like sodden ghosts. One of Caroline's favored dresses. Annie knew wool was heavy as sandbags when wet; she may as well have wrapped herself in an anchor.

Caroline's face was blue in the starlight. Annie was holding Ondine over her shoulder—the baby was crying in her ear, but she couldn't hear it—the world had gone silent. Caroline was speaking, but Annie couldn't make out what she was saying.

"Save her," Caroline seemed to mouth. "Save her."

A memory came to Annie, even as she tried to yank at Caroline's collar, to keep the woman's mouth above the salty waves. Caroline was tiring. She looked exhausted. She was swallowing so much water. . . .

The cardinal rule of survival in the sea, Annie. Beware a drowning person. In their panic, they will pull you under with them. She'd heard the sentiment many times, but when Des had said it to her, he'd meant something else by it. He'd meant, *I can't save you, Annie.*

He'd meant, *God can't save us all.*

He'd meant, *It's either you or me.*

And he'd chosen.

Distress rockets flared and sputtered suddenly overhead, illuminating the sea, and for a brief moment, Annie thought she saw Caroline's face change. The water lapping over her distorted her features, so it was hard to know for sure, but she looked like a different person. A pretty girl whose face had been ravaged by angry slashes.

A name reverberated through her mind: *Lillian.*

Annie felt such a strong sense of recognition at the face and the name that she let out a cry and let go of Lillian.

No, of Caroline.

And then, Annie knew. Lillian was haunting them because she wanted her daughter back.

The water had jolted her awake and alive, for what seemed like the first time in days.

By now the lifeboat was in the water and was headed toward the two women. Sixty feet away, fifty . . . but it was too late. They would not reach the pair in time.

Lillian was gone and Caroline was before her but falling through the water, slipping out of Annie's hand. She had closed her eyes and now her whole beautiful face drifted under the water. Annie gasped, treading water, balancing the baby, crying out silently even as Caroline's billowing dress and darkened hair swirled into the inky black, a final flag of surrender, and gone.

Chapter Forty-Six

William Stead leaned over the railing. It was almost impossible to fathom what was happening. He'd known these people only a few days, but he felt close to them, and now they were in peril.

He could hardly believe what he'd just seen: his stewardess had leapt out of the lifeboat heroically to save Caroline Fletcher and her baby. Along with every other person on the port side, he watched as Annie Hebbley tried to keep Caroline Fletcher's head above water, holding his breath as the waves washed over the young woman's head time and again. He squinted to focus on Caroline's face, afraid for her, wanting to remember her . . . and was surprised when he thought he saw Eliza Armstrong instead. Eliza bobbing in the water. Eliza slipping through Annie Hebbley's hands . . . It had to be his eyes playing tricks on him, or his mind. There in the water, Eliza in peril. She would always be in peril, in Stead's mind.

"Why doesn't she take the baby to the lifeboat?" the man next to him growled. "The mother is a lost cause. That's damned irresponsible of her. They could all drown."

They could all drown. It was a slap to Stead's face, jolting him awake.

That heroic young lady could drown.

Was she the only hero on this ship?

Do not think about what you are about to do. Just do it.

His life belt hung in his hand; he hadn't put it on yet. He tore off his overcoat and tossed aside his hat, then slipped the clumsy life belt over his shoulders. He climbed over the railing and, before any of the people standing next to him realized when he was doing, jumped.

You are not a young man, Stead. This is madness.

He couldn't even recall the last time he went in the water. Maybe ten years ago, he had taken a vacation to Brighton and done a bit of bathing at the shore. He still remembered the gray bathing suit he'd worn. He had never been one for vacations, let alone the seashore. It had been an anomaly.

He couldn't believe how cold the water was. He was surprised his heart hadn't stopped. His mouth had been open when he leapt and he'd swallowed a good deal of seawater. None of that mattered. *Move, and keep moving, or you shall die.*

By luck, he wasn't far from Annie Hebbley. She'd given up on Caroline Fletcher and—Stead realized with horror—for some inconceivable reason, was trying to swim to the *Titanic*. She could use only one arm, the other holding the baby to her shoulder, keeping the head out of the water.

She'll never make it.

He managed to swim next to her. "Miss Hebbley, what are you doing? There's a lifeboat not a dozen yards behind you—you must go to the lifeboat."

Her face had a strange set he hadn't seen before. "No—I must get back to the ship. I must get to Mark."

"Think of the baby. The baby will die."

Stead could see the girl was thinking, as tired and dazed as she was. Listening. He was able to nudge her toward the lifeboat, which had kept doggedly rowing toward them. Between the two of them, they were able to keep the baby's head out of the water. But as soon as Stead delivered the baby into the outstretched arms of the people in the lifeboat, the stewardess turned away and began heading again for the *Titanic*.

Fool girl. Addled by the cold. I should swim after her. But the cold water was leaching the last of his strength away and the stewardess was swimming like a woman possessed.

Something flashed overhead in the light from the ship—a deck chair. Someone had thrown it, perhaps thinking Annie Hebbley could use it to float, but it fell on her. She'd been unprepared and disappeared beneath it. For a long horrible moment, Stead held his breath, waiting to see if she would resurface. But there was nothing, just the wooden deck chair bobbing on the waves.

He swam toward her as quickly as he could. By the time he reached her, she had floated to the surface. He managed to wrestle off his life belt and put it on her. The lifebelt was quickly becoming useless, but it would help keep her afloat. She was unconscious and unable to swim so he paddled back to the lifeboat, pulling her behind him. Women reached over the side of the lifeboat and hauled her on board.

But when Stead started to hoist himself over the side, the crewman at the rudder stopped him. "I'm afraid there's no room for you in the boat," he said. "We're over capacity as it is."

"But he's a hero," one of the women said. "We have to bring him on board."

"Hold on to the side," another woman said to him. "You shall be safe enough."

The woman had no idea how cold the water was, Stead knew. She was wrong, ridiculously so. His teeth chattered uncontrollably as he treaded water. His mind started to cloud, he was aware of that much. He was so cold and so weak that he could no longer feel his body.

He started to get drowsy. He'd lost track of how long he'd been in the water. Ten minutes? *If I fall asleep, I'll drown*—but he couldn't see how he could possibly stay awake.

He tried to watch the events unfurling on the ship. The lifeboats being lowered. The increasingly rough struggles on the *Titanic* as panic set in, as men realized there would be no last-minute rescue. Eventually, it was too painful to watch and he had to turn away.

He held on to the lifelines dangling from the side of the lifeboat as it rowed away. "You don't want to be sucked under as the ship goes down, do you?" the man at the tiller snapped testily to the women who thought they should stay and rescue more jumpers as the two crewmen pulled at the oars. The argument continued as Stead's fingers slipped off the lifeline, and no one noticed when he fell behind and sank beneath the surface of the water. *I loved you, Eliza,* was one of his last thoughts. And: *I would have protected you forever. All this time, that's all I wanted you to know.*

Diary of Lillian Notting

8 January 1912

My daughter.

You're finally here.

And now that you're here, I can only wonder how I could've been so afraid of you, afraid of what you meant for my life. Mine and your father's.

How beautiful you are. You deserve to have a good life. I know what people would think of you if I kept you. How you would spend the rest of your life disgraced for being a bastard and treated differently because of it. How your prospects would shrink. How much smaller and harder your world would be. How unfair, and all because of me.

How could I, your mother, do that to you?

This is why I am agreeing to my end of the Bargain.

You deserve to be in a better place than this.

My greatest hope is that you remain untarnished by the past that brought you here. That you remain safe and innocent forever, as I was not.

1916

~ellee~

Chapter Forty-Seven

20 November 1916
HMHS *Britannic*

Annie's hands shake as she carries Lillian Notting's diary to the edge of the railing. Below her the sea is dark and winking. She has read all of the entries, up to the last one, which ends abruptly on January in 1912. Just three months before the *Titanic* set sail on its maiden voyage.

She couldn't face her shift after the argument with Mark, so she told Sister Merrick that she's not feeling well and asked for the evening off, before creeping out of the ward under the matron's suspicious and watchful stare.

Annie thinks about climbing the railing and jumping into the sea.

With no cloak, she hugs herself for warmth. How could she have been so stupid as to get her hopes up? Mark never felt anything for her, apparently. *Was I mistaken?* It hadn't felt wrong. It had felt—at the time—like he really had been drawn to her. The warmth of that feeling was the most real thing she had ever felt.

And without it, she feels lost. Having read the diary, nothing makes sense. The world is turned upside down. She opens the diary and in the dim light emanating from one of the windows nearby, she once again scans its passages.

17 May 1911

Fate has spared me, though I do not know why.

My closest friends are all gone. Beth, Tansy, Margaret. I keep thinking of Margaret's little boy—motherless now. I keep thinking how Tansy must have screamed. She was so timid, scared of everything. She had said the building was unsafe. I never considered she was right.

Now there is nothing left of the factory girls whose voices once filled my days. Nothing left of the mill except a husk of charred brick.

23 May 1911

I realized something today: I am alive because of Mark's gambling. If it weren't for his disastrous night—the sobbing for forgiveness, the waves of fury—I would not have been left quite so desperate and penniless. With the comfort of my meager savings, perhaps I never would have been brave enough to ask for a better wage, and if I hadn't asked for more money I would not have been brought before the mistress herself. She would not have deemed me "presentable" enough to meet clients and sent me to the house of Caroline Sinclair to do a fitting. I would not have been on my knees taking up Mrs. Sinclair's hem when the fire broke out at the old factory. I would not have been in her parlor, laughing at her witty comments and greedily accepting her gifts of candy and praise. I would not have been holding her hand as she dragged me through her spacious mansion, showing off the purchases she'd made on her European tour, the vast array of dresses in every color and modern style you could dream of. I would not have been drinking her tea and listening, rapt, as she told me her theory that life is for living and that women have as much right to life and liberty as a man. She told me that every article she commissioned for herself is an assertion that she matters in the world. I would not have been eyeing her in the mirror as I measured her waistline, thinking I had been introduced to Caroline Sinclair for a reason, catching my own reflection beside hers, and seeing two women so very different, yet drawn to each other immediately.

In this way, it is both Mark and Caroline who have saved me.

14 June 1911

Caroline's rented home is in Hampstead Heath, on a hill overlooking the park. We sometimes sit for hours in her front room, the one with the best view of Kenwood House, just watching the people coming to visit the famous Russian couple living there, and talking. Talking nonstop—about love and life and all of our trials. About her late husband. About sex, even. Of course, I have told her all about Mark, too. I love spending time with her. We don't even bother to pretend that she has me making her clothes. That is a mere formality, a tiny part of what really brings us together.

And I have fallen in love with this house, because it is the place where she lives. I hope she never goes back to America. I have by now memorized all my favorite sitting areas, all the best of her dresses—one in every color, to celebrate, in her words, a modern widowhood.

She may sound crass this way, but she is anything but. An heiress in her own right and now inheritor of her late husband's estate, I know she must be wealthy beyond belief, but there's a sweetness to her, a freshness, that just seems so pure, so good. So unlike the society ladies I have known in London. I cannot help but think that just one of her fine dresses could wipe out Mark's debt. Not that I would ever mention it to her. I don't want her pity.

1 July 1911

It was my destiny to survive, Caroline tells me every day. I mustn't feel guilty for having lived when my friends died. If this is true, though, then why do I have these debilitating pains every morning? The headaches, the bone-deep ache, the stomach cramps? I believe it is guilt, but Caroline will have none of it. She wants me to see her physician and insists on paying for it. I must take this seriously, she insists.

So, I have relented. I am to see her physician tomorrow.

5 July 1911

I have not yet told Mark. Telling him will only make it real. And besides, I fear he'll guess at the dark thought I keep turning over in my mind, the thought I'd only share in these private pages. The thought of making it go away.

I've heard of such things. Witch doctors and the like, who can give you an elixir, a little dose of poison just enough to make the unborn thing bleed out of you in a rush. Painful but over in a matter of weeks. Though sometimes they say it sweeps the mother away, too. You can never be sure what's safe.

Caroline—sweet Caroline. She says she will help me. Help *us*. She has asked Mark and me both to move into her home. I will have better care there. And though it is unusual—crazy, even—I am tempted to accept.

2 September 1911

It is all very unorthodox. I know this. But these past months have felt like a summer out of a bewitching novel. Caroline worries that once the child is born, I will want to change my mind, but she is wrong. She can give the child a life that we could not. And in exchange, we will have enough to live comfortably forever, to pay off all Mark's debts and put the ugliness of the past behind us for good. This is the Bargain we agreed to. I do not go back on my word.

Mark, too, is flourishing. He has not set foot in a gambling den in over two months. And while he resisted living under the same roof, he has finally given up the charade of returning to that dreary flat of his in the evenings. He has taken up with us, and it makes me so happy. Our walks in the garden. Our late nights in the west-facing parlor, the one full of outlandish art. And though Caroline has given him his own rooms, he spends many of his nights in mine.

Sometimes I think I see something like envy flit across Caroline's face, and I do not blame her. To bask in a love like ours is to be blessed. I know it's unlike anything she experienced with Henry, her late husband. I know she, too, longs for that love in her life. But in a way, she already has it, for I can feel how Mark's heart is widening toward her more and more every day, just like mine did. We are both in love with each other and in love with her. It is a wonderful thing.

1 November 1911

This is hard. I don't know where to begin. First, my body is not my own. I hate this giant *thing* I have become. I crave Mark more than ever, but my body refuses his. I feel cramped and sick all the time. And the ease of Caroline, the very thing that has always made me love her so, now makes my heart feel wretched with jealousy. I can't say what for—is it that perfect, unblemished body, or the smile that has never known the kind of doubts and worries that I have seen, or that eternal optimism that smacks of privilege? Or is it the way Mark sees all those things, too, only with a sparkle in his eyes, with the swallow of lust in his throat. I've always told him that I can read his mind, and I can. I know what he wants.

He wants what every man wants—the gamble, the risk, the thrill of potentially losing it all.

He wants what he can't have.

He wants *her*.

12 December 1911

They think I don't know. It's absurd, outrageous. Mark says that it is only the pregnancy making me out of control. He wants me to doubt myself. How dare he? After everything he has put me through in the past? After I've agreed to trust him, again and again, no matter his past deeds, his failings—how I've held him when he wept with apology. After he spent all my money. After he begged me to take him back. After he threw himself on the floor and kissed my knees. After we've made love a thousand times—in his flat, in his office when the rest had gone for the night, even in the park once, last year. We've laid claim to all of London with our love. We used to laugh, holding hands and racing the streets, pointing out places we'd like to christen with the act of our love. He knows every part of me. Every willful, rageful, wild, and prideful flare to my being. He has seen my best and my worst. I will love him to the ends of the earth, and he knows it. Even if he breaks me. No matter what he has done. No matter what he does now. I would do anything—give up anything. I would give up my *child*.

I would even share him.

So, how dare he lie to me.

I know what is going on.

And I know, too, that if I were Caroline, I would not be able to resist him, either.

It's too much. Annie slams the journal closed again and presses it to her chest, finding it hard to breathe. *What happened to you, Lillian?* The child was born in January. There are no entries after that, but Annie can feel the rage and fear and love of this woman as though it were her own, and it's unbearable. Lillian may have made a bargain with Caroline, may have promised away her baby with goodwill, but something changed. She died wanting that child back. Annie is sure of it. That is what keeps her lingering here, in Mark's wake, all these years.

She is about to let the pages flutter out over the Atlantic when she feels the presence of someone approaching, and quickly slips the journal back into her apron pocket.

She turns to see Charlie Epping, the wireless operator, sidling up next to her in his easy, warm way. Since the day Annie came on board this ship, Epping has tried to get her attention, smiling at her, trying to engage in small talk. He seems a nice man and is universally loved by the nurses, who treat him like a little brother. They say he is very smart, most likely a genius.

"Taking the air, Nurse Hebbley?" he asks. He tosses his cigarette over the railing, then looks at her intently, trying to read her face. "Had a rough day on the ward? Though I suppose they're all tough."

He invites her to the radio room for a drink. Helplessly, with a hollowness inside her, she follows.

Perhaps the ghost of Lillian cannot find her in here.

Perhaps she just needs a man to protect her from all of this—from herself, even. From the darkness and fear that curl up on all sides when she is alone with her thoughts.

The wireless operators live in the radio room; she remembers this from the *Titanic* as well. A quirk of the position, someone needs to be near the equipment at all times. The hospital ship has only one wireless operator and so Epping is the only man beside the officers to have his own living quarters.

They hurry along silently to the boat deck and the small room behind the first funnel, a stone's throw from the bridge. He takes a bottle from one of the cupboards—the room seems fitted with many secret little compartments holding all manner of equipment, little tubes and wires and such—and pours two tiny glasses of amber liquid.

She sniffs and winces at the medicinal smell, like the rubbing alcohol she uses on patients and to clean the counters and equipment. He raises his drink to her before throwing it back in one fell swoop. She does the same.

Within a few minutes, she feels like she is floating. When she turns her head, the view doesn't change right away but lags. Everything is stilted—removed and abstract. The weight that she normally feels pressing down on her chest every minute of every day has lifted. She starts to laugh for no reason.

It is a delightful feeling.

Epping pours another drink for her.

An hour later, the room is spinning. She is having trouble with the tiny, fold-down perch next to Epping's worktable, sliding off it suddenly, as though the ship is rocking. She's having trouble, too, putting words in their proper order and getting them out of her mouth without erupting into laughter. Also, she is hot. She's had to remove her apron and loosen her collar, and has taken off her starched cap. Her hair billows down around her shoulders.

Charlie sits on the other side of the table, within easy reach. His face is red and he is sweating, but his smile is big and loose and easy. It has been so long since someone *saw* her. Noticed her. Appreciated her. Wanted her. For four years at Morninggate, she had been as invisible as a ghost. She was not a person but a shadow. Here, with Charlie Epping, she is light.

The rest is a blur—how his hands tug at her buttons and she doesn't stop him.

How his lips find her throat.

How even as he moans against her, all she hears is Des's voice. *What have we done, Annie? What have we done?*

She's not sure how many hours have passed. Annie wakes with Desmond Flannery's whispers still ringing in her ear.

Where am I? The cramped room smells of musk and sweat. There's a young man sleeping next to her and then she remembers. Charlie Epping. Cheap whiskey. Clumsy kisses.

She slips out of the bunk and gathers her clothing. Epping sleeps on, the deep slumber of the satiated. Annie puts her clothes on slowly, as though she's forgotten how things are supposed to go. She doesn't feel well. She is feverish and achy; even the bottoms of her feet are tender.

She staggers a step or two, steadying herself on the furniture, and her hand lands on paper. It's large, covering a quarter of the table. In the dim light spilling from the hall, she sees that it's a map. It reminds her of that night, four years ago. Maps and coordinates and knowing *precisely* where things were had been very important. She'd seen the numbers, but she hadn't known how to find those coordinates on a map, so once the numbers were lost the knowledge was, too. . . . She can still picture those tiny white squares disappearing in the blackness of the Atlantic Ocean, and she's still filled with regret for what she did.

She feels as though she's still adrift in a dangerous sea and there's something about the map that makes her feel safer. It is protection, a talisman like a rabbit-foot or a four-leaf clover, so she rolls up the map, squashes it flat with both palms, then folds it until it's small enough to fit in her apron pocket.

And then she leaves.

She is far from the nurses' quarters when she realizes she is burning up with fever—or something like it. She's dizzy, afraid she will faint before she gets to her room and they'll find her in the morning sprawled out on the floor not far from the radio room. Afraid not of death but of the scandal. Of everyone knowing what she's done.

She's near a tub room, where they immerse patients in water to flush out wounds and take down runaway fevers. There's a big metal bathtub inside and barrels of water.

Normally, for the patients, they heat up the barrels of water, but Annie doesn't bother with that: it would take too long and besides, she is burning up. The last thing she wants is hot water. Then she strips off her clothing, which is damp with her perspiration, and steps into the tub. It reminds her of wading into the ocean back home, the cold bite of the sea on her feet, then her calves. She lowers herself into the water, slowly at first, then quickly.

It feels good at first, countering the fever inside her. For a minute, she feels in perfect balance. But then the cold sets into her extremities, chilling her fingers and toes, nipping at the flesh of her buttocks, tickling her armpits. She wishes the cold would take her away. It feels oddly familiar, like being in the arms of a lover.

Annie closes her eyes and starts to drift. Snippets of memories come to her. The shimmering surface of the bathwater reminds her of the scrying bowl Mr. Stead used for the séance, its brilliant mother-of-pearl lining flashing silver and white. . . . Steel-gray and periwinkle shells washed up on the beach outside her childhood home . . . As a child, swimming for what seemed like miles with fat gray seals, past the tiny rocky outcroppings that dotted Ballintoy's coast.

The next thing she knows she is standing, water coursing off her like rain through the downspout, drops hitting the surface of the bathwater so loud that it hurts her ears. Her teeth chatter furiously, her lips numb. How long has she been asleep in the cold water? She could've frozen to death.

And then she sees her reflection in the front of a dispensary cabinet, so mirrorlike that it's caught soldiers off guard, too, when they rise out of the tub. Only this isn't *her* reflection. It's the reflection of a woman whose face has been all cut up and her hair chopped off like a prisoner or a penitent. An angry young woman with murder in her eyes.

Annie staggers backward a step, then clambers out of the tub. She is going mad. She must be losing her mind.

"It's you," she whispers. "Lillian."

"No," a voice answers, slightly mocking. "That's *you*."

The voice is coming from behind her.

Annie turns to see a specter rising from the bathwater, the figure of a woman that shimmers brightly like morning light on dew. She stands tall, towering over Annie. The sight of her paralyzes Annie, but it resonates with her, too. A dim, old memory skitters through her mind.

I know you.

It's the woman she met on the beach years ago, when she was a child. The dubheasa of her grandmother's stories. Annie can feel the truth of it rattling her bones.

"Turn and look at the reflection. You recognize that body, don't you, Lillian Notting? That is the woman you once were."

Staring, Annie reaches to her hair, expecting to find it chopped away, but in her hand is a long, wet twist of strawberry blond.

It's not a reflection.

"I'm here to remind you who you are, and of our Bargain. I've been waiting a long time for what you owe me, Lillian Notting, but I'll wait no more."

That horrible pain in her head comes back, a pain to split her skull in two.

The shimmer gets brighter, so bright that Annie cannot look at it. "That nice body—I gave it to you, don't you remember? Yours was destroyed. . . . Oh, you did terrible things to it, didn't you? You wanted to come back, but you needed a new vessel."

Annie runs her hands over her naked body. This is her body, the only body she's ever known. "I'm Annie Hebbley," she says, more to herself than the spectacle beside her.

"Sometimes there are problems when you take another body. Sometimes the old spirit doesn't want to leave. Sometimes the mind is still cluttered with the old life, the old memories. It's up to you, Lillian Notting. You must take control."

The pain gets stronger, more insistent, making it impossible for Annie to think. She shakes her head as though she can shake the pain loose. These aren't memories; they're just stories she's heard from Caroline or Mark, or even quite possibly read once in a book or overheard from a neighbor. It doesn't matter where they've come from: she knows she is not Lillian. That's impossible. She's Annie Hebbley. It's just that she isn't feeling well.

Other memories come at her, ones she tries not to acknowledge. From the unhappy times at Ballintoy. She remembers opening an old tin throat lozenge case, filled with tiny white pills that she stole from a sick neighbor. She doesn't know what the pills are for, only that they are deadly if taken in quantity. In this memory, Annie Hebbley wants to die. There is no future for a ruined woman with a strict father in a small Irish town.

Not when the father of your baby is a priest.

But the pills aren't working the way she thought they would. Annie starts to bleed between her legs and she knows what that means because it happens to the women of her village all too often: she is having a miscarriage. This is the last place she would want this to happen. Not in the house. Her mother and father will see the evidence and they will know their daughter is not a good girl.

She has no choice but to go down to the beach and wade into the pounding surf, and surrender to the mercy of the sea.

Annie rocks unsteadily on her feet. The shimmering woman in the metal tub has vanished. The scary image reflected in the medicine cabinet is gone, too. Annie is alone, standing in a puddle.

Is either story she has just seen real? Or are they just stories her mind created to keep her from remembering something worse? She remembers what Dr. Alice Leader had told her on the *Titanic*: *The troubled mind can never know itself. That is the sad truth of madness.*

She is so, so tired of being mad.

There is only one course of action open to her, as far as she can see. Only one thing she can control.

The enemy of water is fire. The dubheasa may rule water, but she has no dominion over fire.

First, Annie puts on a dressing gown, taking one off a stack of military-issued ones for the wounded men. It hangs off her like a horse blanket, but at least it's dry—so dry that it will, in fact, make good kindling. Then, she searches the cabinets until she finds a box of matches. Her head is pounding so badly she can barely think, but that's all right. She doesn't want to think. If she does, she might not go through with what she knows *she must*.

Snick, snick. Annie runs the phosphorus match head down the strip of sandpaper on the side of the box. Sparks fly promisingly, but at the last second, the wooden stick breaks in her hand. She tries another. The next one lights but goes out just as quickly. Then more sparks, more broken sticks. Is she gripping too hard? Maybe the matches are damp, gone bad. All gone bad. She doesn't notice the faint ocean breeze creeping in from under the door that seems to blow out each match right before it ignites.

Should have died in the fire. The thought moves through her, smoky and dizzying. The fire. The factory fire all those women died in—all but her.

All but Lillian.

She looks down at her trembling hands and for a moment, sees not the matchbook but a men's razor, sharp and gleaming.

She screams.

Chapter Forty-Eight

20 November 1916
Ballintoy, Ireland

The fine sand from the beach gets everywhere in the house, even in a room that's not been used in four years, Mrs. Hebbley thinks as she runs a feather duster over a chest of drawers. She'd use a cloth but then the sand would scratch the wood. It's not fancy furniture, but it is all she's got, and she knows her husband will not replace it.

She's in her daughter's room. She means to pack away Annie's things and let two of her sons move in. The youngest, Matthew, has gotten so big that it really is a punishment to make him share one room with his three brothers.

Finally, the day has come when Theresa Hebbley is ready to let her daughter *go*.

The thought makes her heart tighten, like someone is squeezing it. She can still remember the last time she saw her daughter. She'd been in this bed. The girl could've been asleep, but a mother knows. It wasn't sleep. It was the middle of the day. She'd pulled the blanket back to wake her and that was when she saw the terrible things. What kind of pills they were, Theresa Hebbley had no idea. She didn't believe in modern medicines. They were the devil's work and here was the proof.

There had been blood on the sheets, too. Where had the blood come from? There wasn't a mark on Annie, not a cut, not a bruise. Theresa Hebbley had shaken and slapped her daughter in an attempt to wake her up. But there was no waking her.

Was she dead? Theresa hadn't known that day. There was no one home. The boys were out doing odd jobs, and Jonathan was still at work. Theresa had no idea what to do. Run for a neighbor? She had a vague sense of shame—How could she explain how Annie came to be like this? Should she hide the pills?—and hated herself for dithering, for not knowing what to do. *Go for the doctor*, was her next thought, but the doctor was in Dunseverick, a good hour's trip on foot.

She got so flustered, she did what she always did in times of stress and indecision: she went to church to pray for guidance. Jonathan wasn't here to tell her what to do, so she would look to God. The church wasn't so far and so she ran. Down the street, as fast as her feet would carry her. That quiet young priest, still new to their town, Father Desmond, was there, replacing the tapers in all the candelabra, and he asked if there was something troubling her, something he could help with. She couldn't bring herself to tell him because he was so young—it didn't seem possible for him to be a priest yet, not a full-fledged one—and she didn't want to embarrass Annie in front of a stranger.

Because she knew why her daughter had taken those pills.

The blood, that much of it—with no cuts or wounds—meant a woman's weakness and shame.

She knelt in a pew in front of the altar, closed her eyes, and started reciting the Lord's Prayer in her head. There was comfort in repeating the familiar words. They helped to steady her heartbeat and slow her breathing. Now her heart didn't squeeze as badly. And once things slowed, she was pretty sure she heard God speaking to her, and he was telling her to go back home. Her daughter needed her *now*.

She ran back down the street, sure her neighbors (if any saw her) thought she had gone mad running back and forth to church so quickly, like she was dropping off a loaf of bread.

When she got to the gate, she knew the awful truth. She remembers it to this day: the white curtains flapping in the wind, the front door standing ajar. The small footprints in the sand—small like Annie's—going from the house to the water's edge.

Then nothing but sea.

For four years, this memory has haunted her. She cries every time she remembers, but today she wills herself not to cry. She has always told Jonathan and the boys that Annie isn't dead, but she has started to allow herself to believe that there is the slimmest possibility that this is not true. She knows she failed her daughter that day and it is time to start admitting as much, and accepting the punishment that goes with it, which is that she'll never see her daughter again.

She wishes she knew the father of Annie's unborn baby, but no one has ever stepped forward. No one has ever come to the door pale faced and hat in hand, asking where Annie has gone off to and whether there might be a way to get in touch with her. No one in the village has asked about Annie at all, except for Father Desmond, and she's certain that's only out of consideration for her, seeing her praying for her daughter's soul every day in the quiet solitude of church.

Theresa Hebbley figures the father to be a coward, plain and simple.

She opens the drawer of the nightstand. Inside are girl's things, things Matthew and his brother Mark will not want to see as they will only remind them of their lost sister. Ribbons and hairpins, illustrations of a pretty dress or hairstyle torn out of a newspaper or magazine. A single white glove, the kind meant for wearing to church, its twin lost. A small pot of carmine for the lips—not that Jonathan approved of his daughter using cosmetics.

Pushed to the back of the drawer is Annie's Bible, the one given to her as a First Communion gift years earlier. The plain leather cover is dried and cracked, the onionskin pages yellowed. Theresa Hebbley hefts it, remembering the many times she saw Annie hunched over the book, reading it not because she was so devout but because there was nothing else to read in the house. She was so hungry for stories, particularly after her father banned her from going to see her grandmother, Theresa's mother, for filling her head with nonsense. Fairies, selkies, the dubheasa.

The ripped edge of newsprint peeps out from inside the book. Another illustration that Annie fancied, Theresa thinks, and opens the book to see what it is. But it's not an illustration: it's an article.

An article from not so long before her daughter disappeared, about a fire in a factory in London. A tragic story, Theresa sees as she reads. Hundreds of girls died in the fire, unable to get out of the death trap in time. Instinctively, she wonders why her daughter had saved this story; had she been thinking of running away to London, to work in a factory like this one, and been stopped in her tracks when she saw this story? It doesn't seem likely, but Mrs. Hebbley's mind has run in a thousand different directions since Annie disappeared. She knows it's only the mind's refusal to accept the truth and a mother's wanting for her daughter to be alive, the evidence be damned.

As she goes to tuck the clipping back into the Bible, she notices that it's been annotated. A faded stroke of ink underlines a name: Lillian Notting, lone survivor of the fire. Could her daughter have possibly known this woman, Mrs. Hebbley wonders? Impossible; how would Annie ever have made the acquaintance of a London girl? And there have never been Nottings in Ballintoy, not in all the time Theresa has lived in the village.

So, this must have simply been a fascination of Annie's. Another girl who had survived something, perhaps a trial as terrifying as her own. A kind of heroine.

She tucks the clipping back into the Bible, swallows hard, and continues to make the room ready for her sons.

Chapter Forty-Nine

21 November 1916

HMHS *Britannic*

Door after locked door. This blasted hospital ship is all locked up at night, and Mark's fumbling search for more alcohol has led him down a long, empty hallway, dark but for one flickering bulb at the far end. The Glen Albyn has long since abandoned him, and Mark can't get the urgency of Annie's whispered voice out of his head. Her accusations, terrible and yet not far from his own suspicions.

Except it wasn't Caroline he suspected of wrongdoing.

His foot slips in something wet. He grips his cane, and for a fleeting moment, he is certain the ship has taken on water. That they are sinking.

But, no—the spill is seeping out from under a closed door. Could it be a burst pipe or ruptured tank? He shoves open the unlocked door, and there is Annie: unconscious on the floor.

The shock of it wrestles a gasp from his throat. Surrounding her are an array of broken matchsticks and her discarded nurse's uniform, sopping wet.

"Annie?" He sets the cane on the floor, kneeling beside her. The water—overflowed bathwater, he sees now—soaks into his trousers. He turns off the still-running faucet, then tries to lift her into an upright position, gently slapping her cheeks in an attempt to wake her. He catches the faint smell of alcohol on her, something raw and unpleasant.

She wakes with a violent start—and looks at him curiously. In this moment, she is so fragile and afraid that the dark suspicions he'd entertained only moments ago flee from his mind. His urge is only to protect her.

"What are you doing in here?"

She looks about, taking in the disarray: water everywhere, supplies knocked off shelves, a dispensary cabinet thrown on its side. She must've had a fit of some kind—there can be no other explanation. She starts shaking. His chest aches for a moment, remembering what he said to her. She confessed to loving him and he threw it back in her face. Then again, one couldn't just dismiss her mad rantings about Caroline. He must remind himself that she is untethered from reality. She is dangerous.

Gently he drapes a towel over her. "Let's get you to your room."

She whimpers. Her eyes are red rimmed. Her wet hair is awry. Her lips are raw, and her normally fair Irish skin is fiery and splotchy. It's hard to believe that she's the same girl he met on the *Titanic*.

"Please try to believe me." She clutches his forearms as though she fears he will run away—as though she anticipates he *will* try to run away. "I'm not Annie—I'm *Lillian*."

He freezes. "What?"

She goes on with a story of ghosts and sea spirits and more Irish superstition, but Mark isn't following her because he is thunderstruck. He is certain he never actually spoke her name to Annie. How does she know? Chills rattle down his spine and he lets go of her as though she is on fire or crawling with snakes.

"Annie, listen to me. You need help—"

"I need *your* help." The girl, perhaps heartened that he is still speaking to her, lunges for him. "Mark, I've done a terrible thing. In order to be with you, I've traded away Ondine's future. I made a deal with the dubheasa and I can't take it back. As long as I'm here, our daughter is in danger."

He doesn't believe a word of it. It's all nonsense, a childish fantasy. The girl needs a doctor. He will keep her quiet until morning, when the doctors are back on duty. If word were to get out, it would be demoralizing to the patients, to think that a nurse had gone mad. . . . But where to take her? He can't bring her to the nurses' quarters. She needs to calm down first, before her colleagues see her. He passed a few empty quarters when he was searching for drink. No one would think to look for her there.

Once he's got her situated in one of the empty rooms, he persuades her to try to sleep by promising to stand watch over her. He dusts off a camp stool and sits with his back against the wall to watch her sleep. *What happened to this girl?* He remembers the letter he'd found in the fireplace of the *Titanic*'s smoking room. It had been too burned to yield much, but he only had to read, *I was wrong to leave you to deal with this particular problem alone*, to know what this was about. She'd been pregnant and abandoned.

Mark looks uneasily at the sleeping girl. *She's mixed the story up in her mind*, he thinks, scrambling her past with what happened to Lillian. She wants to forget her own past by stepping into the life of another.

But he doesn't believe it, no matter how much he'd like to.

The living are often anchors for the dead. The old newspaperman Stead's words come back to him, how the dead want to lay down their troubles and escape to the next world, but it's the living, unable to let go, who keep them here. Love and desperation like heavy chains lash them to the earth. Has he been Lillian's anchor? Is he to blame? Has she come back in this poor, weak vessel?

No, this is nonsense. Ghosts are not real.

He rises from the stool, anxious to keep busy. He'd hung Annie's wet clothing to dry and he checks them now, putting his hand to the skirt and apron. Still damp. There's something bulky and stiff in the pocket of her apron. He pulls out a clumsily folded paper packet. He unfolds it: a map of the Aegean Sea and, more specifically, the Kea Channel, which the ship must sail through to get to Mudros. He'd spoken to one of the officers last night on the promenade over a cigarette and the officer had told him the Kea Channel was difficult to navigate, full of narrow straits and rocky shoals. But this—this is marked with mysterious symbols and codes.

His stomach sinks as he looks on Annie one more time. He remembers all the times she prepared warm milk for Ondine. Remembers how Ondine had seemed so sick, so . . . *altered*. He remembers Caroline's misgivings. He'd thought it was just another case of female jealousy. Now he wonders if he was wrong.

He has no idea what to make of Annie's rantings, why she wants to think she's Lillian. Something to do with him, no doubt. Wanting to step into Lillian's shoes. It's terrifying, what the mind can do. He's seen men snap in the trenches, suddenly believe they're seven years old again playing hide-and-seek in the forest and their mummies are looking for them.

In the end, he takes a cue from her own actions, and knows exactly what to do. He reaches for his belt.

~elle~

Chapter Fifty

Where am I?

She remembers being walked by Mark down a passage, her arm slung over his shoulder, her feet barely touching the floor. Then being eased gently onto a bed. And that is where her conscious memory ends.

Annie is a passenger in her body as she descends into sleep. Unable to speak, unable to control her thoughts, unable to make her body obey.

Images appear in her mind—she's immediately aware that they're Lillian Notting's memories—like a moving picture that's playing just for her.

The nightstand on Mark's side of the bed. A book sits at an angle, like it was recently discarded. A plain cream-colored envelope juts out of the pages, holding his place. She doesn't recall Mark reading last night or any night. . . . Lately, he has not been coming to her bedroom, and so she has crept into his. Only he isn't here. She knows what that must mean. She knows where he must be.

With Caroline. She touches the book—no doubt one lent to him by Caroline—and as she lifts it, the envelope falls out.

She picks the envelope off the floor. The upper-left-hand corner reads *White Star Line.*

Inside, there is a ticket. *Titanic. First-class passenger: Mr. Mark Fletcher.* Rubber-stamped in red, sprawled over the words: PAID.

She runs her thumb over the red ink. There is only one other person Lillian knows with a ticket for the crossing.

The pain she feels is immediate, a dagger plunged into her heart.

Mark's straight razor lies innocently within reach. She does it not just for the release from the anguish—the blood a distraction from her inner pain—but to defy the world. So much for a woman's beauty. *We are nothing without it.*

Her hair comes next—hacked off in rough patches, her hands trembling with a white-hot rage that burns the despair, turning it into determination, into a strange and eerie focus.

Like this, a monster, she leaves the house. Walks down the lane for all to see.

It happens in a blur. The outcries and whimpers from those who notice her. But no one can stop her. She is racing now, frantic, still bleeding, and people draw back as she passes, a nightmare in the flesh.

She follows the scent of water on the wind. Standing on a bridge, the wind scuttles over her near-bare head. The coolness, where before there was only the fire of her agony, brings momentary relief. For a brief second, Lillian smiles. This is what freedom feels like.

And then she steps into air. People on the street below her gasp as . . .

She plunges into the frigid Thames. The water surrounds her immediately, merciless. It grabs her nightdress and pulls her down, down. . . .

She swallows a bellyful of water, sucks even more into her lungs. . . .

Her brain floods with panic, fights to make her wake up. . . .

No, no, no . . . What have I done? . . . But it is too late. . . .

Mark is all she can think about, all she can see. Even now, she forgives him. . . .

She wants all of it back, her man, her baby, her life. . . .

But the pressure in her chest is unbearable. She tries to fight her way to the surface, but it only seems to fall farther and farther away. . . .

And then, in the darkness, in the lung-shattering pain, comes a voice, pure as music, sweet as an angel's. A voice that sounds like innocence itself.

I can give you a second chance, the voice says. It is the voice of the water, the voice of something vast and invisible. But in Lillian's last gasps, she sees the glitter of two green eyes, the splay of wild hair. A sea goddess, or a last hallucination, a passing vision, she can't be sure.

I'm everywhere, the vision seems to say. *I am the great mother witch of the sea, able to hear the drowning no matter where they are. You want to live? I will grant your wish, but you will owe me something in return: an innocent soul.*

You cannot return to your body. It is destroyed beyond use. But I will give you a new one, a fresh one. She has just died. The body is perfect.

Go now. Reclaim your love, if that is what you desire. Just do not forget: you must make good on your part of the Bargain. I will have my innocents, and they will live with me in the depths. Protected and loved forever. This is a bargain you cannot undo.

Lillian opens her eyes and she is standing before the gangplank leading to RMS *Titanic*, battered suitcase in hand, Annie's aunt Riona's shoes, hand-me-downs, on her feet. These are Annie's memories: meeting Violet Jessop. Claiming the more cramped of the two bunks in the tiny cabin they must share in order to ingratiate herself with Violet. Trying on the White Star Line stewardess's uniform, tucking in the gold crucifix so no one will see it. Learning to fold napkins and make beds and serve tea the White Star way.

Standing on deck on April 10, 1912, watching the first-class passengers come up the gangplank, wondering which ones will occupy the rooms that have been assigned to her, twelve cabins in first class.

This is when she sees Mark Fletcher, looking prosperous in the fine new suit Caroline has bought for him. And he is distracted, because the baby in his arms is spitting up on the front of his overcoat.

The baby is Ondine.

Annie wakes, drenched in a cold sweat. But even awake, images continue to play against her mind's eye. Writing a note to herself in the night, desperately trying to tell her waking mind the truth. The nights of roaming the ship, looking for Mark, listening for Mark, waiting for Mark. The way she savored the times he held her in his arms.

The dubheasa is right.

Annie is Lillian.

All this time, she has not been haunted. She has been the one haunting.

She came back—not for the child taken by Caroline. But for the man.

She came back for Mark.

But the thought that burns the most sickening in her mind is what she agreed to give up in exchange for love.

A clue—the vital clue all along—swarms into her mind: the brooch. The brooch that had been in her pocket all that time, with its little hidden latch.

A latch she *knew* was there all along, would thumb absently as she went about her work, for comfort. Because, once, the brooch had been *hers*. Caroline had given it to her—to Lillian, as a little gift.

And then comes the worst part, the dark, sickening tide of truth, as Annie watches herself—Lillian—pouring and warming the child's milk morning after morning. Afternoons, too. In a hidden corner of the *Titanic*'s kitchen so as to stay out of the cook's way.

Ever so subtly, flipping open the brooch and sprinkling powder into the warm, white liquid.

A pinch at every feeding.

Yes, she, *she,* had been the one, all along.

She had been the danger to the child.

She had been trying to make good on her promise.

After all, she owed the dubheasa a child. An innocent. That had been the Bargain.

She remembers going to Mark, desperate to get his attention. Telling Mark he's not paying attention to his daughter. *Doesn't Ondine look unwell to you? I think she's taken a turn for the worse.*

I think Ondine is in peril.

I think you should listen to me.

You need me, Mark, don't you see?

Me, Mark. Look at me. See me.

Choose me.

Now: she tries to leap from the bed, to find Mark and make him understand. He needs to help her end this nightmare.

But something is holding her down. A belt, wrapped tight around her wrists. She is lashed to the bed.

Or at least, Annie Hebbley is lashed down.

But Lillian Notting is not.

~elle~

Chapter Fifty-One

"Caroline is a better match for you than I am," Lillian said, touching his shoulder. They were sitting together in the breakfast room of Caroline's house, looking out the window at Caroline with the baby in the garden.

Lillian missed nothing. Her big blue eyes seemed to take in everything. Mark cursed himself; had she caught him looking too intently at the way Caroline moved through the manicured rows of flowers? He could always claim he felt indebted to Caroline—which was true. They owed her much and there was no arguing that. But Lillian was no fool.

"No woman could compare with your beauty," he said, kissing her hand. It was true: Lillian could be a model for illustrations in women's magazines. If she chose, her face could sell tea, perfume, soap. Except that it was hard to imagine her sitting still. She could perform on any stage in the West End (if she could act, but alas, she could not—she was far too dramatic for it).

"Beauty fades," she said, her voice tipped with the silver of need. "Will you still love me then, I wonder? When I am old—"

He laughed. "To me, you'll always be this young and this beautiful." He could tell she wasn't satisfied by his flattery. Lillian had changed over the past few months. Ever since Ondine had arrived. Her mood shifted without warning. She cried at the sight of a stray kitten, at a rain stain on her sleeve, at *anything. He'd always loved the dark, complex winding of her thoughts, but now they seemed always to tremble at the edge of an abyss. She never slept, even when the child did.*

The thing was, she wasn't wrong to be uneasy. Mark knew he was changing, too—and he blamed her for it.

Mark had resisted joining the two women for as long as he could, in this perfect house, where the outside world could be shut out at the gates. Eventually, he could resist no more and left his lonely rooms to live with them, and then he could barely stand to leave them to go to work. His days were perfect. He had Caroline at dinner and for long walks through the woods, Caroline's educated mind and clever tongue to entertain and engage him with fascinating stories about life in America. At night, he had Lillian in his bed. Lillian racing through his veins.

He knew he was being selfish and that it couldn't last, one man with two perfect women, but by the same token, he couldn't walk away from it. The longer he indulged, the harder it would be to give up—it would take some external force to pry him out of this love nest.

That force was Caroline's imminent departure for America.

The lawyers had finished their work. Caroline had the necessary documents ready and could finally return home. For this momentous occasion, Caroline decided to book passage on the maiden voyage of a new passenger ship, RMS Titanic, said to be the biggest and most luxurious liner of the day. It was expensive, yes, but Caroline wanted to celebrate what she saw as the turning point of her life. Mark wouldn't admit it, but he was a little jealous. What he wouldn't give to start a new life in a new country, and to do it in luxury, not to have to scrimp and struggle as he and Lillian had done before Caroline entered their lives.

That evening, as their stroll was drawing to a close, Caroline had handed him an envelope. "If I have misread your intentions of the past month, please forgive me," she said, her cheeks coloring. "But if I let this opportunity slip through my fingers, I'd never forgive myself."

He opened the envelope: it held a first-class ticket for the Titanic.

"Join me—or don't, and I will know your answer," she said before running away, leaving him openmouthed at the garden gate.

He spent the night and the next morning in a daze. It was as though Caroline had read his mind—but now he doubted whether he knew what he wanted. He'd held Lillian in bed that night, wondering if he could bear to leave her. He tried to picture life as Caroline's husband—in America, no less. Would he be expected to run her business interests? What would be his role, when he understood nothing about America, its laws or its ways? He could end up Caroline's lapdog, a conversation piece ("an English husband, how interesting!") for her American friends.

And there was Ondine to consider. He had grown to hate the thought of parting with her, of sending her off to America alone with Caroline. The more he thought about it, the more heartless it seemed. Was he that kind of man? Lillian slept unaware while Mark tossed and fretted. At one very dark point, he almost rose to pick up his straight razor and slit his own throat. What kind of man had he become? This was intolerable, insane. Impossible.

He was hunched over his ledger at work the next day when the solution came to him: we shall both go to America with Caroline. He no longer cared about what he would do—he and Lillian could become Caroline's servants, lady's maid and butler, in order to remain close—but he would not abandon his daughter. During his tea break, he went to a pawnshop and asked how much he might get for the first-class ticket, then ran to the White Star Line office to see about prices of second- and third-class tickets. Only then would he tell Lillian about his plan. He didn't want to get her hopes up, not when she had been so black of late.

But when he returned home that evening, Lillian was not there.

The first-class ticket sat on the nightstand, pulled from its envelope.

She'd discovered where he'd hidden it hurriedly in the pages of a book. She'd always been suspicious, even before. He should've known.

But the worst was yet to come.

It was a horrible scene, one his mind could not make sense of. Refused to make sense of.

What have you done, Lillian?

It was a misunderstanding.

He would find her. Make every apology, every assurance ever known to
a man.

He loved her. He'd marry her, at last.

They would find a way, no matter what.

Except that they would not. Because he never saw Lillian alive again.

Mark lifts the bottle of Scotch and tips it upside down over his glass,
for the last streaky drops of amber. The whiskey was good, a bottle
found hidden in a drawer in one of the doctors' offices.

He leans over the map he found in Annie's pocket. It's almost dry
now, laid out on a table and its edges weighted down with books. It's
crinkled and there's some bleeding of the ink, but it's legible. He's
looked it over for the last hour and thinks he's made sense of it: it's a
chart of the Kea Channel off the Greek coast. It's in the Cyclades,
which has the reputation of being windy and hazardous, considered
an ancient Greek curse upon sailors. He's no seaman, but the chart
certainly looks treacherous, dotted with many islands and the space
between them marked with quickly changing depths and soundings.

Most troubling are the notations—freshly made by hand—that, as
best Mark can figure, mark the location of sea mines. The German
mines have been an increasing threat to ships in the area, he's heard.
And now: the *Britannic* is steaming up the southeastern coast of
Greece, bearing down on the Cyclades, at this very minute. The captain needs to see this map right away.

As he rolls it up, he can't help but wonder how it came to be in
Annie's possession.

He steps into the alleyway, wondering where he might find Captain Bartlett at this hour of the morning, when he hears muffled singing. He recognizes the tune: it's "Nearer My God to Thee" and then
he remembers: the morning church service is going on, probably in

the mess hall, the largest gathering place. Captain Bartlett will surely be there, perhaps even leading.

Mark tugs at his clothing, unchanged since the day before. He feels rumpled and untidy, and his mind swims in the whiskey. He tries to smooth down his hair. Its natural curl has been unleashed by sweat and humidity and it makes him look like a madman, one of the many unkempt shell-shocked.

He lurches toward the service as fast as he can with his injuries, but it's hard to navigate the ship with a cane and he nearly goes sprawling several times, catching the tip on a railing or doorsill. As he makes his way down flights of stairs, he is unnerved by how much like the *Titanic* this ship is—even without the fine touches, servants and musicians, female passengers in silk dresses and wildly plumed hats, alcohol fumes and cigar smoke and perfume. It's like he's stepped back in time—or perhaps is a ghost haunting the present day.

The sound of singing grows closer. He can make out the words now:

Though like the wanderer, the sun gone down,

darkness be over me, my rest a stone;

Yet in my dreams I'd be

Nearer, my God, to thee . . .

He feels the presence of many souls on the other side of the door and can picture them sitting on the benches, sailors in their uniforms, nurses in their pinafores and wimples, soldiers in dressing gowns, sleeves or trouser legs pinned up and neatened for a missing arm or leg. The smell of breakfast, long past, lingers on the air. Fried kippers and beans, coffee and tea. Human smells. Such human affairs, even the worshipping of a God is quintessentially human. The wavering sound of unaccompanied song.

The presence—of life, of faith—emanating from beyond the door is strong and thrums with heat and life—while he is dead and cold and has been these four years since Lillian's death.

Stop thinking about Lillian. We are sailing into danger. I must tell the captain. Mark wills himself to push everything else out of his head.

Annie, Lillian, his daughter. He clutches the rolled-up map tighter to his chest and reaches for the door.

But it doesn't budge. He can't open it.

It wouldn't be locked, not for a church service. That's absurd. All are welcome.

He tries again, but the handle merely turns in his hand. Spins loosely at his touch. He bangs on the wood. They must be able to hear that inside—why doesn't someone get up and open the door for him? But nothing happens; it's as though they can't hear him, as though he's in another dimension. As though he's a ghost.

Or as though the church won't allow him in.

He remembers from a childhood story that witches and demons can't cross the threshold of a sacred place.

It's all in your head, old boy.

But it's not, and he knows it.

He bangs on the doors some more, rattles the handles again, but still no one comes to his aid. Finally, he stumps back out into the alleyway until he can no longer hear the singing. What sounded sweetly human moments ago, now sounds eerie, threatening, and deafeningly loud. A cacophony of innocence.

In his frustration and confusion, a crazy idea flits through his head. *Maybe Annie is telling the truth.* After all he's experienced the past few days, he must admit that Annie's story is the only thing that makes sense.

And what's more—maybe she's not the only ghost.

He starts to come alive, reverberating with a new thought. Maybe there is one last redemption. It's his fault Lillian is dead, he's known that all along. Living with the guilt, trying to hide it by marrying Caroline. He killed her with neglect. This *dubheasa*, this sea witch or whatever Annie called her, may have claimed Lillian, but fate has given him the chance to save his daughter. What was it Annie said— the sea witch wants her innocents? Ondine is innocent, but he'll be damned if the sea is going to claim her.

If everyone is in the service this morning, that means the wheel-house and bridge will be minimally staffed. There will be few men to get in his way. Mark knows what he needs to do. To end this curse at last. To end it all.

That's why the map ended up in his possession. It was important that he knows where the sea mines are.

Rising again to his feet, Mark Fletcher starts off for the bridge. And his destiny.

Chapter Fifty-Two

Am I dreaming?

Annie flexes her biceps, making her arm rigid—and it jerks at the end of its tether, like a dog chained to a tree. A leather strap is wrapped around her wrists, the other end tied to the metal bed frame. She pulls with increasing ferocity, but the frame is attached to the wall and will not budge.

She has no recollection of how she got here. She cannot remember which ship she is on. Time has bled together, her lives flowing one into the other.

She remembers the feeling of floating, the feeling of movement without her feet touching the ground. Drifting through the corridors of the ship—the *Titanic*, not the *Britannic*, evidenced by the beautiful appointments, surrounded by the ship in all its glory—she sees the people she knew then, now dead and gone. They turn their faces to her as she drifts by, William Stead, Benjamin Guggenheim, John Jacob Astor. She pities them in retrospect: such self-important men, playacting right up to the end. If they had known they'd only had days to live, what would they have done differently?

And then there is Caroline, her sweet face turning to her, shining with genuine love. Her beloved friend. A pain shoots through Annie's chest. Heartache, wrenching and true.

And now she sees herself, able to look down at herself in this moment, tied to this bed, her hair wild like a bird's nest, her face dirty and tear streaked. How can she be seeing this? Because she isn't Annie—not right now. She is Lillian.

As if in reaction to this sudden truth, she feels a lightness. She feels . . . *free*. The tension at her wrists lessens. Almost imperceptibly at first, then it slackens, until she is able to pull her hands free.

She is both in this body and not.

She sits up, rubbing her wrists, and looks about the room. She sees her clothes laid out to dry, sees that the map is gone. And knows, instantly, knowing without knowing, where it is. Who took it.

And what she must do.

Her feet, it seems, don't touch the floor as she makes her way to the bridge. Funny, for a large ship, it is surprisingly quiet and empty, as though a sorceress has put this kingdom under an enchantment, a sleeping spell.

She knows what she will find on the bridge and there it is: Mark, standing near the wheel, staring at the battered map stretched between his hands. On the floor at his feet, the two men who were left in charge while the others were away, the two men fallen under the enchantment and now asleep. Or has he harmed them?

Mark looks up when she enters, but his surprise and confusion quickly melt away. She knows that he is seeing not Annie but Lillian, and not the angry, vengeful Lillian he had betrayed but the Lillian of before. Beautiful and radiant, unscarred, with her glossy dark hair piled high on her head, lovely as the dawn.

He reaches for her hand, his eyes wide and filled with tears. "It's *you*."

She can see the red in his eyes—knows he has been drinking. Knows he is barely holding on. She has seen him this way many times before, though. He has always needed her. Needed her forgiveness.

Their fingers entwine. His are warm and strong, whereas hers feel as weak as water. She wishes she could hold on to him harder. They are together. At last. *At last, he sees.* "I've never left you," she says, realizing it's true. "It's always been you, Mark. You are all that matters to me. You know that, don't you?" She can't tell if she's speaking the words or if they are just moving somehow between them, from her heart to his. Through the inexplicable connection they've always had. And though she can hardly feel the body she is inside, still, something pinches in her throat. Something painful and hard and full of feeling. "I gave everything, Mark. I gave—I gave my *child*."

"But we agreed to it."

"Not to Caroline, Mark. Not to her. I gave Ondine to the dubheasa, don't you see? It was my . . . my promise. The Bargain."

"I don't understand." His voice is a low murmur, and he is staring into her eyes as though pinned in place by her gaze.

"So I could return to you, don't you see? So we could be together again. Finally. Forever."

A worried look flits across Mark's face but only for a second. *Ondine.* His child, but a child he has not seen in four years. The mother, however, is standing before him. Holding his hand.

He pulls her into his arms, crushing her body—no, *this* body—to his. His hands find her jaw, the back of her neck, her hair, like they always had when she was alive, and she feels as though she is made of pure flame. She has waited so long, so long for this. The idea of him—the need for him, for a second chance, for *this*—pulsing and aching inside of her.

"I love you," he whispers again, as if still in disbelief. "You came back for me, and I love you. I love you so much." When his lips touch hers—salty with tears—she feels the kiss making her light again, light as wind, feels the way it pulls something out of her, feels her soul finding his and swirling into it. All the pain, all the anger and fear, all the compromises and betrayals, all the *waiting*. The horrible dark promise she made. All of it has led to this.

And then—then she steps back. And in the place of that momentary bliss, there is only loneliness.

"That's right," Mark says, not noticing the change in her. His eyes search her face, taking it in, a long satisfying drink of water for a man dying of thirst. "You are the one, Lillian. You've always been the one." He almost laughs. "It was always us. You were right. You were *right*."

With one arm still around Lillian's waist, Mark reaches for the ship's wheel, his eyes sparkling and wild—unhinged, almost. "Let's finish this, then."

"Mark, wait. What do you mean, what are you—"

"It's better this way for Ondine, too," he murmurs, studying the map again now. "She is safe, with the only family she has ever known. It's better if she never learns of us." And in that instant, she knows what Mark intends to do.

With a harsh gasp, Annie returns to her own skin, fighting down the mournful ache of Lillian within her.

Once, when Annie was a child, she'd gone swimming off the coast of Ballintoy. Gotten caught in a riptide and sucked under, felt the air thrown out of her chest, felt the sunlight disappear as she was flung upside down and pulled far out—so far out. She'd been too young, then, to think of death. She hadn't even dreamed up the Vanishing Game yet. There had been panic, and confusion, as she thrashed beneath the waves . . . but beneath all that had been something automatic and constant—the belief in the surface; the certainty that light, and breath, would return. As a child, you do not imagine anything other than life, other than light, other than another chance, and another, and another.

In this moment, as Mark grabs, wild-eyed, for the wheel, Annie comes to that certainty again. Even now, after everything that has happened. The awful narrowness of her life under her father's watchful eye. The intensity of Desmond's attention, of his touch, of his ultimate betrayal. Of *God's* betrayal. The pregnancy. The humiliation. The desire to die. The dream of escape. After all of it—even becoming the unwitting vessel of another lost soul—there is still some bit of the real Annie, and some bit of that truth, that belief: that light. There is still some kind of certainty at her core.

And she clings to it, as her consciousness bursts through the surface of the enchantment and she takes in her surroundings, takes in the truth:

They are in the channel. She can see the angry whitecaps as the water crashes and swirls in the narrow strait. If the ship doesn't run into the rocks hidden beneath the waves, it will strike one of the German mines.

He means to take the ship down. To damn the thousand souls aboard, asleep and unaware of what waits for them. Like the people aboard the *Titanic*.

Yes, a voice inside her says. *We'll be together forever*. But these are not Annie's thoughts. This is what Lillian wants, but Annie cannot kill everyone on board this ship. She cannot be responsible for so many deaths a second time.

"Mark, you can't do this," she says as she wrenches out of his arms. "You can't mean to kill them all. They're innocent."

His look is pure confusion. "What do you mean? I'm doing this for us. To free you from this Bargain. It's the only way we can be together, don't you see? This life—it's over for me. But for us, for us—it's just beginning."

He is intent. But she cannot be that selfish. She is a good girl.

She tries but cannot wrestle the wheel out of his grasp. This body is still not—never quite was—her own. Maybe it never belonged to her, even when she was born. Maybe women's bodies never are. He pushes her away—manic, now, and desperate to hold the wheel against the bucking force of the waves smashing against the ship. *Britannic* is rising and falling and juddering like a toy boat trying to navigate a raging river. There are flashes of the *Titanic*'s last night, the feeling of being batted about, of falling. The electric charge of impending disaster crackles in the air.

Annie swears she can smell the whiff of explosives a split second before they hit the mine.

In the last moment, she does the only thing she can do: she frees the enchanted from the spell, waking them so they can try to save themselves. She may have done everything wrong, but she can still do one last right thing.

The pulls for the alarm bells beckon from the far side of the control board, the switches and levers, gears and slides that the captain and crew use to control the ship. She lunges for them, praying that Mark does not come after her, that he doesn't try to stop her, doesn't have time.

She grasps on and yanks the pulls, even as the alarm bells peal throughout the ship, their sharp cries cutting through the fog of enchantment.

Even as they cut through her own.

Even as the first of the blasts shudders through the wall of the ship.

She rings the warning until the water takes her, until the bells—and she—can scream no more. Until she can no longer hold on. Until she is no longer Annie or Lillian. Until it is over.

~eeleee~

Epilogue

The Daily Mirror
23 November 1916

Hospital ship sunk by torpedoes;
53 dead, count rising

London, Thursday, Nov. 23, 1916—In a terrible tragedy and af-
front to Her Majesty's government, HMHS *Britannic* has been
sunk on November 21 by German mines off the island of Kea in
the Aegean Sea, according to the *Daily Mirror*'s Athens correspondent. The ship was hit and began to take on water at 8:12
a.m. and reportedly sank within the hour. It is believed that two
German submarines were positioned in the Kea Channel in
waiting for the famous hospital ship, sister ship to the tragic
RMS *Titanic* and the largest hospital ship in the British fleet.
This latest German outrage against humanity is all the worse for
knowing that the ship, heading north, had not yet taken on its
full complement of wounded soldiers, so mainly noncombatants—
doctors, nurses, and crew—were on board.

Survivors reported that the ship sank very quickly, with an
hour elapsing in total from when the ship began evacuation proceedings to when it slipped beneath the water. Because of the
quickness, not all lifeboats were able to deploy in time and this

is partly blamed for the loss of life. Survivors credit the relatively limited loss of life—only 53 unaccounted for at this time—to the sounding of the alarms by someone on the bridge just as the mines were struck. Without the alarm bells, survivors agree, the loss of life would've certainly been higher, perhaps even approaching the catastrophic levels of the sister ship. The ship is believed to have been carrying approximately 100 doctors, 200 nurses, and 200 crew, in addition to about 500 wounded picked up in Naples, Italy. The ship, which is fitted to carry up to 3,000, was en route to pick up another 1,000 wounded in Mudros when it was struck.

Our correspondent spoke to one of the survivors, nurse Violet Jessop, who had also been on the *Titanic* when it sank. She reported that in comparison, the sinking of the *Britannic* was more violent. "There was a great explosion, then a second one. The ship rocked like a toy boat in a child's bath. We were all in the mess hall for daily service, and ran up to the boat deck. That's when we were told we were sinking and to man the lifeboats." Miss Jessop found she was not clear of the horror, however, when her lifeboat was drawn in by one of the ship's massive propeller blades, stuck up out of the water. She had to jump to keep from being killed, hit her head, and nearly drowned.

"Someone hoisted me out of the water. I don't recall a thing," she said of the harrowing experience, "except that I heard a woman screaming from inside the *Britannic* as it was going down. At the time, I thought that was impossible, as they'd surely evacuated the women first, but later I found out that one of the nurses was unaccounted for, and it was all the worse for being one of my dearest friends, Annie Hebbley."

Due to the angle of the explosions, all those in and near the captain's bridge died on impact.

The captain has made claims it was a miracle that he was conducting Mass at just that moment, and thus survived.

~~~ellee~~~

ACKNOWLEDGMENTS

One thing I learned while touring to promote my previous book, *The Hunger*, is that readers are very interested in the research that goes into a historical novel. At every stop, the majority of the questions had to do with my research process and how an author decides how much fact goes into the making of fiction.

While a lot of work went into *The Hunger*, it was dwarfed by *The Deep*, and that's because of the special place the *Titanic* holds in the imaginations of many. There's an avalanche of material available on the *Titanic*—a boon but also a challenge to the novelist. Then there's a second ship, the unfortunate *HMHS Britannic*, to factor in next to its more famous, flashier sister. A huge number of resources were consulted in the writing of *The Deep*, but I'd like call out a few in particular: the online reference *Encyclopedia Titanica* was an invaluable first stop when I needed to look up crew and passengers. *Olympic, Titanic, Britannic: An Illustrated History of the 'Olympic' Class Ships* by Mark Chirnside (the History Press) provided a treasure trove not only of history of the ships but of photos, blueprints, data, and statistical information. And lastly, *Titanic Survivor: The Newly Discovered Memoirs of Violet Jessop Who Survived Both the Titanic and Britannic Disasters* by Violet Jessop, edited by John Maxtone-Graham (Sheridan

House) gave me greater insight into the life of Violet Jessop, whose curious claim to fame as survivor of both *Titanic* and *Britannic* provided the spark of inspiration for *The Deep*.

Once again, I'd like to thank my partners at Glasstown Entertainment—particularly Lexa Hillyer for whom this was, I believe, a labor of love—for their help in bringing the story to life. Thanks are also due to Glasstown editor Deeba Zargarpur, to Emily Berge-Thielmann for her help with all things marketing and publicity, and to Alexa Wejko for her work in the early stages.

Thanks to the team at Inkwell Management—my agent, Richard Pine, Eliza Rothstein, and Glasstown's agent Stephen Barbara—for their able stewardship on this project.

Once again, heartfelt thanks to Sally Kim at Putnam for her steady hand and keen eye in getting the manuscript to the finish line. Her prowess as an editor never fails to amaze me and I am grateful to be the beneficiary of her talent. Thanks, too, to the entire team at Putnam: Ivan Held, for making me feel like family, Alexis Welby, Ashley McClay, Emily Ollis, Gabriella Mongelli, with a special shout-out to Bonnie Rice and Jordan Aaronson.

ABOUT THE AUTHOR

A graduate of Johns Hopkins University, **Alma Katsu** worked briefly in advertising and PR before moving into the intelligence world as a senior analyst for several US agencies, including the CIA. The author of the acclaimed historical horror novel *The Hunger* – called 'deeply, deeply disturbing' by Stephen King – Alma lives in the Washington, DC area. To find out more, visit www.almakatsubooks.com and you can follow her on Twitter @almakatsu.

THE HUNGER
Alma Katsu

PILLGWENLLY

Having journeyed west for weeks, they have reached a crossroads.

Two diverging paths lead to the same destination. Desperate to cross the mountains before the weather turns, George Donner's decision will affect the lives of everyone travelling with him.

Minor disagreements turn into violent confrontations as the ill-fated group struggles to survive.

And a few begin to realize that the threat they face is something primal, and far more deadly, than the fury of the elements . . .

Based on the true story of one of the most infamous events in American history, *The Hunger* is an eerie, shiver-inducing exploration of human nature pushed to its breaking point.

'Deeply, deeply disturbing, hard to put down'
STEPHEN KING

'Like *The Revenant* but with an insistent supernatural whisper . . . utterly chilling'
SARAH PINBOROUGH

'Astonishingly atmospheric . . . an enthralling and chilling read'
GUARDIAN